T0302886

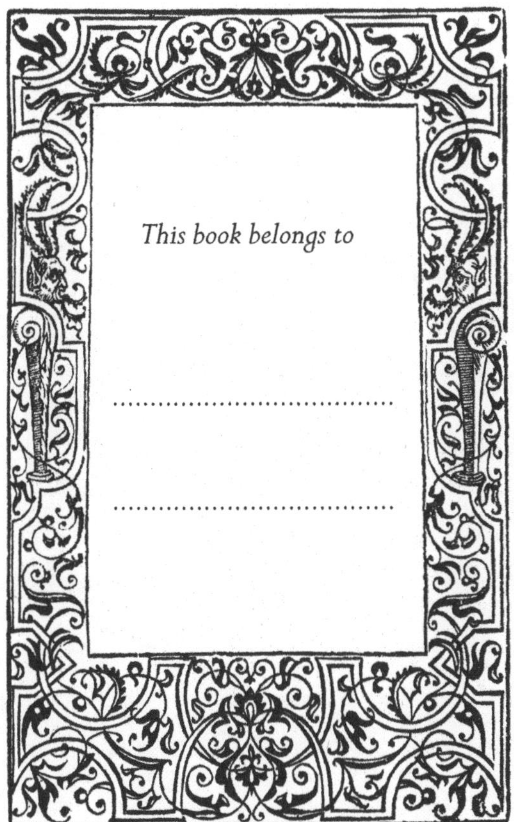
This book belongs to

TALES *from the* TOWER

The WICKED WOOD

VOLUME 2

TALES *from the* TOWER

The WICKED WOOD

VOLUME 2

Gathered by

ISOBELLE CARMODY
& NAN McNAB

This project has been assisted by the Australian Government through the Australia Council, its arts funding and advisory body.

First published in 2011

Allen & Unwin
83 Alexander Street
Crows Nest NSW 2065
Australia
Phone: (61 2) 8425 0100
Fax: (61 2) 9906 2218
Email: info@allenandunwin.com
Web: www.allenandunwin.com

Cataloguing-in-Publication details are available from the National Library of Australia
www.librariesaustralia.nla.gov.au

ISBN 978 1 74237 441 3

Cover and text design by Zoë Sadokierski
Set in 13/16 pt Perpetua by Midland Typesetters, Australia
Printed and bound in Australia by the SOS Print + Media Group.

10 9 8 7 6 5 4 3 2

The paper in this book is FSC® certified. FSC® promotes environmentally responsible, socially beneficial and economically viable management of the world's forests.

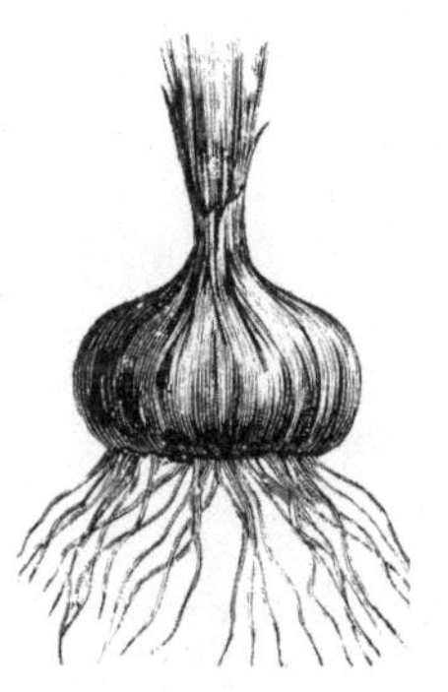

For Bet
who read me the Brothers Grimm and gave me the world.

If life were a fairytale, you would be the swan mistaken for an ugly duckling.

NMcN

CONTENTS

INTRODUCTION

Children, sooner or later, realise that adults keep secrets. Those who seek answers listen at doors, spy, probe, stickybeak, hunt out forbidden books and ask endless questions:

Where do babies come from?

The stork brings them.

What are you making?

A wing-wong for a goose's bridle.

Why won't you tell me?

Because Y's a crooked letter and you can't make it straight.

Curious children look for clues anywhere and everywhere, and hone their instincts for the cryptic and the mysterious. They want to *know*.

I was a curious child, preoccupied with notions of secret knowledge, and I poked around until I found it. On a high shelf I came upon the St John's Ambulance Association's *First Aid to the Injured*, with a whole section on childbirth which I read with appalled delight . . . several times. The faded blue cloth-covered volume of Grimms' fairytales was not forbidden, and yet the stories seemed full of secrets, hidden meanings and immutable laws. I could not understand their harsh wisdom, or their strange power, which I still find difficult to explain. Despite their apparent simplicity, they felt dark and deep. I recognised but could not name a quality that was lacking in other stories, and I listened to them with dread and fascination.

I wanted to understand *life*, but nobody would answer my questions, and school was clearly no place to begin. By university, I knew I'd taken a wrong turn. The big narratives of history – politics, wars, the Church, the state – did not interest me as much as the traces left by ordinary people. When I should have been translating the Battle of Maldon or the Venerable Bede in Anglo-Saxon, I would flip through the riddles and charms. There were charms against a wen or boil, against swarming bees, delayed childbirth, even something called water-elf disease. These, like the fairytales of my childhood, seemed to be full of ancient knowledge, unscientific but enthralling. I especially liked the charms that required herbs or the plants we call weeds. The names were evocative – venom loather and hare speckle, dragonwort, ironhard and mare gall – and seemed to retain some of the lost herbal lore of the women who must once have used them. One charm, the Holy Salve, required almost sixty different plants – plus some black snail's dust – which you mixed with butter from a cow of a single colour, 'red or white and without deformity'.

Another charm, 'Against a Stabbing Pain', required you to boil butter with feverfew, red nettle and waybroad, which is plantain, the long 'soldiers' we used as children in swishing fights, trying to decapitate our opponent's 'head'.

The charm diagnoses the cause of the pain as a wound from the nasty little iron knives or spears of hags, smiths, mighty women, gods or elves. In Germany, these sudden pains are still called *hexenschuss* (witch shot), a word linked to hex, witchcraft and hags, but more on them later. The charm's chorus – '*Out, little spear, if it be in here!*' – along with the herbal butter, will drive out the demons and cure the pain.

Fairytales spring from the same soil as these charms: girls like Briar Rose or Sleeping Beauty also receive magical wounds, not from knives, but from spindles or needles, and are transformed. Stay with me; sometimes hidden insights can be uncovered by pursuing instincts and hunches, by musing on the elements of these old tales.

Both charms and fairytales use powerful numbers: *three* pigs, wishes or tasks; sing the charm *nine* times; 'The *Six* Swans'; 'The *Twelve* Wild Ducks'; and so on.

The herbs and weeds of the charms also figure in fairytales. Rampion or rapunzel condemns a girl to life in a tower; parsley in the Italian version dooms Petrosinella. Nettles must be spun into garments if the sister in 'The Wild Swans' wishes to turn her brothers back into young men. Roses figure in 'Rose Red' and 'Sweetheart Roland'; hazels in 'Cinderella' or 'Ashputtel'; not to mention fruit and vegetables such as apples, turnips and beanstalks.

Some old plant names carry clues to their earliest uses, and understanding those uses adds meaning to fairytales. For example, hazel, sacred to Thor amongst others, was used to cure the bite of an adder, and was the wood of choice if you wanted a divining rod to find hidden treasure. Not surprising then that Ashputtel goes for help to the hazel tree that she watered with her tears to say, 'Shake shake hazel tree, gold and silver over me.' The hazel obliges, thus doing away with the need for a fairy godmother. If we only had the key to unlock all these secret meanings.

Fairytales are both extraordinary, and ordinary, rooted in the everyday; never far from either the hedgerow or the kitchen garden. They happen to everyman and everywoman, everywhere at everytime. The cast includes millers, poor peasants, frogs and donkeys as often as kings, queens and princesses, and only luck separates the king from the peasant: both are susceptible to magic spells; both must obey the deep, hidden rules of life. If these characters are named at all, their names are often descriptive: Little Red-Cap or One Eye rather than Rosalind or Robert. The setting is often a cottage, whether of gingerbread, straw or bricks; a tower; or a wood or forest, where danger lurks but also transformation and new possibilities. Kindness, loyalty, even simplicity are set against pride, greed, and envy.

As I sensed, fairytales, like myths, legends and folktales, carry some of the oldest and deepest insights into the dramas of everyday life: birth, coming of age, sex, motherhood, fatherhood, jealousy, greed, goodness and evil. Psychoanalysts from Freud and Jung onwards have found rich pickings there – the Oedipus complex, Narcissism, the Electra complex – but the insights spring from countless common people, the nameless storytellers who passed on these tales. Perhaps something akin to the wisdom of crowds was at work over the centuries, or a Wikipedia-like process that filtered out any details that did not resonate and passed on only those that did, subtly shaping the stories until they carried profound meanings beneath their apparently simple exteriors.

Fairytales can be many things, but they are almost never sad. Sadness grows out of incompleteness, a sense of 'if only', a yearning for resolution, and in fairytales there is a remorseless sense of completeness, of everything being in its proper place. Hans Christian Andersen's sometimes maudlin retellings and inventions are the only exception, often infused with his own sentimentality and beliefs. His stories can be freighted with morality, whereas fairytales are rarely moral or just in any sense we would recognise. Nevertheless they satisfy something deep within us; they tell us about life.

Traditional fairytales are told plainly, without unnecessary detail. They were part of a rich oral tradition for centuries before they were written down, and any repetition no doubt served as a mnemonic for the teller: 'What big eyes you have . . .', 'I'll huff and I'll puff . . .', 'Mirror mirror on the wall . . .' But an oral tradition is difficult for us – children of the book and the internet – to imagine or really understand. We no longer have to remember much at all, except our passwords. Oral traditions still exist, though, as I discovered when I met an Englishman whose mother was a McNab, like me. I mentioned a story I'd heard in childhood that involves a stolen Christmas feast and some burly McNab boys sent to the neighbouring loch by their father to fetch it: 'Tonight's the night if the lads are the lads.' Led by Smooth John, a name that would not be out of place in any fairytale, they carry their own boat overland to reach the island of the Neishes.

It is a bloody tale, and the McNab lads not only bring home the remains of the Christmas feast but the heads of the clan who stole it, leaving behind their boat on the top of a hill because they couldn't carry everything. 'Here are some bowls [balls] for the bairns to play with,' the Englishman chimed in at the appropriate point in the story. I was astonished. He knew the story, and the pivotal phrases within it, though we had learned it on opposite sides of the globe.

Long unbroken chains of story like this must have stretched back in time to prehistory. Neolithic peoples must have been telling each other creation stories, law stories, stories that explained themselves and their world to their children and each other. One of the questions that intrigues me is just how old fairytales might be and what lost clues they might contain about our ancestors.

One place to look is in the language of these stories. I like browsing through etymological dictionaries; they're like an archaeological dig through the history of words and meanings. Sometimes you can climb down to ancient Indo-European roots, then follow their derivatives up through synonyms and words with no obvious connections, imagining the branching ideas and metaphors that once connected them, and the changes in thinking that brought about changes in meaning. To take three examples, *fairy*tales often contain *witches* and *spindles*. *Fairy* comes from Old French *faerie* (land or place of fairies, enchantment or magic) from *fae*, or *fats* (plural), meaning the Fates, from the Proto-Indo-European root *bha* – to speak. The Fates appear in Norse and Germanic mythology, both of which inform Anglo-Saxon culture; they are usually women; and you don't have to look far before you find them associated with thread. One of the Fates spins the thread of life, the second measures it, and the third cuts it. In Anglo-Saxon, fate is *wyrd*, which gives us *weird*, as in Macbeth's three weird sisters, the witches. *Wyrd* is linked to words meaning to turn or come about, in other words to spin. Goddesses used a *spindle* to spin the thread of fate, and the words for spindle come from the same root.

It's only a small hop to one of the old words for witch. *Hag*, originally *haegtesse*, was used by Anglo-Saxons to translate *goddess*, and the three *Fates*, but also for a mortal prophetess or witch. The coming of Christianity erased much of the knowledge of these pagan beings and their powers, and blackened their reputations; victors write history, and old religions always get a bad press. Hag is also connected to *haw*, meaning hedge, which links it to *haw*thorn. Like hazel, it was a sacred tree associated with holy wells, and safeguarded against witchcraft. Hawthorn was linked to the Tuatha dé Danaan of Irish mythology. One of them, Mac Cuill, was named after his god Coll, the hazel. By the time of Oisín, the Tuatha dé Danaan had become the fairy folk, and solitary hawthorns were believed to mark faerie territory. *Haegtesse* means hedge-rider, which not only brings flying witches to mind, but loops back to the hedgerows, sacred trees, herbs and plant lore for which these women were renowned. It's possible to keep leap-frogging from one word or concept to the next, in an unsystematic and unscholarly way, slowly building up a sense of the network of secrets and meanings hidden in these old tales, remnants of an earlier time.

I was in the midst of this meandering hunt when I thought to check on the sound shifts in words such as *pater/father* or *pedem/foot*, word pairs that derive from single roots. To my surprise and delight, I found that the law I needed was Grimm's law. Jacob Grimm not only collected fairytales, but studied corresponding consonants in Indo-European, Low Saxon and High Germanic languages. He was equally fascinated by the origin of his native language and German folklore and fairytales. (In German, fairytales are called wonder tales, and almost always contain magic.)

Grimm said, 'My principle has always been in these investigations to undervalue nothing, but to utilise the small for the illustration of the great . . .' This sounds like an excellent way to approach fairytales. Often undervalued as simple stories for children, they are distilled from the insights and preoccupations of numberless ordinary and not-so-ordinary people. They are the concentrate of much of our culture's wisdom and insights about life, and receptive readers sense this and are unsettled by it. Artists, writers and poets know they have struck a rich vein.

In *The Wilful Eye*, the six fairytales are familiar: 'The Tinderbox' (Andersen); 'Rumplestiltskin' (Grimms); 'The Snow Queen' (Andersen); 'Beauty and the Beast' (French); 'Babes in the Wood' (English ballad); and 'The Steadfast Tin Soldier' (Andersen). In *The Wicked Wood*, some of the stories are more unusual: 'The Wolf and the Seven Kids' (Grimms); 'Otesánek' or 'Little Shaveling' (Bohemian); 'The Little Mermaid' (Andersen); 'Cinderella' or 'Ashputtel' (Grimms); 'The Fairy's Midwife' (English); and the Irish Tír na n'Óg, which edges from fairytale into myth. Here you will find stories as bewitching and powerful as any fairytale, monsters with benign human faces, heroines gutsy enough for any era, and people like us, who find themselves suddenly entangled in magic, or confronted by the terrible, bewitching world of Faerie.

The forest has always been a place of danger, mystery and transformation. Lose yourself in *The Wicked Wood* and you may discover new and magical secrets.

Nan McNab

SEVENTY-TWO DERWENTS

by Cate Kennedy

Mrs Carlyle has given us all exercise books and said we are going to try to keep a journal this term. This is mine. She says it's better if we don't feel self-conscious so we don't have to put our names on the journals. They will be anonymous. She says she would just like to read them.

Mrs Carlyle has two budgies, a boy and a girl, and they have built a nest. If they have baby budgies and if I'm allowed she will give me one. You have to wait until they're old enough to leave the nest before you can take them away from their parents because they need special looking after. In my mind I can picture this. The babies would live in a soft little nest inside the milk carton Mrs Carlyle has put inside their cage as a nesting box.

The nest for the budgies is soft because I think the mother bird pulls some feathers out of her chest to put inside. This seems cruel but Mrs Carlyle says she put other soft things in the cage and the mother budgie didn't want any of them. She is using instinct. The babies would all be snuggled up inside. If she will give one to me, I would like a girl budgie. I think I would name her Alicia. When I think about teaching her how to say her name I can nearly hear it. I have to wait, Mrs Carlyle says, because she's not sure her budgie is even going to lay eggs yet. She says not to tell the other kids because they would get jealous. After she says this, when I walk back into class and down to my desk, I feel my skin buzzing like someone has stroked it. I hope Alicia is blue.

My mum says do you like him? Shane I mean. She has on her nice earrings. He's OK, I say. Later on when Shane comes over, Mum is in the kitchen cooking dinner. She's made homemade lasagne and now she's heating up oil in the deep saucepan. She calls to Shane, you haven't lived till you've had my home-cooked chips. I'm famous for them. Isn't that right Tyler? My home-cooked chips?

Once I asked if I could get some money to go and buy a hamburger and she suddenly jumped up really angry and said why do you need a crap takeaway hamburger? I can make you a much better hamburger here at home. She got mince out and made a hamburger in the frypan with onions.

It took forever. Finally she gave it to me with two pieces of bread holding it all together. Isn't that better than Maccas? she kept asking. Isn't it? Answer me.

Now I just say yes. Mrs Carlyle told us that when you are training your dog you need to say the same thing over and over until the dog gets it. He wants to do the right thing, he just doesn't know at first. She says it's the same with training a bird to talk, you have to say the same thing again and again so they learn. That's true and maybe it's true for people too.

I'm starving, says Shane, and looks over at me with a smile. He is just out of the shower and there are comb marks in his hair. He says you wanna change channels? and leans over to give me the remote. You have to press the button really hard to make it change channels now because it's wearing out. So I change it over to Simpsons.

What grade are you in? he says, and I tell him grade six, Mrs Carlyle's class. Six C. She comes in and says how are you this morning my treasures? My lovely Six Cs. I've missed you!

I don't tell Shane this. Grade six, he repeats. When Homer and Marge talk to each other their whole heads move to ask a question and then answer but when Shane talks to me just his eyes move sideways, his head stays watching TV.

He says I bet you've got a boyfriend. I can hear my mum clattering oven trays in the kitchen. On the TV Bart is climbing up into his tree house. He can go really fast, much faster than I could in real life. Just a few steps and he's there. But I always like to see the inside of his tree house. I wish I had one. And I don't want a boyfriend. I want the set of 72 Derwents.

They are in a tin that opens out with all the sharp points of the pencils in order and in every colour you could ever think of using. Georgia has some at school and even when you sharpen them they feel special, the wood is so soft and it peels back to leave the pencil good as new. My grandma asked me what I wanted for my birthday and I took her to the shop where they are. The art supply shop smells so beautiful inside, all clean new pencils and paper and brushes. She had a good look at them. For your colouring in? she said. I felt happy when we walked out again, imagining. They have names soft as feathers. Pale Mint. Sea Green. Grey Green. French Grey. Rose Pink. Cloud Blue. Iced Blue. Kingfisher Blue. Prussian Blue. Indigo. Sometimes just when I am walking along the names come into my head like a rhyme in time with my footsteps.

I will put them into my denim pencil case and only take a few at a time to school, but I will invite Georgia over to my house and open up the whole tin so we can do drawing and colouring in together on the table on the weekend. Mrs Carlyle has a special Stanley knife and she could scrape some of the paint off the end so I could write my name on each one. On the tin is a picture of someone's sketch they have done of an old stone bridge going over a rocky creek. It is a very good drawing and it looks like a picture from the old set of encyclopaedias in the library. When I go in there Mrs Bradbury says it's good to see someone still uses the reference section Tyler. I think she means the lovely way the books smell, which is true, I love that too.

You have got a boyfriend, haven't you? says Shane. I can tell. Cause you're blushing.

Bart and Milhouse are in Bart's tree house and they're talking about staying out there the night. I'm watching and I know that in a few seconds it will be night and you will see the moon and they will get scared.

In cartoons time passes really fast and sudden. Also, things happen that aren't true. Like a cat will be running along and will go through the wall and there will be an exactly cat-shaped hole left behind in the wall. Mum's old boyfriend Garry threw a bottle at the wall once and it didn't leave a shape like that it just smashed.

Bart and Milhouse are still in the tree house but it's night and there are big shadows that scare them. They race down the rope ladder screaming. When they scream on the Simpsons their mouths open way up and their little tongues come out and wriggle and you can see their tonsils. That's meant to be funny, and it must be because Shane laughs. Bart runs back into his room and hides in his bed. I like Lisa but she's not in this one.

I'm not blushing, I say to Shane. Sure looks like it to me, he says. What do you get up to with that boyfriend of yours? See, you're not looking at me, so I know it's true.

I try to think if I've ever seen a Simpsons where a human goes running through a wall and leaves a person-shaped hole.

Wait till you taste these chips, calls my mum.

Shane is under my mum's Subaru in the driveway. What a shitheap, he says. I ask him what he's fixing up and he says the carby. He's out there for a long time even when Mum tells him to come inside and have dinner, which is just pasta tonight. It is those little shell ones. I get a clean one onto the side of my plate and imagine it is something in the sea where an animal lives. Ellie is working tonight at Subway. Shane and my mum argue outside about the car and something in the garage gets knocked over. Whatever you've taken out you'd better put back in because I need it tomorrow says Mum, and Shane says look it's just not that simple. I could curl up inside this soft shell and it would be like a hammock in there, all warm. That's all I want to write for today.

If Georgia came over to my house we could make hot Milo and some of that popcorn that you cook in the microwave. She told me she was on camp once and they had toasted marshmallows on sticks on the fire. We could do them under the griller. We have a packet of wooden skewers. We could draw horses and do the colouring in and then we could watch *Saddle Club* and if she wanted we could put on some of Mum's nail polish. Even just do our homework together. I always do my homework when I come home from school. Mum says I sure didn't get that gene off her. I like to sketch but Mum says that's not going to impress the teachers and she wasn't still paying off a colour printer and a computer with internet so I could just do drawings.

First there is *Home and Away* then *Deal or No Deal*. If Georgia came over we could go into my room and Mum wouldn't keep knocking and asking me what I was doing because when you have a friend over that explains it.

And if Shane came over he would leave us alone I hope.

OK goodbye for now.

Mrs Carlyle said who's been writing things in their diary and nobody put up their hands so I kept mine down too, just in time. Someone said there's nothing to write about and Mrs Carlyle said why not write about something that happened to you when you were little, like learning to ride a bike, or Christmas, or a favourite toy.

I have a doll that my Aunty Jacinta gave me for Christmas two years ago when we went to their place in the country. The doll has a long dress and hidden under the dress instead of feet is another doll and you can pull it all inside-out. She is first of all like Cinderella when she was dressed in patchy clothes, and when you pull the dress over the other side has Cinderella in her ball gown and she has a crown on her head. The whole doll is knitted. When my mum saw it she laughed. My older brother Zac had come with us for Christmas and she rolled her eyes at him and nudged him and said see, told you it would be like the Waltons, but Zac just said who are the Waltons? and he wouldn't look at her. I don't know Zac very well because he has lived with another family since before I was born. There's just been Ellie and me even though Mum had three other children before us, Dylan, Zac and Tegan. Anyway Zac was there and it felt strange because the cousins were all like new kids at a strange school, not talking, and my mum said I had so many dolls at home already I was just getting spoiled, and to say thank you to Aunty Jacinta for the homemade one.

I said I love her, I love her crown, thank you. Aunty Jacinta leaned over and gave me a hug and she smelled so nice, not like perfume but just cups of tea and shampoo, and she said softly she doesn't have to be Cinderella, Tyler, you can give her a new name if you like. Then my mum jumped up and said are we allowed to have a glass of wine or do we have to say grace first round here.

After lunch when we got into the car to come home Zac said just drop me off at the station and Mum said I thought you were staying for a few days and he just shrugged and shook his head. Mum said there probably won't even be a train on Christmas Day and he said I checked and there is.

After we dropped him, Mum said he always was an ungrateful little shit wasn't he Ellie? Do you remember Ellie, how he always took his father's side? Ellie said no she couldn't remember. I wished she had just said yes because then Mum wouldn't have kept going. I knew she would and she did. All the Christmas lunch in my stomach turned into a hard cold stone as she started talking on and on about how Aunty Jacinta and Uncle Matt thought they were so great and they didn't even have a plasma and they'd always been like that, always judging her, and Jacinta had always been the favourite with Grandma and how neither of them had given her any support when she'd got pregnant with Tegan and she'd had to move out of home too young and that's what had started all the problems. Mum said they both denied it but she was sure either Jacinta or Grandma had been the one to dob her in to the Department and that was how she'd lost Tegan and she couldn't trust anyone, they were all shits to her even her family.

I looked at my doll's wool hair which Aunty Jacinta had sewed on and made into two little plaits, they were so neat and perfect, tied with thin red ribbon.

When I look at my doll now I remember all this exactly like it happened.

I wrote a card to Aunty Jacinta last year and she wrote a card back to me, here is what she said: *Dearest Tyler we missed you this year and we're sorry you couldn't make it back here again for Christmas. Remember Ty, we think you're wonderful and would love to see you again any time.* On the bottom of the card was a little arrow pointing to the back where she'd written her phone number and small writing saying: *if you ever need to ring me for anything at all, here's the number.* Mum already had that number in the phone book, but Aunty Jacinta must have forgotten. I put the card in my box. I called my doll Calypso. It's just a nice word.

If I had a bike I would of written about that instead.

On Saturday mornings early my mum says I'm allowed to watch cartoons then she goes back into her room. When I peek in as I go past I see an orange shawl over the lamp and a bare foot sticking out of the bed from under the doona. It is Shane's foot, he has a snake tattoo on his ankle. Do you like my tattoo? he said once, lifting up his foot to show me. I said, didn't it hurt? and he said, yep it sure did. He made me read out the words under the snake and said and don't you forget it, that's the truth babe.

If you get something written on your skin it's like you imagine yourself blank like a piece of paper, ready for words, but the bones in Shane's ankle bumped up underneath so the letters were crooked. The snake had fangs that were much too big, like a cartoon snake, when they open their mouths their jaw goes right back and the fangs fill the screen and that's impossible. The person they're attacking starts running in midair without going anywhere and first you hear bongo drums and then the noise they're supposed to make when they run really fast.

One thing about the early Saturday cartoons is that sometimes they show the old ones about the cat chasing the mouse. He makes up all these plans to get the mouse but never gets him, then they wreck the house again, running over and over again past the same lamp and the same chair. Sometimes the cat or the coyote gets big red sticks of dynamite and it always happens that they get it wrong and the dynamite blows up their head. Anyone knows you wouldn't survive that, but they do. They just shake their heads, which have gone black like someone's dropped a packet of black powder onto the floor and it's split open, then suddenly they're back to normal. They can still run so fast they're a blur.

Live fast die young leave a pretty corpse is what Shane's tattoo says. A corpse is a body like on NCI. I don't know how you'd stay pretty if you were dead. I watch the cartoons listening for when Shane gets up so I can run and get dressed because I don't like being just in my pyjamas when he's here. It just feels funny.

My birthday today. I got my present from my grandma. As soon as I saw it I knew it wasn't the tin. It was a long plastic packet of coloured pencils all different colours but when I coloured with them it wasn't the same. With Georgia's Derwents it feels soft when you colour, and it goes on dark and strong. These pencils feel gritty, like there was sand in them, and no matter how hard you press the colour isn't very good. Say thank you to your grandma, said my mum, for your lovely pencils. Grandma said they're just what she wanted aren't they Tyler?

Mum said that next year I can have a party and we can go to Lollypops Fun Centre. Ellie said that place is for pre-schoolers and Mum said well Maccas then. We had a birthday afternoon tea because Ellie couldn't stay home for dinner, she had a shift at Subway till 9.30. She whispered to me in the kitchen sorry Tyler we'll do something good next year, just you and me, don't worry. I said I didn't care because I had cupcakes at school today. Shane wasn't there tonight because Grandma doesn't know about him yet, Mum says she'll introduce them when the time's right. She says Grandma always interferes and wrecks her chances when it's none of her business so don't tell her yet. Ellie asked her why not and she said first Shane has to get his parole period out of the way and get his gold star for staying clean. Maybe that's why Shane comes over to our place to have a shower and get changed, to stay clean. Otherwise I don't get it. Much later when I was in bed Ellie came in and woke me up and said come into my room. We lay in her bed and she opened a bag from the mall and inside were two little mirror disco balls and two torches. We put batteries in and shone the lights on the mirror balls and sparkling dots went everywhere, all around the corners of the room, spinning. It was like we were floating in the solar system. It was lovely and warm in Ellie's bed.

Thank you for making the cupcakes today Mrs Carlyle. It was great when everyone sang.

My mum says she is going to have a new job. Centrelink is running it and it is sewing. She is good at sewing and she already has the overlocker Aunty Jacinta gave her to make tracksuit pants and tops two years ago.

It is very heavy and she has to lift it up onto the kitchen table. Ellie asks her what she's sewing and Mum says designer things. She says it is support to start her own small business.

She shows me a pattern and it is not clothes, it is a doll. Sort of like a doll, anyway; like a prep kid's drawing, just a round soft shape with big eyes and two useless little arms sticking out the side. Mum has rolls of felt and soft velvet, and stretchy fur material for the clothes. The dolls are called Glamour Plushies.

Designer plush toys, Mum says, reading from her pattern page. They're just for fun. I'm going to sell them in that shop with the cushions and teak furniture in the mall, that Asian one.

Are they the scissors? is all Ellie says. The ones that cost 45 bucks?

Mum says I told you I would pay you back so lose the attitude. She lines up material on the table and Ellie just turns away rolling her eyes.

Mum tells me the scissors are just for special sewing, not for my school stuff or craft things. She says that will wreck them. There is a special tag that gets sewn on to the dolls when they're finished, with a card tied on it that says: *Glamour Plushies are soft, loveable critters that teach us that beauty is only skin-deep. When you adopt one of these adorable soft monsters you are showing your warm-hearted side, a valuable lesson presented by cutely irresistible toys designed and created with great care.* Mum says you will have to help me round the house more Tyler so I can get my first order finished for the assessment. I have to make twelve.

So I cook the chicken with the simmer sauce while she cuts out the pieces and says we will eat dinner on our laps tonight so I can leave the overlocker and all my work on the table OK? And I say OK even though we always eat dinner on our laps anyway because Mum is hooked on *Survivor.*

The stuff for the Glamour Plushies takes up all the room on the table so I have to do my project on the glories of Ancient Greece on my bed after dinner. It's hard to write neatly.

Mum hears me snipping and rustling when she comes down the hall to her room and calls out they better not be the good scissors.

They're not. They're the plastic ones that don't cut. Pictures stuck down with the glue that doesn't stick, coloured in with the pencils that don't colour. Sorry, Mrs Carlyle.

Mum had nearly finished two whole dolls today when I got home from school. She said the overlocker doesn't really work properly on the felt so she's worked out how to do the blanket stitch by hand. The dolls have big round eyes and little mouths like cats or big open mouths with teeth and they stick their arms straight out the side like they're running towards you afraid. Out of like a fire or away from a scary thing. They are not dolls, they are more like cartoon monsters. Ellie was doing her homework in her room and I went in there. Her room is nice and she bought some curtains for herself at Spotlight and a hot-pink mosquito net. I looked at Ellie's homework which is so hard because she is in Year 10. It was science and she had written *red blood cells plus white blood cells plus platelets plus water equals blood.* There was a picture of platelets and they looked like biscuits. When I get to high school I want to do art in the art room where they have easels. I saw them when we went to Ellie's school for parent–teacher. You stand up and paint and they have huge pieces of paper you're allowed to use, as many as you like. And also a pottery wheel. It's those things that make me want to go to the secondary school even though there's hundreds and hundreds of kids there. I get worried I might forget where my locker is in all those corridors. You get a locker with a combination so that only you can open it. Maybe the other kids want to steal your stuff. You would never know who because there are so many kids there is no way a teacher would notice that or even remember everyone's names. Ellie says she just does the subjects that are going to get her good marks, not art, so that she can do something at TAFE or uni. That is why she works part-time too, to save all her money. When she and Mum fight Mum says set your sister a good example, and Ellie says I'm setting her the best example I can, which is how to get the fuck out of here.

When we went back into the lounge room for dinner Shane was there. He said here they both are how are you Tyler babe? All the cans of beer he has brought are stacked in the fridge when I get out the cheese for the spaghetti. He is in a mean mood I can tell because even though he is smiling his mouth is wrong.

He picks one of Mum's dolls out of the box and looks at it and says you've got to be fucken kidding me.

People pay $40 for these, says my mum without looking at him and he laughs and says jeez they saw you coming didn't they. She just keeps sewing the hair on one of her dolls and says you wait.

When I go to bed I hear him and Mum laughing and bumping into the walls as they come down the hall and my mum sounds happy but it makes the stones feeling come back to my stomach. I must have fallen asleep because I feel a hand on my shoulder shaking me and I come awake and my stomach is squeezing so suddenly like when you're sick. It is Ellie and I feel her hair brush my face as she leans over me and says get up and come and sleep in my room. I say why and she whispers just come on.

In her bed she lets me have the purple heart-shaped pillow. She shows me a little smooth stone in a box she puts under the pillow and I ask her what it's for and she says bad dreams.

I didn't know Ellie has bad dreams too. Sometimes I dream of a wolf. He's coming for me and his eyes are on fire and he's looking everywhere for me but he can't find me. I don't tell Ellie about this but I say sometimes I feel like I have a stone inside my stomach. Ellie doesn't say anything for a while then she says hey what are those pencils called that you like? I tell her Derwents and she says we'll get those, you wait.

Today we did mammals. Mrs Carlyle said she got a puppy once that was homesick leaving its mother and it cried. She said she wrapped up an old clock inside an old fur collar she had and tucked it into the puppy's basket with a hot-water bottle. The puppy thought the clock ticking was its mother's heart beating and the fur was her warm furry coat next to it. It seemed like a mean trick but Mrs Carlyle said soon the puppy went to sleep and learned to sleep by itself after that. She said it seems cruel but all animals have to learn that and some leave their parents the day they are born, but not mammals because they have to drink milk. That puppy used to like to sleep in the laundry basket full of dirty clothes. When the bell rang she said whoops we forgot to do our worksheets, all I've ended up doing is telling you stories because you are such good listeners.

That puppy thought the clock and the fur and the hot-water bottle was his mum. And maybe the clothes in the clothes basket had a smell that made him feel better. The Plushie dolls are supposed to make you feel warm-hearted too, so maybe people will buy them to cuddle like a puppy. Birds like budgies can't be cuddled but they must still know you love them. Ellie says we used to have a cat when Dylan and Zac were still here before I was born but it ran away. Ellie says, I don't blame it.

My mum is still sewing the Plushies. She says she has a deadline and she has to prove she can do it so she'll be accepted on the job-creation program. She said if Shane thinks he's so shit-hot why doesn't he fix her car and do something useful? Shane is nearly living at our place now and she said if he thinks all he has to do is turn up with pizzas and five weekly DVDs he's got another think coming. But then when he comes she goes quickly into her room and comes out with perfume on.

While she is in there Shane beckons at me and when I go over he leans down close to me and whispers I've got something for you, but don't tell the others, hold out your hand. He gives me a Mars Bar. His voice is so different when he is telling a secret. It is all soft and like you're best friends and I want to believe everything he tells me. He says don't tell Ellie because she will get jealous. Next time I might put it under your pillow, so always check when you go to bed OK? In case I've left a surprise for you. Then when Mum walks back in again he says sshh, here she comes and I can't help it, I smile. I hide the Mars Bar in my bag.

Ellie did a magic thing tonight. Mum had the five Plushies she had finished laid out on the table and she was painting their lips red like in the photo and Ellie said do you want a cup of tea? Mum was just sitting there not saying anything and I realised she had stopped painting and was scratching at her hair like it was itchy just scratching and pulling, not answering. Shane was in the living room watching TV and Mum was just sitting there with her chin tucked down all hunched and sad with the dolls lined up. Her hand scratching harder and harder in her hair. I felt like when I turn the key in my music box until it's really tight and if you kept turning one more time it would snap and break, just one more twist. But Ellie came over very quietly and looked down at the monster dolls that were meant to make you feel warm-hearted. They all had big black eyes that just stared and I could tell Mum was thinking they looked creepy or dead and it's true, they did.

Ellie put a brush in the white paint and put a little dot of white in the dolls' eyes. I don't know how she did it but it changed everything. It was like a little speck of shine. I heard Mum sigh then her hand came down and felt around for her cigarettes. I felt loose again like remembering that inside the music box the ballerina is waiting to dance to the whole song and it will just get slower and calmer all the way to the end.

Just before when I was going to bed Mum said let's have a secret you don't have to go to school tomorrow Tyler, I will ring up and tell them you are sick and you can stay here and help me finish the Plushies. It is the same as when Shane leans down and whispers, grown-ups can make their voices go all soft and excited like it's a big special secret to share just with you, they know just how to make kids feel happy but it's never what you think.

I felt the stones in my stomach because I remembered that tomorrow is the first orientation day for year sixes to go over to the senior campus to visit but I just said yes. Mum still has five dolls to make and she said she will show me how to do the blanket stitch.

I woke up in the night and I saw someone was standing in my doorway and at first I thought it was my mum. Then I heard a sniff and I got a shock because it was Shane. When I said what, he pretended he'd been sleepwalking and said sorry, wrong room.

Ellie was mad at Mum today when she went to school she said you're supposed to have a doctor's certificate if you're sick and Mum said she has a temperature so mind your own business. Ellie said is Shane going to be hanging round all day? and Mum said of course not he's going to his job with the house painters and Ellie said he'd better. Mum got really angry and said who are you to talk you've got that gormless bloke who can't do anything better than work at a takeaway and Ellie said if you mean Luke he's store manager and he's going to uni next year. Her voice was trembling but I never see Ellie cry. Mum just said oh uni is it? That's typical you'd pick him, now you can both be up yourselves together. When she gets angry she just says things that don't make any sense. Ellie just said he's a smart, nice guy who likes me so no wonder you don't get it. And since your useless boyfriend ruined your car, it's Luke that's been driving me home, so thank goodness someone's there to make sure I make it home OK, not that you'd care about that.

Mum just went red as a beetroot and said just get out and get yourself to school so you can do what you're good at and that's show off.

Ellie just looked at her and said is that the best you can do? Like she was tired. On her way out she said to me use the phone I got for you to text me at school if anything goes wrong, OK? I said, like what and she said if you get the stones feeling.

Shane was still in bed when Mum got onto the phone to my school after Ellie had gone. She could swap straight away from shouting at Ellie to putting on a phone voice. I had to unpick one of the Plushies and put more stuffing in when I finished because its arms were too floppy. We sewed them in front of the TV and Mum kept going back to check the instructions to make sure we were doing them right even though she's made five already. She said you don't understand Tyler it just keeps slipping out of my brain. We watched

The Morning Show and *Dr Phil* while we sewed. Shane went out at lunchtime but he didn't say anything about going to work. By four o'clock we'd finished six more Plushies and my fingers were all pricked and tingly but the dolls all had different personalities now because we were getting better at adding little bits and making them different. Their arms looked like they were about to hug you rather than sticking out straight because they were scared. Mum laid them out in a line when they were finished and said you put the little dot in their eyes Ty, my hand is shaking too much. So I did Ellie's magic trick and the Plushies stopped being scary and all of a sudden looked alive. Mum will take them to the shop tomorrow while I am at school and maybe somebody will buy one who wants a *cutely irresistible toy*.

I was in bed when Ellie came home and she woke me up. She said do you want some of this meatball sub and I said no then she said well you can sleep in my bed if you like. I said I wanted to sleep in my own bed and she said well how about I get in with you.

When I made room she sat down and I whispered who is Luke? and she laughed a bit and whispered back oh just this guy. I asked is he good-looking? and she said I think he is, I'll show you a photo of him tomorrow on my phone. I think she was going to tell me more but then she stopped and said hey did Shane do or say anything weird today? I said he just sits with me when the cartoons are on and she said does he get you to sit in his lap? If he does anything like that you come and tell me straight away. I said why not Mum and I could see Ellie's face go sad and tired and she said no, just tell me.

She said Zac and Dylan went to live with other families because they had police records when they were just kids and they ran away thinking they wanted to live with their dad but they didn't really because their dad was hopeless, but Tegan went because of Ian, Mum's old boyfriend before Garry. Mum had a screaming fight with Child Protection and said everyone was lying but it didn't stop Tegan going. She got taken away and Mum didn't stop it. I felt the heavy, heavy weight in my stomach as she whispered. Like when you sit in the bath and all the water drains out. Ellie said you have to be careful of him and I said but I'm just a kid and Ellie said that's why, Ty, that's why.

There wasn't much room in my bed when she'd squeezed in and I smelled her hair which smelled like the bread in Subway and I said that's why you're saving up isn't it so you can go too, and she didn't answer for so long I thought she must've started going to sleep. Then I heard her say Tyler, she might have left me but I'm not leaving you, not ever.

I asked Mum if she would drive me to the mall today. Georgia told me at school that at the arts supply shop there they have Derwents and she thought you can buy them just one at a time. Mum drove me there and it was a bit scary driving in the car because she had to keep revving it up at the traffic lights to keep it from conking out. What Ellie said is true – it's not going well since Shane fixed it. Mum said never mind Tyler it's still good having a guy around the place isn't it and I said yes and she said it makes you feel safe doesn't it and I said yes again. She said he's going to be on the straight and narrow now but he's had his problems like all of us. At the mall she said she would meet me in half an hour and I went to the art supply shop and I had enough money to buy five pencils. I couldn't decide which colours I wanted first. Finally I picked out my five. Scarlet Lake, Oriental Blue, Deep Cadmium, Lemon Yellow and Cloud Blue. If I did a picture of a blue budgie it would be Cloud Blue and Iced Blue with extra grey on the feathers. When I close my eyes I can see exactly how that drawing would look, like the picture I did of the running horse I drew in science and the teacher said where did you copy this and I said I didn't copy it, it just came out of my head. It was Mr Godfrey and he said are you saying you did this freehand? I said yes, even though I wasn't sure what freehand was, and he said OK then let's see you draw one now on the whiteboard, in a voice like I was in trouble. I felt angry instead of nervous because he didn't believe me so I just started drawing a horse with two huge wings coming out of its back, right to the edge of the whiteboard. He didn't say sorry for not believing you he just said well then, I think I've found the student who's going to decorate the board for parent–teacher night. Except for Mrs Carlyle I never want to tell the teachers if I like something because this is what happens, they use it to make you do something they want.

I think sometimes about what you would have to do to be an artist, for example how would you make money. My pencils have 'student quality' written on the packet but the Derwent pencils are for real artists and that is why they're special. I would feel special and proud to have them, like when Aunty Jacinta wrote in her letter 'we think you're wonderful'.

It's like you're not really allowed to feel proud. I said to Mum I wanted to look at our Plushies in the gift shop and first she didn't want to. She said she'd be too embarrassed and the lady would think she was a loser, hanging round looking at them only a few days after she'd dropped them off. She said it would be more professional to stay away until she got a phone call or something. But I wanted to see something I had made for sale in a real shop.

Finally we went up there and looked in the display window which looked so nice with embroidered cushions and wooden carved elephants and Mum said it's not here, it was right here in front of that basket and she's taken it out.

Her voice had gone flat and far off and she was chewing on her lips and breathing hard. She said she must have only left it there to shut me up for a while, it was the good one I made Tyler, with the stripy shirt. I said I want to go in and see if they're inside sitting in a basket or something and Mum said no don't, we're wasting our time here. I thought about all that sewing and Centrelink giving Mum the test and suddenly the lady who owned the shop saw us and her face changed when she saw Mum and Mum said come on we're out of here.

But the lady came running out calling Mum's name and said I was about to call you and tell you. Mum said: are they inside? and I could tell how much she tried to keep her voice normal. Because my little girl here helped me make those things, if you didn't want them you should have just said. But the lady said they're not inside, they're all gone. We both just looked at her and she said it's amazing the whole lot have sold out in three days, I was going to ring you to tell you to come in and I'd pay you.

We didn't say anything we just followed her into the shop and she had a receipt and an envelope for Mum there with her name already on it and she said I'll take as many as you can make. Mum just nodded and grabbed my arm really tightly and steered me out of the shop. We went down the escalators and she opened the envelope without saying anything and bought two Krispy Kreme doughnuts and we went back to the car and got in and we still hadn't said a word. As she was trying to start the car I was thinking that I could have bought another pencil for the same price as my doughnut and the car revved then rattled like it was laughing at us and then stopped.

We sat there with sugar all round our mouths then Mum looked down at the envelope in her lap and tears dripped on it. She kept crying and shaking and not even wiping the tears and snot away then she took out thirty dollars and said Tyler this is for you this is your share.

Today Mum went to do the supermarket shopping and I was home watching TV when the phone rang and someone said is Shane Smyth there please? He was asleep but Mum says never tell a stranger on the phone that anyone is asleep so I just asked if I could take a message and the person said: please tell him someone from the Community Offender Services Office needs to speak with him. When I told Shane that he got straight out of bed and pushed past me and just listened on the phone saying yes yes sure thing yes. When he hung up he said to me Tyler do you like to do your friends favours?

I said yes. I didn't really know what else to answer. So many of Shane's questions you can't really answer, like he'll say wassup Tyler baby? And, all good eh Tyler? but there's nothing really to say to those questions.

But I said yes and he smiled and said that's good, because you can do a little favour for me. It's a simple thing. It's something so simple you won't believe it.

I was watching him smiling and nodding at me and even though his voice was friendly his hand was in his mouth and I could see his teeth biting the bleeding cuticle down the side of his thumbnail all the time he was talking. The stone in my stomach was squeezing and pressing, sending a taste up into my mouth. Not a taste. Like when you have an easter egg and the foil gets bitten onto one of your fillings. Like fingernails on the blackboard.

I said what is the favour? I kept looking at my sandals. I liked them when I got them in Target because they had small pressed-out daisies on the top but now they just looked stupid and babyish. My toes were hanging out over the edge all grubby. I swallowed down the foil taste.

He tells me what it is and it's like the words he's saying don't make sense, like they're broken up in a box and I can't start sorting through them to put them back together. And the stone shifts and slips and I feel sweat on my skin because my heart jumps up into the back of my mouth.

He says Tyler I need you to piss into a cup and give it to me. I know it sounds crazy but it's just a surprise trick I'm playing.

All the muscles go stiff on my face and Shane is smiling so wide his mouth is big and stretched. He says hey, you're blushing! It's just for a surprise. You can't tell anyone.

I say why not Mum? and his face closes up like a window and his lip gets that mean look and he says I thought you were my friend, I thought you would be a good person to ask, because you can keep a secret. But can you, Tyler?

I say yes, I can.

He says you have to do it in a special cup, with a lid. Well, so the piss doesn't spill out, and so that I can carry it, I just put the lid on, OK?

I say OK again, and my mind is picking up one piece, searching, searching for another piece to make sense.

And Shane looked at the time on his phone and said do you need to go now, Tyler baby? Because if you can go right now for me, that would be great, and I can get the surprise going.

I get up and take the cup, walk out with my jigsaw-box head and my foil mouth. Ellie tried to tell me to watch out for him, but not for this, not going to the toilet. Not sitting trying to catch the wee that gushes out of me, seeing my white legs jiggling on the toilet seat. I go out and his hand is already stretched out waiting for me with the fingers going come on come on come on. I give him the cup and I see the face he makes when he feels it's warm and I get really small and a thread is pulling through me like I am one of the dolls stitched up tight and stiff.

He says that's perfect, I owe you one, Tyler babe, and he screws on the lid and runs out of the house. I am putting this in my journal for Mrs Carlyle because she said it's good to write about things even if they make us feel ashamed or like we want to cry. Now I don't want to write any more.

My mum has worked out how to make the overlocker do blanket stitch and she says check this out girls I've got a sweatshop going here. She says it's so much quicker now Tyler and if you can just help me do the hair and the faces I'll be able to do stacks of them. She has put colour in her hair and it is a red-brown colour. Vermilion plus Burnt Umber. The internet is back on for the computer so Mum says there's no reason why Ellie has to hang round to use the ones in the school library which means I won't be able to stay there with her after school and read *Charlie and the Chocolate Factory* in the beanbag in the story corner.

This morning Mrs Carlyle said now my dearest Six Cs, I'm going to put this box here on my desk and if anyone would like to take the opportunity to put their journals in so I can read them, I would be so happy and honoured.

I am just waiting after school for Ellie to walk across from the senior campus to come and meet me and there's no one else here so I'm going to put mine in.

I've checked in the box already and it's empty but maybe Mrs Carlyle has already taken the other ones out.

On Monday night and Tuesday night I didn't have my journal to write in and it felt strange, like waiting for a phone call with news to tell the person but they don't ring. Now it's Wednesday night. I want to tell Ellie about Shane making me do a wee but just thinking about it makes the stone come up into my chest and neck and it jams my throat shut so I can't talk.

My journal was back inside my work folder this morning and when Mrs Carlyle asked me to stay behind the same thing happened. She said she had to make an appointment for me to be interviewed by someone and I couldn't speak, just shake my head, because my throat felt all squeezed up. She said it's about your journal Tyler, and I kept shaking my head and she said: your mother . . .

I felt everything go blurry then because it would be the police, like what happened with Tegan that Ellie told me, and I just said flat out no.

She said, what are you doing this afternoon? I was meant to go to the mall and wait for Ellie to finish an after-school shift because Mum was going to her Centrelink course so there would be nobody home except Shane. So I said the mall.

Mrs Carlyle said would you like me to give you a lift to the mall then? And I said OK. We walked down the empty corridor to the teachers' car park and it felt really strange. I stopped and she said would you rather I drove you straight home and I said no, not home, and this sounded so stupid but the thought of Shane sitting there watching cartoons made the stones grind together so that I just couldn't move or make myself get into the car. Then Mrs Carlyle was crouching down next to me and she was saying Tyler, if you could go anywhere now where would you like to go? My voice came back and I said I want to go to your house and see the budgies. It just came out in a rush because it was exactly what I did want.

She was quiet for a minute and then she said right let's do that. That's how I ended up visiting Mrs Carlyle at her house. She had a great front door with a big knocker on it like a hand and you had to hold the hand to make it knock back and forth, tapping on the door. I said I love that and she said so do I. We had Milo and biscuits in her kitchen and then she showed me the spot in the back garden where the budgies lived. It was not like I imagined, I thought they would be in a little cage, but it was a big space with a net around it. It took up almost the whole garden. Mrs Carlyle said she wanted them to have an aviary because she didn't like to think of birds not being able to fly around. The nest inside was made out of a plastic milk bottle cut open and stuffed with soft hay and feathers just like she said. She said the mother bird is in there, Tyler, so we'd better not disturb her. But it means there are eggs and I haven't forgotten my promise to you.

We sat on a seat in her garden under a tree and I wished I had one of those too. She said do you think we should ring your mother and let her know where you are Tyler? and I said no, she won't be home. I said if it was OK she could drop me back at the mall and I would go to meet my sister to get the bus. She said that's Ellie, right? and I felt all hot thinking she had read that in my journal. For a long time we didn't say anything then Mrs Carlyle said I just want to do the right thing by you Tyler, I just don't know exactly what that is. She reached over and took my hand and said the school rules are so insane, I'll probably get reprimanded by the school board for even bringing you here, it's the Department's policy. I felt the stones squeeze up remembering what Ellie had said about the Department. I don't want to get taken away, I said and my voice was all stupid and high and squeaky like a cartoon. I won't tell anyone we came here to your place. Mrs Carlyle kept holding onto my hand and said that won't happen Tyler, but I'm bound by mandatory reporting so I don't have any choice. And I felt my stomach gulp like I was one of her birds swooping through the air in their big home she had made for them.

Their aviary. She said do you trust me Tyler? and I looked in at the milk bottle nest cut neatly open and tied so carefully onto the post inside and the tray of soft straw and grass she had found for them to use and I said yes. I said if I put my hand into the nest now would the mother bird bite me? And she looked so sad at me and nodded. We fed the birds, and then she drove me back to the mall.

I was in our backyard. It was funny but when I'd been at Mrs Carlyle's I'd kind of imagined my backyard to be different. Like it had trees where I could nail up netting in a corner and make a kind of aviary so I wouldn't have to put my bird in a tiny cage. But I'd remembered it wrong and there were no trees. Just bushes next to the fence and the clothesline and the paving. Mum was inside working on finishing off the dolls. On Thursday night she had come home from her Centrelink course with a sort of artist's smock her case worker had given her, she said it's a real tailor's apron for people who work in fabric, and she showed Ellie and me the pockets at the front where the scissors and cottons and pincushion went and Shane came in and said well lookie here it's Doris Day and burst out laughing and Mum stood there for a minute then she laughed too and pulled the apron off and said you're right it's stupid.

I said Mum, that colour is a Derwent colour and it's called Pale Mint and she just nodded and went into the kitchen. But she had the apron back on today because Shane wasn't here. I was standing looking at the bushes and the fence wondering how I'd remembered them so wrong and thinking about the weekend and I didn't know it but it was the last minute of everything being the same.

Ellie was in her room and I could hear her voice through the window just very softly singing along to the song she loves playing on her iPod, 'Three Little Birds', she was up to the chorus where the words say you don't have to worry because every little thing is gonna be all right, and then I heard the front door slam and Shane's voice shouting where is she where the fuck is she? Then Mum shouting what? what? but her voice not angry enough, not enough to stop him, and Shane saying I've had my parole officer on my back and that dumb-arsed brat of yours has fucked everything up for me because she ran and told her fucken teacher. I could hear him going down the hall and I heard his voice say I'll kill her. And Ellie screamed and that's when I ran into the laundry and climbed into the clothes basket. It is a big cane basket with all the week's dirty washing in it and I pulled some clothes over me and lay still. Everyone was screaming now and I thought, all jumbled up, of Mrs Carlyle telling the principal and Aunty Jacinta's phone number folded up in the box on my chest of drawers and how my mobile phone was lying on my bed with a flat battery so I couldn't of rung the police anyway. My whole stomach was full of stones now, gritting heavy together, and I shut my eyes and thought Cloud Blue Kingfisher Blue Oriental Blue Iced Blue Prussian Blue Indigo. I heard Mum say she's not here and Shane said bullshit and Mum said OK OK calm down and her voice was all scared and hopeless and I knew she wasn't going to be any good to me. I just hated her then and I went to burrow down deeper into the clothes. I felt something sharp sticking into my hip as I curled up my legs tight and I put my hand down very carefully without making a sound and felt around. It was something hard and plastic in the pocket of the shirt my mum had worn the night before to her class and I could just see it, a square white badge that said 'Student of the Week'. I thought Grey Green Sea Green Light Sand French Grey Rose Pink and my breath was coming out funny and then I got up out of the basket and even though my legs felt like jelly I walked into the living room.

Right, said Shane when he saw me. You. I've breached my parole conditions now thanks to you you interfering little bitch.

I looked at Mum and she just stood there in her green apron and I could see her shoulders hunching and her face closing up and Ellie stepped in front of me and said good, because I already called the police, and Shane turned around to her and grabbed her and threw her hard against the wall and I heard her head bang against the plaster and it's not true what happens in cartoons, people don't leave a person-shaped hole in the wall when they hit it.

But as soon as Ellie falls on the ground she stands up again grabbing onto a chair and Mum says in a voice like something far away don't touch my kids.

Shane turns back to her and his mouth goes scary and he says I should have known, everyone told me I was crazy to get involved with you. Everyone. They all know you're fucked in the head.

Mum is like one of the dolls without enough stuffing, loose and floppy, her hand on the bench to help her stand up. She's going to fall over and then we will have to see what he does to us. All the things she doesn't see, she will see them now but she will be too weak to stand up.

I feel Ellie behind me now, I smell her Oil of Olay and her lip gloss. My sister.

And this one, Shane says, pointing behind me at her. This little prickteaser here, she's going to turn out just like her mother, that one. Just like you – five bastard kids to five different blokes, can't look after any of 'em. And too dumb to charge for it.

Mum is still hunched up with her mouth open like she can't make it say anything.

She'll be a chip off the old block, he says to Mum.

Ellie doesn't say anything and I know why. I can hear her in my head, saying *Tyler let him just spew it out don't say anything or he will hurt us*. I hear her voice like when she is singing in her room, small but clear.

Mum turns and stares at us, Ellie and me. Then words come out of her mouth again, tired and flat: you'd better get out of here now. I think she means us to run and get away, but I can't move with Shane watching us, holding us frozen there.

Look at her, says Shane, pointing at Ellie. Crawlin' up to me. She hates you. Don't you, Ellie?

I turn around and Ellie shakes her head *no no no*. Tears fill up her eyes. Mum just stares at Ellie and I feel everything rock for a minute, back and forth. Then Mum flinches and blinks like something has just brushed across her face.

I mean it, out right now, or else, she says. But she's not saying it to Ellie, she's saying it to him. A quiet voice. And she's reaching into her apron pocket and she brings out the big silver scissors, the good scissors.

You've got to be fucken joking, says Shane, laughing like she's just said something stupid. On the bench is the big square knife and he slides it into his hand, and now the stones in my stomach are so heavy I just want to sink down and sit on the floor, because he does it so easily, you can see he's not scared at all of just sticking it in her.

I'm warning you, he says, you're making me have to defend myself. His wrist comes up, and he's pointing to the small blue tattoo on his neck, just a blue and blurry smudge. See this? he says, that means I done this before and believe me bitch I got no problems doing it again.

He did that himself, I hear Ellie say inside my head. *He's never been in jail. What sort of loser boasts about jail, and it isn't even true. Sad bastard with homemade tattoos. I'm right behind you, Ty. Right here.*

I warned you too, says our mother, and she steps forward with a little sigh as if it's all finished for her and she wants him to do it, but it's like my mum's arm has got strong hauling up the sewing machine every night and lifting all those rolls of material onto the table, she swings quick and easy like she's pushing the car door closed, then she steps back again and the scissors are buried in his stomach, just with the handles sticking out.

Shane looks down, amazed. Here's the part I don't understand Mrs Carlyle, he could have still stabbed us all to death then, but he didn't even look up. He just started crying. Then he sat down on the floor with his head down and held his stomach crying and my mum said Ellie, time to phone the police for real now. And she wasn't like a doll anymore. Someone had come along and put the white dots into her eyes and they were bright as black glittering glass, and her mouth was like the line you cut in the felt, one hard snip straight across the pattern, across the exact right spot. She held out one arm, and Ellie went into it.

Look, Mrs Carlyle, I am writing this in Prussian Blue. Guess what Ellie got me for Christmas, yes! it was the Derwents and all the blue ones are still my favourites. When you told us to write the journal you were still my teacher but I missed the last two weeks of term when I went up to Aunty Jacinta's place after all this happened. My mum asked me where did I want to go and I said her place and Mum didn't even argue, she said I think you're right, we all need a holiday. When I opened my present there at Christmas and saw it was the pencils I nearly cried and Aunty Jacinta showed me something I'd never noticed before. She said look at that drawing of the bridge on the tin, Ty. The artist has drawn it so carefully you can see how all those stones fit together to make that arch over the water, and then she opened the tin and said, look, on every single one of your new pencils they have stamped the word <u>artist</u>.

I only realised at the end that next year when school starts again I will be in secondary school across the road so you won't be my teacher anymore. But when you gave us the books you said it didn't matter where we started and finished and maybe the journal will never be finished but it doesn't matter. I kept writing mine these holidays so that you will know you were right. I have been thinking and thinking about when we went to your house to see the budgies and they ate seed out of your hand, and you said Tyler our true friends never ask us to do favours as a test and you looked so sad. I want to say, I hope you are not sad now because you helped me and I tried to be brave like you said and now I think I'm going good.

I still remember where you live. I'm going to put this in your letterbox. I hope that is OK. I hope you are still living there. If your budgie's eggs hatch please will you call one of the babies Alicia. One day I will get an aviary and then I will come and get her, Mrs Carlyle. That's my promise.

AFTERWORD

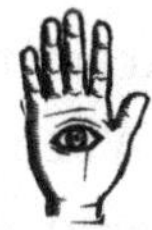

Bruno Bettelheim would strike my name from the Fairytale Teller's League, I'm sure, but when I read my daughter fairytales I find myself automatically censoring and sanitising some of the more nightmarish bits – girls dancing on hot pokers, mermaids having their tongues severed and having to walk on legs that felt like knives, woodcutters being ordered to cut out a child's heart – no wonder they were called the 'Grimm' brothers! Even before my daughter could talk I'd expurgate nursery rhymes. 'She gave them some broth and she gave them some bread,' I'd chant, smiling, 'then she kissed them all soundly and tucked them in bed.'

I rationalise by telling myself that it's the twenty-first century now and life is different for children; they don't face the same life-threatening perils. However, the more

I thought about the story of 'The Wolf and the Seven Kids', the more I was persuaded that even in contemporary, ordinary suburbia, where I wanted to set my story, the perils for some kids are all too real.

In the fairy story, a mother goat leaves her kids to go shopping, warning them not to let the wolf in. He tries to trick them into opening the door, disguising his voice as their mother's by eating chalk, but they recognise his dark paw on the windowsill. He covers his paw with white flour and returns, speaking in his softened, disguised voice and holding up the white paw as proof, and this time they open the door, thinking their mother has returned. He chases and eats up all of them except the littlest kid, who hides in the grandfather clock. When the mother goat returns she finds the smallest kid and they go together and find the wolf sleeping by the riverbank, his belly full of the other kids. The mother goat takes her scissors and cuts the wolf open and all the kids jump out unharmed. They each find a big stone and they fill the wolf's belly with them, and the mother sews him up again with her sewing kit. They make their escape and reach home safely. When the wolf awakens he's so thirsty he leans over the riverbank to drink. The heavy stones overbalance him and he falls in and drowns.

In one version, when the smallest kid tells the mother goat his siblings have been taken by the wolf, she says shortly: 'We'll see about that.' My daughter always waits for that line and recites it herself with great relish. I feel something of what she's feeling, I think – a relieved, exhilarated sense that even though the mother's unwisely left her children unprotected and a predator's got them, he's messing with the wrong goat, and now it's payback time.

Why did I choose this story, apart from the genuinely unforgettable creepiness of the wolf's sly, premeditated imitation of someone trustworthy? Because it came to mind when I was sitting with my sister-in-law watching our children splash in the pool last year. We sat there, drinking in their graceful freedom, and she said out of the blue: 'You know, I always considered myself a pacifist, but the moment I had kids I realised I was wrong. If someone hurt my children I would kill them. I wouldn't even need a weapon. I would kill them with my bare hands.'

I looked at her and nodded. Then we both looked back, eternally vigilant, at our swimming, carefree, oblivious children, and I thought we were like two grim lionesses there in the sun: *vigilant*, from the same root word as both *vigil* and *vigilante*. So I wanted to write about contemporary peril, and the guises a wolf might come in, and who, in spite of everything, might be keeping watch, grimly thinking: *we'll see about that.*

GLUTTED

by Nan McNab

She stunned the pig quickly, to spare them both, and stuck it while it was still rigid, opening the throat in a welling slit. Its trotters paddled in a pitiful attempt to flee – or so it always seemed to her – but it was dead, or as good as. Sprawled on its side, it ran on. She attached the chain quickly and hauled the pig aloft by a back leg, glad to use her muscles freely after clenching herself for the killing. Then she shoved a drum under the snout as the pig bled out.

'Excuse me.'

A jolt of horror stopped her – did the pig speak? – but she turned towards the doorway of the shed and saw that it was a sturdy child silhouetted against the flare of light. For a moment she was speechless, her heart thudding in her chest, then she stumbled to one side so she was not dazzled and saw that it was not a child but a little man. What was he doing here?

'Oh, look out!'

She flinched, but it was the pig that had convulsed, knocking over the drum.

'The blood,' he said. 'What a shame.'

She re-positioned the drum beneath the thrashing pig, steadying it with one hand. Steadying herself.

He was watching the pig with keen interest, not her, and her breathing eased a little. She saw that her mistake came from the childlike proportions of his body, the large head.

'We would make a blood pudding, where I come from,' he said, and she noticed the accent now.

Her heart was still pounding, but she found herself saying calmly enough, 'And you're—'

'Bohemian,' he said, then held up an expensive-looking black camera and fiddled with the lens. 'Would you mind?'

Ah, tourist, she thought, and wiped her forehead with the back of a gloved hand, conscious of her lank unwashed hair and flushed skin. *Lost tourist.* She stepped away from the corpse, turned her back and took out her steel to put a keener edge on the skinning knife. She disliked cameras.

'Please, don't let me interrupt. Go to your verk. Forget me. I will be silent. Do not think of me at all.' Snap.

But she did think of him, a strange man appearing as if by magic in her shed, and she alone. *I'm the one with the knife,* she told herself. Yet something childlike about him disarmed her.

'This is wonderful.' Snap. 'The afternoon light is so beautiful, don't you think?'

She reached for the hose and began to sluice the pig, glad of the fine mist on her burning face while he framed and shot. In spite of herself, she ceased to mind the camera, and they moved around each other in a sort of minuet, she thought, as she worked on the pig, slicing along the seams of the carcass to peel away the skin, hooking off the hooves, delicately opening the belly. Gutting required all her attention, and she soon forgot everything else.

Later, when she had done all she could, she straightened and saw him, surprised all over again at this little man in her shed.

'So. Hello. Good afternoon,' he said. He was wearing a pale linen suit and a beret, as if he had stepped out of a French film. It was not a labourer's beret like the leather-trimmed one her father had worn. For a moment she felt a stab of grief, remembering his smell, his forearms – brown and stringy with muscle – straining a fence, tending an animal.

When she did not respond he went on smoothly, 'I am forgetting my manners. Allow me to introduce myself. My name is Sanek. Otto Sanek. My friends call me Otik. How do you do.'

'How do you do,' she said, peeling off a glove and feeling his warm, smooth hand in hers. His formality was catching. 'My name is Greer.'

'Greer?'

'Yes, it's Scottish.' She smoothed her hand over her overalls and felt her work-hardened palm jag minutely on the cloth.

'Scottish?' He was smiling again. 'I have not been to Scotland, but I hope one day to go. I hear it is beautiful.'

'I wouldn't know.' Her real origins – here, the farm, these pigs – seemed too drab to own.

Now what? He was standing before her in his little suit as if there were nowhere he would rather be.

'Perhaps, if it is not too much trouble, I could ask you for a glass of water.'

'Oh, yes.'

She indicated the door, infected by his civility, and followed him out of the shed. The dogs were dancing on their chains, so she let them loose and they bounded round her, sniffing at the blood on her overalls, wagging their tails and waltzing in circles. She saw that he was chary of them, even little Molly, who was a scruffy charmer and accustomed to being petted. She ordered them to stay.

'You are wery kind.' He took off his beret and she noticed that his head was as flat as a flounder, the hair pressed to the back of his skull and dark with sweat. 'May I?' He nodded towards a worn backpack and a battered folio under one of the pine trees.

'Of course, bring them onto the verandah.' She waited for him, then opened the screen door, and they did an awkward little dance on the threshold as he pressed past her, each of them trying not to touch the other.

'Please, take a seat,' she said, and crossed to the sink to fill two glasses with water. 'There you are.' She dragged a chair out from the table and sat opposite him.

'Your health.' He drank it down in a single draught, and smacked his lips appreciatively. 'Aaah, thank you so much.'

She noted the wide forehead and the strong clean planes of his face, as if they had been hewn from wood. It was a head that belonged on a big, strong, handsome man.

'It is rainwater?'

She nodded, rotating her glass. His skin was fine-grained, spared the desiccation of an Australian childhood.

'There is nothing like it. Delicious.'

'Another?'

'If it's not too much trouble.'

She leapt up, conscious of his eyes on her back, her buttocks. This time she filled a jug. Jumping up and down like this was ridiculous.

She poured him another glass and he tossed it back. His face reminded her of the bust of Cicero on her tutor's bookcase, with its intelligent brow and soft loose mouth.

'Ah, so good. I am on a long and hungry journey – oh, I beg your pardon, a *thirsty* journey.' He laughed, and this time she smiled back.

'Are you hungry?' she asked.

His eyes slid away, and he said, 'Actually, I am famished.'

She was on her feet again, bringing bread and cold pickled pork, a board and knife, a plate. Her own appetite would take some time to return. It was always the way when she killed a pig.

When she began to slice the meat he took the knife from her, but charmingly, with an 'Allow me' and another smile, as slice after slice peeled away, moist and pink.

'None for me,' she said hurriedly. But he sliced more anyway, then slabs of bread.

'Do you have – what is the word? – lard?'

And she was off again, bringing the lard pot and setting it before him.

'Wonderful,' he said, his eyes gleaming. 'And a little salt perhaps?'

She fetched the salt and placed it near him, white and crusty in her grandmother's old crystal dish, the little silver spoon tarnished, she noticed. How she let things go, living alone. Her mother would never have been so careless.

As he ate, he told her stories, about himself, about the pictures he painted, about books and music and films, all the while biting and chewing, digging lard from the pot with his bread and salting it generously. His gusto, his pleasure in the food – in everything – seemed to loosen a knot somewhere within her. *This is what I've missed*, she thought. *This talk about the wider world, about art and ideas rather than just the price of wool and the cost of feed.*

She watched him, intrigued, and scooped up his stories, saving them for later, when she had time to think. She tried from long habit to find words to describe him, but he was too strange, too new, like a piece of music heard for the first time, and so not heard at all. And he made her laugh, pretending his command of English was less than it was, flattering her and offering little wordplays and jokes. She did not know what to think.

When at last he stopped talking, the plates were all empty. Not a crumb was left of the loaf, and the pork bone was clean and white.

'You *were* hungry,' she said.

'I am always hungry,' he said simply.

And yet you're a good doer, she thought, hearing her father's voice in the words and having to steady herself. How long until she stopped mourning for her parents, dead over a year now? After the accident Charlie had picked her up from university and brought her home. Dear Charlie, her neighbour and friend since primary school, with his slow smile and steady grey eyes. He'd seen her through those first stunned days and months, helped her with the farm, yet it wasn't enough. She was young; too young to be stuck out here alone. She still hankered for that other life she'd glimpsed at university, of ideas and books.

'Allow me to give you a little gift, to thank you for your kind hospitality.' He sounded rather grand as he said this, grand and generous and fine.

She blinked, unsure how to respond.

He went to the pile of his belongings and fetched the heavy cardboard folio.

'My verk,' he said, his voice weighty now. He untied the tapes and laid it open before her, lifting aside a sheet of tissue paper carefully.

They were small paintings in rich, intense colours, of things she had never seen or imagined outside of dreams and nightmares. She looked at them, entranced, drawn into a land she knew from childhood tales. If there were figures, they were solitary and stiff, like toys or dolls, their faces vacant, their eyes blank, peopling fantastic cityscapes, towers and empty squares. They reminded her of the grotesques of Hieronymus Bosch. She struggled to name the disturbing feelings they evoked: loneliness, isolation, rejection, yearning?

As she laid each one carefully aside, landscapes and abstracts replaced the figurative work, pigment bleeding into fantastic plants or meadows, domes or spires. These she loved. The less he put into the paintings, the more she saw, and the more room there was for her to imagine and dream.

'They're strange . . . but very beautiful.'

'Thank you,' he said. 'I would like you to have one, for the meal. A little one. These big ones are for my show.'

How could she choose? She went through them carefully once more, setting aside the bizarre figures and keeping the smoky landscapes.

'Or if you do not find one that you like, perhaps I could paint your farm, or your livestock . . .'

'My pigs?' She snorted.

'Your pigs are beautiful! I love the pigs.' He laughed at her reserve. 'Mr Orwell was not kind to the pigs, but we know better.' At the 'we', she felt the hard knot inside her slip a little more.

'Please, show me your farm.' He pulled a small sketchbook from his pocket, and a mechanical pencil of some sort, and said with another charming smile, 'I am ready.'

'What do you want to see?' she said, grabbing Spinner by the collar as he pranced up to the door with a stick in his mouth.

'Everything. Everything on this very fine farm.' He quickly took command of their walk, opening gates and doors with a flourish, gallantly ushering her into her own sheds. All of it was wonderful – unlike his own country, but magnificent. The orchard, that was a little like home, but there they had cherries, whereas here? Yes, Greer assured him, there were cherries, planted by her grandparents. The hens scratching under the trees were very nice – how many eggs each day? And the pigs, such fine beasts. He lingered over them, especially the piglets.

'Do you eat them?' he asked.

'No! They're only babies.'

'But with the apple? Suckling pig – she would be delicious.'

When he said *delicious*, he made a wet sound with his mouth that Greer found slightly repellent, but she quickly smothered the feeling. Here was an artist, a real artist, admiring her pigs, her farm, giving it back to her transformed.

She laughed. 'I'd soon be poor if I sold them off at that size.'

'Yes?' He nodded, and began to question her about the price of full-grown pigs, her profits, the living she made here. She would have minded if it were anyone else, but there was something so open, so frank about the questions that they seemed guileless.

'May I watch?' she said as he sketched one of the sows. Piglets were lined up along her belly suckling and nudging at the soft dugs. He nodded, concentrating. His hand was deft and quick, and he drew with a sureness that made her marvel, the lines economical and expressive. And yet the piglets looked strange when he had finished. *Exotic*, Greer told herself, as if he saw them through an old-world filter. She thought of the sinuous eucalypts in early colonial paintings squeezed into the mould of a birch or alder because their forms and colours were too novel for European sensibilities. For a moment she thought she glimpsed things through his eyes, and saw her farm grown suddenly unfamiliar. *Do we always see only what we expect to see?* she wondered. *Even the artists and poets?*

She wanted to ask him, to say that making poetry was like drawing or painting, that it required the same fresh glance, the same sifting and shaping, but she could not find the words. Often days passed on the farm when Greer spoke to no one but the pigs and the dogs, and when she did meet someone, her voice felt rusty and dry, and she could think of nothing to say. Small talk had never been small for Greer.

Since her parents had died, words had sometimes deserted her utterly, and she worried that she would become mute. Yet on good days, when she sat at her desk to write, words came unbidden and she folded them into her small, spare poems with a deep pleasure.

The old smokehouse her father had built sent him into ecstasies; it was just like the ones at home. She smiled at his enthusiasm. Charlie, however much he'd admired the farm, would never say much more than, 'You've got a nice set-up here.'

'Do you make sausage? Salami? Hams?'

'No. When my father was alive, he—'

'But Greer,' he cut across her, 'you could make much money from selling these . . . these . . .'

'Smallgoods?'

'Yes, these small goods. Much money.'

She wanted to laugh. Raised never to discuss religion, politics or money, Greer felt suddenly liberated by his complete indifference to social niceties. He was like a child who says loudly what everyone is thinking but is too afraid to utter.

Then they were back at the killing shed, and he hesitated outside the door to the cool room.

'The blood will still be good,' he said. 'Shall I show you how we make blood pudding? Blood pudding you could sell, also.'

She felt a warm rush of nostalgia. 'My dad loved black pudding.'

'Barley first,' he said, once they were back in the kitchen and the blood had been salted and thinned with vinegar. 'It must be soaked. Do you have . . .?'

She didn't.

'But you will have oatmeal. Good Scotch woman will not be without oatmeal.' He grinned at her, another little joke.

She returned the smile and brought the rolled oats.

He scooped up a quantity with both hands and dropped it into a bowl, passed it to her and indicated the tap. 'Plenty of your good rainwater to soak . . . no – more, more.'

She did as she was told, and had just set it down when he said, 'Now fat. That beautiful fat I saw on your pig this afternoon. It is perfect. We need—' He indicated with his hands the amount, then said, 'And bring belly fat. I will show you how to make škvarky, another very good dish.'

She strode out to the carcass, aware of every inch of her body, feeling that she might skip, or dance, or run for the sheer delight of it, as children do. She remembered the story of stone soup her mother had told her when she was a little girl, the cunning stranger drawing what he needed from his witless host. They had laughed about it, both confident that they would never be so gullible. Greer cut away enough of the creamy fat to fill a basin, then some liver and lights for the dogs, and strips of belly fat.

His eyes glistened when she gave him the basin, and he sank his hands into it, slicing and cubing the fat in a trice.

'Onions now, please.'

Greer fetched the basket and he took three large ones, cut them in half, slipped off their skins and sliced them with startling haste.

'Butter next, and your biggest frying pan.'

The kitchen soon filled with the smell of frying onions, and he issued more instructions: the oatmeal drained, a large bowl, salt, pepper, paprika?

Greer shook her head.

'I have my own supply,' he said. 'Don't worry. You are not the first in this primitive country to lack paprika!' He slipped outside and returned with a small tin of reddish spice which he sprinkled over the oatmeal. Then he tipped the onions into the bowl and blended everything together with his hands.

'Now, blood, please.'

She obeyed.

'It is best to use before it . . .'

'Clots?'

'Yes, clots. Pour it in until I say no.' She did so, her stomach turning at the texture, which reminded her of curdling milk. He began to mix and squeeze the bloody mass, and Greer realised she had only ever seen someone use their hands to mix scone dough or pastry. This looked alien and slightly disgusting.

'Ah, this reminds me of my papa. He made the best blood pudding – *No!*'

She stopped pouring at once.

'This is enough.'

'And your mother?'

He frowned. 'Mother is dead.'

'Oh. I'm sorry.'

'No need. She was mad. Best she is dead.'

When he had worked the mixture to an even consistency, he set the bowl aside, spread a tea towel over it, and said, 'While it cools, we will prepare the . . . what do you call this?' He indicated the mound of his belly.

'Stomach?'

'No, within.'

'Oh, guts?'

'Guts? No, I don't think so.'

'Intestines, innards, entrails.'

'Intestines.'

'I feed them to the dogs, or bury them.'

'Greer, you must not. You need them for your sausage! Come, I will show you. They are not yet given to the dogs, I am hoping?' Seeing her expression, he waved a hand. 'No matter, we can use cloth instead. We need no intestines, then.'

The blood pudding was finally seething in a pudding cloth when he sat down to paint. He unpacked a small travelling paintbox, the colours vivid as gems, and opened a cloth pouch of brushes.

'May I verk here? On the kitchen table?' he asked politely, sliding the lunch dishes to one end.

'Yes, of course.'

'Please, some more water. Two jars is enough.'

She fetched them, and sat opposite him.

'This pudding,' he declared as he loaded a brush with crimson, 'is not traditional way. But this is good for you Scotch people. Haggis, you call it?'

'Yes, I think so.'

'Next time when you kill the pig, you must have tubes all ready. Waste nothing, my father always says.'

He seemed to forget her then, concentrating on the paint.

What could she offer him in return for all he'd brought her? What did she have that would do?

'I write poetry,' she said. It came out baldly. 'I—'

'So, a poet. "Here with a loaf of bread beneath a bough, a flask of vine, a book of werse . . ."'

She laughed.

'You have a book of werse?' He smiled broadly. 'You are published poet?'

'Yes.'

'You must show me this book.'

His attention shifted to the stripped ham bone before she could get up and fetch a copy of her book. 'Will you make soup?'

'Maybe,' she said, awed. His appetite for food – for life – seemed unquenchable.

'The pudding is done, I think.'

Greer fetched plates, forks, knives and napkins, the sight of the two settings on the kitchen table lifting her spirits as it always did, even when it was only Charlie dropping by for lunch.

'Beer is the drink to have with blood pudding,' Otto said rather wistfully.

'I've got beer. In the cellar. Wait a bit.' Charlie was the only one who ever drank her father's home brew.

By the time she returned with a bottle in each hand, the plates were piled with slices of steaming pudding, its strange cloying smell filling her nostrils. She poured them a glass each, and set the bottle between them.

'Bon appétit,' he said.

'Cheers.' She heard how casual that sounded, almost childish, and speared a slice of the pudding, tasting it. It was good, livery, rich and savoury, but with a bitter aftertaste, and too strong to eat alone. She left the table and brought tomatoes and salad greens, a handful of little carrots, and her last loaf.

'Good?' He smiled at her.

'Yes, good,' she said, and returned the smile. It was a long time since she had sat with someone at this table, and she felt a sudden wash of happiness.

After the meal they sat and talked. He had finished the blood pudding and half the bread, emptied both bottles of beer, and they had begun on a bottle of whisky her parents had kept at the back of the pantry. Bolstered by the generous slug Otto had poured them both, Greer remembered studying

Holan and Seifert, the only poets she knew from his part of the world, and offered them to him as a sort of surety, but when she moved on to the Russians he stopped her.

'Russians I hate,' he said.

'But surely their writing . . .'

'Yes yes, but still I hate them.' He smiled. 'At school we must learn Russian language, Russian books, Russian music. Enough!' He laughed. 'I still remember the smell of Russians in my country.'

'Surely not.'

'Surely yes. They stink of cologne.' He poured more whisky for himself. 'Will I tell you how I escaped from them?'

Greer nodded, with some of the gleeful anticipation she felt when her mother asked her, 'Will we have another chapter?' Perhaps she was drunk.

She listened while Otto told the story of his escape, full of bravado and audacity and humour, and she found herself laughing, then almost at once pitying him, and soon after admiring his courage. Surely no one she knew had ever had to make such decisions, or risk so much. It was . . . heroic, she thought rather muzzily.

The night ticked by, and what would happen next loomed between them, but Greer was unable to speak, despite the whisky. Eventually, he drained his glass, rose to his feet, bowed, and said he would be on his way.

'Where will you go?'

He smiled at her winningly. 'That depends rather much on where I am.'

She ran a hand through her hair. Why hadn't she washed it? 'Well, it's a good hour to town if you go by the road.'

'I see.' He was serious now.

There was an awkward silence.

'I will go. You have been wery kind. I have been wery happy today.' He got up and cleared the plates. 'But first I will vash the dishes, as my mother taught me. Verk first, with Mother, always verk.'

'No, please don't worry. I'll wash them with the breakfast things. Saves water.' It sounded too curt.

'Of course.'

'If you would like to stay here, there's a spare room,' she blurted. 'It's late to be walking, and where would you stay when you get there?'

'Ah, you are far too kind, Greer, but thank you. I would like that very much.' His lips formed a little moue, as if he were savouring that last word, as he had savoured the blood pudding.

She woke late. Greer, who never overslept, who was at her desk before the sun rose, woke to sunlight streaming through the window and groaned. She leapt up, guilty, climbing into her work clothes unwashed, unbrushed – the hair would have to wait another day.

The kitchen smelt of fat, and the table was set with food from the pantry. Had he eaten breakfast? There were no dirty dishes, but he had left his crockery and cutlery in the dish drainer, neat in all things, and in the sink were the shells of half-a-dozen eggs. The bread tin was empty, but on the bench there was a bowl with a few cubes of greasy crackling – what had he called it? Škvarky? Weighed down with a knife was a small sketch of the dead pig, with a few touches of colour and an inscription – *Thank you Grir* – in a baroque hand.

She stared at the sketch. Did she like it? The disturbing slit in the pig's body was black and ragged, the gash in the throat a charred scarlet. Was it weirdly erotic or weirdly perverse?

He had gone, and taken his paintings with him. Why hadn't she chosen one when she had the chance? He had appeared and disappeared so suddenly she might have conjured him up, were it not for the empty plates in her pantry and this one small sketch. It was as if the little man had come from the land of wonders, of reverie and art, his paintings like souvenirs from that strange and marvellous place which she, a simple poet – no, be honest, a farmer – had only glimpsed now and then. Still, she believed she could recognise the signs of it in his work. He had the secret, she was sure of it.

She propped the picture carefully on a shelf, downed a glass of water, fighting the undertow of disappointment and self-doubt that seemed to be her lot now that she was alone. Why had she slept so late? She should not have let him slip away.

The dogs were scratching at the back door, and she stepped outside and squatted down to them, burying her face for a moment in Spinner's silky coat. *Count your blessings*, she told herself in her mother's no-nonsense voice, but there was only the clamour of the pigs for their food, and the dogs' polite hints, and this huge thirst in her. *Salt or alcohol*, she thought, draining another glass of water, *or both*.

Molly and Spinner wolfed down their dry tack, then followed her to the pig paddock, where the weaners were pressing their snouts through the fence and shrilling to be fed. She banged the slop bucket, calling, 'Pig, pig, pig,' and they followed her to the troughs. The farm had long outgrown slops, but still she took her peelings and kitchen waste and added it to the grain and pig feed. Yes, the pigs were beautiful. She could admit it now that he had said it, the artist. The smell, too, was part of the odour of childhood, familiar. For a moment she watched them, leaning over to scratch a scaly neck or two before heading back to the house and her morning's work.

Watching the black-and-white pigs rootling for tender shoots, she wondered what her parents would have said about letting them wander, and what they would have made of the artist, but the dead keep their counsel. At times, even now, she felt their deaths as a dragging weight, and missed their steady love and clear good sense. Month by month they faded. Perhaps she had rubbed away the lustre from her memories as she worked them into those raw, abrupt poems. She had been surprised when they were published, and then favourably reviewed, surprised they were reviewed at all. Best, though, was the note from a favourite poet expressing his admiration. He wished he had written one of the poems himself, he said. She kept the letter in the old blackwood box of her father's, along with her mother's rings and the single strand of pearls that Greer could still not bring herself to try on.

Eat, she told herself. *You are just hungry. Eat and then work.* But today her commands could not contain the wash of yearning that stopped her for moments and left her staring at nothing, or rather at fragmented images, flickering like an old black-and-white film: a toddler with flaring sun-glitter on her hair, the dark bulk of a man. That day she felt chock-full of longings, for a family to wrap around herself, replacing all she had lost.

She was driving back from town a week later when she saw a figure on the side of the road, hefting an assortment of bags. *Otto!* She swung the ute off the road and braked hard.

He leant in at her window, smiling broadly, and she smelt his sweat.

'Greer. I am coming to see you. I have the photographs. May I?' He piled his belongings into the back and bounced into the passenger seat.

'Look at this!' he exclaimed, waving a hand at the bleached summer paddocks. 'This grass you must paint with Naples yellow and white, and perhaps a very little Payne's grey. What a landscape!'

'I always think summer grass is the colour of sheep,' she said, and smiled at him. She could not say such things to anyone else.

All the way home he exclaimed at the beauty of the high clouds, the line of hills, dropping the names of painters into the conversation which she pretended to recognise, or knew a little.

'Such a long walk,' he said with a sigh, easing his bags down beside the kitchen table.

'Have a seat,' she said, dropping her own bags beside the fridge. 'I'll put the kettle on. Are you hungry?'

'I am always hungry,' he said again, grinning, and this time she laughed. 'But I will cook, and you will see what I have done. Here, you sit down and look at these.'

He busied himself while she set out the photographs on the kitchen table, disappointed for a moment that they were all black-and-white. She had been expecting the same gorgeous colour as the paintings. But soon she forgot, and when he placed an omelette beside her, she ate absently, her eyes on the pictures of what must be her farm, for the images were cryptic, the light mysterious. In one, the pig's body lay on the heavy drape of its own skin, its fat creamy and pure. In another, rosebuds of raw flesh gleamed on trotters where the hoofs had been hooked away. The entrails were like a Dutch still life, glistening, coiled and weighty. And most surprising of all was Greer herself, suddenly beautiful, the sheen of sweat on her arm as she turned the carcass, the line of her back, ribs corrugating the old singlet as she bent over the cavity to free the lungs. She had never seen herself like this; never seen her place like this. He had given it back to her renewed.

'You see, this is very beautiful,' he said, running a finger over a photograph to trace the line of her neck. 'You have a long neck—' He repeated the gesture, almost touching her, and she went still and held her breath, heat flooding through her.

Next morning, she lay in bed, sore and dull, the sheet pulled up to her chin and one hand cupped between her legs. None of this had she imagined, even in her most florid fantasies. Such . . . *greed*. He had wolfed her down when she had wanted to be tasted and savoured, to be touched tenderly, appreciatively, to be known.

When she had sought his mouth he had turned his head sharply – almost in disgust, she thought now. 'I don't like to kiss,' he'd said, and rolled her away from him, butting at her from behind.

Grow up, she told herself now. *This is a man, not some timid romantic boy.* But she felt her throat constrict as she pressed the weal on her shoulder where he had sunk his teeth into her. The bones of her pelvis ached and she needed to cry.

Now the sun was up and she could hear busy, cheerful sounds from the kitchen. Soon he appeared with a laden tray – fragrant coffee and slabs of fried bread giving off the savoury stink of garlic. He was happy, and seeing him, Greer had to smile too.

'I am thinking all night of the smokehouse,' he said, giving her the tray and taking his own plate over to the window. 'Salami, prosciutto, sausage, hams—' he waved his fork, '—you can do all. Greer, you have the goldmine.'

It was not what she had expected.

There was a small silence, and then he said, 'You are very beautiful woman, Greer. I have made picture of you. Would you like to see?'

It was in his sketchbook, a Neolithic Venus, breasts and hips amplified, head shrunk to an apple on a long stalk. Was that her – Greer, the artist's muse? There was something in the proportions, in the distortions, and the lines were sure and elegant. She was flattered.

And so the little man crept into her heart, and into her bed. Never would he tolerate her kisses or caresses, starting away from her as if her touch burned him. But she told herself it was early days – a man and woman needed time to learn about each other – and perhaps, in some dark place, she welcomed the brute force, the compulsion.

Each evening when she came in from work, the smell of

linseed oil seemed like the smell of promise. They ate vast meals and he talked about the smokehouse and the market for smallgoods. She studied him, enjoying his enthusiasm and the pleasure he took in everything. And they talked, about books and philosophy, art and music, the old cities of Europe and their bloody history, skating over them at dizzying speed. This, at last, was life. Greer wanted to dig deeper, to develop her ideas, but he was always off on something new.

She loved to see his paints and jars and brushes, the sketchbooks open on the kitchen table, the sequence of bizarre still lifes he was creating. In his paintings, Otto transformed the contents of her cupboards: her grandmother's yellow porcelain bowl supported a nesting bird with extravagant plumage; a grove of old bone-handled knives, silver spoons and forks grew from the hill at the back of her farm; her cast-iron pot became an unlikely vessel afloat on a darkening sea; and a pig flew over a pile of her books. They were images from a child's fantastical world, and Greer was entranced to see the stuff of her life, grown invisible to her through long use and habit, transformed into art. She puzzled over the paintings but could find no meaning in them. Poetry often required effort. Like all good art, it didn't always open itself on a first reading, but demanded something of the reader. Why could she not see beneath the surface of his paintings? Art for her demanded the deepest honesty and the clearest sight, or it failed. *There must be some lack in me*, she thought, but still she was captivated.

Sometimes he would be there, bent over his small easel; at other times he would disappear for half a day, or a whole evening, coming home long after she'd gone to bed. Perhaps he went in search of new things to paint or to photograph. Greer felt unable to ask yet, her own place in his life still tenuous and undefined.

Within a month she found herself able to pack up her parents' clothes and possessions and store their bed in the barn. 'It is best, Greer,' Otto had said kindly. 'I help you. It will be my studio, this room. Something new. You will see. It is best to forget the past.'

The dressing table would be good for drawing, he insisted, and his pleasure in the room carried her along as she collected her mother's few cosmetics and tipped them into a bin. The brush, still smelling faintly of her hair, Greer pushed to the back of her own underwear drawer.

As she sorted and packed, she told him stories, to make him a gift of her childhood, and the parents he would never meet. She showed him her mother's few bits of jewellery, catching the worn ring in her palm and giving it a squeeze, rubbing the pearls with her thumb.

'I used to fiddle with this ring while my mother read to me. It's one of my earliest memories. Those magical stories, and her warm weight on the bed . . .'

'It is gold?'

'Mmm.'

She told him about the rare times her mother had worn the pearls to a dance or a wedding, and how beautiful she appeared to her small daughter, her dark eyes gleaming, her lips an unaccustomed red.

'They are valuable?'

'I don't know. I've never had them valued. I always put off wearing them until . . . I don't know . . . until I became a woman, I suppose.'

'This room is good for me,' Otto mused. 'The light is excellent.'

The strand of pearls trickled through her fingers into their case and she snapped it shut.

'This warze will do for my brushes.' He indicated a vase with a rich green glaze.

'Oh, that one belonged to my great-great-grandmother. My mother used to fill it with blossom – she had a knack with flowers – and hawthorn berries in autumn. I don't think . . .'

'Ah, Greer, you are such a bourgeois,' he said. 'It is only a warze – so ugly.' He smiled. 'These things, they do not matter.'

And they didn't, because Greer was happy, busier than she had ever been, but able to watch Otto while he painted, increasingly confident that he possessed the key to a door that would open onto that larger and more intense world which she had glimpsed in her single year at university. Both her parents had been readers, and she came from generations of self-taught farmers, but she was the first to go to university, and had always felt the two parts of herself, daughter and student, chafing against each other. In the grief and shock of her parents' death, she had done what was necessary. The poems had been both a way to honour her parents and an attempt to regain some of what she had lost, to reinsert herself into the world of poetry readings, small-press magazines and slim, hand-stitched chapbooks.

Otto talked of the smokehouse often. His best memories, he told her, were of his father smoking sausages when he was a boy – the mingled smells of garlic and pork and wood smoke, and the taste – there was nothing like it. Greer thought she recognised the voice of longing and loss, and pitied his homelessness. She wanted only what he wanted, but she was practical, and began to anticipate what must be done to please him. 'We must make it modern, though, Otto. It must be clean, and it must be bigger than your father's to make sense commercially.'

She did her research in the evenings, when she came in from work. Otto would have a joint on to roast, the kitchen smelling wonderfully of garlic and onions and spices. He would pile their plates with meat and potatoes, and they would eat and drink until Greer pleaded satiety, then, feeling heavy but content, she would return to the computer until late.

Soon people from the city began to call to see the artist at work, or people Otto had met at a gallery, or on a bus, old friends perhaps. Often she would come in from mucking out the pens to find her kitchen full of people, all talking and laughing and admiring his latest paintings. The air smelled of cooking and fresh coffee and he would pour her a cup, solicitous and kind in front of them. 'Greer, sit here. Would you like water also?'

'Thank you.'

She felt shy, clumsy in her soiled work clothes, and unused to so many people and so much chatter. But it had been one of her secret wishes, for a world where people talked about more than the drought, or the price of fertiliser; where they lived different lives from her parents, from Charlie; where she was not so odd. Perhaps this was the beginning.

Often they talked late into the night, wine bottles accumulating on the table, the coffee pot refilled. When she woke, bleary and thick-headed, in the morning, humps of bedding would cover the sofas and the door to the spare room would be shut. She would tiptoe outside into the day, closing the screen door carefully behind her.

Her poetry notebooks were untouched – she had neither the solitude nor the energy for her early-morning drafts, but she kept a small pad in the pocket of her overalls to jot down fleeting images and lines, hoping that one day she would have time. Each night she fell into bed too exhausted to read, but life was good, life was rich and exciting with Otto. The house filled with the things he made or found. He hewed firewood into crude beasts, torsos or heads and set them in the garden and beside the drive. He lined a discarded mudlark's nest with a lace doily and displayed it on the mantelpiece, and wove corn dollies out of straw, hanging them in the window. His view of the world was as fresh and unspoilt as a child's, and she loved him for it.

Some nights she woke to pain, and found him pressed against her back, his thick fingers clutching her breasts, kneading her flesh. Why did he have to ambush her like this, drag her back into her skin from the deeps of exhausted sleep? Why when she came to him in the evening did he turn away from her? But in the mornings he would smile like a child, delighted with what the day presented, and she would remind herself that his appetite for life, which she so loved, was the same force that drove him to bite her shoulder and tug at her hips in the night, the same force that produced his art. Looked at another way, it was energy and fervour – passion – that he brought to their nights, and she told herself she was squeamish and prim.

The smokehouse plan quickly became burdensome, but she pressed on, reading about meat mincers, brine injectors, smoke generators, sausage fillers until her head spun. Then there were the legal requirements, inspectors, standards, registration, packaging, labelling. When she tried to talk to Otto he poured scorn on her concerns. His father had never needed these permits. Pah! So many laws and rules, it was not necessary. 'Here, I will draw you the smokehouse; it is all you need. And the labels, I will do. They will be the most beautiful of any.'

She would smile, and resolve to keep these concerns to herself in future. She needed more than pretty labels and picturesque wooden buildings – she needed money. Otto was an artist, an innocent, with an artist's view of the world. She was the practical one.

And so she found herself before very long sitting opposite the bank manager and asking him for a large overdraft. Otto was at home, painting. It was his work, he explained, and could not be set aside, even for a morning. 'You go, Greer. It is your farm. I am not good with the money.'

Her family had been thrifty and modest, yet the bank manager made her feel like a beggar and a fool. Did she have a business plan? he asked her coolly, peering at her over his rimless glasses. Had she investigated the market for these products? Were there hygiene issues? His nostrils flared minutely, as if he could smell pig on her.

She answered his questions, listed her assets, pressing on mulishly, and he was cold and disdainful and uncompromising. She despised him, but in the end he drew up the documents and made her sign – here, and here – indicating the places with a manicured finger.

Her farm was mortgaged.

She spotted the green vase as she was on her way from the bank to the store. It was in the window of the gallery cum antique shop, alongside a set of cream-and-green canisters, some old green enamel bowls, and a couple of lime-green linen tea towels. Greer was shocked by the price tag.

At home, she walked into her parents' old room and placed the vase on the dressing table beside his paints. 'I found the vase, Otto.'

He glanced up, then bent over his painting, concentrating on a detail, ignoring her.

'Warze?'

'This vase. It was not yours to sell.'

'Still so worried about your china cabinet?'

'It's been in my family for—'

'I needed paints. Until my show I cannot pay.' He sounded furious.

'If you need money you only have to ask—' She heard herself placating him, reassuring him.

'I do not like to beg.' He jammed his brush in the preserving jar of turps she had given him and washed it thoroughly.

'It's not begging. Otto, you know I begrudge you nothing.'

'But you begrudge me this ugly old warze.'

'No, I—'

'This is bourgeois bullshit, Greer. I have told you.'

'But it was my mother's.'

'Do not speak to me of mothers,' he hissed.

One day, she recognised a journalist amongst the throng seated around her table – Evonne, Eva, something. They had both written for the university newspaper, although she must have been in her final year when Greer was a first-year.

'Ah, here is Greer. Speak to Greer,' said Otto, beckoning her over. 'She has a book of worse.'

'Worse?'

'Poetry,' she said quietly, filling a glass and drinking it in two long swallows. The woman barely looked at Greer.

'You can write about my paintings and Greer's worse,' Otto insisted, good-natured as ever. 'Greer, get your book while I show Eva my verk.' He pronounced it *Ever*.

She fetched it, but when she returned the food had been pushed to one end of the table and Otto's little jewelled paintings had been spread out for their admiration.

'Do you like this?' Otto said, indicating an abstract in rich crimson and umber. 'This I will show, I think.'

'You're having an exhibition?' Eva sensed a story. 'How marvellous.'

'Yes, very soon. You will be first to know.'

'Otto?' said Greer.

'And this is mother,' he said, pointing to an old woman clutching an axe, like a Judy puppet with her stick, about to beat Mr Punch. Her clothes were primitive, her face a rictus of rage. Everyone laughed, and he leafed through others. The old woman figured in several – Greer was surprised to see how many. Here she stood before a burning house, flames like red hair bristling from the windows; in another she wore a white coat stained with blood and carried cutting implements – the paintings were nightmarish, but he hurried past them, saying with a smile, 'Mother . . . mother again . . .' until he came to a painting of the orchard, all the trees dotted with picture-book fruit.

'Oh, that's really lovely!'

'Do you think?' Otto seemed suddenly uncertain.

'Yes, beautiful, really, you're so gifted.'

He smiled. 'Thank you. You are very kind.'

Greer noticed a painting of the green vase, with a tree sprouting from it, shedding leaves that turned to play money as they fell. Her face burned.

'Oh, this is *gorgeous*!' Eva pounced on a funny little painting of a flying pig that he had promised to Greer for her labels and advertising. This one flew high above the farm, the town tucked into the hills in the distance.

'You like it?'

'I love it. How much?'

It's not for sale, Greer thought, *it's my trademark*, but Otto mentioned a ridiculous figure for such a small work, and Eva pulled out a cheque book. 'Sold!' she said jubilantly.

'You see, Greer, I too can make the money.'

They visited the bank together the following day, and Greer was astonished to find the bank manager a changed man: where she had expected contempt, she found instead a clumsy bonhomie. It seemed that no one was immune to the artist's charm. She wanted to add Otto as a signatory to her account to grant him some financial independence, but found herself listening to a conversation about art, in which the bank manager paraded his knowledge, and Otto flattered and encouraged. Behind the cold façade was a connoisseur, apparently, and one eager to see Otto's paintings. The paperwork was dispatched within minutes – 'Sign here, and here, and you'll need a debit card of course, and a cheque book? Credit card? Of course.' Nothing was too much trouble. And Otto, at his most winning, promised to bring his work in to the bank for a private showing before it went to the framer.

Outside in the sunshine, Greer didn't know whether to laugh or grind her teeth with rage. 'Otto, how did you do it? That man's a supercilious, cold-hearted . . .'

'No, no, he is fine. You'll see. Come on, now. Let us drink to our success.'

'Our what?'

'To my show.'

Greer had rarely been to the pub. Her parents had never drunk much, and it was not a place she could visit alone without causing a minor scandal. But Otto was obviously well known, and was greeted warmly by the publican and most of the drinkers. Greer noticed one of his paintings hanging in the bar.

'Usual, Otto?'

'Thank you. And for Greer, champagne. And one for you, my friend. One for all! Today we celebrate.'

'Sure thing. So what's this in aid of?'

'In aid of me, my friend. My new show. It will be big success, you'll see.'

The publican laughed, setting a pint of beer on the bar for Otto, and starting to pull beers for the other drinkers. Soon Otto was surrounded by well-wishers, and Greer found herself edged along the bar. She reached for her champagne as he proposed a toast, raising his pint pot and shouting, 'To art!'

'To art!' they cried, surely the strangest toast ever made in that small country pub.

An old man on her left, his nose crimson with grog blossoms, mumbled, 'Who's Art?'

The barman totted up the bill and Otto took out the new credit card and slapped it onto the bar. 'Can you make the tab?'

The barman nodded and scooped it up. 'Cheers.'

Otto insisted the exhibition was a triumph. He had sold almost a third of his pictures, and many people had expressed an interest, especially in the flying pig, which he had painted again, changing it slightly. He'd sold one version to the bank manager for a hefty price, who insisted on calling it 'Pigs Might Fly' and made a ponderous joke about farmers and overdrafts. Greer flushed, but Otto laughed immoderately.

Afterwards he told Greer, 'It is kitsch, this flying pig, but they do not see it. I paint it fifty times and still it sells. These people, they know nothing. Philistines! Art-lovers the worst . . . no, amateur painters – *they* are the worst,' he said with relish.

'Why do you bother with them then?'

'Because they are useful, or they may be.'

But in spite of the failings of the townspeople, and the gallery, which was nothing more than a 'pretentious craft shop', Otto pronounced himself well pleased.

Greer cast her eye down the catalogue and did some quick arithmetic. The gallery took half – *half*, and for what? – then there were framing expenses, the cost of canvas, stretchers, and those wickedly expensive little blocks and tubes of paint . . . After they subtracted the cost of all that, there would be nothing, less than nothing, left. This was success? This was the life of art?

'Always with you it is money!' he shouted. 'This is bourgeois bullshit, this always worrying about money money money!'

'I *have* to worry about money, Otto, or we won't eat.'

'We have big farm full of things to eat. Don't give me that.'

But it's my *farm*, she thought. *And it's my hard work. If we keep on like this you'll eat up everything I have.* She began to cry, silently, shamed by her weakness.

He snorted contemptuously. 'It is always tears with you women. Tears and money. My mother is just the same. "You must work, Otichek. I cannot do all. Art does not fill our bellies, Otik . . ."' He minced and mimicked savagely, then suddenly barked, '*All* from my show will go into your bank. *All*. You are happy now?' He slammed out of the room and she heard him thumping and banging around in his studio and finally the sound of the front door slamming.

Greer, replaying the exchange later, wondered if his mother was alive after all. Was her resurrection no more than a grammatical slip? Was she still in Europe, or out here? Did she know about Greer? But what did it matter, if Otto had left her?

Days passed, then weeks. Otto didn't return. The exhibition money did not appear in her account. People dropped by to see him, or called, and she made excuses. 'He's gone away. No, I'm sorry, I can't say when he'll be back.' She let Spinner and Molly in again at night for company, as she had done in the past, and they were ecstatic, then hastily sober and polite, as if good manners might stave off banishment and keep them there by the fire forever with their beloved mistress.

Time seemed to slow and thicken. The days shortened and she felt again, as she had after her parents' death, that winter was her enemy, sucking warmth from her. She worked to stop her thoughts, oversaw the building of the smokehouse, did what she could herself to cut costs, but she had no enthusiasm for it anymore. The paperwork and red tape were maddening. Everything exhausted her, and she was off her food, feeling a faint nausea whenever she thought of eating. What was the matter with her? *You're tired*, she told herself. *And you're sad. Work. Sleep. Forget.* And so she plodded through each day, hoping that she would look up from her books and see that blocky little figure standing in the doorway of her kitchen and they could start again, and talk.

The first postcard came in the same mail as the bank statement, which she opened at once. Casting her eye down the withdrawals for builders, concreters, plumbers, smoking equipment, she found a cluster of expenses from a city in France! And wait, there were more. For an instant her throat closed with panic – someone had stolen her bank details – and then she knew. Her account was almost empty, and here was confirmation, a postcard with a foreign stamp and the familiar extravagant hand.

My favourite painting in whole Louvre. I am reborn after visit to this my true home. Thank you Grir. Back on 30th. I have much to tell.

Greer felt a spurt of laughter catch in her throat, then turn to a sob. She cried tears of fury and fear and joy. He was coming home. But he had emptied her account. What would she do? He might have much to tell, but Greer had news of her own: she was pregnant.

Otto arrived one evening, luggage stuffed with books, prints, small sculptures, new camera equipment, brushes, paints, liqueurs, chocolates and other little luxuries. He was in high spirits, showing her his work, telling her stories about what he had seen and where he had been, what he had eaten, the wines he had drunk, and the promises of exhibitions in Paris, Milan and Bratislava. They would be rich! It was his big break. They would go together, travel the world! She listened, waiting for the right moment. But there was no right moment, and he seemed oblivious to her silence. Instead, she told him at dinner, abruptly, when his mouth was too full of food for him to talk.

'Otto, I'm pregnant.'

He stopped chewing, frowned. 'Oh, I'm sorry.'

She felt a sudden chill, then a wave of heat. 'Why are you sorry? I'm not.'

'Greer, don't be stupid. This cannot be.'

'But—'

'No. I am artist, Greer. I am not caught so easily.'

Caught? *Caught!* Greer was speechless.

'You are poet!' he went on. 'You do not want babies. How can you have babies and be poet and farmer?'

Why did he mention her poetry only now? She had not written a line for months, and he had always been indifferent to her work. She stood abruptly and went to her bedroom, shutting the door firmly. She lay on her bed, her mind threshing between impossibilities as the hours ticked by, and he did not join her.

In the morning Greer made him coffee, feeling too queasy for anything more than weak tea. When it became clear that she would not be cooking breakfast, he slammed into the pantry and came out with eggs, bacon, garlic, onions and bread. The smells sickened her, but she sat there as he listed his requirements and fried up a pile of food for himself. She would have her little baby, but he would need a studio, a large studio, big enough so he could show his work. A studio gallery. There must be room for him to paint and draw, and for a press – he had decided to return to printmaking since his trip – and space for him to sleep if he needed peace and quiet. His first European show was in six months' time. It was necessary that he attend, and he would be away for at least six weeks. It could not be helped. And if Greer insisted on such foolishness, she must understand that he could not be trapped like this. 'You must pay all, Greer, if you want babies like every stupid woman.'

'I do want babies,' Greer said quietly, 'and I hoped you would, too. But if you don't, then I will have this baby alone, and I will care for it alone.' For a moment sorrow welled in her, but she fought it down. There at the kitchen table she determined that she would ask him for nothing. She would manage as she had always managed, and he could have his studio.

'The orchard's the obvious block to sell, Greer, if you must.' Charlie's voice was kind, but he was frowning.

'I've got no choice. I can't go back to the bank, and I've got feed to buy and bills to pay, and the mortgage, and

I'm . . .' She couldn't say it, couldn't tell him. Even asking his advice seemed unfair.

'I could—'

'No, Charlie. It's my problem.'

He sighed, nodded. 'Well, the orchard, then. It's on its own title, there's easy access from the road, and it'd make a nice weekender for somebody, although the pigs might be a problem.'

'I can keep them further to the south. That next paddock can be used for crops. I'll figure out something.'

'Greer, I'd buy it myself, but it's too far from my place, and you'll get more if you sell it as a house block.' For an instant she slipped into a parallel life with Charlie and a baby, finding to her surprise not tedium but safety and kindness and ease. Almost, she thought, love, then shook herself.

It was decided, the orchard had to go, the trees her grandparents and parents had planted and tended must be sold. It felt like cutting away part of herself.

Greer felt better and stronger in her second trimester. The smokehouse was finished and the product trials had been surprisingly successful; she had more orders than she could fill for her hams, farmhouse sausage and salami. Business was looking good, and she began to feel more hopeful. She caught herself whistling or singing as she worked, something irrepressible rising in her. She hadn't felt as buoyant since her parents were alive. It was the child growing steadily within her, she was sure.

Otto had produced an etching of the flying pig for her labels, which managed to look both elegant and rustic, but apart from that he took no interest in the business, only in the smoked meats. His appetite was prodigious. Greer looked at him crossing the yard, and saw that he had ballooned into a humpty dumpty; face round as a plate, the strong planes of cheeks, forehead and jaw blurred. His clothes no longer fitted. *More expense*, Greer thought. Each day he would cut slabs of bread and ham or salami for his lunch and take them into town, where he rented a studio. It was necessary, he said, until his new studio was built. Her parents' room where he had painted for months no longer sufficed. 'I must be seen. The farm is too isolated, too quiet. I need people, Greer. People will buy my paintings.' And he needed to go to the city regularly to negotiate with one of the big galleries. Once he signed with them, he would be rich. 'Money for studio is investment, Greer. Like smokehouse. You have to spend money to make money.'

The half-built studio was on a rise overlooking the orchard, which had been sold to people from the city. They had pulled out half the trees to clear a large building site, but left most of the rest, for which Greer was grateful, as she was for the money, but she felt a deep shame over the loss of the orchard. She had failed her family, failed herself. The rustic building she had envisaged for the studio, with its recycled timber and second-hand windows, quivered and dissolved. Otto insisted on double-glazed industrial windows from floor to ceiling, 'for the light'; masonry walls for a stable environment for his papers; water was necessary, and a toilet, and also a small kitchen. And proper heating. Greer tried to talk to him about the mounting costs, but he flew into a rage. 'You who have so much begrudge me this? How can I paint if I have no studio? I am an artist! Where can I work? I cannot print in your little kitchen! It is dirty. Painting is dirty. You do not want me and my dirty paints when you have your little baby.'

He was jealous, Greer reasoned, and felt touched. She'd be less blunt when next they talked, she promised herself. But each time they fought, she would find something broken, or missing. The shattered green vase she found pushed to the back of the wardrobe. Her mother's pearls, gleaming in a dark still life with a china teacup and a silver spoon, simply disappeared. When she asked about a crystal ewer, he looked at her with such loathing that Greer, worried she would drive him away once and for all, learned to be mute. Children needed two parents, she was convinced. Her baby must have a father. She should practise detachment, like the Buddhists. She should not put such store in mere things.

'You are losing weight, Greer. Are you eating sensibly?' The midwife jotted down the figure with a frown.

'Yes, I . . .' In truth she was often too tired to eat, or felt too unsettled.

'You are pregnant. You need to eat and rest. If you don't, you will endanger the health of your baby.'

Greer's eyes prickled with tears and her hands, gripped in her lap, blurred and swam. She nodded. There was nothing to say. She had to work, now more than ever. Otto was travelling again, organising exhibitions he said, in a chain of galleries in several big cities. He had to be there in person to close the deal. Without Otto to share meals with, she often fell asleep in her clothes, too exhausted to eat, and woke later, shaking with hunger and fatigue.

Greer had been to the bank manager to try to extend the term of the mortgage and borrow a little more, but there was no sign of the warmth he had shown Otto. 'If you need to borrow money for daily expenses, you are not managing your finances or your business properly,' he said coldly. 'No offence.' This time there was no convenient block to sell. The rest of her land was on four large titles and if she sold one of them, she would have to rearrange the rotation of her paddocks and lose good cropping land, but it was that or lose the farm, which secured the mortgage. She sold one, and somehow it was Charlie who managed to buy it, and pay a fair price, even though he knew she was desperate.

When Greer's waters broke, almost a month early, it was Charlie she called. He did not mention his own farm, or the shearing waiting for him, or Otto, a capable man, living with her but apparently unable to work, and now gadding around Europe . . . He just came when she needed him and said nothing. Charlie would never understand that Otto was an artist, and therefore exempt from the rules that governed the lives of others, but the effort of explaining it all was beyond her.

On the trip to hospital, feeling her body in the grip of a powerful spasm that she had seen often enough in her labouring sows, she remembered to tell him that her best sow had just farrowed, and needed to be watched. 'Not to worry,' he said, 'I'll keep an eye on the litter and I can feed the pigs and the dogs till you're back on your feet.'

The baby was born underweight but healthy, his little limbs thin as twigs, his old man's face rehearsing expressions from the grandfather he would never know. Greer loved her son with a ferocity that frightened her. When the midwives carried him off to the nursery and exhorted her to rest, she felt a painful tug in her chest, as if there really were heartstrings that could stretch unbearably.

Three days after the birth, she woke to sunshine and the sound of Otto's laugh. 'You are too kind,' she heard him say. Then there was more laughter, and one of the midwives showed him into the room bearing an enormous bouquet of brightly coloured flowers.

'Aren't they divine! I'll get a vase for you while you meet your beautiful son. We'll need a big one.'

'Ah, please. I am so grateful.'

When she had gone, he walked to the window and said, 'So, you are okay here, in a private room?'

'Yes, they want me to rest, and it was too noisy in the ward.'

'And the food?'

'Yes, it's fine. Do you—'

'Thank you, but I have eaten. You know how it is on planes; always they feed you.'

'I mean, do you want to see the baby?'

'I have, I have. The nurses showed me. Look, I have already made a sketch.'

He took out a beautiful leather-bound sketchbook and flipped through until he found the page, holding out a drawing of a waif, the little wisp of baby hair transformed into a ragged crest, the mouth lolling open.

'Oh, may I?' The midwife set the vase down on the floor and hurried over. 'You're an artist! How wonderful. Oh, what a lucky boy to have his portrait painted before he's a week old.'

Otto smiled modestly. 'Look through it if you would like,' he said. 'Most are from Paris.'

Greer put her baby to the breast as she had been shown, self-conscious now that Otto was sitting opposite her, sketching. Everyone, it seemed, had been in to marvel and exclaim over the drawings, and now it was the turn of the lactation consultant. 'Look,' Otto said, holding up his latest sketch. 'Greedy Otichek.' The baby's mouth was enlarged, his cheeks ballooning, as if he would swallow his mother whole.

Greer felt tears threaten, for in reality her milk had not come in, and the baby fretted, which made her anxious and clumsy.

'This is quite normal,' the lactation expert reassured her. 'Nothing to worry about. Just relax and you'll be fine.' But Otik continued to lose weight, and Greer felt that she was failing him.

Otto was ebullient when he came to collect her. 'Wait till you see,' he said, shepherding her out of the ward.

'Are you sure he'll be all right?' she asked the midwife escorting them to the door. 'He's so thin—'

'He is fine,' Otto said with a broad smile. 'Isn't he fine?'

'Yes,' the woman said, smiling back at him. 'Don't worry so much, Greer. Go home now. Rest, and enjoy your baby. He'll soon be back to his birth weight.'

On the drive back to the farm Otto said, 'I have painted little Otichek. A whole series. It is my best verk, I think. Wait till you see.'

Greer clutched at this sign of paternal feeling. Such a warm, generous man could not fail to be a good father, she thought, given time. She turned in her seat to check on the baby, and smiled to see him sleeping.

They pulled up by the house and Otto leapt out of the car. 'Come, you will see.'

'But the baby . . .'

'He is sleeping. Let him lie. Come on. This is my baby.'

Her raw senses recoiled at the reek of linseed and varnish as he opened the door, but she followed him through to the living room, ignoring the fumes. The paintings were propped against the walls, and her first impression was of rich dark surfaces slashed with scarlet.

'This is old story about foolish woman,' Otto said, 'who wanted baby most of all. Here she is. And here she finds baby – you see? It is piece of wood . . .'

'A stump.' Her voice came out flat and dull.

The nuggety baby had roots for legs and branches for arms; the fingers were twisted twigs, the head a block.

'He cries for food, all the time. See, he is greedy like little Otichek.'

Now the stump was slashed across in red to form a gaping toothless mouth. Around him were scattered broken plates and cups. Greer thought she heard a faint cry and turned her head.

'The more he eats the more he wants,' said Otto, 'until he has eaten all.'

The stump baby confronted his foolish mother and

father, who stood side by side looking almost as wooden as their son.

'Still he cries, but there is no more. So he eats up Father.'

Greer had fallen silent, listening as she stared at the painting of the father half engulfed by the monstrous child, his face impassive.

'Next he eats up Mother. That is the thanks she gets.'

'Otto, I think I can hear—'

'And now he goes outside to eat more. He eats up all the pigs . . .'

Greer saw that the pigs were her own Wessex Saddlebacks, their black-and-white bodies despoiled and bloody, crammed into the giant mouth.

'Then off to the village to eat more. First a girl . . .'

The girl's face, frozen in horror, filled much of the painting, her upper arms gripped by the twig hands of the monstrous infant. Was it Eva? The baby was crying, she could hear it clearly now.

'Next he eats up horse and cart and farmer with it. And then sheeps and sheep farmer and dogs.' There were Molly and Spinner; a trotting horse and sulky from the stud across the road, driven by an old man; Charlie and his merinos. Greer felt her breasts prickle and sweat dampen her face, but Otto seemed unaware of her silence, gazing at his work with pleasure.

'Ah, but here is trouble. Next he meets the old mother.'

Greer recognised the Judy character with her axe, but her whole attention was on the cry, which had intensified and now pulsed through her. She felt a cramp low in her belly, and half turned towards the door. 'Otto, I can hear the baby. Just wait a moment and I'll fetch him.'

'He is fine. You will spoil him if you run to him like this. I am showing you my work. Look.' He took her by the arm and turned her back to the pictures. 'Here he says, "I have eaten up all the food – mother, father, pigs, girl, horse, cart, farmer . . ."' he pointed to each painting as he listed the gargantuan meal, '"sheeps, farmer again, dogs, and now you, old woman."'

Greer took in the old woman standing on the monster's shoulder with her dripping axe, the wooden chest opened from gullet to guts. She felt milk leak from her and dampen her shirt.

'"No, you do not eat me!" she cries, and she splits him open with axe.' Otto chopped at the palm of one hand with the side of the other, and Greer flinched. The baby's cries had risen to such a pitch that Greer could hardly endure it.

Animals and people tumbled out of the sooty red cavern of the monster's chest and belly, like entrails from a butchered carcass, or a parody of birth.

'And never more does mother say "I want little baby",' Otto concluded. Greer turned and rushed out to the car, fumbling over the capsule straps, haste making her clumsy, and gathered the hot little sobbing body to her chest, crooning and swaying as she walked back into the house.

Otto was still studying his pictures when Greer returned and settled herself in her father's armchair. Struggling to make her voice calm, she said, 'You've painted your mother? With the axe?'

'Yes, and Father, too. See, in the cart with the horse. He is Grandpapa now. I have told him about little Otik.'

The baby was hiccuping, pressing his cheek against her,

so Greer pulled up her shirt and put him to the breast. The baby cast around for the nipple, a stuttering cry starting up. She cupped his soft head and guided him onto the breast. Was he attached properly? Her hands were trembling, but she looked up and smiled. 'I'm glad you've told him. You must tell me what he said.' Little Otik was suckling, and she knew that she must calm herself, must live these days to the full, and enjoy her baby as the midwife had said. She smoothed the pale down on his head and watched the tiny fist curling against her breast. Something would happen.

And it did. Greer came down with pneumonia, a virulent form of the disease that had her back in the small local hospital before she'd had a chance to settle little Otik into the nursery. This time it was the intensive care ward. Her fever was so high that she felt ethereal, thin and hot and free from care, as if the dross in her were being burned off. Her dreams were vivid and strange, and full of fire. The smokehouse was burning, tussocks of flame sprouting from the windows.

She woke once, weeping, because her dead parents had come to her, had looked down at their new grandchild as if to bless him, and had laid their hands on her bowed head in a sort of benediction. 'I'm sorry,' she said, like a refrain, 'I'm sorry. I've been such a fool.'

She had woken again to a baby crying, or so she thought confusedly, but there was no baby, and she wept and tried to submerge herself in the same dream but dreamed instead of little Otik. In the nightmare he was glistening with lard, lying trussed on a baking dish surrounded by chopped vegetables. The heat radiating from the dish beat against her forehead and cheeks and neck, and she woke gasping, sticky with sweat, her heart hammering. Otto was there, at the nurses' station, with the baby capsule on his arm. He was laughing with the nurses, his round face shining and taut, as if the skin were stretched tight enough to split, and yet still he charmed them. When had he grown so fat? How had she not noticed? The baby was crying. She knew the baby was crying, she could feel it in her breasts, in the prickle and leak of milk. Where was he? Who was feeding her baby?

When she dreamed again, she was in a forest, the trees reaching down their gnarled branches to catch at her, tangling in her hair, scrabbling at the infant in her arms. She recognised her own orchard, transformed by sleep. She had betrayed the trees. They stooped to engulf her, but she struggled to escape, plucking at her arm to release a clinging tendril; then the old Judy was there, with her axe on one arm, and a tightly swaddled baby on the other. Her face was riven by creases and cracks, as if she had endured a lifetime of care and hard work. Greer was glad to see the axe. 'Who are you?' she croaked, but the crone did not speak.

She woke to find an old nurse thumbing the tape on her intravenous drip.

'You mustn't pull it out. Leave it be now. Try to sleep.'

The mild words filled Greer with sorrow, and tears seeped from her eyelids and ran down into her ears, wetting the pillow under her neck. It was too hard. Life was too hard. She wanted to rest and let someone else shoulder these burdens for a while. Just till she was well again. She wanted to lie with her small son and gaze into his smoky eyes and think of nothing.

Greer returned to herself slowly, and as she did, the ache to see her little boy, to be home again, became almost unbearable. The nurses taught her to express milk herself, now that she was feeling stronger, but why didn't they bring the baby to her? She asked for a phone, but nobody answered when she called home. Where could he be? She called again an hour later, but the phone rang out. He had not been to see her, apart from that one hazy visit, and as the afternoon and then the evening passed, she became first anxious, then panicky, then frantic. How many days had she been here? Who was caring for her little boy? She had to get home. But the nurse absolutely forbade it. 'You will not move from that bed until the doctor has seen you in the morning. What nonsense is this? Your husband is caring for the baby, he has formula, and the milk you've expressed, there is absolutely no cause for alarm.'

'But he doesn't—'

'He can learn the same way you'll have to learn. Now go to sleep and no more chatter.'

Greer waited until the change of shift, feigning sleep. She could be cunning, if that's what it took. She slid open the drawer silently and felt for clothes – hospitals were never dark, she could see what she needed in the fluorescent twilight – now shoes. The public toilet was just down the corridor. A murmur came from the nurses' station, no more. One quick sprint and she was in the toilet, but her knees were weak, and heat washed over her. She dressed, shoved her pyjamas behind the toilet seat and straightened her hair – ugh, it was plastered to her head.

Outside the night was crisp with stars. Everyone was watching television, judging by the blue light leaching the curtains and blinds. Fine, she would walk home.

The tilting world slowly righted itself and the wind cooled her hot cheeks as she set out across country – she could cut off a third of the journey at least, and it was light enough for her to find her way. But after a short time she had to stop and rest, weak and breathless. *Slow and steady*, she told herself, as her father used to say when they were tramping across the paddocks. *What's the rush, missy?* But there was a rush. She walked on beneath the whorl of the night sky and over the jarring clods and tussocks of the paddocks. Pressing the tiny wound on the back of her hand where she'd pulled out the cannula was like pressing a bruise to test the ache; it grounded her. Her breasts dragged and throbbed, and she tried walking with her arms crossed over her chest, but feared she might fall. Sometimes one leg would give way, and she would stumble to a stop. Shaking, she would lock both knees to teach them strength – standing to attention, she thought irrelevantly.

It was past midnight when she stumbled onto the road leading to the farm. The closer she got to the house, the more she was plagued by dream scraps. Breath sawed in and out of her lungs and she shivered and sweated. It's fever, just fever, she told herself. Otto would never harm a baby. And the paintings of that monstrous child, that's what was giving her nightmares. But with that thought came the red-and-blue flash of a police car or ambulance. It was heading towards her – had they come to fetch her back? Trailing its skirl of sound, faint and distorted by distance and wind, it rushed along the home road and turned in at the farm gate. She hurried on, stumbled and fell heavily as it careered past her. An ambulance. Oh God, and not for her. One of Otto's woodheap sculptures had felled her and now her shin burned with pain. The siren wound down to silence but the lights continued to pulse.

She ran – staggered – up the driveway, dread locking her throat. The house was ablaze with light, but there was no welcoming racket – *where were the dogs*? The lights on the ambulance revolved endlessly, painting her hand on the doorhandle red and blue by turns. Then she was in the kitchen. Muffled voices came from one of the bedrooms. Her fingers fumbled for the light switch. She heard each breath as a high keening cry, but it was distant. Was it coming from her? And that smell – an odour of roasted bones and glutinous flesh.

The globe was slow to warm, and she saw first the roasting dish and in the blue-and-red strobe a small rib cage picked clean. The tiny vertebrae were set in congealed fat and meat jelly. There was a skull, and slender arm bones. Greer stared and felt her gorge rise in horror. Heat broke into fresh sweat on her face, then ice spread numbingly through her body. Faintly she heard something shuffling towards the kitchen door, and looked up to see the old Judy, her face creased with anxiety and her eyes sharp and hostile.

Greer could not speak. She had woken into nightmare.

'Grir? Is you?' the crone was speaking to her, knew her name. Greer stared.

'Com. Com. Sit.' The old woman pulled out a chair beside the hideous remains.

Greer backed away, and the old woman, seeing her fixed stare, picked up the roasting dish to move it to the sink.

'He say you no want kill bebe but he kill. He eat. It kill him maybe.' Her lips pursed and she shrugged helplessly, indicating the murmured voices somewhere in the house. 'No can help him.'

Greer tried to breathe, to weep, but a black tidal bore was sweeping through her, engorging her skull. In a dozen strides she was at the woodheap, grasping the axe, the smooth wood fitting her hand like an old friend. She swung it up and gripped it behind the head, then she was in the kitchen, the darkened hall, with the old grandmother at her heels gabbling and shouting and plucking at her.

'Otto!' It was the voice that quelled dogfights, dragged up from the pit of her lungs. Two uniformed figures were bent over the bed, working at something, one of them glancing up at her, alarm rounding his eyes. She hefted the axe, but a knobbed hand caught it and held it and would not let go.

The cry was lustier than she remembered, and she thought, this is madness then, but was glad of it, glad to hear her little son one last time. She relinquished the axe and slumped in the doorway, confounded. The old woman shuffled from the room, muttering to herself, the axe gripped to her withered breasts. As she stared blankly at the stooped backs of the paramedics, the crying stopped and she heard only strange crooning words she did not understand. There, almost as she had dreamed it, was the old Judy with a tightly swaddled baby in her arms, coming towards her in the dim hall.

'Otik!' She snatched the child away, scrabbling at the cloth that bound him as she hurried down the hall and shouldered open the kitchen door. The little face was pinched and thin, but his colour was good. Greer laid him on the kitchen table and unwrapped him completely, needing to reassure herself that he was truly there, alive and healthy. The old woman watched, clucking with approval or disapproval, Greer had no way of knowing, as she unfastened the last folds of cloth, and there he was, coated in something white and greasy, like vernix, as if he were newly born. And for Greer he was. Risen from the dead. Plucked from the belly of his father, still coated in lard, for that was what it was, she could smell it. Perhaps it was a peasant remedy, or a salve against starvation.

The old woman extended a gnarled hand and gently pinched the soft arm, which was furred with hunger hair like a famine victim. 'No fat,' she said. 'Papa too much fat.'

Greer wrapped him up hastily and fumbled to free her breast for him. She could feel the milk tingling through her, rushing to the nipple. 'Milk com,' the old woman said, her voice crackling with age. The work-roughened hands clasped Greer's breast as she brought the baby's head firmly towards it, pressing the clamouring mouth onto the nipple. 'Good. Is good.'

And it was good. Greer felt the milk being pulled from the roots of her heart, but it was there, and it would be there in greater quantities if she could but rest and eat and recover. She turned her back on the pitiful remains of the suckling pig, and understood, at last, why the ambulance and paramedics were here.

'Sorry, ma'am.' One of them stood in the doorway. 'The old lady thought he'd just overdone it, but it's a bit more than indigestion, I'm afraid. We've got him stabilised, so we'll be off now.'

Greer looked up at the paramedic and nodded. 'I should come, but I can't. I'm sorry.'

He gave her an odd look and said only, 'Righto. Probably have to shift him to the city pretty soon. Not looking too hot.'

Greer phoned Charlie as soon as it was a decent hour. She was shuddering with fatigue, but she had slept for a few hours, and so had little Otik, his belly full. And here was his grandmother, neither mad nor dead, come just in time to care for her grandson, fretting over the poor starved scrap. The hospital must have provided formula and bottles, but still the baby had lost weight. Now the old Judy muttered over the tins and bottles, encouraging Greer to put the child to the breast again. It was difficult to understand what had happened the previous night, but it seemed Otto's mother had been convinced that he was suffering from nothing more than indigestion until he collapsed; then she had called for help. How she had come to be here, Greer could not discover. She spoke very little English, and although she talked volubly in her own language, Greer could understand not a word of it, apart from names.

She heard the dogs first, scrabbling at the back door and yipping to be let in. 'Is it okay?' Charlie called. 'Can they come in? Can I?'

Spinner bounded up to her, and Molly wagged herself in circles, but they quietened when they smelt the baby, stretching their noses to take him in, this new creature. Greer thought *gentleness*, then *reverence*. How much did they understand? She looked up at Charlie with a tired smile, and he smiled back, embarrassed to see her breastfeeding, but pleased that she was back.

'The dogs turned up at my place. They were pretty hungry.' He would say no more. 'And I guess you know you're one piglet down.'

Greer nodded. 'Could be worse,' she said. 'Can you drive us back to hospital, please, when he finishes feeding?'

She saw Otto for the last time in a small bare room in a city hospital. His mother stood beside her, weeping quietly, but Greer was dry-eyed. It was hard to recall the small energetic man who had so beguiled her. There was a long gash down his sternum that had been stapled together like a crude drawing of a wound. The bloated belly, once tight as a drum, was flaccid and yellow-grey. *Naples yellow*, she thought absently, but couldn't name the grey. She reached out and touched him very lightly on the shoulder. It felt like the trunk of a gum: cool, unyielding, wooden.

Greer recalled his painting of the gutted pig's carcass, and imagined an empty cavity beneath this zipper of flesh and steel. He had crammed himself with so much, she thought, that it had clogged and curdled in the vessels of his heart. Still light-headed and disoriented, Greer pictured the surgeon levering open the cage of ribs to find a cart and a horse, a girl and a sheep. Or perhaps just the remains of one small black-and-white piglet, too young to leave its mother.

AFTERWORD

The story of Otesánek is simple enough: a childless couple long for a baby; the husband finds a root or stump that looks like a child and shapes it roughly with his axe, then presents it to his wife. She coddles it, and it transforms into a baby with an insatiable appetite. It eats all the food in the house, then turns on its parents, gobbling them up, then their neighbours, the livestock and crops. This monster of greed eventually tries to eat an old grandmother, but she hacks him open and out pours all that he has swallowed, unchanged. The couple swear that they will never again long for a child, and order is restored.

I first read 'Otesánek' in manuscript, submitted to me, disturbingly, by a new father, but it was not until I saw the Svankmajer film of the same name that I understood that 'Otesánek' was not an original work, but a traditional Czech fairytale. Perhaps I would not have found it so unappetising had babies not been so much a part of my own life then.

For Svankmajer, it was a cautionary tale about humans assuming godlike powers of creation, similar to Adam and Eve's impertinence, and perhaps the arrogance that led to the Tower of Babel. These 'religious' interpretations didn't interest me, nor did they seem particularly illuminating. Not all men who breathe life into their creations offend the gods: Cadmus created soldiers from a dragon's teeth; Pygmalion sculpted his beloved Galatea from stone; Hephaestus created his automata and handmaidens; the giant Hrungnir built his helper, Mökkurkálfi (Mist Calf), from clay and gave him the heart of a mare; and Rabbi Loew of Prague pressed his golem from clay, predating Karel Capek's robot (the word comes from the Czech, *robota*, meaning to work or slave). Closest to Otesánek and expressing the same yearning for a child, is the story of Geppetto's Pinocchio, and there is lastly Frankenstein and his pitiable monster. Some of these 'fathers' and their 'sons' come unstuck, but the gods don't punish all of them.

There are similar tales of monstrous selfishness that lack any element of hubris or human transgression, such as 'Tiddalik the Frog'. Tiddalik drinks up all the water in the land and must be tickled into returning it to the rivers and waterholes so that all animals can drink and survive. This creature puts itself before others and its selfishness threatens the survival of everyone. For me, much of the power of Otesánek came from his relentless greed and complete disregard for those around him, not from his origin as a rough stump artfully shaped by a man.

To be honest, I loathed the story, but my reaction was immoderate. It's always worth investigating such visceral responses: they can tell you much about what you've locked away from the light. Like the couple in the story, I had longed for a child, and been lacerated by envy at the sight of women with babies and children. I well understood why this sad couple had shaped a clumsy infant for themselves.

When I first read the story, I was breastfeeding. I'd already noticed the curious hostility or discomfort in some people when confronted by the unfettered desires of a hungry baby, and the deep pleasure it takes so unselfconsciously. Most adults have learned to mask their greed and pleasure; perhaps the sight of it in an infant is unsettling. When I came to write this story, I wondered if this was enough to explain the amplification of a baby's natural hunger in this story? So much is tied up in hunger and its satisfaction: nurture, love and generosity run as deep as selfishness and greed.

My next thought was that Otesánek might be a famine tale. If times were hard enough, a new baby really might threaten the life of its starving parents or even the survival of the tribe or community. Perhaps desperation turns babies into monsters in their parents' eyes. Was hunger the key? What lost meanings did this repellent little story carry?

In the original tale, the father shapes Otesánek from inert matter. This act goes against nature in another way, because the mysterious ability to bring forth life belongs to the woman, not the man. She creates new life from her flesh, from the food that she eats, from the water she drinks. This is the true miracle of transubstantiation, universal and banal, but miraculous nonetheless. Otesánek himself 'gives birth', although by brutal caesarean section. Life springs from his belly after he is cut open by the grandmother–midwife, and he manages to usurp the powerful magic of women for himself, although it costs him his life.

I began to wonder hazily about eating, and the transformation of food, about metamorphosis. I thought about the broader meanings of consumption and production. To consume means not only to eat or drink, but to buy, to use something up, to destroy. But consuming necessarily produces something, even if it is only manure and heat, and production is close to creation, so do the farmer and the artist share some common ground? I was fumbling with images and ideas and getting nowhere.

I looped back to transubstantiation (the changing of one substance into another), but in a broader sense than the theological or even the biological. I wondered about change, about taking in or consuming experience, sights, sounds, objects. I thought about the mysterious metamorphosis that occurs in the production of art from these same raw materials. The monstrous baby absorbs everything that surrounds him, as any artist must, but he fails to transform it. In the original story, all that he eats re-emerges unchanged. The only act of transformation is from stump to baby, the father's act. So he is the only artist in that tale.

I considered the life of artists, their place as outsiders, the overwhelming selfishness of some of them, justifiable in those who produce great art, or even good art (how many of us would save the Leonardo from the flood rather than the baby?). But who pays the piper, the poet, the painter, when they can't earn their bread? How does one live the life of art without becoming a monster of selfishness?

Otesánek never doubts that he is entitled to all he takes. He is made monstrous by his appetite, but also by his selfishness, a thing apart from his community, unable to postpone his gratification for an instant, even when it leads inexorably to his own destruction. He stands for competition rather than cooperation, the individual rather than the collective. The natural greed and hunger of babies, their need for nurturing, becomes grotesque in a being like Otesánek, and distasteful in an adult. Nobody would argue that Otesánek's short brutish life was good, and yet he snatched everything he desired and nobody could stop him. All that went into the mix, too, because I am curious about what it is to live a good life.

'Glutted' was originally called 'The Life of Art'. I wrote it to try to understand why Otesánek preoccupied and repelled me, and to elaborate on some of the themes that had occurred to me as I puzzled over this fairytale of greed and self-indulgence, which could as easily be a parable for this era of rampant consumption.

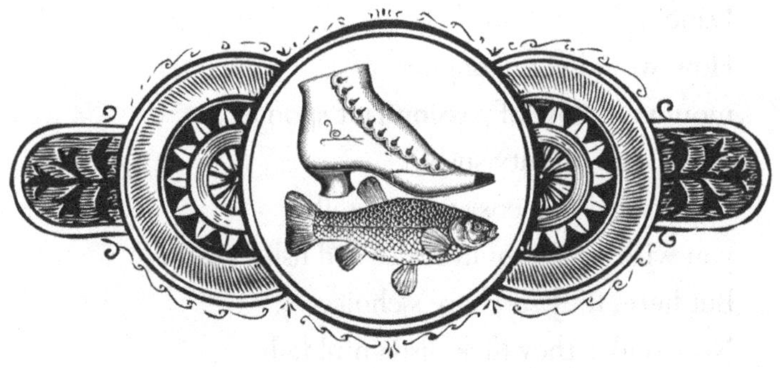

LEARNING *the* TANGO

by Catherine Bateson

{A Tourist in Normal}

If you're Amish, you're given the world
outside as your eighteenth birthday present –
here you go, fall in love with a stranger at a bar,
go to parties, drop e,
you with your quaint rustic accent
and last decade's clothes.
A tourist in Normal.

The grandmother sends the mermaids up at fifteen –
Look, my mermaids:
there's land, there's the Love Boat
watch the couples dancing.
Dancing!
How would your tongue
mouth a pillow of passionfruit sponge
after years of salty sushi?
How could you cosy up to a sailor
you with your sequin scales and fish-breath?
But here, they say, here's choice.
No wonder they flick disdainful tails
flipping back under faster than whitebait.

One to five – basked on a sandbank, star-gazed.
Knew that the sky belled around them
that air smelled green and that sailors
hungered – but for what?
One to five didn't know.

The youngest mermaid was hollowed out by hunger
already.
In her sea garden she'd sharpened her desire –
the beautiful marble boy she swam loops around
the boy who, in her rocking dreams,
tiptoed to the clamshell bed, bent over
his eyes full of nothing but her and then
his mouth, fluttering
like delicate fins, then firm
and then – oh she was starved and her yearning
sang her own heart siren songs.

There's always one. One colt-boy or gawky girl
looking at life through the keyhole of a different world
who says, yes, yes.

We grow old, hunch-backed, rheumy-eyed
but we said it once.
Yes. Yes. Paid whatever it took
to squirm us through from one world
to whatever it was we saw –
love, fame or magic.
Look at me now wearing my boa
of seasnakes, my fat toad familiar
squat on my shoulder.
Yes, I said, yes.

{My Childish Days}

I played in the garden
where the marble boy
was king to my queen.
One by one my sisters went up
for their days in the sun.
They came back. Yes, there were lights
and people, birds flew, so?
I was as patient as the moon.
I knew what I'd find –
a sky wide as the ocean
filled with flying and –
passionately real, no longer stone
but warm skin and heartbeat,
the king to my queen.

{Witch of the Love Boat}

Mostly they plop to the surface
like baby seals, wet behind the ears,
get bored and go back home.
It's not what they thought it would be,
land ahoy but out of reach,
the passengers on the Love Boat
standing awkwardly on their two legs.
Give up sequined flip of that sparky tail?
They cover their yawns with a dainty hand.
Not number six.
Surfs up on a wave and spies
the Lurve Boat and who on it
but him, languidly leaning on the rail
watching for whales or mermaids
or staring vacantly out to sea.
(I'd guess the latter.)

She loved his eyes, brown as earth
the waves of hair the wind lifted
his dinner shirt strained just so
across his biceps.
He'd caught her in his net
and he wasn't even fishing.

There's always a catch –
he's married, she's emo
the internet dating site crashes
just as he hits her profile.
You think you have trouble?

Imagine a tail. How to tuck it under
the wedding dress. How to waltz?
Then think of it slipping between silk
sheets, the scales catching.
No joy there.
Enter me, Witch of the Love Boat.

{The First Chorus}

We saw her longing and knew her lost.
Oh little sister, would you leave us for a man?
What has he, that we can't offer?
Come, let us braid your hair,
let us sing together,
swaying like soft weed to the songs
that loop and flow, ribbons of seduction,
velvet handcuffs that lock
each of us fast to the other.
Why would you leave us,
little lost note
in our loving harmony?
We reach for you
but you evade our pale fingers
as though they were sticky tentacles.

{The Storm}

Who questions the storms and rips of Fate?
Destiny pulls the carpet from under

our questing feet – or tails –
and suddenly we're shoved off course
or back on if you're an optimist.
So there she is, my sixth little one,
all hair and silver,
all ache and emptiness,
but with a heart full as an old sea boot.
She'd watched him watch the horizon.
She'd watched him dance with the lucky ones,
his cheek – a little manly stubble – to cheek
with powdered softness, she'd seen his hand
tighten around a waist, bunching up the satin.

A squall of darkness on that particular horizon,
a rough swell, monstrous under the surface,
thrashing upwards under the ship,
a whipping foam frenzy, the fairy lights
extinguished, then lightning and *crack, crack,*
the captain hears the great bow sunder.
Life boats – but it's too late. The girls go down
shrouded in party frocks. Some call out
feebly and bob about like tossed seabirds,
some cling to broken planks or each other
but soon the ocean closes over all,
sailors and revellers alike.

The sixth one, the littlest, dives deep.
She's looking for one man only,
leaves the rest – takeaway for night foragers –
strikes for the shore in her best bronze medallion
rescue stroke. She's got him,
her pale arm looped around his neck.

But will he ever be so docile, so needy
so much hers
again?

{The Rescue}

As soon as I saw him dancing on the deck
I knew it in every silver bone
that he was mine.
I cursed my spangled tail,
flapping around on the sand
like a dying fish.

When the storm came I was pleased.
I heard the mast snap, the great ship groan.
I saw the people flounder and sink.
All the girls he'd danced with,
their pretty dresses wrapped around their useless legs.

I found him, mouth and fingers blue
his chill skin white as marble.
I swam him right through the night.
Let him live, let him live,
I begged the moon and stars
but they shone for themselves
not for me, not for him.

When I reached land, I hauled him in,
always my tail tripping me up –
how I hated it! I breathed into his mouth.

I lay over his body until I felt it grow warm.
Then I slid back to the sea,
leaving a slick of salt on his skin,
a hint of silvered scale, the smell of me
on his breath.
Enough for a man in love
to find his heart's joy, his heart's own.
Other men have done it with just an old shoe.

He woke to *her* touch. Some beach babe,
cheap sunblock and attitude.
He reeled with love.
Not for me.
Never for me.

I took my shamed heart home.
My arms ached
from tugging him towards life.
My mouth stung
from the chill I'd kissed warm.
But still I was tossed up
and abandoned by his heart's tides –
not even remembered.

{The Prince Speaks}

As I sank into the dark I saw odd things –
the steam-train cake my mother made
for my first birthday, my father polishing
his boots, the girl with red hair

who sat behind me in school.
I'd loved her that first year and the second.
I had forgotten how red her hair was,
how it was a fire around her face
I longed to touch.
I saw my dog waiting at the gate,
his old tail flicking up dust
as I got nearer. Then
a great rush of water or wings
lifted me up.
A speedboat's no way to get to heaven
but I couldn't say that for the water
poured back into my mouth and out
and the words flicked away like minnows.

Woke on the cold beach, most of the ocean
vomited up beside me and there she was –
that blaze of hair, that fire,
all I'd loved. And me, shaking and puking
like a puppy, but she didn't care.
Wrapped me up in a towel that smelled of
coconuts and jasmine and shooed off the
crows who were gathered like widows at a wake.

{The Second Chorus}

Sister, the beach is littered with broken shells,
bones and washed-up hearts.
Don't lean too closely over him.
Don't press your mouth against his
and breathe your breath for him.

He'll take your voice, clip its wings
so it sits on his finger
croaking platitudes.
He'll want a cup of tea,
the news at a certain time
and legs against his, warm in the bed
and all the better
to wrap around him
against the cold night and old age.

If he sees you at all, little sister,
he'll want you in his image,
softer of course and a little mysterious,
but not unknowable, unchanging
or wild.

Sister, your heart's washed up with the wreckage
and we can do nothing but sound our warnings
surfing them into the shore, mournfully,
wave after wave.

{Without Him}

The colour's leached
from every living thing,
even the morning's bleached bone-white.
I can't carry a note, my voice
is a toad croak, a gull's hoarse caw
and all songs sound like a scavenger's dirge,
my sea garden withers,

shells crumble, the anemones droop,
there's no salt in the sushi,
no sparkle in my tail swish,
no light, no joy, no life
without him.

{The Third Chorus}

There's a murder of crows
on the beach little sister,
brooding black
against the white sand.
They're looking at you,
little sister, with their abacus eyes.
Slide back in to the sea.
Sing with us – no missed notes,
no broken chords.
Don't look at the crows
looking at you,
don't look at the prince.
Sing little sister
so the crows don't know
how you'd let them
slit and slice, twist, wrench
tug and dice until they had your heart
laid out on a stone.
And all for love.

There's a murder of crows
on the beach little sister,

a feathered dark, waiting
on the white sand.

{His 'n' Hers}

She thinks love is a piece of wedding cake,
matching His 'n' Hers bath towels
always fluffy on a heated rail.

Let me tell you about the word *lover*
– rhymes with *smother* –
take away the *l*
and it's all over, red rover.

She's a pretty little thing –
with her cost-a-fortune smile.
The tail's an obstacle
we agree, but one we can sort
with a large enough fee.

I read her the health warnings:
searing pain with every step
bunions, corns, blisters
and little bloodied footprints,
but she hasn't dodged
the seasnakes, the
guard toads and deadly coral
to go away fainthearted, tail intact.

Falters only when I demand her voice –
    my payment.

Everyone's entitled to a
lullaby or two, even the toads.

How will I talk to him?
Look, miss, there are other ways,
you know what I'm saying? You don't have
to talk all the time. Most men would rather
you didn't. You want legs. I'll sell them for a song.
She doesn't get the joke.

But will I be beautiful?
As you are now but with ten toes to twinkle,
and twinkle you'd better – it's marry or burn.
If he chooses another, you're dead in the water.
Forgive my frankness. It's just the way I'm wired.
You say Valentines. I think massacre.
I hand over the potion. She gives up her voice.
Now, who got the best deal, my wise children?
I'd almost feel sorry for her
if she wasn't so painfully stupid.

{The Fourth Chorus}

Oh sister, little lost note,
what have you done?
Why let the witch clip your tongue
from your throat?

We've sung three ships down
with our keening, but you're deaf

to all love save his.
Remember your troth
little lost love –
it's marry or salt tears to ocean
delicate bone to sea lace and foam.

Oh sister, pinned to the ground
by your infant legs,
dancing in blood for your life –
he calls you dumb foundling.
Take warning, lost note,
that's no name for a wife.

{The Prince's Little Foundling}

She arrived with a change in the weather,
my pretty dumb foundling,
problems with her feet
and no voice to even state her name.
The ideal listener,
in love with me, of course,
but what can I do?
Friends with benefits, sure,
but I want a partner
with some snap and sizzle,
standing equal and firm.
Adoration has a strictly limited season.

One more kiss, little mute,
my sweet dumb foundling,

one more turn round that dance floor.
Then I'll let you down gently.
It's not you, it's me,
too young, too soon, too much,
but best friends on Facebook, oh yes,
your number on speed dial,
your photo on my phone –
until the contract's expired.
Adoration has a strictly limited season.

{The Supplicants}

Here come the fishtailed five,
lamenting the loony lovelorn one,
the singing sisters,
all doleful minor chords today.
And what can I do for you, my little aquatic sprites?
It looks as though you're not quite the full
    complement?
A sextet reduced to a quin – stop thrashing your tails,
I know what you want. There'll be a cost,
and no guarantees.

Minutes later I'm left with five kilos of hair
and they've got the spell to set her free –
if she consents.

Oh my wise children,
you know she'll not do it.
Martyr herself. Tick.

Die for love. Tick.
Sacrifice herself on the glossy double-spread
of honeymoon tips for newlyweds? Tick.
Kill for life?
Not on your red-heart helium balloon.
Not even for the keening quintet,
now quite bald.

{The Wedding Night}

I'm good as dead and he doesn't even know.
They're at it again. I'd scream at them –
Break it up, have a rest, get some sleep –
but I gave away my voice.
I gave it all away for what? My ear pressed
to the wall, hearing her show-off moans,
his sly love-whispers, the lip-suck and swell of them,
poisoning my air. I've been so stupid.
I flee the loving noise,
each step a knife-thrust. I may as well die, I think
when I see my sisters. I'd laugh at their egg-heads
shining in the moonlight, but my heart is shattered
and my life ebbing out with the night.
I can't even say goodbye but they're all talking at once.
They've been to the witch, they sold their hair –
for me? For a knife. Sharpened with spite,
honed on hate. I'm to plunge it deep,
right through his heart, then let his blood
flow on my feet. I take the blade.
With each step it grows heavier.

They're sleeping now, spent.
It should be my head on his shoulder,
my hair shawling his chest,
my legs wrapped around his.
Instead I'm here with death in my hands
and dogging my steps.
What is love? My sisters' hair? My voice?
The way he holds her?
I can't strike. Look,
dreams move under his eyelids.
I tiptoe out, knife in hand,
to wait for the sun to rise on my last morning.

{The Fifth Chorus}

Bald for no reason
we sulk in the shallows,
scalps prickled with cold.
There's always one sister –
the baby, the spoilt one –
who refuses to play
except by her rules.
Her choice, after all.
Why then do we bicker?
Why do we pick at our tails,
flicking azure blue scales
into the air?
Are legs so in fashion?
We don't want them,
but our voices waver.

We're disconsolate, quarrelsome
and sadly out of tune.
Her stumbling world –
impossibly – seems
grand and postcard-bright.

{The Prince on Love}

I'm not the main player –
although indispensable –
what I don't do
moves the story inexorably on.
But if I could have your attention
I'd like to talk about love.
How it's not always convenient –
you don't make an appointment,
you don't say, not this week, thanks,
I'm busy. Love knocks you off your feet,
leaves you winded, lost – or found.
Steals up and kidnaps you.
It can happen at the wrong time
to the wrong people.
It doesn't come with a lifetime guarantee.

I fell for a secondary character –
it was written in my stars.
Am I a villain?
More the callow ingénue
saying the lines
love told me to.

{The Mermaid's Last Word}

Every little girl
wants to be a mermaid.
See how they flip and flop
in the swimming pools,
feet together until they forget,
dolphin-kicking down at the shallow end.
I longed to be a girl.
What was between those legs,
I wondered, what power?

Don't think the story ends with me
waiting for death like a fish on a hook.
I'd bargained once – I could do it again.
It's not all about men. I knew what I'd miss;
wiggling my toes in the sand
knee-hi striped socks
how tall I looked in heels
and the way boots make me swagger.
I knew what I wanted – my legs
wrapped around another's,
my hair on his chest, my name on his breath.

I worked out my time with the seasnakes,
grew fond of the toads and the witch.
Now I'm at Sea World – the seal girl –
feeding them fish from my mouth.
I'm dating the trainer – the one
with the mermaid tattoo – not my idea.
We're learning the tango.

He doesn't talk much but has eloquent eyes.
When we kiss, I stand on tiptoe,
tasting the ocean
and the flight-filled sky.

{The Witch's Postscript}

I know you think I'm getting soft
but I always liked her. She knew what she wanted
and exactly how far she'd go.
Wasn't going to settle for siren songs
on a cold damp rock, all that endless
brushing of hair. I did the others a favour –
knots every hint of a breeze
and split ends from the salt.

I always loathed the ending that boy
put on the story – silly Hans,
a sentimentalist, of course.
The daughters of the air
three hundred years of good deeds
the tears of sorrow and extra days
for a wicked child – please!

Better she stands on a diving board,
fish between her teeth,
loved by the crowd, the seals
and their trainer. He paints her toenails,
rubs her feet. What better ending than this?
Look at them, practising the tango,

how he dips her and lifts,
how her legs slide
between his.
Then the kiss.

AFTERWORD

I discovered feminist poetry in my teens. In Brisbane in the late seventies, this was no small achievement. There was no feminist or gay and lesbian bookshop in Brisbane. There was no www.amazon.com or any other internet resource. Bjelke Peterson was the premier and nearly everyone I knew risked jail at various public protests.

The poets who congregated in our second-hand bookshop were, for the most part, male. I grew up in a household that read and recited poetry – W. B. Yeats, John Donne, Ernest Dowson and Robert Browning. My mother and I loved Judith Wright and Gwen Harwood. Later I read the Mersey River poets, Adrian Henri and Roger McGough, loving their pop culture references thrown so irreverently into what I had regarded as a rarefied art form.

The anthology *No More Masks: An Anthology of Twentieth-Century American Women Poets*, edited by Florence Howe, was electrifying. I can still feel the thick, yellowed paper under my fingers and how I held my breath at each turned page. Here were voices I had never before heard. The poems were immediate, urgent and revolutionary. They were playful and sexy. They simmered with angry energy. They were fearless. They were mine.

This is a long way from 'The Little Mermaid', sacrificing her identity for love, and then sacrificing it all over again to conform to a patriarchal religious ideology and gain an immortal soul! Or is it?

Second-wave feminism challenged women to re-vision fairytales. Even poets such as Anne Sexton, who never identified as a feminist but was nonetheless a bold foremother of the next generation, put her own inimitable spin on the tales in *Transformations*, her cackling, streetwise witch-voice rocketing the stories into the twentieth century. She used the fairy stories to further her own personal mythology – a mythology with a foundation in mental illness, therapy and a dark family history undercut by Sexton's sly, black humour.

I knew from the outset that I wanted to write a poetry sequence for this project. I wanted to be able to give more than the central character a voice and I wanted the poems book-ended by the witch-storyteller. 'The Little Mermaid' appealed to me because, while the mermaid appears on first reading passive, she's actually very brave. After all, she alone of her five siblings falls in love with the world above the sea. She's an intrepid explorer. Sure, there's the prince – but isn't he just part of that great tug of the unknown? In our contemporary world she'd be the one falling in love with a Masai warrior, Indian swami or an eco-activist living a life of subsistence. We shake our heads at their folly, but marvel at the optimism and sense of destiny that leads to such adventures. It will end in tears, we say wisely, and it does of course. But after the tears have been mopped up, a richer, less predicted life remains.

Could I find this life for my little mermaid? I was hampered by Hans Christian Andersen. Fortunately, I wasn't also influenced by Disney, having escaped ever seeing the Disney version, by luck rather than intent. However, Hans Christian Andersen was a problem. His Little Mermaid was courageous, certainly. She defies her grandmother and her siblings to visit the witch. She braves the sea serpents and the line of toads that guard the witch's watery residence. She gives away her tail and her voice with scarcely a backward glance, subjecting herself to constant agony and stripping herself of one of her best assets – mermaids sing siren songs. She rescues the prince only to watch him fall in love with the girl he believes rescued him from the shipwreck. She mutely worships him, sleeping like a cat at his feet. She suffers him saying that if it wasn't for this other girl, he'd marry her. Her sisters bargain for her life but she refuses to murder him and save herself. She'd rather die.

Hans Christian Andersen's version ends with an odd coda, bringing in the mysterious daughters of the air who can prevent the little mermaid becoming nothing but sea foam. They can give her a chance to earn an immortal soul.

This was my stumbling block. I didn't want the daughters of air in my take on 'The Little Mermaid'. I didn't like them or what they stood for. They made my little mermaid a namby-pamby goody-goody two-shoes. Even though she'd give up everything for love, I wanted my little mermaid to be worthy of the poets who had influenced me so much with their fierce forgings of identity in *No More Masks*.

My answer was in what I'd just called her. Goody-goody two-shoes. What was a flippy tail compared to the joy of shoes? Purple stompy boots for winter, teetering in your first high heels, slipping on strappy sandals on a warm day in summer – would my girl give up all that? I remembered shoes I'd loved – some fringed suede boots I'd worn going out with a motorcycle-lover, a pair of T-bar high heels that made me feel so French, and way back, my first heeled sandals, white leather with a flower, bought for me by my father. Shoes or immortal soul? No contest.

From there it was plain sailing – forgive the pun. I knew she'd have to go back to the witch, but hey, the witch was on her side. I knew the sisters would lament, but that's what sisters are for. I'd get my girl a job and give her a life – not the life she would have chosen initially, but richer, unpredicted. My Little Mermaid stands firmly on her own two feet.

the UGLY SISTERS

by Maureen McCarthy

{PROLOGUE}

You think you know this story, don't you? You think you know who did what to whom, and why, and how it all turned out. You think you know who was bad and who was good, and every time you remember the ending you feel glad that all involved got their just desserts. Am I right? Of course I am!

But there is a whole other side that you don't know about. How could you? You weren't there. I was, and I'm prepared to be honest if you promise to withhold judgement until the end. Some of what I've got to say isn't nice – in fact, it's distinctly gruesome in places – but rest assured I've already been punished. My sister and I have been through enough public humiliation to last us the rest of our lives. Just remember this isn't about you; it's *my* story, and I'm not looking for anyone's approval or understanding or forgiveness.

No one ever bothers to ask where we ended up, do they?

It's impossible to say exactly how many people are in the ward with me, but by the constant moaning, the clearing of throats, the hoarse whispers and foul stinks, I guess that all of them are old and horrible. My surgeon was just in here with one of his sidekicks – an Indian, judging by the accent.

'So what have we here?' the sidekick asks in that hearty way doctors have. I am immediately alert. Surely the bandages on my eyes, the cuts and scratches on my face and throat and hands tell him enough. The surgeon mumbles something to deflect him, then bends to fiddle with the bandages. He is so close now I smell him over the sharp tang of hospital disinfectant and urine and the disgusting mince we had for lunch. He has a nice fresh smell, like mint, and I'm tempted to grab his hand. *Am I going to see again?* My heart pumps with the enormity of what I want to know. *Tell me, please, doctor, will I see again?* Perhaps he plans to take the bandages off. But after a few moments I realise that he is just checking to see that they're secure.

'So how are you, Skye?' he asks quietly.

'Okay,' I say, stiff as a pole.

'The operation went well,' he tells the other man. 'We just have to wait.' He takes my hand and squeezes it briefly. 'Try to be patient.'

'Will I . . . be . . .'

But the word *blind* swells in my throat like rising dough and jams my mouth.

'You know I can't promise anything,' the surgeon says gently. 'It could go either way, but . . . we remain hopeful.'

'An accident?' the Indian murmurs.

'Not exactly.' The surgeon puts a hand on my shoulder and leaves it there a moment. Against every brittle instinct in my miserable soul, the gesture comforts me. This man wishes me well. I can feel it through his fingers.

'So what happened?' the sidekick asks. I turn away, steeling myself. Whoever he is, I hate him. Why doesn't he go back to where he came from? And take that soft singsong voice with him while he's at it! Do I have to lie here and listen to strangers discussing what happened to me yet again?

The surgeon mutters something, but the only word I can discern is *attacked*, nothing else. I can feel a stillness between them and I know they are looking at each other and that all manner of information is being passed between them silently.

'But *how?*'

Tears tighten my throat, but I hold them back by imagining how I would throttle this underling, how I would wrap these big ugly hands around his fat little brown neck and squeeze! Hands that I tried for so many years to make soft and creamy and white. What a surprise if a nineteen-year-old blind girl reared up in her hospital gown and attacked him. Oh, the idea of it comforts me mightily.

But my surgeon, bless him, doesn't answer. He picks up my hand again.

'Three, maybe four days,' he says quietly, 'and we'll know. Try to be patient.'

'I will.' I try to smile. 'Thank you.'

'Good girl.'

I had a dream last night, a dream so vivid that it is with me still. I am walking along a dirt road under a hot blue sky with hardly a cloud apart from a few high wisps like skeins of ashen hair. Then a sudden heavy shadow cuts out the light and warmth. I look up and see a thousand huge birds quietly circling above, with no sound at all except for the flapping of their wings. How ominous is that sound! *Swish . . . swish,* the beat of their wings like the rhythm of a terrible doomsday opera. *Swish . . . swish.* Round and round they fly, steady and silent, watching and waiting for the right moment.

Reine and I came from money, heaps of it. Our father was in real estate and he'd made a fortune. He was a wheeler and dealer at nineteen and had made his first couple of million by twenty-eight, a self-made man, real entrepreneur, hard-nosed, loud and generous to a fault, especially with us. It seemed like he'd only just finished buying one business and setting it up with the right people and equipment when he was taking on another.

We'd lived all our lives in beautiful houses. My favourite was the apartment we had on the twenty-first floor right across from the Opera House. Whenever we visited Sydney we stayed there. First-class air travel for everyone, including our friends. When we grew older there were parties and fabulous clothes and any luxury we fancied – beauty treatments, massages, holidays . . . Our home in Melbourne was a three-storeyed mansion in Toorak. Then there were houses in Noosa and Portsea. Our mother had never done a day's paid work in her life. Come to think of it, we always had housekeepers and maids, so it wasn't as though she did any unpaid work either, apart from picking us up from school occasionally if there was no one else around. My parents were negotiating to buy land in Italy, right next to Lake Como, for their latest dream home when . . . when it all started to unravel.

Not that it happened all at once, or that we had any idea that the demise would be so . . . complete. I suppose it took nearly two years for everything to go down the gurgler. One after another, each piece of the business fell into insolvency. Unbelievable! It began with Dad making some very bad financial decisions. He borrowed too much from the wrong people, sold at the wrong time and then . . . well, I don't pretend to understand all the details. All I know is that his affairs featured prominently in the financial pages for about twelve months before the end, and then, to our complete humiliation, on the *front page*. He was being sued left, right and centre and it seemed he'd become everyone's bad boy overnight. All his dodgy dealings and desperate attempts to stem the flow of money by borrowing more were paraded in the media for every cretin to pore over and discuss.

Reine and I were in our last year at the top posh girl's school when the shit began to seriously fly. Suddenly there was no actual cold hard cash for anything, including school fees. We were allowed to see out the year, but everyone knew.

'Is that your father in the paper today?'

'Did you know he was a . . . crook?'

'Is your family going to be . . . all right?' our classmates whispered, their eyes wide with fake concern. Did they really think we couldn't hear the gleeful undertones? Or see the merriment in their eyes or the furtive glances of amusement? Other people's woes are always so amusing, aren't they? We knew that. What we didn't know was that one day our family would take centre stage.

Our parents screamed at each other behind closed doors, but at least we were still in our lovely home in Toorak. We had our clothes and jewellery, the beautiful cars and furniture. The fact that it was all on credit wasn't really our concern. Our mother was the same. *Daddy is going through a bad patch and everything will be all right soon.* I suppose none of us quite believed that things could get worse. We were going to wake soon and everything would be back to normal.

The truth hit the day the trucks arrived and all our furniture was carted off to an auction house. It just seemed so totally outrageous that a gang of horrible little men in dusty shorts and sweaty T-shirts with cigarettes hanging out of their mouths could pick up *our* stuff and put it in *their* trucks. We begged Dad to do something, but there was nothing he could do. Out went my sound system and my huge flat-screen. The antique sideboards, the solid oak antique French beds and dressing tables, even that exquisite Venetian light from the sitting room, all the beautiful leather furniture from the downstairs study . . .

When the last truck had left and the four of us were standing in a more or less empty shell, I remember Dad turning to us.

'I'm sorry,' he said, holding out both arms helplessly, 'girls, I'm so sorry.' It was the first time we'd ever heard him apologise for anything. His face was grey and drawn, and the clothes that used to fit perfectly were now baggy. In fact, he had aged so much over the preceding year that he was almost unrecognisable.

We just sniffed and walked out of the room. I see him still: my father's stricken face as I turned my back on him. It is the most vivid image of my life. As far as I'm concerned, nothing we did to her comes even close to what we did to our own father.

He walked out of the house with nothing that day, not even his wallet or phone. He must have had some cash in his pocket, because we found out later that he hailed a taxi. But from that day he just disappeared out of our lives. His body washed up eventually, in a little backwater of the Goulburn River near Yea in central Victoria about six months later. Apparently he'd been dead for five days when they found him under overhanging trees, wedged between a rock and a couple of old tyres.

The three of us, Mum, Reine and I, moved into a two-bedroom flat out the other side of town. Reine and I had to share a tiny bedroom. There was nowhere for our clothes or cosmetics, or for anything much, really, except the two beds. And there was only one small bathroom. Our mother had to go to work for the first time in her life, answering calls in the office of a business that we used to own. The three of us were at each other's throats most of the time.

Neither of us had the brains or the inclination for university. We'd grown up believing Dad's promise that there would be jobs for us in the business as soon as we finished school. It went without saying that we would eventually nab a wealthy younger version of our father who'd provide everything we were used to. So we sat at home and moped and waited for phone calls that never came.

Then Mum brought Jack home . . .

She met him in a hotel one Friday night after work, and after knowing him for just on three weeks she told us that they were going to get married.

'Jack says there's room for all of us in his house,' Mum gushed with that mad, half-drunk look in her eye that told us she was putting a scheme together. 'So we can move out of this flat.'

'I know it's very sudden,' the poor sucker added, reaching out to squeeze our mother's arm, 'but neither of us is getting any younger, are we sweetie?' Reine and I looked at each other and said nothing. Was it our responsibility to warn him? I don't think so. Anyone with half a brain could see our mother was more reptile than human. Any man would need all his wits just to survive her, and this idiot obviously had none. We found out later that his wife had died only eight months before, so he was *emotionally vulnerable* – is that the term? Whatever. In short, he didn't know if he was coming or going.

'So when do we move?' Reine asked stonily. She'd seen the guy's car and told me it was a piece of crap – a Commodore, I think – so it wasn't like we had any illusions about the house. On the other hand, anything would be better than living in that poxy little flat.

'What about tomorrow?'

'I've seen the house,' Mum whispered later, 'and it's much better than this. You'll have a room each.'

'Okay,' we mumbled in unison. What she was telling us was that this guy Jack would be the first step on our climb back to the world we once knew. We trusted our mother. She'd always had an eye for the main chance.

They forgot to tell us that Jack had a daughter until the day before we moved all our things over to his house.

'Ella,' he said, squeezing the last load of Mum's clothes into the car. 'The sweetest girl in the world.'

'Oh?' I said warily. 'Does she mind us . . . coming?'

'Not at all,' Jack smiled. 'As soon as I told her you'd be coming to live with us, she offered to move out of her room so you two could have the two rooms near each other – they're bigger, too.'

'What room will your daughter have?'

'There's a spare room at the back of the house.' Jack hesitated. 'It's been a junk room, but we cleaned it out. And it's only a stopgap until I get the bungalow built.'

'How nice is that?' Mum turned around in the front seat and gave us one of her vicious little smirks. 'You girls will be sure to say thank you, I hope,' she added in a syrupy voice.

Reine and I mumbled something, but we were both suspicious. What kind of a *retard* would willingly give up her room?

'So she *offered* to move into the *junk* room?' Reine asked unbelievingly, 'without having met us?'

'Yep.' Jack smiled proudly. 'She's always been like that, generous to a fault, just like her mother. She just loves doing things for people. Wanted to make you both feel welcome.'

'How old is your daughter?' I asked, trying to keep my voice serious. Reine was doing her squashed-spider mouth, all tight and pursed up, and it never failed to make me laugh.

'Seventeen,' Jack said, eyes on the road so he didn't notice our sniggers. 'There'll be no problems, I promise. She has never given me a moment's worry.'

'Lucky you.' Reine's voice was dripping with sarcasm. 'So what school does she go to?'

'The local high school's just down the road,' he said. 'It's a wonderful school and she always gets top of her class.'

'Really?'

'She's loved reading since she was tiny, and she's a great little writer,' he blathered on, oblivious to our stifled hilarity. 'She writes plays, too. Last year the school drama group chose one of hers for their end-of-year performance.'

'Oh, that's sooooo nice.'

'Wow! She must be talented.'

Reine and I had her sussed and we hadn't even met her. *Reading and writing plays, eh?* We looked at each other with raised, knowing eyebrows. We knew the type. Every school has them – tedious, bright-eyed, studious geeks. At school I hardly even *saw* those girls until they stood up at assembly and started crapping on about some boring play or wacko author the library group had invited to the school. *So come along and get your books signed!* Yeah right! It was either that or Indigenous rights or climate change. My friends and I would be down the back paralytic with laughter or boredom as those total losers blathered on. The incredible thing was that they had no idea how totally . . . uncool they were, with their witless little battles to save the world. They were continually bugging people to join their clubs and buy tickets to their stupid performances or raffle tickets for their good works. As far as we were concerned, the world as it was was totally fine. Why would we want to change anything?

'Ella is going to have a special dinner ready for us,' Jack said when we asked if we could stop for takeaway.

'Oh goody,' Reine muttered under her breath. 'She sounds like such fun.'

'Yeah,' I muttered. 'God, I'm *dying* to meet her.'

{1}

It has to be said right up front that as soon as I saw her I hated her. My sister Reine and I both hated her on sight. When she opened the door to welcome us into that poxy little vanilla-brick nothing house in that nowhere suburb surrounded by other shitty little houses with low fences and dreary gardens and muffled dirty traffic noise . . . we were overcome by it. I remember the way we snorted and chuckled as soon as we were out of earshot. 'Oh how nice! She wants to show us around!' my sister sniggered.

'Like there's anything to see!' I giggled, glad to be brought back to reality after the shock of actually meeting the girl. Reine had always been a brilliant mimic, and she'd got the deep breathy voice just right.

She was beautiful, you see, startlingly so, if you want the truth. Funny that I can admit that now, because there was a time when I was unable to say her name without the green monster sticking so hard in my throat that I almost choked. Her hair was deep titian bronze – that colour that you just can't get from a packet or a bottle – full of depth and natural highlights. In one light it was almost blonde but in another quite a deep red. Anyway, it was long and thick and curly. Her eyes were so blue and bright that you couldn't, even if you tried, look away from them, especially if she had them trained on you, and they were surrounded by thick, dark lashes. Above them were perfectly arched eyebrows that had obviously never even been plucked! *Oh God.* Ditto for the rest of her! That was the truly sickening part. Not a hint of contrivance or a trace of makeup.

We hadn't been warned, not by our mother or by the hopeless idiot who was to become our stepfather. No one told us that our stepsister was this incredibly hot chick or tried to prepare us for how it would actually feel to *live* with that every day.

She was in baggy jeans and a torn old red T-shirt and rubber thongs if you don't mind.

'Hi, I'm Ella,' she said, 'it's so good to meet you both. Welcome!'

It makes me laugh to remember how damned *friendly* she was, right from that first meeting, smiling shyly, holding out both of her soft white hands as though she really had been looking forward to meeting us! How dumb would you have to be not to hold back a bit? The three of us – Mum, Reine and I – were about to move into her house permanently. She'd never met us before, so how completely stupid not to be just a teeny bit wary. She could have had the upper hand if she'd wanted it! That's what I always come back to when the buckets of blame pour over our heads. She could have had the upper hand! She was seventeen, for God's sake, not ten.

We stood there – Reine and I – transfixed by the perfection before us. When she turned away to close the door behind us I couldn't look at my sister, but I remember praying, *Please let her have heavy legs and thick ankles under those jeans. If not that then at least give her some other awful defect or better still some fatal disease that will kill her off soon, because I'm not going to be able to handle living with this . . .* But I could already see that her feet in those old thongs were small and dainty, and before the day was out I knew that she had the lithe athleticism of a ballet dancer and lovely, shapely legs as well. After we'd been shown to our rooms and checked out the bathroom and the kitchen, which was in the middle of the living area, she was still all smiles.

'Come and I'll show you out the back.'

Outside was even more boring than inside if that was possible. The yard was neat, with a huge gum tree in one corner and a fruit tree in the other, a couple of beds of roses and coloured flowers in the middle of the lawn and some sort of vegetable patch along the back fence, as if they were peasants. A row of small trees and bushes lined the side fence. A wire-netting enclosure attached to an old disused laundry was the only thing that was even vaguely interesting.

'It's a hospital for birds,' Ella said proudly as she led us over to it. Reine and I, raised our eyebrows behind her back and Reine pretended to throw up. *Oh wow! How totally wonderful! A bird hospital. Can't wait to see that!*

'People bring sick birds from all over the country for Dad to heal,' the girl carried on, oblivious.

What could we say?

There was nothing to look at anyway. Nothing interesting. At the very least I thought there might be an exotic species – like the coloured ones you see in Indonesia and Thailand with the weird beaks, or some of those bright pretty twittering things that would at least be amusing or decorative. But no, there was just this huge, black, morose-looking thing sitting like a lump of wood on a low branch. And a few very ordinary-looking pigeons in a cordoned-off section in one corner, but who'd want to look at them?

'Is that an eagle?' I asked, pointing to the big mean one with the yellow eyes and hooked beak.

'No,' she laughed, 'we're not sure what he is. Dad knows every species of bird but he can't pinpoint this one. We've got a guy coming from the university to check him out next month.'

'Looks so . . . mean.' I shuddered.

'Mean,' she agreed, 'but wonderful too. Look at his beak and his legs, so powerful and they . . .' She stopped, sensing that we didn't really want a lecture on how wonderful the ghastly creature was. 'It's really important to keep this gate shut, okay?'

'Why?'

'Well, he's a scavenger. We know that much. He'll attack other small creatures like cats or other birds.'

Reine looked at me blankly and put her fingers through the wire. 'Like we were planning to walk in,' she whispered to me.

'Don't do that,' Ella said quietly.

'Why not?'

'It's a wild creature. It will attack if it feels threatened.'

Reine left her hand exactly where it was.

'It doesn't look too wild to me,' she mocked. But just as she said it the gross black thing turned its head, fixed its bright yellow eye on us, then opened its beak wide and let out this incredibly loud, long screech. It was like someone's nail sliding down the blackboard at school, only much worse.

'Yuck!' Reine pulled her hand away.

'How come your dad knows so much about birds?'

'It's been his lifelong passion,' Ella said proudly.

'Has he studied them?' I enquired suspiciously.

'Some people just have a feeling for particular animals.' She obviously thought this was enough of an explanation. 'Birds have been his thing since he was a kid. He knows a lot of stuff by feel.'

'Feel?'

'Remember the horse whisperer?' she went on.

We shook our heads and stared at her. *What the hell have horses got to do with birds?*

Ella sighed, like it was *us* being stupid, and I didn't take kindly to that. 'Dad didn't do formal study,' she went on defensively, 'and it made the university people a bit wary of him when he asked for help with this bird. They kept suggesting that it might be something ordinary, like a giant eagle or a hawk or something.' She laughed. 'Like Dad wouldn't know that.'

'If he's not properly trained, then . . . he's *not* an expert,' Reine snapped and turned back to the house. I followed, leaving miss lovely-goody-two-shoes to trail in after us.

Did I tell you that her skin was beyond flawless? It was as fine as silk, with the faintest pink flush on both cheeks, which of course made us both feel like lizards in comparison with our greasy spots and Noosa tans. She had a long, swan-like neck and when she pulled her hair back into a loose ponytail you immediately noticed the high cheekbones that all the models have (or dream of having *or* have painted on *or* cut in by the surgeon's knife), not to mention the small, straight, slightly upturned nose and wide mouth. God, she was . . . *gorgeous!*

Reine and I were not ugly – at least we weren't until we met *her*. We were short, though – stocky rather than fat – and we both had long noses, biggish hands and ugly feet. Reine had good eyes, and I've been told I've got a nice smile – if only I'd use it more – but my eyes are too close together and there isn't much you can do about that. I was booked in for liposuction because my thighs and bum are too heavy, but that never happened because of the money issue. Reine had already had it done at sixteen, along with a nice boob job, but I'd decided to wait for all that. A few of Mum's friends had had dodgy jobs that made them look weird, so . . . yeah, I was putting off going under the knife.

I guess we were just two ordinary-looking chicks who had to work hard to make ourselves attractive, and spend a fortune on it, too. It figures that what you haven't been born with, you have to cultivate or create or buy if you can. Mum, Reine and I dieted constantly and spent heaps on skin treatments, massages, hair and nail products – so what? We thought nothing of it; it was just what girls like us did. Our father was rich. We had friends. We went around with stylish people. Okay, we weren't up there with the really hot chicks, but . . . we'd never considered ourselves *ugly*! We'd both had guys ask us out – not exactly the guys we wanted to ask us out, but hey . . . we were *on the map*, definitely part of a scene. Life was bearable.

But by the end of that first day, after meeting her, things had changed – we were ugly. It wasn't fair that just because of her we had to feel like that every day. So . . . we decided we'd keep her out of sight as much as possible. Not that Reine and I sat down and talked about it exactly. It was just understood. Life would be better if we didn't have to look at her.

{2}

The surgeon was in again this morning. No sidekick this time. I must have frightened him off. He sat on the bed and started to loosen the bandage over my right eye, then I felt some sort of cold instrument slipping under it and pressing gently around the area. It didn't hurt but I couldn't tell what he was doing. Was he shining a light in? I still couldn't see.

'Are you going to take them off?' My heart was pounding, though I'd managed to keep my voice even.

'No no,' he murmured and he taped back the bandage and did the same on the other side. 'We'll wait for tomorrow or the next day. Try to be patient.'

I nodded meekly. This guy doesn't know it, but he is the only person in the world I trust.

'So how are you sleeping?' he asks.

I shake my head and turn away.

Last night a sudden rush of wind and a terrible sharp cry woke me. Was it human? Suddenly there was a crushing weight on my chest. I struggled but couldn't move. But I could see. A huge bird with a long hooked beak had landed on my chest. I felt the sharp talons pierce the flesh as it folded its wings into place, bouncing slightly from side to side as it took hold and settled itself. All the while its huge head was turning casually from left to right, so utterly *indifferent.*

'Oh God, please.' I couldn't move. 'Help me!' Confident that it had no competition, it lowered its head and started to pick delicately at my right eyelid with its sharp beak.

'I sleep okay.' I tried to smile at him. 'But I look forward to the morning.'

'Ah yes,' the surgeon mumbled, as if he knew exactly what I meant. He rested one hand on my shoulder for a moment.

'Always give thanks for the morning,' he said softly. And you know I've found myself thinking about that all day. *Always give thanks for the morning.*

{3}

The temptation is to gloss over this next bit; just throw it away with a few lines like 'we were mean to her right from the start' or 'for some reason we felt the need to belittle her' or 'baiting her became fun for us'. It would be the truth and we could get on with the next bit, but . . . it would be weak. Real life is in the details, so I must tell at least some of them. Looking back, I see that it got pretty bizarre. I could point to many reasons, but why make excuses? None of them are adequate.

I guess the room thing gave us the idea from the start that she was pretty malleable. You could spin her a line and she'd believe it. First off it was innocuous enough. She'd come home from school and we'd be sitting about doing nothing and I'd raise my eyebrow at Reine and say, 'God, I've had this terrible headache all day.'

'Do you want an aspirin or something?' Ella would say, all concerned. She was always sort of tentative, as if she was still working out how to please us. I don't know why, but it brought out the worst in both of us.

'No, but I haven't had any lunch,' I'd say. 'Reckon you could bring me a sandwich and a coffee?'

'Oh sure,' she'd say, 'no worries.' She was so gullible you see, so eager to please, and she kept coming back for more. Baiting her became a kind of sport for us. Neither Mum nor Reine nor I knew the first thing about cooking, so it wasn't long before we started to expect her to do it all.

Her presence at meals used to annoy Reine and me because she ate everything she felt like without ever putting on any weight. And we had to look at those dainty hands.

'Look, why don't you have your meals later,' Reine said at last. 'I mean, it's annoying having to look at you eating like a pig when we're all on diets.'

'That's a good idea,' Mum said sharply. By this stage she hated her too.

So that's what happened. Not only did she do all the cooking, she wasn't really allowed to eat with us either, except when her stupid father was around. He used to get home late most nights and seemed unaware of what was going on. He'd come in and do the big cheery act, kiss Mum and ask if we'd had a good day, then he'd make himself a drink and head out to tend to his sick birds. Anyway, sticking up for his daughter would have meant crossing our mother, and he must have decided by that stage it wasn't worth it. For some reason Jack was in absolute thrall to Mum. Reine and I used to snigger together as we speculated about what she must be giving him, because he was constantly trying please her. Sometimes we'd get scared that Ella would tell him about how mean we were, but although she looked miserable sometimes, she never said anything. I think she didn't want to ruin his happiness.

That suited us just fine.

The three of us weren't used to doing housework, of course. We'd always had someone do it for us and Ella acted so willing and able at first that it seemed natural for her to keep doing it all. She'd rush home from school to get the dinner on, and there would be dishes all over the sink. Once she asked us to clean up after ourselves.

'Why should we?' Reine said.

'Well, I do the cooking and the rest of it,' Ella said in that soft way she had. 'It's not fair that I should have to do everything.'

'But you're good at it,' I said. Believe it or not, little miss prissy-pants started to cry.

'What's up?' I said.

'Why do you have to be so . . . horrible?' she whispered.

'Look, it was a joke, okay?' I said uncomfortably. But Reine flew at her, quite unfairly I guess.

'Horrible?' she shouted, jumping off the couch and advancing on Ella menacingly. 'I'll give you horrible. You think we care about this shitty little dogbox of a house? Well, we don't. We hate living here. We hate your stupid father and his ridiculous birds and we hate you. So if you want the dishes done, do them yourself!'

Ella ran off to her room and Reine and I were left looking at each other. Reine was feeling it even worse than me, if that was possible.

'God, I hate living here,' she said before switching on the television. Then Ella came back out, tears streaked across her face. I have to say that there was a determined look about her.

'Why?' she said. 'Why do you hate it here? Why do you hate us so much?'

I remember being on the point of apologising. We'd gone too far. But Reine had other ideas.

'You're just too dumb to take seriously,' she sneered. Then she picked up one of the cushions and threw it straight at Ella's head. The girl gave a startled cry and retreated to her room.

It wasn't just her looks that made us jealous. Oddly enough, it was her life as well, even though by our former standards it was totally pathetic. But at least she had a life, with friends and homework and school choir and drama club. Sometimes she helped her father with the sick birds before she left for school. After a few weeks, more birds were brought into the cage, none of them as big or mean-looking as that huge black critter who continued to stay in his little fenced-off section looking horrible – but we never asked about them. Nothing about any of it interested us. Reine and I would watch Ella and her father working together inside the wire enclosure, chatting away as they cleaned out the feed bowls and mucked around with medicines like all that stuff really mattered. When they were in with the birds they both wore ridiculous big leather gloves and masks, which made us snigger. Ella's interests and activities were complete crap, of course, but at least she had something to do. Reine and I had nothing. Mum had enrolled us into a shonky business course, but we soon dropped out when it became obvious we'd have to work. So we spent our days sitting around watching television, bitching at each other, eating and getting fat.

After a few months Ella began staying back late a couple of nights a week for choir and theatre rehearsals, and that's when we really felt it. Apart from the fact that she wasn't on duty to cook and clean and wait on us those nights, it seemed unfair that she had outside interests when we didn't. But it wasn't like we could stop her going to school. So we took advantage of her absence to poke around her room and go through her things.

There was only one small bathroom in that ridiculous house, which we were all supposed to share. One morning when Ella was in there getting ready for school and Reine wanted to use the toilet, she had the bright idea that the bathroom was way too small for all of us to share. There was a cold shower in one corner of the old laundry out the back near the bird enclosure – no curtain or towel rail, but a big sink and an old leaky toilet that you had to pull a chain to flush. The floor was concrete, the door was battered and cracked and the whole place was covered in dirt and dust because it had been used to store bird feed, straw and medicines for the birds. After checking the place over, Reine declared it Ella's 'new' bathroom.

By the time Ella came home that night, Reine had moved

her few things out there along with an old chair and a small cracked mirror.

'You've got your own private bathroom now,' she said.

'But there's no hot water.' Ella seemed more stunned than anything else.

'So you bring it out in a bucket if you need it.' Reine sniffed, as though she didn't have a long hot shower every day herself. 'But we thought you'd be keen to save water. And you'll be near your beloved birds.'

Ella stared at her silently for a few moments, then went to her room. We only just managed to wait until her door had closed before we doubled up with laughter.

'God, it worked,' my sister chortled.

'But she'll tell her father,' I said under my breath.

'No, she won't. She doesn't want to upset dear Daddy,' Reine chuckled, 'and he won't do anything to upset Mum.'

It was true. Jack seemed oblivious to anything except what was right under his nose. So from that day, Ella used the old laundry as her bathroom. I must admit to a twinge of guilt when I'd see her heading outside with her bucket on cold mornings!

The day we decided we'd destroy the stash of journals hidden under her bed was a kind of watershed moment. Naturally we read them and hooted and chortled about all the crappy poems and deep-and-meaningful rubbish she'd written there, but it was when I found the huge, bright pink *Live Your Dreams* sticker on one of them that I lost it. I'll be honest here, that little motto sent me completely *spare*. It had silver stars all around it and little girly flowers, and not only that, she'd written it out again a few times underneath. It was too much.

Live Your Dreams.

I guess I was thinking about what had happened to Dad and to Reine and me and Mum, and the way our dreams had fallen right through the cracks of life. This girl's constantly sweet and positive attitude to everything, even us, was driving me crazy.

We had planned to torch the lot before she got home and pretend we knew nothing about it, so when she came home early it threw us a bit. My sister was inside trying to find the matches when Ella came around the back of the house to find the pile of her precious notebooks on the lawn. When she realised what we had planned, her face went white.

I held one folder up in front of her. 'Why do you write this crap over your stuff?' I sneered.

'What do you mean? Why are you doing this?' she cried.

'Haven't you worked out *anything* yet?' I yelled, dropping the book with the sticker on top of the pile. Reine watched this from the back step, a broad smile on her face, then she came out with the matches.

Ella was more upset than I'd ever seen her. So *this* was her raw nerve. I felt glad we'd hit it, but another part of me was on some kind of ride that I couldn't seem to get off, and it was going faster and faster. *Why were we doing it?*

Ella lunged forward to snatch some of the books and I soon forgot about any misgivings and became incensed all over again. This time she didn't give up so easily, but kept trying to save her journals – even managed to grab a few in spite of my best efforts to shove her back. We always got them away from her, and in the end Reine and I were shrieking and screaming and chucking them back and forth like frisbees, the pages flying out in the breeze as she raced between us sobbing. She was outmanoeuvred as well as outnumbered.

'No one gets to live their dream, and if you don't believe me, then here's the proof!' Reine had her in a tight grip and she threw the box of matches at me. 'Go on! Do it!'

With fumbling fingers I pulled one out, struck it and set it to some newspaper we'd scrunched up beneath the pile. The flames flared in the wind, quickly spreading from one notebook to the next. They didn't immediately catch, but it didn't take long. After a while Reine let her go and she just stood there staring at her smoking journals, tears running down her face.

Live Your Dreams.

Then the three of us stood around watching the flames take hold. It was late afternoon at the end of winter, still cold. Reine and I were laughing meanly as we kicked in the books around the edges, making sure the fire got everything.

'Oh, poor little Ellie!' Reine crowed. 'She won't know what to do with herself now.'

'All her lovely journals,' I joined in. 'She'll have to save up and buy herself some *special* ones now.'

'Maybe she wants to jump on there with them!' Reine suddenly grabbed one elbow and motioned for me to take the other. Ella struggled against us but didn't scream, and we soon had her.

'One, two, three!' We shoved her towards the flames, but although she stumbled and fell onto some burning ash, she got away before any real harm was done and ran for the back fence. Reine was all for dragging her back for a proper burn, but the ferocity in my sister's eyes frightened me a little.

'No,' I muttered and Reine acquiesced, although she seemed disappointed.

Without actually speaking about it, we must have agreed to keep our hands off her at that point. Apart from a slap or two along the way, that was probably the most physical we ever got. We didn't want to end up in jail!

After it was all gone she edged back to the smouldering remnants of the fire, squatted down and hid her face in her hands. We smirked as we watched her from the back window. Reine nudged me and pointed at the bird enclosure. There was a dark shape moving up and down against the wire. I went out onto the back porch for a better look and felt a slight shiver down my spine when I saw it was the big bird, his eyes gleaming yellow in the dim light, clawing the wire to get out.

Two hours later she was still outside sitting by the remains of her books, poking through the ashes as though looking for something. When she came in again she had ash all over her hands and face.

'Hi Cinders,' I said breezily, laughing at her mucky face. She said nothing, just passed us on her way to the bathroom. 'Hey, that can be your new name,' I said.

'Yeah, Cinders,' said Reine. 'And don't use our bathroom, thank you. You've got your own.'

{4}

Invitations to parties with our old crowd were few and far between. In fact, just about everyone we knew had forgotten us, or pretended they had, so when we got Joshua Hogan's invitation Reine and I were excited. It was a big glossy black-and-red number, the details printed in scrawling silver letters. His parents wanted to celebrate their son finishing university, or some such crap, with a big party. It was to be a night of *ultimate fun and mystery*, with everyone in masks and dressed as their favourite character from history.

The thing about Josh was that in spite of his being born into a famous family – his father was a film producer and his mother had been a well-known actress who now ran the most prestigious acting agency in the country – *and* in spite of him being very clever and handsome, he was actually a genuinely nice guy. Amazing, isn't it?

I'll never forget his reaction the day Dad's face was plastered across the front of every paper in the country. Reine and I had cleared off into the city to see a film, just to get away from it all, and quite unexpectedly we'd run into him outside the cinema. Eyes downcast with shame, we mumbled hello and walked passed quickly, assuming he'd be loath to be seen with us like everyone else we knew. Not so. He deliberately came after us and tapped me on the shoulder and made me turn around.

'Hey, you two!' he said. 'I'm really sorry that things are so tough for you at the moment.' There was real sympathy and kindness in his voice and eyes. We just stood there staring at him, not knowing how to respond. 'Things will get better,' he added seriously and then he grinned, put his arms around both of us briefly and said, 'You always think they won't, but they do. I'll bet you anything!'

'Thanks.' We both managed to smile.

'Got to go now,' he said, 'but I'll be in touch.' Then he actually got out his phone and punched in our numbers! With that he was off, but that minute-long exchange meant so much to us. We talked about it for weeks afterwards. And, true to his word, Joshua occasionally sent us a funny text message or a bit of news about someone we knew. Once he rang us to see if we were interested in coming to Bali with a group of the old gang for a couple of weeks. Of course we couldn't – there was no money – but it felt good to be asked. Hardly anyone else had called, much less asked us anywhere, after we'd had to move out of our house in Toorak.

Anyway, I stupidly stuck the invitation on the fridge. Sometimes I wonder if any of what transpired would have happened if we'd kept the invitation to ourselves.

Unfortunately Joshua had scrawled a little note along the bottom of the invitation.

I'm expecting to see you both here – dressed up to within an inch of your lives! Josh.

P.S. Someone told me that your mum has remarried and you have a stepsister. Be sure to tell her that she is welcome too. In fact, tell her I'm expecting her. Three fantastically adorned chicks from your house will be just what my party needs!

That night Mum had gone through the motions of making a pissy little salad, but Cinders had made the bulk of the meal as usual. We were sitting at the table waiting for her to bring us the knives and forks when my mother snapped, 'Why don't you set the table *before* we sit down, Ella.'

'Iced water!' Reine demanded as she served herself some of the delicious-smelling lasagne. (Did I mention that along with everything else, the girl was an excellent cook?)

Cinders went back to the kitchen and saw the invitation on the fridge. She stopped to read it and looked at us, her eyes shining.

'So I'm invited too,' she said in her deep, soft voice.

Reine snorted. 'No!' she snarled. 'You're not.'

'But it says . . .'

'You don't even know the guy.'

'But he says he wants me to come.'

Reine and I snickered and rolled our eyes. *As if!*

'He was being nice!' I said, faking a sweetness I didn't feel. My God! As though we'd want *her* there!

'Why would he say it if he didn't mean it?'

'And why would you want to go to a party where you know no one?' I snapped.

'Because it might be fun,' she said with a touch of vehemence in her voice that I'd never heard before. 'I love fancy dress. It's my favourite thing.' Reine and I looked at each other and burst into a fit of giggles.

'Have your own party here then!' I waved my arm dismissively around the humble little kitchen. 'It's such a great venue.'

Suddenly we heard her father whistling in the hall. The door opened and he said jovially, 'How are all my gorgeous girls?'

I have to say that I wondered sometimes if Jack was a full-on mental retard. He was certainly thick, no question about it. No one answered, of course. We didn't even look up from the table. He threw his bag down and put his arm around his wife, *our mother,* who deigned at the last minute to offer him a cold upturned cheek. Then he kissed the top of his daughter's head.

'Any tucker left?' He was almost shouting. 'Smells good!' Maybe he *had* picked up on the vibe. His jovial tone might have been an attempt to break through the unpleasant fog that was hovering over that table. Cinders went to get him a plate, and of course Reine and I assumed the whole matter was over. But no.

'I really want to come,' she said, turning those incredible bright eyes from one of us to the other. Mostly we kept things sweet in front of him – it was his house, after all. I almost burst out laughing as I watched Reine switch on her concerned expression and nice warm voice.

'But everyone will be older than you, Ella,' she said sweetly, helping herself to another serve of the delicious lasagne.

'I don't care,' Ella said stubbornly and then went to the fridge, plucked the invitation off and handed it to her father. 'I'm invited too and it would be such fun to go.' She looked around at us challengingly. 'I haven't had any fun for ages,' she said doggedly.

'Forget it,' I said icily. I was almost reeling from her absolute cheek. If her father hadn't have been there I would have screamed at her or slapped her face. As it was, everyone's eyes were on their plates. We were shovelling food into our mouths at a great rate, but I was aware of the glistening in Cinders's eyes and the determined set of her mouth. Finally Jack looked up from reading the invitation.

'Why can't she go?' he asked quietly, looking around at the rest of us. 'She's been invited.' He did a small thing then that seemed extraordinary at the time. At least it did to me. He leaned across the table and touched his daughter's face briefly with one finger and smiled. I saw one bright tear spill out and roll down her cheek. His gesture was like a sudden sharp jab in my guts; it took my breath away. I had a moment of the most terrible shame, piercing my chest like a poisoned arrow and then seeping slowly out into my head and arms and legs. *He loves her. He really loves her.* But the insight didn't last long. It soon turned to contempt. So how come this fool had no idea? Were men so stupid that they couldn't pick up the most obvious dynamics of a household? *All my girls indeed!*

We turned to our mother. Something had to be done . . . *now.* Mum would know what was best.

'Jack, I think this is something that the girls have to work out between themselves,' she said sweetly. 'You know what girls are like.' She giggled and ran one painted fingernail up from the inside of his wrist to his elbow. Her ridiculous simpering usually melted him immediately, but this time he looked up at her with the strangest expression. Almost as though he'd never seen her before in his life. He shrugged unhappily before turning back to his food.

'I just don't understand,' he said quietly.

Mum waited a couple of moments, then said blandly, 'Well, girls, please keep an open mind about it. It *might* be entirely appropriate for Ella to attend.'

Jack nodded seriously, as though satisfied, and bent his head over his plate, and Mum gave us a quick wink. It was all I could do not to laugh. *Nice one, Mum!*

{5}

At last the day arrived and I have to say that Reine and I ended up looking pretty fantastic even if we broke the sucker's bank doing it. Mum managed to wangle her way into his special savings account on the pretext that, as his wife, she should have access to *all* his money in case of an emergency. Of course, up to this point she'd been spending every cent of his wages, but this account was set aside for his little princess's tertiary education and for the bungalow he planned to build in the backyard. Mum understood how important it was to do the party right. She knew that if we were a success at Joshua's then it could put us back on the social map with the people who mattered.

Reine and I dismissed all the obvious costumes – nuns, queens, witches, cowgirls. This was our chance to really shine. Sure we would dress up as *characters*, but sexy and glamorous characters. We wanted to look *hot*.

So while Jack was at work we spent his money. After much ringing around we ended up heading out to the other side of town by taxi to a really classy costume-hire place. The picking and choosing and trying on of outfits took one whole day. The manicures and pedicures and hairdressers and makeup took another. Reine, who has nice full tits thanks to the boob job, and a decent waist, went as Scarlett O'Hara. Her cleavage was stunning and the big, hooped skirt hid her heavy bum and solid legs. I went as a Greek goddess in a long, simple red dress that disguised my bum and thick waist. It was held at one shoulder with a gold brooch, showing off my nice olive skin. We hired good hair pieces to enhance our outfits – mine was a thick dark plait which I planned to adorn with a string of tiny white flowers, with the help of a hairdresser who we'd booked, along with a makeup artist, to help bring it all together on the day.

We knew it was probably going to take all afternoon to get ready but we were both happy and excited about what we'd decided. By this stage Cinders seemed to be over the disappointment of missing out on the party and was willing to help us get ready, running and fetching for the beautician and even biking to the shops for some anti-frizz serum for the hairdresser.

{6}

The makeup woman had just finished with me when the doorbell rang. I thought it would be the tiny flowers for my hair, special delivery from the florist, but standing on the doorstep was Dorothy, Ella's weirdo old drama teacher, dressed in white as usual. Reine and I had met her a few times. She never said anything much, but we didn't like her. Too sure of herself. Acting like she was somebody when she was only a teacher. She had this long silvery-grey hair, and a million tiny wrinkles around her eyes. Cinders told us early on that Dorothy and her mother had been best friends. Like we were meant to care about that!

This day she was wearing a white linen tunic dress and wide pants and she was holding a shiny white box and leaning on a slim silver cane.

'Hello Skye,' she said in her weird stage voice.

'Hello?' I was not in the mood for diversions.

'May I see Eleanor?' she asked. 'I have something for her.'

'Hey, Cind . . . ers,' I called back into the house. There was no answer, so I held out my hands for the box. 'I'll give it to her,' I snapped. 'She's pretty busy right now.'

'Oh no,' the old woman laughed, as though I'd said something totally outrageous. 'Definitely not, my dear!'

'*What?*' I stared at her, furious. *Go play Shakespeare somewhere else, why don't you!*

'I will give it to Ella,' she said calmly.

'But we're all busy, okay?' I snapped. Who did this old bird think she was?

'I can see that.' She laughed again and stepped towards the threshold, as if she wanted to come in. But I held my ground. For some reason I really didn't want her inside the house.

'Hey Cinders!' I yelled again. 'Someone for you!'

This time Cinders poked her head around the door and when she saw who it was, her face lit up and she came over at once.

'Hi Dot,' she said joyfully.

'For you, sweetheart.' The woman thrust the box into her hands.

'What is it?' Cinders asked curiously.

'You must wait until night falls before you open it.' The old bird chuckled.

'But what is it?' Cinders asked again childishly. The woman just smiled.

Even though I was so caught up with getting ready, this old chick made me wary.

'The instructions are inside,' she said in a low voice, like she didn't want me to hear. 'You will understand when you open the box.' The woman raised her two old hands to Cinders' head and ran them briefly down over her hair to her shoulders. 'But you must wait until tonight.' Then very abruptly she turned her back and began to hurry away down the path. Cinders stood watching her disappear.

'Remember, not until tonight,' she called from the gate. 'Obey the instructions to the letter and all will be well.'

'Okay.' Cinders was still bewildered. 'I will.'

Then the woman was gone.

Cinders raised her eyes from the box, a tentative smile of delight on her lips. Needless to say, I did not smile back.

'Open it now,' I commanded coldly. But Cinders shook her head and immediately retreated towards her room, holding the box tightly to her chest.

'No,' she said firmly.

'That woman is a nut!' I yelled after her. But the truth was that she'd made me feel uneasy.

'I don't care,' came the muffled reply.

I was furious that she would defy me like this.

'Come out, Ella!' I yelled. 'Let's see what it is.'

There was no reply.

I stood outside her door fuming, listening to her shifting things around in her little boxroom, knowing she was probably searching for a safe hiding place. I was toying with the idea of barging in and snatching the thing when the doorbell sounded again. This time it *was* my flowers.

'Cinders!' Reine roared from the other room as I took the flowers from the delivery boy and signed the docket. 'Hurry up! This nail polish is dry and I need the top coat.'

'Coming.' Cinders edged out of her room warily and went to Reine. If it had been any other day I would have made damned sure I found out what was in that box right away, even if I'd had to break through whatever barriers she'd set up, but I was diverted by the party preparations. By the time the hairdresser had started threading the flowers through my hair, the whole incident had simply slipped my mind.

{7}

It was so wonderful to be back in the world of huge houses and exquisitely decorated rooms, the world of enormous gardens all lit up with candles and lamps, of beautiful champagne and tables groaning under the weight of delicious food! Best of all it was wonderful to be back among the silly talk of rich people. I'd missed it so much!

Reine and I entered tentatively. We weren't sure how the old crowd would treat us. But you know, just being there seemed to make us respectable again! The fact that Josh, whom everyone loved and admired, had invited us was enough. No one brought up Dad or our diminished circumstances. No one asked any awkward questions about where we were living now. It was like they'd forgotten what had happened to us, and the odd thing was that it didn't take us long to forget, too! In fact, after the first glass of champagne the last eighteen months slipped away like a bad dream.

It was a lovely warm night and everyone was wearing masks. Reine's and mine were black with some diamantés around the edges, but so many of the others were more ornate, decorated with fake jewels, gold and silver thread and tiny mirrors. All of this added an air of mystery to the night. Reine and I had judged our costumes perfectly. There was Henry VIII and Joan of Arc in her helmet. There were nuns and queens, popes, clowns and two Florence Nightingales. One girl came as a panther because she couldn't think of anyone from the past she wanted to be. Another came as the devil's wife in a shiny red catsuit, horns and a pinned-on tail, with a pitchfork hooked to her back that looked like the real thing! Another came swathed in yards of black muslin and coloured veils, unable to say quite who she was: Mary Magdalene one minute, an Islamic terrorist the next! Although we knew most people – it was our old crowd, after all – it took everyone a little while to work out exactly who was who, but that only added to the fun.

'Hey, it's Reine and Skye!'

'The sisters extraordinaire.'

'No shit, so it is!' William Hollis, whose father owned most of Sydney's water supply along with half the office real estate on the North Shore and who had just flown in from a trekking holiday in South America, was so glad to see us that he was virtually shouting. 'We haven't seen you two chicks for ages!'

'You both look *soooo* amazing.'

'Why thank you, sir!' Reine, in full-on Scarlett mode, was fluttering her eyelids and waving her fan around like crazy, making everyone laugh.

'Listen to her!'

'Having a bash next weekend to celebrate the new pad!' This from Karl Peters, whose old man ran Macquarie Bank.

'Oh?'

'You've both got to come.'

'Love to!'

'Scarlett O'Hara, eh?' Marcus Brown, from Brown's Australia-wide Plumbing, which had just expanded into South-East Asia and was taking the stock market by storm, took Reine in his arms and waltzed her around the room.

'Frankly, my dear,' he said after they'd circled the room in front of everyone, 'I *do* give a damn!' There were whoops of delight and shouts of laughter as he knelt and kissed her hand. And so it went. From one group of old friends to another we were welcomed with pecks on the cheek and cries of delight.

I was standing with a group in front of a huge gilt-edged mirror having my photo taken when Kara, my one-time best friend, nestled in beside me.

'So great to have you back,' she whispered in my ear. (I'd stopped hearing from her about the time Dad hit the front pages.)

'It's great to *be* back!' I murmured, smiling for the camera and trying not to remember the three-bedroom shit-box in Epping.

'So everything is . . . okay now?' She had on her wide-eyed expression that meant she actually did care. Absolutely. No matter that she'd cut me at the last party; she cared. She must have forgotten all the times I'd witnessed the same look changing to one of amusement as soon as some poor loser's back was turned.

'Absolutely.' I gave her an extra-bright smile just to let her know that I believed her *absolutely*.

'We all have hard times,' she murmured, before slinging one arm around my shoulders. 'The main thing is to rise above them.' *Jeez!* A bit rich from someone who was Sienna

Miller's clone and had been given a Porsche Boxter for her eighteenth birthday!

'You're right,' I murmured, deciding then and there to forget about the way she'd cut me dead. 'It's a matter of *moving on*.'

'Absolutely. You are going to have to come and stay soon, Skye.'

'Love to,' I said, meaning it. 'Absolutely love to.'

After the group photo I caught Reine's eye and we each raised an eyebrow. It was all working out better than we'd expected. In fact, the night was turning out to be a raging success.

The party was held on the upper floor of Josh's family home and it spilled onto a large balcony. It was lovely standing out there with our glasses of champagne, looking out over the city skyline. Waiters in black-and-white uniforms brought around silver trays piled with delicious food. The music was good – a very cool DJ sat in the corner in his sunglasses spinning tracks – but the chatter and laughter were better. They bounced and sang around me in that warm air like sweet rain after a long dry summer.

When I turned back to the house I noticed a small huddle of people surrounding my sister. She was regaling them with funny stories about the business course we'd gone to for the first few weeks of the year, staying well clear of the facts. Then I heard the words *stepsister* and *moron*, followed by hoots of laughter. I didn't bother to listen too closely. Reine had always been able to spin a good story. What did it matter if she exaggerated and lied? Our sharp tongues had always made us popular.

'Can you believe this?' Reine grabbed my arm on my way back from the toilet. Her eyes, ablaze with her success, darted hungrily over the drapes and furnishings and crystal.

'Oh, I know,' I murmured and took another glass of champagne from a tray. 'We had all this—'

'And more,' she finished my sentence, 'remember?'

I nodded.

'We *will* get it back,' she said earnestly, 'I promise you.'

'How?'

She took my hand briefly and smiled into my eyes.

'I promise you,' she said once more, 'it will be ours again.'

'But how?'

'We *marry* it,' she hissed, just as though she were telling me some state secret. I began to laugh, then saw she was deadly serious. She was surveying the room slowly and carefully like one of those big cats you see on the nature channel stalking prey, her eyes narrow and cautious under the heavy brows.

'Right,' I said, trying to sound as confident. Reine was so persuasive, and at that moment I actually believed her. We *would* marry it.

'See all these hot chicks,' she whispered, waving her fan dismissively at the crowd. 'Most of them are too stupid to use what they have. Most beautiful girls have no idea where their best interests lie because they've never had to worry – it all falls into their laps. Whereas you and me, babe, we know, right?'

'Right.' I edged away from her a little, wanting to get back to the fun group I'd been with. The big doors into the adjoining room had just been opened to create a huge space for dancing. A stage had been assembled down one end and a live band was tuning up. I'm a good dancer and I was itching to get onto that polished floor and show everyone what I could do, but Reine held me back.

'I want you to know that I saw Josh looking at you before,' she said. 'I mean really looking at you, like you were . . . *interesting*.'

I was dumb with surprise, but I believed her. Reine didn't tell lies about that kind of thing. This was exciting news.

'So use it,' she said quickly. 'See, he's over there. Go and join him.' I looked over and saw Joshua laughing and talking to a small group of guys and a few girls. Reine sniffed and clicked her fingers. 'Those little chicks are nothing. No competition. Too dumb for a guy like Josh.' One of the girls was dressed as some kind of fifties tennis star, another as a medieval matron and the third as some kind of explorer. Reine seemed to be right, the guys weren't paying them much attention.

'Maybe I will,' I murmured.

'Attagirl!' She smiled. 'I wonder what our lovely step-sister is doing right now,' she said lightly.

'Well, it's Saturday,' I replied, 'so she might be taking out the rubbish.' We both began to laugh.

'Or she might be writing in her new journal.' Reine's eyes were bright with malice, and for some reason that sent a shiver up my spine. I stood tall and pushed my shoulders back. It didn't do to be on the wrong side of my sister.

Holding my head high the way Reine had taught me, I crossed the floor to where Joshua was standing with his friends. He turned to smile at me and the rest of the group moved aside to let me join them, but just then the band launched into their first number. Perfect timing! I took a deep breath and smiled straight up into Josh's face. 'I simply have to dance,' I said, feigning a confidence I didn't feel. 'The question is, do I have to do it on my own?' He hesitated for a beat – was it shock or was he annoyed at being interrupted? At that moment I wondered if Reine had fabricated the story of him looking at me with interest. But then his expression changed quickly to a warm smile and he held out his arms.

'I'd be honoured, Skye,' he said simply. 'Let's go.'

{8}

Joshua was a good dancer and I'm a *really* good dancer. We were the first out on the floor and we really hit it off. Everyone was looking, which was a buzz for me. Within a couple of minutes I began to show off and so did he. By the end of the first number everyone was whistling and clapping and even though a few others joined us on the floor, we were the only ones with style. We were the couple everyone was looking at.

I'd never felt particularly talented before, but this night I was a star. I was out on the floor with the most desirable guy in the room and he was *loving it*! None of the other girls, including my sister, could dance like me, and the envy on their faces worked on my psyche like rocket fuel. In other words, I let it rip. I rocked, jived, shimmied, dipped and soared. I showed off like crazy.

When we'd both completely had it, he took my hand and led me over to the drinks table.

'We're going to have to go out dancing again, you know, Skye,' he said, grabbing me some water and grinning down into my face. 'You're really good.'

'So are you.' I smiled at him. 'So many guys can't dance.'

'There lots of things I can do,' he said cheekily. I laughed and pretended to be embarrassed, and before long we were back on that floor spinning and careering around each other.

When the lights dimmed and the music changed he reached for my hand and pulled me to him. It was a lovely long slow number, and by the end we were clinched together tightly. At one point I looked over his shoulder and saw my sister watching us. She gave me her small secret smile and then turned her back.

I have no idea how long we danced like this. It felt like hours and yet it was over too soon. All I know was that I couldn't have wished for anything better, and as each number ended and another began I fell deeper and deeper into the spell of it. In the end we were barely dancing at all, it was more like swaying in time to the music. I let my head rest on his shoulder and drifted off into La La Land. Joshua would be my shining knight. He was going to rescue me from that terrible house in the burbs. I was going to marry him just as Reine had said, and this very house would be mine one day! All would be well.

All would be *very* well indeed.

I *felt* him lose interest before I saw anything. I'd been having such a good time that I suppose it took me a while to twig. Nothing was said. We were dancing another slow number and – I know this is weird – although I couldn't see his face I felt his attention spin off away from me to another place, even though his mouth was near my ear and his arms were still around me. There was a hesitation, then a few slight movements over perhaps a minute, and suddenly we weren't clinched together anymore. We were still dancing but I knew he was pushing me away, as nicely as possible – still dancing, still smiling, but he'd stopped meeting my eyes.

When I eventually turned to see what had caught his attention, I was so shocked that I became mute. Standing just inside the door was this stunning girl who seemed to be glowing from within. Was she meant to be a fairy or a princess or some kind of exotic gypsy or maybe an angel?

The small black velvet mask covering her eyes did not in any way obscure the loveliness of her face. Her perfect skin, pale gold in the party lights, was like some glorious work from one of the Old Masters; her smile was full of life and excitement. The most glamorous guests present looked somehow jaded by contrast. A small band of glittering stones held her hair away from her brow. Her dress was a soft clinging ivory with tiny seed pearls trimming the wide neck and sleeves. Although not tight, it hugged her lovely slender figure down just past her hips then it spun out from there into a froth of soft waves that ebbed and flowed as she moved – so elegant, but at the same time so simple. Where had she come from? She stood in the doorway looking around her just as though she'd arrived from another planet. I could feel the frisson in the air as one by one everyone noticed her. She fitted in and yet somehow she didn't.

The band faltered right in the middle of a song, mesmerised by her along with the rest of us. Maybe a whole minute went by with everyone waiting for something to happen.

Joshua wasn't rude. In fact, he turned to me with a smile.

'Hey, thanks, kiddo,' he said warmly, giving my hand a quick squeeze. 'You're a great dancer! But I'd better go welcome the newcomer . . . whoever she is.'

Kiddo!

I nearly wept as I watched him walk off across the room towards the creature in cream as though propelled by some force quite outside his control.

Gradually the silence gave way to a low rumble of conversation as people came to their senses and resumed their conversations. Or pretended to. Witnessing the girl's arrival had been an almost surreal moment and the crowd was waiting to see what might happen next. The band started up again, and so did the chat and the laughter, but it was quieter and more subdued than before. Glances constantly flickered over to where Josh was standing with the girl. When he held out his hand to her it was like the rest of us stopped breathing. We all watched as she smiled shyly, looked away and then after a few more moments turned back to him and took his hand. Together they glided into the middle of the dance floor and began to dance . . .

Do I need to tell you what happened next? Surely no one needs a picture of me running off to the toilet to sob? The world I'd built up in my head out there on the dance floor had come crashing down like a hastily built wall at a dodgy building site. I probably would have stayed in the toilet all night, except Reine stormed in and insisted I pull myself together.

'These things happen!' she hissed. 'Get over it! He isn't the only fish in the sea. A big part of being a success is acting like one! Get back out there *now*!'

So I washed my face and reapplied my makeup and then got out there again on the dance floor and tried to make the best of it. I made myself smile at the idiots I was dancing with and I made myself chatter like a maniac as I died inside. All the time, like everyone else, I was aware of the golden couple. Apart from their hands their bodies did not touch, but their eyes . . . their eyes! They had eyes only for each other. Nothing else existed.

Then, amazingly, it was over. The girl – whoever she was – picked up the front of her dress and began to run back through the main entrance. It was totally weird to watch! Taken by surprise, Josh was left looking after her, completely dumbfounded. I edged nearer and watched him try to gather his wits. Frowning, he shook his head a couple of times, folded his arms and half-laughed in disbelief. Then after the shock he made a wild dash through the crowd towards the door. A few of the guys looked at each other to shrug and grin as though to say, *Well, that's the last we'll see of him for a while!*

But he was back after ten minutes, looking decidedly crestfallen. Glee rose in me like bubbling froth. She was gone! I edged nearer and saw he was holding a lovely little red leather shoe with a low squash heel and a soft bow on the front. Joshua turned the shoe around in his hands for a few moments before slipping it into the pocket of his jacket. The party went on, but although I made sure I was in his line of vision, hoping that he'd suggest we resume dancing, he seemed not to even see me. Speeches were given and toasts made, but he didn't dance with anyone else that night and nor did I.

{9}

Most of the way home in the taxi Reine tried to be positive, telling me about all the invites she'd got to parties and weekends. We both knew that most of them were spur-of-the-moment suggestions and that we'd be lucky if one or two come to anything. The nearer we got to that poxy suburb the lower our spirits fell. It was such a downer having to leave that beautiful house and all our old friends. By the time we let ourselves in through the front door we weren't even bothering to talk. We just set about the business of getting ready for bed. I knew I wouldn't sleep, though. I was still secretly fuming about that strange girl turning up to ruin my night. *Who was she?* I went to the kitchen, hoping perversely that it might have been left in a mess. I wanted to bang on Cinders' door and scream in her face. But the place was as neat as a pin.

'You have a good night, girls?' Mum called sleepily.

'Really great,' Reine called back.

'I want to hear about everything in the morning.'

'Okay, Mum.'

I slammed into my room and slumped on the bed, hardly bothering to register that Cinders had cleaned up while I was at the party. Everything was so damned squeaky clean. Rather than feeling grateful, I wanted to kill her for daring to come into my room. Then I remembered that I'd ordered her to clean the whole house while we were out. *Damn.* I pulled at my hair in frustration. The hairpiece I'd been so happy with earlier had begun to feel like a nasty little animal clawing at my scalp. It was so hard to dismantle that I was almost crying by the time I'd pulled out all the pins and flowers and thrown them on the carpet. Then I dragged off the red costume and dumped it on the floor, consoling myself with the thought that Cinders would have to vacuum again the next day.

{10}

Reine and I were sitting around telling Mum about the party late the next morning when there was an unexpected knock at the door. Both of us were totally spent after our efforts, hungover and bleary-eyed, so we were in no mood for visitors. We'd sent Cinders out to buy chocolate croissants earlier and were sitting in the lounge room stuffing ourselves.

'Ella!' Mum yelled over the telly. 'Get the door, will you.'

When there was no answer she sighed and shook her head. 'Where the hell is that blasted girl?' Reine and I shrugged and the doorbell rang again. Mum got up grumpily and we heard her talking to someone at the door but didn't think anything of it until she came back with a rather strained smile on her face.

'Someone to see you both!' she said. Then, with no warning and to our complete mortification, Joshua walked into the room behind her. *Oh my God!* We both jerked to attention. He'd *found* us here in this awful poxy house looking like complete . . . hags! I looked at Reine, whose face had suddenly turned three shades paler. How were we ever going to live this down?

'Hi there, you two.' He seemed a little agitated. 'Took a while to find you. It's . . . a long way out.'

'Well, hi Josh. Yeah, it is.' Reine rallied valiantly and got up to turn off the telly. 'Luckily we won't be here for long, but . . . hey, what a *great* party last night!'

You have to give it to my sister. No matter what the situation, she puts her best foot forward. In her old clothes with no makeup and not enough sleep, she looked as terrible as I did and yet she acted cool, whereas I was simply so horrified that I couldn't move, much less speak. It felt like the worst nightmare. My skin was blotchy, my hair wet from the shower and I was dressed in baggy grey trackpants and a truly grotty lime-green windcheater of Dad's.

'Yeah, it worked out okay, didn't it?' He smiled. 'Glad you both had a good time.'

'Sit down, why don't you,' Reine said, pointing to the battered old couch.

'Thanks.' He sat down on the arm of the couch and looked around with mild interest. 'So you both live here now?' He smiled at me and I tried to return it.

'Just until our new place becomes vacant,' Reine smiled gamely. 'Sorry everything is . . . a mess.'

'Oh,' he waved at her and smiled again, 'don't worry about that.' He slid off the arm and onto the seat and looked around again. My spirits lifted a little. Why did I get the feeling he wasn't even seeing this horrible little room? A bizarre thought suddenly skidded into my brain and stayed there. What if he'd come to see *me* and ask *me* out dancing? Mum must have been thinking the same thing.

'How about coffee?' she simpered from the doorway.

'Okay, thanks.' Joshua smiled at her. Once Mum was out of the room I jammed up again. Josh didn't help things by being so agitated. He was twiddling his thumbs, staring at the ceiling one moment then looking out the window behind Reine the next.

'I need to ask you both something a little . . . crazy,' he said eventually.

'Okay.' Reine tried to smile. 'Fire away.'

He suddenly pulled the small red leather shoe out of his pocket.

'Thing is, I don't know what else to do.' He blundered on. 'This belongs to that girl I was dancing with at the party. I don't even know her name. I'm contacting everyone who came to the party to see . . . if they have any idea who it might belong to. It's my only clue.'

I took a deep breath and tried to swallow the bitterness in my throat. He'd come to our house to find another girl, the owner of a *shoe*!

I watched as Reine leaned across and took the shoe from him and put it up against her big foot.

'Well, I don't think so.' She gave a fake laugh. 'Your turn, Skye!' I scowled as I took the beautiful little shoe and held it up next to my foot. Reine might be smart and tough but she could also be quite thick. Why draw attention to our huge ugly feet? She only had to look at that tiny thing to know it definitely wouldn't fit.

Cinders suddenly came in carrying a basket full of washing. It had started to rain and her hair was dragging all around her face and she was in faded old jeans and thongs. She nodded but hardly looked at us as she hurried through to the kitchen, dumping the washing basket on the table before heading towards the back door again.

'What about her?' Josh asked as the door closed.

'What about her?' I said sourly.

'Maybe she could try it.'

'But why? She wasn't even there.'

'Just for the hell of it.'

'Cinders!' I shouted. 'Come here.'

She came back immediately, her face still partially covered by her hair. There was a hole in her T-shirt, I noticed with satisfaction, and there was grime over her jeans. Mum had told her to clean the oven that morning. At least her beauty wasn't quite as obvious as usual!

Josh held the shoe out to her.

'Will you try this on?' he asked. Without raising her head, Cinders took the shoe and simply held it in her hand, turning it this way and that as though unsure what to do next. Josh took a step towards her, staring intently at her lowered head, as though trying to work something out.

'Quickly,' I snarled, 'he's in a hurry.'

She sat down on the arm of the chair, slipped off her thong and, wouldn't you know, the shoe fitted her foot perfectly! Joshua's mouth fell open and he moved closer, a smile playing at the corners of his mouth.

'I've visited so many people,' he said quietly, 'and not one other girl could get it on.' Cinders blushed, but she didn't raise her head, or smile or look at him. In fact, she looked distinctly uncomfortable. I glanced at Reine. Suddenly we both knew it was very important to get that girl out of the room.

'Go and help Mum, will you,' I ordered, 'she's making coffee.' On cue, Mum appeared in the doorway holding the tray of coffee cups and a plate of the delicious biscuits that Cinders had made the day before.

'Where have you been, Ella?' she said unpleasantly. 'I shouldn't have to do this.'

'I was cleaning the oven, then it started to rain . . .' she protested softly and immediately slipped the shoe off.

'Well, get back to it right now.'

Ella nodded and hurried from the room.

'Hang on!' Josh stood up. 'Please . . . don't go.'

But she had disappeared and Josh was left frowning deeply as he stared after her.

'I guess she's shy,' he said quietly.

'A personality bypass, more like it,' Reine chuckled.

'Okay.' Joshua gulped down his tea and stood up. 'Well, I'll get going now. I'll see you gals soon, eh?' He had a distracted expression, as though his mind was already elsewhere.

'Dancing,' I said cheekily, 'remember? You and me.'

'Sure,' he said, and squeezed my hand. 'That would be fun, Skye.' He smiled at Mum. 'Your daughter is a fantastic dancer.'

'Oh, I know.' Mum swooned under his charm. 'She's always been a natural.'

Joshua looked at his watch again. 'I'd better go.'

Once we'd closed the door on him, the three of us rushed back into the lounge to peer through the curtains and watch him leave. Out on the street he turned to the house and stood looking at it thoughtfully, hands deep in his pockets, then he shrugged and walked back to his car.

'Just look at us,' I wailed in despair.

'And this place,' Reine said furiously.

'Doesn't matter,' Mum said smugly, 'he likes you.'

Of course, we were really pissed off that he'd seen us at our worst. Still, Mum might be right, he was a nice guy and he'd been so friendly. With a bit of luck he wouldn't find the girl who owned the shoe and he'd ask me out instead. We talked at length about the pros and cons of sending him a gentle reminder if I didn't hear anything within the next week. But I couldn't stop thinking about it. Every time the phone rang my heart rose. Perhaps he'd only been shy in front of Mum and Reine . . . maybe . . .

Reine seemed to grow increasingly uneasy as the afternoon continued, and when I tentatively suggested that things just might turn out okay, she wouldn't meet my eyes.

'What is it?' I asked after a while. 'What's on your mind?'

'I've got a bad feeling about this,' was all she'd say.

'Tell me.'

'I need to think.'

There were no phone calls from him but we did get a few from girls who'd been at the party the night before.

Had we had a visit from Joshua yet?

Yes.

The shoe – did it fit either of us?

No.

So we began to make a few calls of our own.

Any idea who that chick was?

No, we thought you might know.

No.

Word got around that the shoe fitted no one who'd been at the party and no one knew anything about the mystery girl.

When there was no busy little Cinders getting the meal together at dinnertime, we were all puzzled.

'Where is she?' Mum snapped. 'Go get her. I'm hungry.'

I went to bang on her door.

'You planning to cook something for dinner?'

'No,' she called back.

The three of us looked at each other. Mum threw down the newspaper she'd been reading and stormed over to Cinders' door. 'Get yourself out here right now, girl!'

But just then Jack walked in looking harried and worn out and wanted to know why we were all standing outside his daughter's room. Of course, we had to back off and make light of it.

'I think she might be feeling *unwell*,' Mum said quickly, changing her irate expression to one of concern. Jack pushed past her and gave a couple of sharp knocks.

'Hey Ellie, are you coming out?' he asked.

'No,' she said.

'Are you ill?'

'I'm tired,' she said.

Our faces dropped in fake concern behind his back and we mouthed, '*I'm tired*,' sarcastically and tried to suppress our giggles. He turned around and almost caught us out.

'She's tired,' he said shortly.

'Oh dear,' Mum said lightly, 'so are we all, I'm afraid.'

'Leave her be,' Jack said under his breath.

'Of course, dear!' Mum said, smoothly magnanimous as she sensed his mood. 'Everyone is entitled to drop their bundle occasionally.' She smiled. 'What say we order in tonight?'

Jack gave a grunt before turning on the television.

We ate takeaway pizza and then watched a show. All the time I was thinking of Joshua. All those phone calls but not one from him. *Oh, why didn't I make myself look reasonable this morning? Perhaps I should have asked him out . . .* Something was brewing in Reine, so I knew I couldn't talk to her about it. I had to wait. Even so . . .

'What is it?' I said to her eventually.

'Talk later,' she muttered.

'Give me a hint.'

'No.'

{11}

She made me wait until Mum and Jack were in bed.

'Okay, we need to see what was in that box,' she said.

'What box?'

'The one that came yesterday, of course,' she snapped.

I'd forgotten all about that stupid woman arriving yesterday afternoon. It seemed such a long time ago.

We crept together up the little hallway and stood outside Cinders' room.

'Are we going to wake her?'

Reign shook her head.

'Not yet,' she whispered. 'Let's just see.' She put her hand on the door and gently pushed it open and tiptoed into the room.

I hesitated, my heart beating fast. If Cinders woke with a start and made a noise, then her father would be out for sure and we'd have to explain ourselves. I had a gut feeling that he'd begun to see through Mum by this stage, and I had no wish to cross him. So I waited, hardly daring to breathe, listening to the noises of my sister rustling about in the room. Suddenly the light went on. *Oh no! She'll wake Cinders.* But when the door opened it was Reine.

'She's not here!' she whispered furiously. 'Quick, come in.' We closed the door behind us and stood looking blankly at Cinders' neat little empty bed.

'So where is she?' I said stupidly. 'It's nearly midnight.'

'How would I know?' Reine was searching frantically under the bed and on top of the cupboard.

'What are you looking for?'

'The box.' She scrabbled through Cinders' clothes drawers, dumping the contents out onto the floor any old way. But there was no sign of the box or anything else to give us a clue. We stood looking at each other, not knowing what to make of the girl's disappearance. There was a sudden gust of wind from outside and a few leaves from the big gum tree fluttered in through the open window. As though suddenly deciding something, my sister pushed past me and climbed onto the sturdy little bookcase under the high window, peered through and gasped.

'What?'

She turned back and held out her hand to me.

'Come up.'

I scrambled up alongside her and we looked out Cinders' small high window into the backyard.

It took a while for my eyes to adjust, but the almost full moon and the bright fluorescent streetlight in the side lane gave enough light. Enough to see the trees near the back fence and the markings Jack had made for the foundations of the bungalow. Over to the left was the big dark shape of the shed and . . . I looked to where Reine was pointing.

Something was moving near the big gum tree. I clutched my sister's arm and held my breath as we watched the lone figure of a man walk out from behind the tree and stand in the exact place where we'd made the bonfire of all Cinders' notebooks. I squinted into the darkness. He was tall and young and . . . oh no! The realisation hit me hard.

'Oh,' I whispered, wanting to crawl away and die, 'it's . . . *him*.'

My sister gave a sour nod.

'But not her . . . *yet*. We've got to get to her first,' she whispered. 'You know where any rope is?'

'Rope?' I said stupidly.

'We'll need to tie her up and gag her.'

'But she's not here.'

'She has to be somewhere.' Reine was frowning deeply, both hands to her temples, trying to think. 'She'll be getting ready to meet him! Or . . .'

We both looked over at the old laundry at the end of the yard. Was that a faint yellow light coming from the window? It was hard to tell for sure because the moonlight was so bright. But without another word we clambered off the bookcase and quietly let ourselves out of the room.

I grabbed a spool of twine from the bottom drawer of the kitchen cabinet and went to the back door. I could see now that there definitely *was* a yellow light coming from the old laundry.

'This way or he'll see us,' Reine whispered, grabbing my hand. We headed out the front door and then crept back down the side of the house. When we reached the backyard we waited until Josh's back was turned, then under the cover of trees ran over to the laundry.

We crept along between the laundry and the fence to the side window and peered in. There she was, dressed in the lovely cream dress from the night before, smiling dreamily as she stuffed a small bag with her clothes. Reine and I looked at each other. So, she was planning to run! *Elope?*

She looked so unbelievably beautiful that a tiny part of me wanted to simply slide away, back to the house and into bed, because it seemed wrong somehow to disturb such loveliness.

But not Reine.

'No noise,' Reine said under her breath, 'we've got to surprise her.'

'Okay.' I was still mesmerised by the sight of her.

'Come on.' My sister nudged me sharply in the ribs. 'Get around to the door. Once we're in there we bring her to the floor, gag her and then tie her up.'

'Right. But what then?'

'What do you mean, *what then*?' she snapped viciously.

'Where do we put her?'

My sister hesitated for only a moment.

'We lock her in,' she said grimly. 'A few hours lying on the cold floor will sort her out, and when she doesn't show up he'll go home.'

'But . . .'

Reine gave me a hard look and I shut up.

But it was Cinders who surprised us. I'm not sure if she

sensed anything, but just as we were about to creep around to the door, she suddenly stopped what she was doing and stood very still in her lovely dress as though listening for something. Then almost in one movement she had the door open and was peering out.

'Now!' Reine said under her breath.

Without a word, Cinders understood our intentions as soon as she saw us, and made a dash for it. Reine managed to grab one arm and hauled her back for a moment, but the girl was lithe and supple, able to slither out of my sister's grasp like an eel. Lifting her lovely skirt, she sprinted towards the back fence. I dropped back instinctively. Josh was out there, not far away. How uncool to be seen struggling with another girl! But Reine had lost all sense. She ran after Cinders and actually managed to grab her, this time by the hair. Josh turned in time to see my sister trip Cinders and then fall on top of her, all the while trying to gag her with a scarf while she was on the ground. He yelled in surprise, rushed over and pushed my sister off.

'What are you doing?' he cried incredulously. 'Are you crazy? Stop it!'

But Reine was beside herself and wouldn't give up. She fought him tenaciously, kicking and snarling furiously, but he was much stronger and she didn't have a chance. Not used to fighting females, he behaved in his usual gentlemanly way, but when Reine kept coming back for more he ended up giving her a seriously hard push, straight into a couple of rose bushes. Reine let out a loud yelp and began cursing like a navvy.

'Skye,' she called furiously, 'help me. I'm being torn apart by thorns.'

But I was rooted to the ground watching Joshua helping Cinders to her feet.

'I thought you weren't coming,' I heard him say as his arms went around her. 'I honestly thought that you might have changed your mind.'

'Of course I was coming!' They were holding on to each other and laughing in relief under the cold bright moonlit night, just as though we didn't exist. 'Here I am.'

'Here you are.' He laughed and kissed her.

'Come on!' Ella said suddenly. 'Let's just go now.'

'Okay. Let's get away from here!'

'I'll grab my things.'

'Okay.'

Arms around each other, they headed back over to the laundry. By the time they came out, Joshua carrying Cinders' bag over one arm, I had my sister out of the rose bushes at last, her legs, face and arms smeared with blood from the deep scratches. Josh and Cinders looked at us coldly as they passed, as though we were beneath contempt. They walked down towards the side way leading onto the street. At that stage I was ready to admit defeat, but when I next caught sight of my sister's face I saw that her anger had intensified mightily. Seething with fury, she motioned towards the garden fork and spade leaning against the garage only a couple of metres away.

'Come on,' she said, her voice ragged, 'we'll get them.'

'Reine, I don't think . . .'

She grabbed the fork and almost threw the spade at me.

'Come *on*.' It was a command, really.

At that point I caught sight of the big mean bird in the cage behind her. He'd moved from his branch and was climbing up the side of the cage, making these horrible, loud distressed squawks and croaks, and I have to say that his yellow eyes in the moonlight looked bright with intelligence and malice.

'Hey, open the cage and let it out!' She laughed maniacally. 'Go on.'

'What?' I asked stupidly.

'That bird! Go on, open the cage.'

'Why?'

'That university guy is coming tomorrow. Be good if it's gone,' she hissed.

I went over and opened the gate, then, picking up my spade again, followed Reine. When we heard the click of Josh's car door opening and then the thump as he threw the bag in, we knew we'd better hurry.

'What . . . will we do?' I was shaking.

'Kill her,' she whispered. 'Him too. Quick.'

The world seemed to close in around me at that point. One part of me knew that my sister had lost it and that I had to make a choice. Was I going to follow her into . . . *this abyss* – because surely that is what it was – or call a halt to the craziness? I hesitated. I couldn't imagine life without Reine. She was my sister and my best friend, and yet . . .

'Reine,' I said, 'I think . . .'

'I'll take the rap,' she snapped. 'Come on. I'll get us off. I'll plead insanity or . . . something. Come on, it will be worth it.'

'But—'

'Why should we sit by and watch her steal Josh just because she's pretty? He's our friend, isn't he?' I nodded and clutched the handle of the spade tighter.

Reine was already a few metres ahead of me with her garden fork, hurrying down the driveway, but some new unease that I can't quite explain made me turn around. The strange ugly bird was out of the cage now and spreading his huge wings.

'Reine,' I called out loudly, 'come back!'

She must have heard the panic in my voice, because she dropped the fork and came back to where I was standing. We both watched in fascinated horror as the huge thing circled the backyard in low swoops, all the while screeching wildly.

'Wish I had a gun,' Reine muttered.

Eventually it settled on top of the cage but the screeching intensified. After a while it began to sound like some kind of weird laughter.

Josh and Cinders were forgotten at that point, because something happened that was so totally weird it's hard to describe, hard to believe even now. There was a noise, unlike anything else I'd heard before. First it was a kind of low shuddering sound, like the beginnings of an earthquake, then the sky suddenly darkened, and except for patches of light from the laundry and the porch next door, the backyard was no longer visible. My sister stopped and so did I. We looked up. The moonlight was being blocked by some kind of fast-moving dark cloud. The bird's screeching had become deeper and more threatening. That's when I realised that the darkness wasn't a cloud at all, but a flock of perhaps a dozen huge black birds like the one I'd let out of the cage. They were all screeching now as they circled us, around and around and around, very gradually getting lower.

So loud!

We'd got used to living on that busy street near a transport depot and a huge public hospital, trucks on their way out to the freeway, trains, police and ambulance sirens going day and night, not to mention the feral cats fighting in the back streets and the mad drunks stumbling home from two nearby pubs. But this noise was . . . something else.

We stood quite still. The wind picked up and the huge gum tree began to creak and sway. Reine let the garden fork fall to the ground, covered her ears and ran for the light and cover of the old laundry. I did the same.

Hunched down together in the corner of the shed, I felt as if the terrible noise would go on forever, but it was probably at its loudest for only a couple of minutes. Gradually it began to ebb away until at last there was silence and the wind died down with it. What a relief. Our hands dropped from our ears; we opened the door and peered out. Ella and Josh had gone.

The back porch light suddenly came on.

'Girls?' It was our mother, out on the porch in her dressing-gown. 'What are you doing out there?'

'Nothing,' Reine called sullenly. 'Go back to bed, Mum.'

'But did you hear that noise?'

'Yes. Just go back to bed, okay.'

But Mum was nothing if not curious. She wanted to see what we were doing, so she stepped out onto the lawn, then looked up and saw the birds circling. One by one they landed on the roof of the laundry.

'Oh, what ghastly birds,' she said in a low voice.

'Yes.'

Like fools the three of us stood there watching as each huge bird circled lower and lower, and eventually joined the original bird. I counted fifteen of them, just sitting, each of them as big as a normal-sized dog, their yellow eyes staring down at us. So repulsive and yet . . . fascinating.

'Where did they come from?'

'We don't know.'

'Why did you open the cage?' I snapped at Reine.

'*You* opened it,' she snapped back.

'You told me to.'

'Enough of this!' Mum said loudly. She picked up the fork and advanced on the birds.

'Get away with you!' she yelled. 'Go on, you monsters. Clear out!'

'Mum . . .' I remembered Ella's warning and suddenly felt afraid. 'Don't do that!' But it was too late.

Without a hint of warning, the biggest bird suddenly flew straight at her face. Totally shocked, she stumbled backwards and fell, screaming for help, trying with all her might to free herself, but its sharp claws had sunk into the flesh of her face and neck. Then a second bird joined the first, then another and another. Within a matter of seconds our mother was lying on the grass in her dressing-gown and slippers trying to fight off six huge vicious birds. Of course Reine and I tried desperately to kick them away and, when we found we couldn't, we ran for the shovel and the fork, all the time screaming for Jack to come out to help us. But he never came. I don't know if he heard us or not. Mum writhed, screamed and cried, but that only seemed to encourage them.

Sobbing with shock and terror, Reine and I fought them as best we could until . . . I can hardly bring myself to recall what happened next.

The sky darkened once again. More birds were arriving. The terrible whooshing sound of wings gave way to raucous ear-piercing screeches. Reine and I had to leave Mum and try to escape ourselves. But we didn't stand a chance.

{12}

I have eaten nothing, nor have I read anything nor even listened to the telly since they told me last night that today would be the day. Morning tea arrived and then lunch and the old woman across from me was sick again. What do I care? I begin to think that he will never come and that I will have to stay in this hospital bed for the rest of my life.

Then at last there is a flurry up the other end of the ward. I can feel the frisson. He has arrived with an entourage of nurses, I guess, because I can hear the murmur of a lot of voices. *So . . . this is it.*

At last they reach my bed and all of a sudden some weird part of me wants them to go away again, even though I've been waiting for so long. *Dread.* I suppose I am filled with dread. Maybe it is better to live in hope than know that I'll never see again.

'How are you feeling?' the doctor asks gently, then without waiting for a reply he speaks to a nurse about bringing some piece of equipment closer.

'So, my dear?' He begins gently to inspect the bandages and whatever is underneath. 'Yes . . . yes, I think we can safely take them off today.' He puts one hand on my shoulder. 'Now we will find out the result of our work.'

I nod numbly, quite unable to speak.

It takes some time for him to get the bandages off. Finally, when his fingers stop, I can feel my face naked and exposed, and a deep silence has fallen all around me. Everyone in that room is waiting, along with me. For once the woman opposite me has her television switched off and all the peeping machines, the grunts and sighs, cheery comments, footsteps and mobiles have magically ceased. I can't smell anything, or feel anything . . .

The surgeon moves first. I feel him step away from the bed, then he murmurs something to a nurse and I remain in darkness as he begins to wipe some cooling lotion over my eyelids.

He is still messing around with the lotion when the first small ray of light appears. I hold my breath and say nothing until it starts to build, more and more light. Then I seem to be blinded with light. It rushes at me like a rising flood. So much light and then . . . *colour*! A blurred blue shape and then something brown, moving. It is so unbelievably wonderful that I cry out without even being aware of doing so. Oh, there are no words for this, no way to describe these first wonderful moments as the world comes into focus again.

'So, my dear?' he says. I see he is an old grey-haired man in his sixties with a craggy, lopsided, beautiful face. He is smiling, smiling! And so am I. He takes both my hands in his and I hold on tightly, hanging on to him for dear life. Eventually I see all those others standing around him, all these smiling faces, blurring now through my tears.

'Thank you so much,' I whisper, 'thank you!'

'Oh my dear,' the surgeon says, 'my dear girl. I am so happy for you!' There are murmurs all around and I see that they all are so happy for me and I know that I don't deserve it.

I stare at all the smiling faces, at the cheap print of flowers on the wall, at the phones, and the pair of pink slippers, and at the poor old woman in the bed opposite, so sick, but sitting up now and smiling at me. I stare at the tall buildings outside the windows, at the pale-blue sky and the drifting clouds, and after so many weeks of being in the dark it all seems so *outrageously* wonderful that I think I might have died and gone to heaven! So . . . I begin to cry.

'No more tears now,' the old doctor says and gently pats my shoulder. 'Time for laughter now.'

'Yes,' I say and continue to cry. He hands me the box of tissues and I take a few and blow my nose. I don't want to keep crying, I want to keep on looking at everything. I want to get up and walk around, go to the toilet without bumping into things, switch on the telly, use my mobile phone. But I can't seem to stop the flow of tears. I cry and I cry.

'What is it, my dear?' he asks, now that the others have gone and I'm still sobbing. The old lady opposite has switched on her television and people are coming and going as before, so it is just him and me and he has been sitting with me for some time now patting my shoulder kindly.

'Are you feeling sad about your poor mother and sister?'

I shake my head.

'If only we'd been able to help them,' he murmurs.

'Yes.' I nod and reach for more tissues. 'If only.'

But in truth what happened to Reine and Mum isn't real to me yet. They are gone. I know that much. The grief, when it comes, will probably bring me undone, but until then I am floating above that particular reality.

'I think I'm just . . . happy,' I manage to whisper.

'Ah,' he chuckles, 'the best kind of tears.'

I clutch his hand again.

'You have given me so much.'

'I have done my job,' he says quietly, 'that is all.'

'No . . . much . . . much more . . . than that.' He smiles and pats my shoulder again and then leaves at last with promises to see me the next day.

Gradually I calm down, and when I do I notice a page cut from a newspaper on my side table. I pick it up, remembering now that one of the nurses had heard the story and left it for me to read if my sight was ever restored.

The caption reads: *Love Survives Ugly Bird Attack*.

It is about them, of course – the beautiful Ella with Joshua's arm around her, both of them looking so very happy. It is mostly about how they were brought together by the 'terrible' incident with the birds. When I reach the bit about my mum and sister being killed I put the paper down. There is only so much one person can take in a single day.

But before long I pick up the paper again. I still can't bring myself to read the rest of the article, but I can't stop looking at the photo. I stare and stare at those smiling faces, mesmerised. How lovely and open and *free* they both look. I am suddenly so grateful that Reine and I were not able to carry out our terrible plan to kill them. *Alive*, they are alive, and so am I. So another miracle is taking place, but this time inside me. It is as though a great heavy chunk of something stinking and putrid is simply sliding away from me and dissolving into the ground.

The old lady in the bed opposite wanders past on her way to the toilet, a plastic wash bag under her arm.

'So, dear,' she smiles at me, 'what does the world look like after so long in the dark?'

'Oh, it's wonderful,' I smile back, 'totally wonderful.'

You thought that you knew where this story was headed, didn't you? Of course you did! And so did I. But it turns out we were both wrong. Endings always promise more than we imagine, especially happy ones.

AFTERWORD

I grew up in a rough farming family with six older brothers, a big-boned, ordinary-looking girl with straight hair. I had to feed lambs and chooks every day, collect firewood and ride to primary school on a sweaty old pony. Yet oddly enough (or maybe not), from a very early age I yearned for glamour, sophistication and romance! In fact I'm told that the first words I said after 'Mum' and 'Dad' were 'lipstick', 'rouge' and 'beads'! (I was constantly teased about this for years afterwards.)

'Cinderella' is one of the first stories I remember reading by myself. I think it was probably the very sanitised Little Golden Book version, but I loved it all the same.

The basic storyline is such a good one. A poor but beautiful girl, downtrodden and ill-treated by her stepfamily, is eventually elevated to her true station in life by a series of magical events. And by the end of the story not only is she happy and free, but she beats her oppressors at their own game by marrying the most eligible man in the country.

Wow! What could be more satisfying?

The story of Cinderella has everything: tension, pathos, drama, magic, glamour, crime and punishment, not to mention archetypal characters and a blissfully happy ending. I can still see the (very ordinary) drawing of Cinderella in the 1950s Little Golden Book version, rushing away down the stairs from the ball in her gorgeous frothy dress, and in the background the clock showing five minutes to midnight and on the top stair . . . one glass slipper! As a very young preschooler I remember staring long and hard at that image – at the slipper, the clock and the gown – feeling anxious every time I read it. *Will she make it? Will the prince find the slipper? Will they end up together?*

How I hated those ugly stepsisters with their scowling faces and huge ugly feet. I prayed that mine wouldn't end up like theirs, prayers that were unfortunately never answered. I have terrible feet! And how happy I was every time I came to the end of the story and there she was, the blonde delicate beauty in lace and jewels, on the arm of her prince.

Oh, how I longed to be her.

Of course, years later I became much more critical. What an utterly regressive sexist storyline! No wonder women are so soft-headed when it comes to love if this is the pap they're fed as children! Cinderella is so damned passive. She doesn't *do* anything except take instructions from the fairy godmother and fall in love with the handsome prince – not exactly brain-taxing! She neither takes initiative nor shows strength of character or even fortitude!

Another illustration I remember staring at, my heart full of sympathy, came early on in the story. It is Cinderella sitting by herself on the hearth crying, while the ugly stepsisters are making merry in the next room.

So . . . why the hell didn't she plot against them or poison their food or . . . at least run away?

Later I also railed against the unfairness of equating beauty with goodness and ugliness with evil when in real life it is often not so. Beautiful girls and handsome boys can be shallow and boring because they've never had to bother being anything other than good-looking. Whereas Plain Janes who are plump with bad skin and big noses, and John Does with short legs and small eyes, have had to develop other sides of themselves to make a success of their lives. Intelligence, humour and kindness to others can help you cope with the vicissitudes of life and love if you're born plain.

Yet I wanted to write this story of Cinderella. And when I read the more grisly Grimm version, where the stepsisters' eyes are plucked out at the end, I became even more keen to write it.

The gruesome nature of the Grimm version seemed a nice foil to all the romance and glamour of the fairy godmother and the prince. For a start, the message is less didactic. The Disney version seems to say that those who are good and meek (and beautiful) will win in the end. But I think the Grimm version is more subtle and true. It points to the arbitrary nature of life – it can be quite unexpectedly wonderful, full of surprises and possibilities, but it can also go horribly, shockingly wrong in a flash – and for no good reason.

And the punishment does not always match the crime. The punishment can be, *and often is*, far, far worse!

It didn't take long to find the emotion in the original story that really interested me. Envy is one of the seven deadly sins that is so often overlooked and so rarely acknowledged. My gut feeling is that envy affects most people and yet they don't talk about it. Consider how we laughingly admit to being lustful, slothful, greedy . . . but who admits to being envious? Maybe it's because people instinctively know how lethal envy can be. The private sphere of love and families and friendships is littered with examples of the chaos and mayhem that envy can cause. But so too is the wider world of politics and international relations.

So we leave it alone.

Yet the truth is that we do so often want what other people have and are often envious when we can't have it. And that envy can quite easily become overwhelming. It can make us lose sleep, appetite and our own sense of self-worth, not to mention all sense of perspective. Before we realise what is happening, it can poison our lives and relationships, and turn us into monsters in the process.

So I decided I would play with envy within the 'Cinderella' framework and see where it took me. Because I wanted to get right inside this emotion, I decided the story must be told from the point of view of one of the ugly sisters. This necessitated playing down or omitting some of the elements in the original story, such as the fairy godmother, who doesn't feature so prominently in my story. In fact, hardly any magic remains from the earlier drafts. By writing this story I learned that, as wonderful as fantasy and magic are, they are not my strong points. I decided that I'd better stick with the world as I know it. I'll leave it to the reader to decide if this was the right choice.

Finally, I hope that those same readers will forgive me for the many liberties I took with a story that is so well known and loved by so many.

BIRTHING

by Victor Kelleher

Strictly speaking, this is not a story about my early years, which were for the most part uneventful. Nonetheless, without some knowledge of a particular childhood episode, the real story can't be fully appreciated.

So, in brief: I grew up as a kind of orphan, my mother having died in childbirth, and my father having disappeared soon afterwards. It fell to my grandmother to care for me, though 'care' is perhaps too strong a word. When I think of her now, words like *stern* and *unbending* spring to mind. As I recall, she had just one redeeming feature: she told me bedtime stories – or, to be precise, stories about the faerie folk – drawing her cast of characters from *A Midsummer Night's Dream*.

Her nightly tales always began in the same way. 'There are faeries at the bottom of our garden,' she would say, and give a snicker of cool laughter.

I laughed too, though not because I shared her wry amusement at those hackneyed words. At the age of six or so, I saw them as the literal truth. There *were* faeries at the bottom of our garden, down in the wild untended part beneath the ancient pear tree. I hadn't seen them exactly, but I'd heard them – the furtive rustle of their footsteps in the leaf mould, the whirr of their wings amongst the foliage. So why did I laugh at my grandmother's opening words? Out of nothing more complicated than joy. It delighted me to think of those tiny beings flitting effortlessly from bloom to bloom.

My favourite amongst them was Puck, the trickster. He was my hero, a creature lighter and less definite than air. Oh, I loved the other characters too: Oberon, with his brooding jealousy; Titania, with her wandering eyes; Mustard Seed and the rest. I even adored Bottom and his friends, whom I wrongly believed to be half faerie, half animal. But out of them all, it was Puck who won my heart.

Alone in my room at bedtime I often opened the window and called to my favourite, using his other, more worldly name: 'Robin, Robin Goodfellow, are you there?'

As a further enticement, I would close my eyes and picture the faerie light which, in my imagination, surrounded him like a halo. Sometimes, at the edge of sleep, I felt its shimmering phosphorescence fill the room, and in a last instant of wakefulness I glimpsed Puck's likeness out beyond the flame.

As you can see, I had become obsessed with Puck and his kind, and by rights my grandmother should have done something about it. At the very least she should have told me the brutal truth: that in ancient stories about the Faerie, they are not pretty and beguiling. More often, they are terrible creatures, fearsome and amoral in their dealings with humankind. But she alerted me to none of this. In truth, as long as I didn't get underfoot she hardly noticed my presence, and left to myself, I developed the odd fancy that if only I had wings – if only I were able to fly – I could somehow enter their magical world and become a faerie of sorts myself.

When you are six, making a pair of wings is no easy task. It took me a while to create something moderately satisfactory out of coloured tissue paper stretched across flimsy loops of bent wire.

I put them to the test on a blustery day in early autumn. Having tied them on with two lengths of string, I made my way to the bottom of the garden. Overhead, the giant pear tree shook and swayed noisily, but I had climbed it before, so I didn't hesitate. Careful not to damage my wings, I began clambering from limb to limb, up through the roaring foliage to the crazily swaying top.

From there I had an unobstructed view of our suburb, with its tree-lined streets and well-tended gardens. Seen through childish eyes, it had the beguiling appearance of an ancient forest, a more than fitting place for Puck and the other faerie folk. And for me, too, once I had passed through that invisible membrane which separated us. All I had to do was trust my winged self to the void, which I knew in my heart would bear me up.

Of course it didn't. As I released my hold and stepped free, I barely had time to think: I'm doing it! Flying! I *will* see the faerie light, I *will*! Then I came crashing down through dense foliage, jolting from one branch to another . . . until, mercifully as they say, I lost consciousness.

The generously spreading branches of the old tree saved my life, for I was still more or less intact when I reached the ground and lay spreadeagled amongst the tendrils of bindweed that had once been the setting of my fantasies. I wish I could say I dreamed of Robin Goodfellow during the hour or more that I lay there unattended – his glowing face stooping over mine, his wings brushing my lips with faerie-like concern – but I had no such vision. He didn't come, nor would he have shown concern had he existed.

In any case, none of that mattered anymore, because when I awoke in hospital, I had suffered more than just broken bones and internal injuries. Something else had happened. Young as I was, I sensed it immediately. The world had changed somehow. It had become flatter, duller, less than it had been before.

Typically, it wasn't my grandmother who confirmed my fears, but the surgeon. I remember him as a kind, patient man. In straightforward language, he explained how a branch of the tree had gouged out my left eye. I would be partly blind for the rest of my life.

'Now here's the good news,' he added with a smile. 'No one need ever know, because we can give you a false eye that looks exactly like a real one.'

He produced such an object from the pocket of his white coat. It was a wonderful thing made of glass and ceramic, with the depth and sparkle of a living eye.

'There's better news yet,' he went on. 'We can teach you to move your head rather than your eyes. In a month or two no one will realise you have a false eye. It will be our secret, one that need never leave this room.'

What he forgot to mention was that 'our secret' would also be recorded in my medical records. As things turned out, that was an important omission.

The 'real story' I referred to begins nearly fifteen years later, soon after I had finished my formal training as a midwife (a natural enough career for someone whose mother has died in childbirth). Like all young trainees, I was required to serve an internship of sorts in a rural community, and I had already given some thought to where I would like to go.

Before I could make any applications, however, I received an offer from the midwife at a place called Little Earth. Her name was Gretel Andersen. She explained in her letter of offer that she was nearing the end of her own career and, having read my file, she was confident I was the person she needed.

Had I been older, I might have wondered why she had sought me out – me in particular. But amongst the young there is a tendency to regard all good fortune as heaven-sent. So instead of enquiring about Gretel Andersen, I merely researched the oddly named Little Earth.

I learned that it was a remote area populated by members of an obscure religious sect. They believed above all in the sanctity of the simple life, and had long since outlawed modern gadgetry, including motor cars and other mechanical aids. For some generations now they had earned a living by farming the land in a completely traditional way. Perhaps typical of such communities, they were also highly superstitious.

To someone as mildly adventurous as I was then, it all sounded charming and intriguing, and a week later, suitcase in hand, I stepped down from a long-distance bus that stopped only long enough to drop me off at the head of a sloping valley.

I don't know what I was expecting. A village, perhaps, or at least a car to take me further. But all that greeted me was a gentle rural scene and, in the foreground, an ancient horse and buggy. The driver, a woman, gestured me over.

'I'm Gretel,' she said with a pleasant smile, 'and you must be Lucy. Welcome to Little Earth.'

My first impression was of someone white-haired and quite bent over, with that gauntness which often accompanies extreme old age. Yet she still appeared fully alert and shrewd, and her face possessed an unmistakable kindness. Even at that first meeting, she radiated the sort of warmth I had longed to find in my own grandmother, and I sensed that we would be happy together. Only one thing struck me as odd: how, in the act of speaking, she half averted her face, as if embarrassed by my gaze. It was a mannerism I would soon grow used to, though at the time I found it vaguely unsettling.

During our slow buggy-ride along the valley, she told me more about Little Earth and its people.

'These are good, simple folk who have no understanding of the outside world,' she explained. 'They live close to the earth and follow the old ways. To them, the midwife represents the traditional wise woman, and they are grateful for our care. We in turn should be grateful for their respect.'

While she spoke, I looked eagerly about me. Already I had spotted several of these 'simple folk' working in the fields: the men dressed in severe black and white; the women in long mother hubbards, their hair pulled back from their faces. Seen against the vivid greens of the unspoiled valley, they looked wonderfully quaint, like figures from a lost past.

'It's glorious here,' I burst out at one point. 'A kind of paradise. Another Eden, almost.'

Her manner changed for a moment. 'Don't be fooled by appearances,' she said, with that characteristic turn of the face. 'Everything has a dangerous side, even this place. Enjoy its beauty, by all means, but keep your distance.'

Then she resumed her friendly chatter, telling me how glad she was to have me there, and how I was to share her house in the heart of the valley – an old-world cottage nestled beside a stream and backed by a stand of whispering poplars.

I was so taken with it all that it wasn't until late in the evening, when she walked me to my bedroom, that I noticed what I should have spotted from the beginning. She was more than just old, she was also unwell, with an unnatural droop to her eyes and a ghostly pallor. Lying in bed, the moonlight pooling on the floor beneath the window, I confronted the true nature of my situation. I was there as more than an intern. I was her chosen replacement.

That fact was made even plainer during my first week in the valley. Our daily rounds, I soon discovered, taxed Gretel to the limit; and when we were called out on a birthing, the all-night vigil proved too much for her. In the end I was the one who delivered the baby – the woman's first – and saw to both their needs. I also reassured the bewildered young husband, whom I found trembling and distressed on the outer porch.

'Her screams,' he muttered, refusing to meet my eyes. 'She sounded like . . . like an *animal*!'

'Hush,' I said. 'That's no way to speak of her. Now go up to them, they need you. I'll be back in a few hours to see that all is well.'

While we were talking, Gretel appeared in the doorway.

'Come, Lucy, you've done enough,' she said, and drew me away. Once clear of the house, with the dawn gathering around us, she added: 'I was impressed by the way you handled things tonight. Especially the father. That was kind.'

'How else should I have handled him?' I said. 'People are people. We are all the same inside.'

She shook her head at that. 'No, some here are different. More different than you can imagine.'

'How do you mean, different?'

But she merely sighed, as though too tired to answer.

I was given some inkling of what she might have meant when we attended the local market, which was held every Saturday in a field beside the church. It wasn't a grand affair, just a modest collection of stalls set up mainly by farmers, there to sell or barter excess produce. Over to one side I noticed a group of people who hardly seemed to belong in the valley. They certainly *looked* different from everyone else: the men dirty and unshaven; the women greasy-haired and slovenly.

'Who are they?' I asked Gretel, pointing in their direction.

She snatched my hand down. 'Tinkers and horse traders,' she said in a half-whisper. 'They live at the very end of the valley. No one mixes with them unless they have to, so don't stare. Don't meet their eye.'

But it was too late for that. One of them – a middle-aged brute of a man, and their leader as far as I could tell – came sauntering over. Ignoring me completely, he gave Gretel a half-bow and touched the knife at his waist in a strangely chivalrous gesture.

She responded with a wary but otherwise friendly smile, and I had the impression that a spark of understanding passed between them.

'All continues well with you?' he asked.

And she: 'Yes, nothing has changed.'

He glanced briefly at me, and back to Gretel. 'So our pact holds?'

'It holds.'

'Then go in peace,' he said, and bowed again before returning to his people.

I waited until he was out of earshot.

'What's this about a pact?' I demanded.

She shrugged. 'He's a trader, remember. It's their way of talking.'

'Yes, but what was he talking *about*? What sort of pact?'

She hesitated, and then nodded, like someone relenting under pressure. 'I've agreed to attend the tinker women if I'm needed. That's all there is to it.'

'So why the big mystery?'

'Because I don't want it generally known. It could harm my standing in the community. Also, I don't want you involved. Not yet, anyway.'

I would have asked her more, but she had already walked off. Again I glanced over at the tinkers. A young woman – barefoot and with mud up to her knees – saw me looking and gave a leering, gap-toothed smile. Was it a lewd invitation, or a warning to keep clear? I didn't wait to find out, but hurried off into the crowd in search of Gretel.

After that I didn't see much of the tinkers for some months. Occasionally I glimpsed them during our daily rounds, sharpening tools in a farmer's barn or tending sick horses. Once or twice we encountered one of their dilapidated wagons on the open road. Otherwise, our paths didn't cross – not, that is, until an evening in early spring, when a loud knocking sounded through the cottage.

I was upstairs at the time, so Gretel answered the door. From the upper landing I heard a childlike voice say: 'We need you. He says to come at once.'

Gretel had closed the door before I reached the downstairs landing.

'Who was it?' I asked.

'The tinkers,' she explained shortly. 'I've been called to a birthing. Can you hitch the horse up for me?'

'Only for you?' I said, surprised. 'Aren't I coming too?'

She turned her face aside, though not in the usual fashion. 'That won't be necessary. Not tonight.'

But I wasn't taking no for an answer. 'Listen,' I said, 'do you think I haven't noticed how unwell you are? What if your strength gives out? At the very least you'll need me to drive you home.'

She couldn't really argue with that, and ten minutes later we were seated together in the buggy, she slapping the horse's rump to urge it into a trot.

We didn't talk much during our starlit journey. I had never been to the far end of the valley, and I watched in silence as the neatly cropped pastures gave way to fields of tussock and thistle. These in turn were soon replaced by rough, broken country in which only gorse flourished. Then, as we neared the rocky crags that closed off the valley – almost in the shadow of those crags – I picked out the vague outline of a dwelling. Close up, it proved to be a tumbledown affair, more a hovel than a house.

The leader of the tinkers, as squat and brutal as I remembered him, stood waiting in the starlight.

'You've come,' was all he said, and motioned her inside.

She held back for a moment. 'What am I to expect?'

'The same as always,' he said, his voice taking on a hard edge.

She made no attempt to hide her impatience. 'This is too high a price to pay! Why don't you control these girls more?'

'And why don't you control those menfolk out there?' he countered.

She snatched the obstetrics bag from me. 'Let's get it over with then,' she said, and pushed past him into the house.

I made as if to follow, but he barred my way.

'Not you!' – the words barked out in a tone of command.

'He's right,' Gretel agreed. 'Wait out there. I'll call if you're needed.'

And the door was closed in my face.

Left to myself, I sat in the shelter of the porch and drew my coat closed, for it was a cool night. Through the flimsy planking of the door, I could hear people coming and going, and voices. A little later the shrieking began – terrible screams the like of which I had never heard before – and I blocked my ears with both fists and willed myself to sleep.

Gretel woke me an hour or so before dawn.

'What of the mother?' I asked.

'She survived,' she said, and handed me a bloodstained sack. 'Don't look inside,' she added quickly. 'Just go and bury it.'

But I had already looked, and despite the darkness there was no mistaking what the sack contained: a jumble of monstrous infant limbs, and an even more monstrous head.

I drew back, appalled. 'My God, what is it?'

'Don't ask,' she said. 'Just do as I say, and then forget this happened.'

'But we have to register births and deaths,' I replied stupidly.

'In this case we register nothing!' she shouted, her voice cracking under the strain. 'Now, if you have any affection for me, any sense of trust, stop all these questions and bury this thing.'

So I did. We always kept a shovel in the buggy, to dig out the wheels on muddy roads, and I used it to scrape out a shallow grave. I was still trampling down the loose earth when Gretel and the tinker reappeared.

'My thanks to you,' he said, and gave one of his formal bows.

'And mine to you,' she answered with a sad smile.

'What of her?' he asked, meaning me.

'She stands apart . . . for now.'

'Ah yes, *for now*.' A hint of melancholy flitted across his brutal features. 'That invisible clock of yours, how it ticks and ticks and carries you along with it.'

Then, without further comment, he left us.

Back in the buggy, the horse plodding wearily ahead, I had so many questions I hardly knew where to start, but she brushed them all aside.

'I'm asking you to trust me in this matter,' she said, much as she had before. 'Believe me, all this will be clear one day. When the time comes.'

When the time comes.

I guessed what she meant by that, and I didn't have the heart to press her further. Not then, nor later. Because the truth is, I did trust her. I had even come to love her, in my way, as the mother I'd never had. So I left her in peace through the remainder of our journey, and on into the days and months that followed.

In all the time I spent under Gretel's roof, she was less than kind to me on only one occasion. It was a short, upsetting episode, soon forgotten, and I mention it here not to diminish her in any way, but because of its bearing on subsequent events.

Some months after our unhappy visit to the tinker hovel, I started seeing a young man, a local farmer. I won't pretend I was wholly serious about him. Aside from mutual attraction, we had little or nothing in common. Yet the body, like the mind, has its needs, as any twenty-one-year-old woman knows. Also, he said he loved me, which I found flattering.

Although not yet lovers, we had begun to keep regular company. Word soon got about, as it must in small communities, and arriving home late one evening we were waylaid by Gretel. Feeble though she was, she dragged me down from the buggy and sent my suitor packing.

I was momentarily incensed. 'What right have you to interfere in my private life?' I shouted at her.

'Every right!' she shouted back. 'Like it or not, I'm here to remind you of your responsibilities. As a professional, you have to stand apart from these people.'

'Have to stand apart?' I took her up angrily. 'Are you my keeper now? Was this the condition of my coming here?'

She answered with disarming honesty. 'Yes, it was.'

I stared at her in astonishment, too taken aback to speak.

'You are here because of me,' she went on. 'I chose you – I alone – and I can *un*choose you if I so will. Remember that.'

I rushed up to my room and very nearly packed my bags there and then. Except where was I to go at such an hour? By morning, of course, I had cooled down. Lying at length in my bath, it struck me that there would be ample opportunity to look for a husband after she had gone. Not that I longed for her death. Quite the reverse. My fondness for her had deepened, in spite of her attempt to control my life. After all, no one else had ever bothered about me enough to try. Then, too, there was the fact that I genuinely respected her. She knew her job, she loved the people she served, and she still had a good deal to teach me.

So, as on the night of the secret burial, I decided to bide my time.

I'm glad I did, because soon after that she went into a slow decline. Day by day more of the work fell to me, until eventually she grew too frail to leave the cottage. I did the rounds alone then, and on my return she was always eager to hear how this or that woman and child were faring. She never lost interest in our work; never complained; never felt sorry for herself.

'In a week or two I'll be up and about again, you'll see,' she assured me more than once.

It was an elaborate pretence, and we both knew it, but it kept us from becoming maudlin and gave a welcome veneer of cheerfulness to our lamplit evenings.

All along I knew we could not go on like this indefinitely. Yet still it came as a shock – a body blow almost – when I returned to the cottage one afternoon to find she had suffered some kind of seizure. It was probably a minor stroke, though it's hard to be sure because she wouldn't hear of sending for a doctor.

'But I have to!' I urged her desperately. 'If I don't . . . !'

She placed a finger on my lips and gave that characteristic turn of the head, refusing to meet my gaze directly even then. 'What would be the use?' she said in a whisper.

'We both understand what's happening. How can a doctor help?'

'He can give you more time!'

She managed a half smile. 'A day maybe. A week.'

What was I to do? Go against her wishes? Fetch a doctor whether she wanted one or not? She must have sensed my indecision and pitied me.

'You can send for one later,' she said. 'Sit with me for now. That's my dearest wish.'

It was a hard request to refuse, and for the rest of the afternoon I remained at her bedside, her hand in mine. Thankfully, she seemed to improve a little as the hours passed, and by evening she had slipped into a peaceful sleep.

Careful not to disturb her, I disengaged my hand and went downstairs to prepare an evening meal. I had barely begun when there was loud knocking at the door. The way it sounded through the house reminded me of an earlier occasion, and I half guessed what awaited me on the porch. It was a small boy, one of the tinker clan, his face thin and pale, his wretched clothes damp with sweat. In one grubby hand he still held the bridle of the horse he had ridden bareback. The horse itself, standing just beyond the porchlight, humphed and pawed the ground as if impatient to be off.

'It's her,' the boy blurted out. 'She's bad. He says the other one . . . the old one . . . she has to come.'

It was more or less what I was expecting.

'Tell him I'll be there as soon as I can,' I said.

He gave me a pinched, doubtful look. 'It's the old one he wants.'

'Never mind what he wants,' I said shortly. 'Just go back and deliver my message.'

With a scowl he sprang onto the horse and wheeled it about. 'He won't like it!' he shouted as he galloped off into the dark.

Having collected my coat and bag, I ran upstairs to check on Gretel. She was still asleep, or so it seemed, but as I turned to leave, her eyes flicked open.

'You're going to them, aren't you?' she said. 'The tinkers. He's called you to a birthing.'

I nodded. 'Don't worry. I won't be gone long. Try to rest while I'm—'

She waved aside my soothing words and clutched my arm. 'When you get there,' she said in an urgent whisper, 'show no curiosity, no surprise, whatever happens . . . even if the child is . . . is not what it should be. Deliver it as you must and be on your way. For God's sake don't linger!'

'I won't,' I said, thinking that would satisfy her, but she hadn't finished.

'And . . . and if the light . . . the light . . . if it flares around you, close your eyes. Ignore it. Pretend you've seen nothing. You must promise me that.'

I had no idea what she was talking about, but time was passing, and a promise was easily given.

'I'll do as you say,' I assured her. 'My word on it.'

She let out a relieved sigh and released my arm. 'Go then,' she murmured, and gave me a strangely squint-eyed look before slipping back into sleep.

Within minutes I had hitched up the buggy and was on my way. It was a warm, still night, with a nearly full moon, so I needed no lamp to light the road ahead. Our old horse seemed to understand what was expected of him anyway, for at the crossroads he didn't hesitate, instinctively choosing the lesser-used track that led westward to the end of the valley. The journey itself proved uneventful, but as I left the cultivated fields behind and entered the scrub country beyond, I felt a chill of loneliness, like someone wandering in a foreign land.

I was almost glad when the dark shape of the hovel came into view. Hastily I looped the reins over the nearest fence-post and hurried forward – to where, once again, he stood waiting. He looked past my shoulder enquiringly, and then back to me. In the moonlight his face was gaunt and hard, etched out by shadow.

'Where is she?' he demanded.

'She's ailing. Too weak to leave her bed.'

'Ah yes, I always forget about you people. What it must be like for you.'

I interpreted his softened tone as a sign of acceptance and made for the porch, but he stepped directly into my path, the two of us so close that I could smell the rankness of his unwashed body.

'Did she send you in her place?' he asked.

'I'm her apprentice. Who else would she send?'

'So she trusts you in . . . in *everything*?'

'Yes.'

He paused for some moments, pensively. With one brawny hand he wiped at his mouth, his palm rasping against the stubble. I took the opportunity to ask a question of my own.

'The woman . . .' I nodded towards the hovel. 'Is she the same one as before?'

'No, but just as foolish.'

'How is it foolish to have a child?'

'You saw the last child,' he answered coldly. 'Wasn't that folly enough for you?'

'How can you be sure . . .' I began, and stopped as he raised his face and his eyes caught the moonlight. 'Come,' I added quickly, changing tack, 'we're wasting precious time here. I need to see her.'

Without waiting for his permission, I eased past him and onto the porch. As I entered the house itself, the foul stench of it hit me full in the face, and I paused for some seconds, gasping. I had hardly recovered when an older woman appeared from the shadows and led me upstairs – our way lighted by a crude lamp which was little more than a wick floating in a saucer of oil.

At the head of the stairs she pointed to a door across the landing. I pushed it open, the stench growing stronger as I did so. Inside, on a bed of filthy straw, lay a young woman. She was naked, her face and limbs bathed in sweat, her belly unnaturally enlarged. She whimpered when she saw me, and covered her face, though not before I noticed her gapped teeth. It was the girl from the market.

By the flickering light of a candle, I squatted beside her and made my initial examination, the woman with the lamp watching from the open doorway.

'Is it bad?' she asked.

Before I could answer, a terrible contraction gripped the girl, so strong that it contorted her whole body. Her moan of pain soon grew into a shriek that went on and on.

And so began the long night of her delivery.

The tinker chief was right, of course. It turned out to be a bloody affair, just like the last, the baby far too big for her and horribly deformed. Had they called me sooner,

I could have got her out of the valley to the relative safety of a hospital. But that was not their way. So given the circumstances – the filth and lack of equipment – I was forced to make a choice that faces all midwives from time to time: whether to save the mother or the babe. It is no choice at all, really, and towards dawn, after a dreadful night, I eventually removed the child in pieces. It was the best and only thing I could do. The head emerged last of all, an ogrish thing that I swiftly consigned to a sack held open for me by the woman with the lamp. Even she was shocked by its distorted features, and fled the room before I had finished.

Working alone, I did what was needful for the mother and made sure there was no haemorrhaging, then stroked her sodden hair to soothe her. At first she shuddered at my touch, as a horse trembles when patted by an alien hand; but exhaustion, rather than trust in me, won her over, and she dropped into a murmurous sleep – muttering words I had never heard before.

I gathered up my bag and the bloody sack and groped my way down the unlit stairwell. On the lower level I could sense figures moving in the shadows. One, an old woman with stringy grey hair, appeared briefly. Reaching out one work-hardened hand, she offered me something that flashed gold in the poor light, but I refused her and hurried out onto the porch.

He was standing exactly where I had left him, the moon now low in the sky, the stars faded almost to nothing by the upcoming dawn. He turned, and I saw him glance down at the sack in my hand. I placed both sack and bag on the ground as we faced each other – I, in the partial shade of the porch; he, with his face exposed to what remained of the moonlight.

'So it's done,' he said.

'Yes, it's done,' I said, 'but should never have happened in the first place.'

He dipped his head slightly. 'We are agreed on that.'

'Why does it happen then?' I pressed him. 'Is it some genetic disorder? Because if it is . . .'

He clicked his tongue impatiently. 'You shouldn't meddle with things you don't understand.'

'That's exactly my point,' I said. 'I *need* to understand. This is the second time this has happened. I can't keep coming here like this. It's only fair that you tell me the truth.'

'The truth will not change anything,' he countered.

'I need to know all the same. Otherwise I can't promise to come next time.'

'Is that a threat?' he growled, his hand stealing to the knife at his belt.

I corrected myself hastily. 'No, I'm *appealing* to you. It's your help I'm asking for here.'

He nodded, satisfied. 'Very well, the simple truth. Our girls like to seduce the young farmers, especially the married ones. It gives them a wicked sense of joy. And they both pay a price for their folly. The farmers no longer delight in their wives, and the girls . . .' He shrugged. 'Well, you have seen the result.'

'But why should it always end like this?' I asked, indicating the sack at my feet.

He swept one arm round in a half-circle, including both the hovel and the rocky landscape surrounding it. 'You have seen where we live. *How* we live. We are the poorest of the poor, the lowest of the low. Different from your kind. As different as night from day, as . . . as past from future. Our two peoples can never mix, our bloodlines never cross over.'

He spoke like a man convinced, and I was too tired to try to prove him wrong.

'You can at least keep your girls on a tighter rein,' I said wearily. 'Stop them stealing out at night.'

He laughed at that, a hollow, unhappy sound. 'Haven't you noticed? We are an unruly people.'

I stooped for the sack. 'So this abomination will continue?'

He shrugged again. 'So it seems.'

Hiding my disgust, I trudged past him, sack in hand.

'My thanks to you,' he called after me, 'and to the old woman too. Tell her she'll be missed.'

After which, the door of the hovel banged shut.

Because of the recent rain, it didn't take long to dig a second grave alongside the first. That done, I unhitched the horse and was climbing into the buggy when I remembered leaving my bag on the porch. I hurried back, tiptoeing the last few paces so as not to disturb those inside. As I stooped for the bag, however, I heard something. The sound of laughter, of merriment; plus a softer, tinkling sound which I took to be some form of music. It was all coming from inside, clearly audible through the cracked, thin planking of the door.

I put my good eye to one of the cracks and peered in. What I saw cannot be easily described. Where there should have been darkness, or at best a dim candle-glow, there was now a shimmering golden light that transformed the sordid interior into a place of splendour. In the midst of the light, equally transformed by it, was a group of stately creatures. I can't say they were wholly human, or animal either. I can say only that they were beautiful beyond words, and also terrible beyond imagining. They were laughing and singing together, like gods at play, and I knew, even as I spied on them, that I shouldn't have been there. I was doing a forbidden thing. Still, it was hard to pull away. The golden light, the creatures themselves, drew me back to my childhood, and to those nights of longing when I had called out to Robin Goodfellow.

One of the creatures, as though sensing my presence, glanced towards the door, and somehow, despite the transformation, I knew him for who he was. Had he recognised me too?

A sudden hush fell on the gathering.

I had been frightened before, but not to that extent. This fear pierced me like a thin steel blade. Scooping up my bag, I turned and ran off into the strengthening dawn. Behind me, the door crashed open, but I didn't look back. Leaping into the buggy, I lashed the rump of the old horse until he broke into a stumbling gallop, and I didn't let up until I could hear his wheezing breaths and feel the newly risen sun warm on my neck.

Then and only then did I look behind. The road, streaked with morning shadow, lay empty. There was neither sign nor sound of pursuit. Yet still I sensed something not quite right. More calm now, less blinded by fear, I surveyed my surroundings . . . and immediately wondered why I hadn't noticed it before! The sky was far bluer than it had ever been; the grass and trees more vividly green; the whole scene shot through by a suggestion of golden light – the same transfiguring light I had glimpsed in the hovel. It was as if, in peering into that forbidden place, I had passed through the doorway itself, into a magically altered world from which there was no return.

I blinked my one good eye, just to be sure, but this newer, brighter world remained. Even my own hands, still gripping the reins, appeared wondrous to me now. As did the steaming coat of the old horse. And leaning back into the padded seat of the buggy – the horrors of the night and my recent fear both momentarily forgotten – I laughed out loud.

I could hardly wait to get home. Gretel, I felt certain, was the one person capable of understanding what had happened to me, for in all likelihood it had happened to her too. Abandoning the buggy at the front gate, I ran indoors and took the stairs two at a time.

But when I burst into the room and called her name, there was no response. A fly buzzed busily at the window, and that was all. As for Gretel herself, she lay stark and still in the wooden bed, both eyes staring blankly at the ceiling.

'Dear God!' I breathed, and in the first rush of grief I bent to kiss her.

What prevented me were those staring eyes – one dull and unseeing, as you would expect; the other as bright and unclouded as ever.

For a moment I thought I'd been mistaken. She was alive after all! Except that when I grasped her hand, the flesh felt chill.

I blinked away tears, too upset to fathom the simple truth.

'Gretel?' I whispered uncertainly, and when she failed to stir, I touched the tip of my finger to the brighter of her eyes. It felt weirdly familiar: rock-hard and unyielding. More intently now – the truth at last beginning to dawn – I pressed my fingers into the surrounding flesh, gently at first, and then more firmly, until the eye eased itself free. It was exactly like my own, a thing of glass and ceramic!

I sat down on the bedside chair with a thump. Here in my hand lay an explanation for her habit of turning her head aside, which had merely been her way of hiding the fact that her eyes did not move in unison. Yet in solving one puzzle, I had raised other, more pressing questions. Had she, perhaps, only chosen me as an assistant because of our shared handicap? And if so, why? It seemed an odd, even self-indulgent reason for making such a choice and didn't gel with what I knew of her.

Not without some sense of guilt, I went to her desk and rummaged through the drawers. In the lowest of them, which I had to force open with a paperknife, I found a copy of my file, including my medical records. A single item in those records had been asterisked and heavily underlined. It read: *Suffered a severe physical trauma at age six which resulted in the loss of an eye. A prosthetic eye successfully fitted.*

So! I *had* been chosen for my handicap, but still I didn't understand why. It seemed too petty a motive for someone as generous as Gretel, too out of character.

However, when a loved one has just died, it is impossible to sit around wondering, or even to give way to grief. There are too many things to be done: the body to be washed and dressed; the funeral to be arranged; food to be prepared for the reception afterwards.

I set about these tasks with a heavy heart, but also an inner sense of elation. Because here is the curious thing: my sudden clarity of sight – or whatever it was that had happened to me back at the hovel – didn't fade with the passing hours. It persisted. The world at large retained its unnatural vividness. The interior of the cottage, my brush and comb, the utensils I used in the kitchen, all seemed shot through with golden light. And when I woke each morning, the gift remained. It was the one thing that made my sombre duties bearable, and kept at bay my lingering fear of the creatures (whoever they were) who lived at the end of the valley.

The day of the funeral arrived. The graveside ceremony, I need hardly add, was well attended. News of Gretel's death had spread like wildfire through Little Earth, and the local families turned out in force – hardly surprising, given how she had touched their lives. Most came on to the reception, and by midday the cottage was full to overflowing, with people spilling out over the porch and down into the garden.

I was kept busy consoling those who grieved, organising the children, and passing around platters of food. As I bustled to and fro, it never occurred to me that the tinkers might appear. Hadn't their leader stressed how different they were from the people of the valley? How set apart? Hadn't I witnessed for myself what that difference entailed when I'd peered through the crack in the door? No, I felt confident that they'd stay away. They would have been out of place there.

Yet when I carried food and drink out to the garden, I spotted them immediately, down amongst the poplars, their presence signalled by a shimmer of golden light. The leader, as magnificent as when I had last seen him through the door, detached himself from the rest and approached me across the lawn. None of the farming folk made way: to them he was a common tinker. But to me, his savage splendour appeared all the more dazzling amongst so many drab, black-clad figures.

As absurd as it may sound, I dipped my head and dropped him a formal curtsey.

'You're very welcome,' I said, taking care not to meet his gaze.

He responded with what I took to be a form of reassurance: 'We are here only to honour her.'

'Then let me thank you on her behalf,' I said, relieved, though still with my eyes cast down.

He clicked his tongue softly, in disapproval, that sound alone sending a jolt of fear through me.

'Come, girl,' he whispered, 'look at me when you speak.'

I couldn't help but obey. Slowly, I raised my head, and as our eyes met, I knew instantly that I had given myself away.

'Ah,' he sighed. 'So you *did* see past our dimming.'

I nodded.

'And now?'

'It's not just you,' I confessed. 'Everything else has changed too.'

He regarded me in silence for some moments. 'This presents us with a problem,' he said finally.

'A problem?' I echoed him, the fear audible in my voice.

But there, on that crowded lawn, he was reluctant to explain. 'You will tell no one about us, you understand,' he said by way of warning. Then, as he turned back towards his people: 'We will meet again later.'

I hated the sound of that word 'later'. It weighed heavily on me through the remainder of the afternoon; and that evening, as a precaution, I barricaded the front and back doors before going to bed. But he didn't come. Not on that night, nor the next, nor in the weeks that followed. I thought to begin with that he was watching to see if I was trustworthy, testing me perhaps; but as the weeks stretched into months I began to relax, even to hope. Until one day I woke without any feelings of dread, and decided:

It's over. He's forgotten.

I was twenty-three years old by then, and had been officially appointed as the resident midwife of Little Earth. Pretty soon, people began looking up to me as they had once looked up to Gretel. Out of sympathy for my single state, they even invited me to their homes, and to services at their church. I knew all along that I could never be one of them – our religious differences were too great – but that didn't stop me envying their close family life. Like everyone else, I had no desire to live alone forever, so I suppose it was inevitable that before too long I again began seeing a young farmer – or 'walking out' with him as they called it in the valley.

Whether it would ever have come to anything I can't say, because we weren't really given a chance. I remember our last evening. We had been out together, walking arm in arm in the starlight as lovers do, and on our return to the cottage I found a message pinned to the door. It was from a neighbouring farm, where a woman had gone into premature labour.

While I collected my bag, he hitched up the old horse. Then we kissed a hasty goodbye, neither of us dreaming we would never meet like that again. As I drove off, my only concern was for the woman who had summoned me.

In fact, it turned out that she was in no danger, and nor was her child, despite being premature. She had had several children already, and with a little help from me she soon produced another healthy babe. Even so, the night was well advanced before I left her.

I reached home at the first hint of dawn. Having unharnessed and fed the horse, I trudged up the path to the back porch . . . and he was there, waiting by the door, his splendour shrouded in a heavy woollen cloak. In the burgeoning light he looked more inhuman than ever, like some mythical creature risen from the past.

'You have heeded my warning?' he asked abruptly.

I shrank back. 'I've told no one, if that's what you mean.'

'What about that young man of yours? Haven't you been tempted to whisper our truth to him? Pillow talk, I believe you people call it. Things confessed in passion.'

'If that's why you've come,' I said, 'then you have nothing to fear, because I've told him nothing either.'

He moved forward threateningly, his gleaming features looming above me. 'Yes, but what of the future? When you two have grown closer? Won't you be tempted then?'

'Never!' I exclaimed. 'I'll always keep your secret safe, I swear.' I edged nearer to the door. 'Now I'm sorry, but

I need to sleep. I've been up all night and I'm too tired for more questions.' With a brief nod of apology, I reached for the latch.

Straightaway he grabbed me by the hair and forced me roughly to my knees. His face close to mine, his breath as rank as any animal's, he hissed: 'Would you have me tear out your tongue?'

I shook my head, too scared to speak.

'Then answer me this. When you visited us last, how exactly did you come to see past our dimming? And tell me no lies!'

'There was a . . . a crack in the front door,' I stuttered out. 'I peered through it and . . . and . . .'

He didn't wait for me to finish. 'Which eye was it that betrayed us? Which eye stole from us our glory, and enjoys it still?'

It came to me then – in the midst of my terror – the truth about Gretel.

'So you were the one who blinded Gretel!' I blurted out. 'But why? She'd already seen you! Who you really are! How could taking her eye change that?'

'She had to learn what we are capable of,' he snarled, tugging at my hair. 'You must too. How else can I guarantee your silence? So I repeat, which eye? Or would you have me take them both?'

I had just enough presence of mind to point to my false eye. The rest – the drawing of the knife, the downward plunge – happened too quickly for me to follow. Yet his reflexes were quicker still. Even as the knife-point clinked against the surface of my eye, he stayed his hand. I felt the faintest jolt, that was all.

He flung me to the porch floor, unable to mask his surprise. 'You lied to me!' he rasped out. 'You have no sight in that thing you call an eye!'

'It happened when I was a child,' I confessed, beginning to cry.

He nudged at me with his foot. 'Tears won't help you, woman. The price must still be paid.'

I crawled forward and clutched him around the knees. 'Please!' I sobbed. 'Don't blind me completely! Take my hand, my arm . . . anything! Not my other eye!'

He gazed down as you would at an insect scurrying for its life, his face inscrutable. 'The price,' he repeated, 'must be paid. It's the only way of keeping my people safe.'

'Didn't I help one of your women?' I implored him through my tears. 'Didn't I come to your house and save her? Surely that counts for something. A life for a life – isn't that fair?'

Ironically, it wasn't my pleading that moved him. It was the tears that seeped from my blind socket. He reached down wonderingly and scooped them from my cheek with one pointed nail, then licked at them, like some mythical beast drinking at the stream of life.

'There may be another way,' he conceded.

'Take it . . . !' I began.

But the knife had already descended, carving a path down my cheek and paring the flesh to the bone.

I clamped my hand to the wound, felt hot blood spurt between my fingers, saw how it splashed crimson-black upon the planking in the dawn light.

He crouched close beside me. 'Hear what I tell you and remember,' he murmured. 'You will not stitch that wound.

Nor bind it closed. Nor seek help from anyone. You'll let it scar over as it pleases.'

'What if it disfigures me?' I moaned, crying from pain now.

He brushed the hair from my face in a sudden gesture of pity. 'That's part of our price,' he went on. 'The other part is this. Even if some man looks past your disfigurement or loves you in spite of it, you'll reject him. You'll live alone for the rest of your days. In exchange, I leave you with the gift of seeing, which you stole from us that night – more than just an eye. Are we agreed?'

'Agreed,' I whispered, and felt for his hand, but he had already gone.

Alone in the cottage I cleaned and staunched the bleeding wound, though that was all. In the clear morning light I could see that he'd done his work well. It was a fearsome cut, as fearsome in its way as his undimmed presence, and I took it as the threat he had intended it to be. Under the guise of suffering from some contagious disorder, I holed up in the cottage for several weeks, allowing the open wound to heal in its own good time.

It left behind a broad, disfiguring scar, as I had guessed it would, a scar that distorted my whole face and more or less ensured that my days of romance were over – soon replaced, in fact, by pitying glances. Strange to say, I didn't overly care. I was alive! What else mattered? And free! Free to relish the gift he had left with me. What had he called it? *The gift of seeing*. Yes, that was it: the ability to view the world as he might view it. Actually to live within the faerie glow I had dreamed of as a child. It is no ordinary gift, believe me. It brought a real joy into my daily life, which more than made up for my damaged face.

As peculiar as it may sound, I felt grateful to him.

I didn't see him again for some time after that, nor any of his people. Months must have passed before our paths crossed again. Fittingly, given our first meeting, it was at the market, where he and his clan were busy trading horses.

He spotted me within moments, and I can only assume that he read the happiness in my face because he soon came striding over, a great golden creature passing unnoticed through the gathered farmers and their families.

'I see you have kept your part of the bargain,' he said.

'It was a good trade,' I replied, and laughed.

He laughed too, a booming sound, also unnoticed, that rang out across the market. Only the singing birds in their cages seemed aware of it, beating their wings against the bars and trilling loudly.

'You have more than a little of Gretel in you,' he observed.

I dropped him another curtsey, but in a playful, half-mocking way. 'I'll take that as a compliment,' I said.

And so we fell into conversation – of the kind that takes place between old friends whose paths have diverged, but who once went through testing times together.

Right at the end I asked: 'So what am I to call your people? You must surely have a name I could use. Between ourselves, I mean, not out there.' I gestured towards the rest of the market.

He considered the question, and while he did so, one of the women sidled up and eased herself into the crook of his arm. She too was a wondrous creature, more fabulous than real, and yet something about her reminded me of the gap-toothed woman I had attended at the hovel.

'We are an ancient people,' he said at last, 'and have answered to many names, but mostly we've been referred to as the Faerie. It's a magical word, special to us.'

'Ah, the Faerie,' the woman crooned in delight. 'I love the sound of it.'

So did I, for it put me in mind of my grandmother's stories and somehow stitched together the two separate parts of my life – bound them far more tightly than the ragged edges of this wound of mine.

'Yes, I like it too,' I said. 'The Faerie.' I paused to savour the word. 'That's how I'll think of you from this point on.'

He gave me his hand in a burning grip. 'Let it seal our pact,' he said.

'Gladly,' I said, and glanced down at my flesh-and-blood hand locked in his golden fist – an unlikely link between alien worlds, severed the moment we drew apart.

We have met frequently since then: sometimes at the market, sometimes on the open road, occasionally at the far end of the valley, when he sends for me. I still find those visits to the hovel hard to endure, and so I'm sure do the women involved. There is no altering the way things are, however; I've learned that much. Whether I approve or not, the faerie women will go on reaching across the gulf that divides us, and our young men will return their passionate embrace; but like our brief handshake – his and mine – the bond can never hold. Always and for ever, it dissolves in the dawn light and leaves behind only the monstrous offspring of a mutual yearning.

AFTERWORD

In its original form, 'Birthing' is not one of those widely known and popular fairytales – perhaps because of its unexpectedly savage ending; perhaps, too, because nineteenth-century popularisers found it an impossible story to sentimentalise. Yet for all that, it has endured, and even the briefest of internet searches soon reveals multiple versions of it. What all those versions have in common is a deceptively simple tale of a midwife who accidentally discovers that the ancient faerie folk are not just the stuff of legend. In the guise of poor fringe dwellers, they continue to exist within her rural community. The midwife soon pays dearly for her discovery when the Faerie retaliate by cruelly blinding her in one eye – the eye which peered in upon them and saw them for who they really are. This savage act usually brings the original story to an abrupt end, and readers are left to make of it what they will.

So what *are* we to make of it? That was the first question I posed to myself when I set out to retell the story. At the most obvious level, it seemed to me that the taking of the eye is a warning of what the midwife can expect if she reveals the Faeries' existence. But it is surely more than just that. It is also an enactment of the ancient lore, 'an eye for an eye'. By looking past the human disguise and peering into the magical world of the Faerie, the midwife has awakened her 'inner eye'; and for that gift, she must give up a portion of her earthly vision. In one sense she still has two eyes: one capable of 'seeing' into the wonderful and terrible faerie realm; the other restricted to the workaday 'surface' life we all lead.

All of which raised a further issue: in the end, is she cursed or blessed? This struck me as a vital question, which many writers before me have struggled to answer. The poet, Keats, for instance, would probably have considered her cursed. In his well-known poem 'La Belle Dame Sans Merci', his 'knight-at-arms', having once crossed into the land of Faerie, considers ordinary existence drab and colourless. All he can now perceive with his outer eye is a pointless wintry landscape in which 'the sedge has withered from the lake, / And no birds sing'.

Frankly, and with due respect to Keats, I find this puzzling. Peering into the enchanted heart of nature, into the vibrant world of the 'other', would surely add lustre to the ordinary, not render it drab, and it is this belief that I've tried to build into my retelling. Despite her suffering, Lucy, my young midwife, is blessed by her new-found vision.

Deliberately, I've avoided trying to describe precisely how she now sees things – the ineffable, after all, can't by its very nature be described. Rather, and in keeping with the unresolved spirit of the original, I've left her transformed world for the reader to imagine.

In part, I suppose, I'm already explaining why, out of a feast of old stories, I chose this one. Yet it did have other attractions. For one thing, it is not so much a fairytale as a tale about the Faerie – and it is the Faerie, that elusive image of the 'other', which I find most compelling. Also, with its cruelly abrupt ending, it strips away that pretty nineteenth-century version of fairies which has so impoverished our reading of old stories. What the midwife sees, when she peeks through the crack in the door, is something both terrible and beautiful. It is akin to the Old Testament prophet Isaiah's experience in the temple, when confronted by the awesome and terrible image of the seraphim. After such an experience, the world can never look the same again.

For this reason I began my retelling with Lucy's naïve, childhood notion of the fairies found in Shakespeare's *A Midsummer Night's Dream*, and then deepened that experience into a moment of tragedy. This is partly intended as a preparation for what is to come; partly as a childlike version of Gretel's earlier encounter; and partly, too, as an ironic means of undercutting later events. For if I'm to be honest, 'Birthing' is more a sequel to Gretel's story than a simple retelling of it – a sequel that contains the original, but takes it several steps further. In my sequel, Gretel, like any surrogate parent, tries to protect her successor by choosing someone half blind. Ironically, that 'someone' has already encountered the true spirit of the Faerie once before, to her cost, and no amount of clumsy benevolence on Gretel's part can shield her from a second encounter. The fact remains that Lucy's subsequent adult glimpse of faerie splendour is simultaneously an act of theft and a moment of transformation, and for both she must pay by giving up any hope of a normal existence.

A final word about the bonds I have invented to tie the two worlds of the story together – bonds that don't exist in the original. First and foremost, there is the bond of honour, symbolised by the handshake near the end, a reaching across the gulf, with human and Faerie pledging their word and thereby guaranteeing their coexistence. Without this act of good faith, there can be no ongoing story, no intertwining of the magical and the real, only the eventual destruction of the 'other' and the loss of all wonder.

There is, however, also a second, darker bond, one of mutual fascination, symbolised by the unnatural lust that draws humans and Faeries into a single embrace. (And on this point, I fancy, Keats and I agree!) Herein, for me, lies the importance of the original image of the midwife. She is the lynchpin of the story, for she is the one with an 'eye' for the needs of both peoples, whose duty it is to deliver the uncertain results of their dangerous union. Lucy's task, in short, is to emulate Gretel and grow into the traditional witch-cum-midwife-cum-holy woman, into the archetypal wise old woman of many old stories; to accept the role of outsider whose secret knowledge alone can ensure the safe passage from one order of being to another.

Or rather, that's what I've *tried* to hint at!

GLAMOUR

by Kate Thompson

{1}

The sound of the key in the door surprises him. He has forgotten that she is coming home tonight. He is engrossed in work, moving sentences around and searching for better words. It is important to get exactly the right words.

No, he has not forgotten that she is coming home. It has just slipped his mind.

He is writing a review. The editor of one of the national broadsheets offers him a review maybe four times a year, maybe six. His reaction is always the same. It is easy money for a few hundred words of prose, and it is good for him to exercise his analytical skills. When he actually gets down to work he discovers, every time, that it is not so easy, and he remembers that it was like this last time, and the time before, and that he always underestimates the amount of work involved. It is not criticism that is the problem. Criticism is the language of the circles he moves in, and he is never short of opinions. It is analysis that is more difficult. Analysis requires a different set of muscles entirely, and his are slack.

He knows immediately whether he likes a person's writing or not. It works for him or it doesn't. That is simple. The reason why is not so simple. But that is what reviewing is all about, and more often than not it's a struggle.

No, it has not slipped his mind that she is coming home tonight. It is just not uppermost in his mind. But earlier in the day it was. When he was waiting at the ATM on Upper Street he was thinking about her coming home. He had got the date wrong, initially, and had bought flowers a week ago; flesh-coloured lilies with a deep pink blush at the centre and a powerful scent. When the ATM rolled out his cash, he went into the supermarket and bought a nice bottle of bubbly to go with them.

The other important thing to be taken into account when writing a review is the tone. The tone has to reflect his position in the literary world. It is important not to be condescending, but at the same time the reader should not be under the illusion that he is considering the work of an equal. He is a statesman of the poetry world, giving a helping hand to both the reader and the young, or not-so-young, aspirant. He is seldom, if ever, given the work of established modern poets to review.

He is surprised when he hears the sound of her key in the lock, but it is a pleasant kind of surprise. He has missed her and he is glad she is back. And it means he can forget about his review, for the time being at least. And later, when she has finished telling him about her time in New York, he might talk to her about the book, because sometimes that helps him to get his ideas straight. A description might come out of his mouth in a way it never came out on the page. Or a comparison, when he tries to give her an impression of what the book is like. 'Kindergarten Freud' came about like that a few months ago, and the editor used it as the title of the review.

He hears the door close and her footsteps in the hall, the pause while she takes off her coat and scarf, the thump as she drops her bag at the foot of the stairs. He comes through from his study at the back of the house into the kitchen.

He probably won't tell her that he doesn't believe women should waste their time trying to write poetry. He won't put that in his review, either, or mention it anywhere in public, though he believes it wholeheartedly. It isn't that he thinks women are inferior. Not at all. But as far as he is concerned, poetry is about men struggling with things that come easily to women. And the things that women poets seem to write about would be better kept as gossip to pass over the garden wall to their neighbours.

He has his face on, his eager 'darling' face, but it freezes when she opens the kitchen door. The shock hits him like a snake-strike in his entrails. Its venom shoots out along his nerves, stretching his scalp, even weakening his knees.

'What's up?' she says.

He opens his mouth. It is not a fair question. She knows what is up because she has done it.

He needs something light. A quip. He needs to toss it off as if it were nothing, rally the nerve-endings and carry on, buying himself a bit of time to adjust. But there aren't any words to be found that are not obscenities. Ordinary speech has abandoned him.

'It's not that bad, is it?' she says.

No. Say no. Of course not. But it is that bad. It's worse. It's so bad that it hurts.

'I . . .' he says.

'Oh, come on,' she says.

He can see that his reaction is frightening her, but he can't fix it. She has brought it upon herself, after all.

'I need cigarettes.'

He can't even pass her to get into the hall. He goes the long way, through the dining room and past the door to his study, then back through the hall and past the door of the kitchen where she stands with that frightened look on her face, watching him as he snatches a coat and scarf and goes out into the night.

{2}

In the jaundiced gloom of the street he turns the wrong way for the corner shop. He doesn't need cigarettes, not yet anyway. What he needs is distance and time, to work the venom out of his system and allow some sense to come in.

Why?

The leaves are dropping. He hasn't noticed until now. He thought it was still summer but it isn't, it's autumn.

Why would she do a thing like that?

The streets are wet, but it isn't raining now. A taxi slows hopefully, then speeds irritably away. Two young women are talking under a street lamp on the other side of the road.

Why didn't she warn him? Or did she? Maybe she did warn him, and he didn't notice. What was it she said in her last email? *Don't bother to come to the airport. You won't recognise me.* Should he have guessed from that?

It's not as if he didn't know. She told him on the first day they met, when they found themselves squashed up against the wall together at the launch of *Turtle Shore*. She did not read poetry, she explained, but she was with some friends who did. She liked to know everything that was going on in the publishing world. That was her job. She even liked to know what was happening on the fringes.

It wasn't a proper party. Publishers of poetry could not afford lavish launches. He had done an after-hours reading in an independent book shop in Camden and followed it with a general invitation to the pub. All evening strangers had wanted to talk to him. Some of them wanted to talk to him about his new collection and about the life of a poet in the televisual world. Some of them wanted to talk about their own love of poetry, and about how sad they were that it was a genre in such decline. But most of them, in the end, really wanted to talk to him about their own attempts to write, and what they wanted him to discuss was not the gritty day-to-day realities of a modern poet but how they might go about getting their own work into print.

So, much as he would have liked to take umbrage at her reference to the 'fringes', he couldn't. This was indeed the fringes, not just of publishing but of society. The people he met on occasions like this were like earnest members of some tiny cult, as anachronistic and out of touch as those head-bangers who dressed up in medieval clothes and played recorders. Poetry was an archaic language, deader than Latin and read by far fewer. It had both feet in the grave, and only that great juggernaut of a life-support system, the Arts Council, was keeping the earth from closing over its corpse.

She loved poetry, she told him, but she had no time to read it. She was busy. She had a hectic job. But poetry was the pinnacle of the written arts and deserved far more attention than it got.

There was, he thought, a little electric charge between them, from the first moment they were washed up against the wall together. He despised people who worked in publicity. They were all, male or female, media tarts. But she had a kind of energy he seldom saw. Vivacity was an ugly and polluted word, not to be touched. Vitality. That was what she had, and that was exactly what he lacked. He was drawn to it like a mosquito scenting blood. It was love at first sight.

{3}

She stands in the middle of the kitchen floor in a state verging on panic. What she needs is a drink. On the table, in a ceramic jug full of melted ice and surrounded by a careful arrangement of ageing pink lilies, is a bottle. It is shaped like a wine bottle but she knows, before she pulls it out, that it doesn't contain wine. There has been no alcohol in the house for more than six years, except for the rare occasions when they hold dinner parties. She has never minded. She likes a glass of wine but she willingly forgoes it so as not to put him in the way of temptation.

There are good neighbours up and down the street, any of whom would happily lend her a bottle of wine without a moment's hesitation. But she can't face anyone now. She would have to pretend to be her usual, jaunty self and for once she finds she can't do it. She is disarmed. Or if not disarmed, then disrobed. She would have to stand naked and vulnerable at her neighbours' door. She would have to face that same moment of shock at what she has done. Not the cruelty, though. No one could deal her the kind of blow that he has just done.

The realisation produces a little surge of anger. She is adept at restraining her temper – any job she has ever had has required it – but this is more comfortable than fear and for once she lets it loose. How could he do that to her? Just stare and stammer and run? How dare he treat her so callously?

Energised, she puts on the kettle for coffee, and for a minute or two she patrols the kitchen, aimlessly opening cupboard doors and slamming them shut again. She picks up the paper and tosses it down. She begins to compose a speech for when he returns, but she doesn't get very far. As rapidly as it arrived, her anger evaporates, and she slumps onto one of the ladderback chairs and rests her head against its top rung.

No, she is not disrobed, she is disempowered. The comparison with Samson is too obvious. Or is it? He didn't look at her as if she were Samson. He looked at her as if she were Methuselah.

{4}

He suddenly realises where his feet are taking him and stops, appalled. Quite unconsciously he has been following the sweet, hop-and-barley scent-trail laid by Dionysus. It is alluring, but he is wise to it as well. He knows the other stinks it masks: the vinegary sweat, the stale bedclothes. His body remembers, too, and he gets a bilious flashback taste in his throat.

All the same, he hesitates for an instant. He doesn't believe that he is an alcoholic but he does believe what the doctor told him a few years ago about the state of his liver and his heart. A unit or two here and there would do him no harm, he was told, but he doesn't take even that. He can't, because if he empties a glass he empties a bottle. If he enters a pub he is always the last to leave, unless someone succeeds in dragging him away. He knows that oblivion is only a short-term answer to the horror that has entered his life, but he still longs for it.

He won't yield. It isn't the fall he fears so much as the long, arduous climb back out again.

The gods are everywhere around him these days. Not just Dionysus, but Eros and Hermes and Zeus and Ares. And the Irish gods, too, and characters from his schoolbooks that he has scarcely thought of since. Fionn and the Fianna, who roamed the ancient forests of Ireland, hunting and hobnobbing with the fairy folk. Bran, the dog with a human mother. The Children of Lír, who were turned into swans for four hundred years, and Oisín, who fell off the horse and turned to dust. Some nights they all crowd round him so intensely that he feels suffocated by them. They enter his dreams and try to elbow their way into his poetry, but he won't allow it. He doesn't write that kind of poetry. He despises that kind of poetry.

He threw off that backward-leaning yearning for the old myths along with his Catholic religion when he was a student. He replaced them with radical politics and a hatred of empire. His early poetry blazed with anarchic rage and idealism. His middle era pulled no punches either; was full of meat and bone and machetes. It writhed and sweated on the page. It prophesied the deadly effects of the capitalist system and free-market enterprise. His best-known collection, the one he was launching when he met her, was written from the viewpoint of an Aboriginal woman who watches the eradication of her people for the sake of sheep and gold, and whose voice he studied during a two-month visit to Australia, funded by the Arts Council.

And his recent work? It unnerves him to see his attention trying to veer away from the subject. He rebukes it. It is true that he has only published two collections since he moved into the house in Islington with her, but so what? They are fine. They are good. He is happy with them.

He just wishes he didn't have to keep reminding himself of the fact.

{5}

How did she expect him to react? She must have thought it through, because she has spent hours mentally composing emails and deciding not to send them. Except for the one that had the hint. She would never expect him to meet her at the airport, any more than she would meet him if he had been away for a few weeks. It's a long time since they have been at that stage of their romance. But she sent the email anyway, just to flag the fact that he should expect a change. So if not this, what had he expected? She hasn't been away all that long. She is hardly likely to have put on four stone, and she couldn't have lost it because she doesn't have it to lose.

The kettle boils but she doesn't get up to make coffee. The most likely thing is that he paid no attention to the email at all. He might have registered the day and the time that she was arriving – he must have, because he has bought the flowers and that irritating bottle – but ignored the bit at the end, or regarded it as a joke.

And what did *she* expect? *Hello, darling. Have you done something to your hair?* (Pause, to pour her a glass of tepid, overpriced, melon-flavoured soda pop.) *How was New York?*

She hasn't changed her hair. What she has done is stop changing it. He has always known the truth about this – she has never lied to him about it. Not only did she take the trouble to tell him about it at the first decent opportunity, but she has reminded him regularly, over the years.

So why didn't she warn him? Why didn't she actually send any of those carefully composed emails?

She knows why she didn't. She was leaving herself room to change her mind. And she still could do that. She hates colouring it herself and always gets it done by a professional, but she keeps a couple of bottles in the bathroom for emergencies. She could go up there now and colour it again and tell him it was all a joke. By tomorrow they could both pretend it never happened.

He could, perhaps. She couldn't. She has been working towards this moment for years, now. And the irony of it is that it was he who set her on the path in the first place.

{6}

He lights a cigarette and turns away from the pub. There are other pubs, of course, thousands of them in London, but none so dangerous to him as his local.

Fifteen years. Can it really be fifteen years since that night in another pub? The one in Camden, after the launch?

No, it was not love at first sight, despite the electric charge. She was tipsy when the conversation began and almost legless by the time it wound up. She touched him more and more often, to emphasise the earnest nature of whatever it was she was saying, and leaned in closer and closer as the evening progressed and her balance deteriorated.

'You need my help,' she said, about once every ten minutes. 'Poetry needs to be rescued from obscurity. It will be my good work capital G capital W. It will salve my conscience and save my soul.' She was a freelance publicist, she told him, and worked for most of the major publishers. Ran some of their big, blockbuster campaigns. 'I know everybody,' she went on. 'Anybody who is everybody.' She laughed at herself. 'I've had a bit too much, haven't I? I'm off duty, that's why. Here, you finish this.'

He took the glass from her and, making sure that she saw him, drank from the very spot her lipstick had stained. Their eyes met.

'You need my help,' she said. 'Poetry needs to be rescued.'

His publisher materialised and pressed a fresh glass into her hand. She really was somebody important, then. His publisher did not readily buy rounds.

'Give me your card,' she said.

Slowly, and with great care, he tore a three-inch by two-inch rectangle from an empty cigarette packet and wrote his name and phone number on it. She read it, smiling, and handed it back.

'And your mobile,' she said.

He didn't take it. 'I don't have a mobile.'

'Better get one, then,' she said.

Then her friend came along and, in a practised manner, took the new glass of wine out of her hand and steered her out of the door. She was still clutching his homemade card, but he didn't hold out much hope that it would survive. He didn't expect ever to see her again.

But the next day, when he was still asleep, the phone rang. It wasn't her, but the call came because of her. It was a researcher for a local radio station who wanted to set up a short interview about his book with the presenter of the evening arts round-up. They did it over the phone that afternoon, and the presenter was young and glib and sounded as if he had just moved from a job advertising cheap lager. His questions were idiotic – verging on humiliating.

'So who reads poetry these days? The spotty young bloke in the corner with the glasses, isn't it? I mean, what's the point of it really, when we have movies and computer games and stuff? What is it saying that all those other things can't?'

It's hard to talk about the soul to gobshites like that. He survived somehow, but the interview wrecked his head and it took him a long time to recover his equilibrium. He swore he'd never do it again, but the next offer was more interesting: a small, serious production company making a documentary for BBC Radio 4 about Irish writers in London. He did well. The documentary used a lot of his comments and observations, and soon after that he was approached by a different company, for Radio 4 again, to take part in a morning panel discussion program.

No, she couldn't have told him about her hair on that first, noisy, bladdered occasion. It didn't fit. The next one then? That dreadful party with all those media people? Surely not. When they went to dinner then, a week later? Their first proper date. He remembered now, or it might be that he imagined a memory. He must have remarked on her hair, or perhaps he leaned across to pick something out of it. Like what? A leaf? A bit of a twig? Or perhaps he was standing behind her, helping her into her coat, and the soft, gleaming mass of it was under his nose, and he said, 'It's such a lovely colour.'

And she said, 'It's out of a bottle. I've been going grey since I was twenty-four.'

{7}

Reading his poetry and getting to know him had made her re-evaluate her life. He wrestled with things she never thought about, with the nature of the human race and our relationships with each other, with the earth, with the stars. There had always been men in her life, but she fell for him in a way that was entirely new. Her analyst told her that he represented her animus, her soul's guide, and that she was attracted to him because he embodied what she wanted to become.

'A poet?' she said. The idea made her laugh, and she left the session full of scepticism. But over the days and weeks that followed, and in subsequent analysis sessions, she came to see that there was some kind of truth in the suggestion. She still had no desire to be a poet, but she began to think in a new way about the work she did and the validity and integrity of it, and her confidence in what she did began to develop cracks. Through them she glimpsed different possibilities about what she might do. Or, more importantly, what she might be.

Her commitment to her work began to slide. She saw the slick and glitzy people around her in a new light; judged them against him, or against her animus perhaps, and found them lacking. Not in glamour or wit or wealth or power. What they lacked was depth.

She began to crave a different kind of life. She sought out his company more and more, and before long they became lovers, and the talks they had went on long into the small hours and made the work she did in publicity feel shallow and mundane. She began to examine the books she represented for their content and not just for their saleability. She was amazed at how much rubbish she had sold in the past, and how repugnant some of the people were whom she had represented. And she saw, as well, how her life and her work had become one and the same thing. All her office hours were taken up with phone calls and meetings. All her meals were meetings as well; a clockwork succession of cafés and restaurants, with a launch or a publisher's party thrown in here and there. Most of the time she had left in the evenings and weekends was given over to catching up on emails and reading the books of the next authors she was going to be paid to represent. But she realised now that she got no pleasure from reading anymore. Or at least, she got no more pleasure than a professional gambler might get from picking up a newly dealt hand of cards and working out how best to play it. The actual content of the book, its essential nature, was irrelevant.

And then there were the authors themselves. She remembers how it was when she started out in business; the thrill she got from meeting these people and dropping their names. She doesn't remember when that changed and she began to view her charges with cynicism. With rare exceptions, these people she once believed to be so fabulous and talented turned out to be neurotics with monstrous egos. She had a huge range of tools in her social kitbox, but the one she used most often with the authors was flattery. A bit of flattery never went amiss on the other side of the fence, either, with the media people who had the power to make or break, but she needed different kinds of tools there as well. She bribed researchers to take little fish on to their shows, with promises of bigger fish to come. She tempted tabloids and chat shows with sordid little details weaselled out of her authors late at night in pubs. And she networked. She got her hair coloured and styled, she painted her face and went out on the town. No one in the business had a nose to equal hers when it came to sniffing out the right parties to be seen at or the latest little out-of-the-way pub where the People Who Mattered could be found.

She was liked, she knows that, despite the disdain with which both seekers and purveyors of publicity view her caste. She was liked because she knew how to be liked and never allowed her personal opinion of others to get in the way of that. It was a deliberate act, a carefully measured blend of servility, competence and frivolity. It never surprised her that her work diary was always full or that she was invited to every party in town.

Until she met the poet, and then she was suddenly flummoxed.

{8}

It surprised him to learn that she dyed her hair, but what surprised him even more was the slow realisation that they were all at it. He didn't watch much TV, but when he did turn it on he saw that almost every commercial break had an ad for one hair colour product or another. They were as familiar to him as the ads for cars and booze and burgers, so he must have known they were there. It just hadn't registered that if these things were worth that amount of expensive advertising, there must be a massive market for them.

When he discovered this, he thought back over his previous relationships. He didn't remember ever seeing any of those advertised colourants in a bathroom cabinet, but did that mean none of his previous partners had used them? He didn't know, because he now saw the stuff in the window of every hairdresser's shop he passed. How could you tell, if you weren't let in on the secret? Were there giveaway signs that he had never learned to read?

And why should it matter, anyway? It was the person who counted and not the colour of their hair. He had proved that to himself, and to her, when they became lovers. He had proved it doubly when he committed himself to the relationship and moved in with her. He didn't forget about it – she wouldn't let him forget – but it had never seemed important.

So why does it matter now? The image of her standing in the kitchen doorway revisits him, and it brings with it a sharp echo of the original shock. He loves her and it shouldn't change anything, but it does.

He has only just opened a new packet of cigarettes, but he goes into a shop to buy more. Wherever his feet carry him, it will be a long night. He buys two packets and a spare lighter, and he keeps his eyes down on the sweets counter so he won't be tempted to look at the shelves of bottles behind the assistant's head. He adds a chocolate bar to the tally, even though he detests the stuff, because it will be such a long night that he may need it.

She rescued his career from the brink of extinction. Everything he has become he owes to her. She turned his life around.

He didn't always like what it entailed, but he had been too long ignored to turn down the chance of a bit of attention. He hated the day of media training she arranged for him (and paid for), but he made good use of it nonetheless. The woman who was giving it took him through his 'back story', beginning with what he knew of his birth and anything he remembered from his childhood. She was thrilled to discover that he had been brought up on a farm in Tipperary, even when he disillusioned her with the information that it was not a miserable peasant's croft but a large, two-storey farmhouse with a courtyard of cut-stone outbuildings, one hundred and eighty-three acres of prime pasture and a similar amount of lovely old native woodland. She picked out a few of the most interesting things and taught him how to introduce them into interviews, whether or not they were relevant to the question being asked. Like the big family running wild in the woods, or being rounded up to help with the shearing and the hay. Or the long walk every day to the village school. The boarding school bits didn't interest her so much, even though he had a string of hilarious anecdotes, but she loved the polio outbreak that hit two of his siblings but left him and the others mysteriously untouched. And she picked up on his father's knowledge of horses and the people who came to him for advice.

'You'd be surprised,' she said, 'how many people know about horses, and even people who don't are often fascinated by all the paraphernalia around them. Like ships. Horse and ships. Can't go wrong.'

Later, talking to someone from the press or the radio, he followed her advice, and even introduced a few funny stories to spice things up, like the time when he was first allowed to drive the Land Rover when he was twelve, and managed to overturn it in a ditch. But he told no one about another, more unsettling thing that her probing had exposed – a memory of the huge house and the silence in it. Of course, it was never really silent, except in the dead of night. There were seven children with only eleven years between them and they were boisterous and given to endless gangings-up and squabbling like all large families. Nonetheless there was a silence in the house that underlay all the noise, like a single, strong background colour, and it was the silence between his parents, who never spoke to each other at all.

He remembers his father asking them, *Where's your mother?* or, *What's your mother up to?* He asked them that because she didn't tell him where she was going or how long she would be. He never told her, either, but she didn't ask. She either knew, or didn't care. She kept his dinner warm for him, and there were always one or two kettles on the range, at the boil or close to it. Everyone knew how to make tea and coffee.

The memory of this silence disturbed him terribly when it came. He mistrusted its sudden emergence and suspected that he must have manufactured it to serve some obscure neurotic purpose of his own. But when he phoned his older sister she confirmed it. Their parents had their own precisely delineated areas of operation and they hardly ever spoke to each other, right up to the time their father died.

It hurt him, this rediscovery of parental disharmony. But over the next few days, he scrutinised the memories more closely and came to realise that the silence was not, as he had leaped to conclude, full of anger and petulance. It was not a refusal to communicate but a demonstration of perfect communication. They didn't need words to understand each other.

He wrote several poems about it, and in the process came to understand that neither extreme of interpretation was entirely accurate, and that the truth probably lay somewhere in between. One of the poems was good, and it led into a series about his mother and father, which became part of the first collection he published after he moved into the house in Islington. He knows that they are not bad poems, but in retrospect he wishes he had held some of them back for a bit longer and worked on them some more. Or, even better, retired them to the filing cabinet along with the slim folder of family letters.

But his publisher, for the first time ever, had been pressing him for a new book. It was amazing what a bit of publicity could do. He didn't fool himself into believing that he had become a household name or anything like it, but he had entered a new realm where he was known to the people who mattered, and the small population of lost souls who still bought poetry. *Turtle Shore* had been slated in Australia, where the Aboriginal sequence was condemned as inaccurate and exploitative, but in the rest of the English-speaking world it had been well received. It was reviewed just about everywhere that poetry could be reviewed, and although some of the interpretations made him cringe, almost all of the critics were positive. It was reprinted, then shortlisted for the Whitbread poetry section and reprinted twice more, and although it didn't win the Whitbread it did pick up two other prizes, both of them smaller and less wellknown, but both more prestigious in poetry circles.

He continued to be invited onto discussion panels and arts programs now that his name had risen up those important lists in important hands, and he continued to experience the enormous pleasure of finding that his books were in the shops. And not only *Turtle*. On the strength of its success his earlier works had all been reissued in new covers that echoed *Turtle's* design and thus gave him his own jacket style. Then letters began to arrive via his publisher, asking him to speak at conferences and to visit writers' groups and schools. She got a designer to set up a website for him, and through that came emails with more offers. He co-tutored a week-long course in Wales on writing poetry, and two weekend ones in Ireland. His publisher sold the US rights to a small press in Boston. He applied for residencies and bursaries as usual. The difference was that now he often got them.

For the first time in his life he was making money. Not serious money, not even a realistic living where Islington was concerned, but he paid his share of the household expenses at least, and it made him feel less like a kept man.

{9}

After she has made the coffee she discovers there is no milk. He hasn't used it since the doctor warned him about his cholesterol levels, and he has forgotten to buy any for her. She finds double cream in the freezer and chisels off a chunk with a carving knife. A large chunk. She puts it in a cup and microwaves it until it bubbles, then she adds coffee to it, and sugar, for comfort. And because of that, of course, guilt interferes with her enjoyment of it.

She considered herself overweight as a teenager and has been obsessed with thinness ever since. At the time she saw herself as massive, with tree-trunk thighs and double chins. But recently, looking through some old photographs, she was surprised to see that the girl in the photos, nearly always trying to evade the camera, was not plump, or even chubby. At worst she might be described as sturdy; perhaps busty. Not fat, though. Nowhere near fat.

And yet the misconception had governed her life; perhaps still does. At college she verged on becoming anorexic. In her first job, as a junior in the publicity department of a large publishing house, she skipped lunches and then sometimes gorged at home, and sometimes vomited afterwards. But when she went freelance she left all that behind her. She was run off her feet, and despite the endless meals and parties she never put on an ounce. It was burned off by the relentless pressure of keeping up with it all, and by the nervous energy needed to present her public face.

The face. The permanent bloody perfect public face. That was what perplexed her when she met him and they became close. She felt that it was obvious to anyone why someone like her would be attracted by someone like him, with his talent and his depth and his moody complexities. But why would he be interested in her? She accepted the label of media tart – that was what she was, and unashamedly so. But surely he wasn't taken in by the bubbles and the smile? Surely he could see right through to the vacancy behind them? She could only believe that he did, and that he saw even further than she could see, to where her true self lay bound and gagged and drugged. And if he saw it and liked it enough to stay around, then maybe she should try to discover it herself.

So with the help of her analyst, she set about rescuing it, and throughout the whole long, arduous process he listened and appeared to understand. He agreed, enthused, advised, encouraged, supported. She was right to undertake the search for her soul; it was the only really important part of a human being. Everything else could be reduced to survival tools and window-dressing, he said. The body was the scaffolding from which the soul is suspended, and as such it was largely irrelevant.

So what was all this about now? Could she have been wrong about him all along?

{10}

Over time he lost his gaunt appearance and developed what he called a beer belly. Although he still hated parties he learned to put up with them, because he understood the necessity of networking, and he no longer planted himself in the quietest corner but stood more centrally, or even circulated. His confidence increased exponentially, and if he never lost his dislike of media types and his disdain for the 'arty' scene, he never let it show.

When *The Turf Shed* came out he was rewarded for his pains by full review coverage and another round of interviews and feature articles. One critic, writing in a prestigious Irish poetry journal, compared him unfavourably with Seamus Heaney and accused him of constructing a mythical 'Oirish' childhood to cash in on the current publishing hunger for 'barefoot misery'. His admirers told him it was rubbish and he would be best to ignore it. He did his best to follow their advice, but it wasn't as easy as it sounded.

He walks north, through London's strung-out villages, each with their own banks and post offices, shops and supermarkets, pubs and restaurants. He passes a Japanese place that was 'in' a few years ago, but when he catches the cooking smell outside it he is reminded not of the food he ate there, but of the drinks he had in its parchment-and-bamboo waiting area. A few doors down, the legs of a prostrate drunk extend across the pavement. He crosses the street and lights another cigarette.

It is after ten, but that is still early for London and he feels safe in the bright high streets and the quiet residential hinterlands in between them. The black wool coat he bought in New Bond Street last year was an inspired choice. Anyone in the know would recognise its designer elegance as soon as they were close enough, but to a passer-by it would look quite casual, even slightly shabby. So although he keeps his eyes open, he does not fear attack. But what he is carrying within him does not feel so safe.

That Irish critic still haunts him. Twelve years on, the words still sting, and he is not such a fool that he doesn't know why. The title poem was one of those he now wishes he had withheld. It contains a lie at its very heart. It was his publisher (who also acted as editor, publicist and distributor for his small press), who suggested the change. His reservation was reasonable. The wood shed was too firmly associated in educated minds with Stella Gibbons and *Cold Comfort Farm*, and the power of the poem and of the whole collection would have been compromised by the comic echoes. He agreed and made the change, even though his family had never burned turf, but ash and beech cut from their own extensive woodlands. It hadn't troubled him at all at the time. No one would ever know, after all. But it now seems to him that the lie was a road sign pointing to greater lies within.

He passes a tube station and thinks, for the first time, of turning back. But the shock returns and the memory of what awaits him there, and he continues to walk, still heading north. In any case, he is struck by a strange sense that he is heading towards home and not away from it. He tries to analyse the feeling, but it is elusive. It is certainly not a blissful childhood hearthrug-and-hugs sense of home, and nor is it his current sofa-nest-and-popcorn one. It's a darker feeling; a primal, disturbing, instinctive kind of longing. For what, though? Death? No, not death. Nothing as dramatic and final as that.

A few drops of rain fall tentatively, the advance party for a deluge, checking that the sky corridors are clear. They are, and the downpour follows. He steps into the doorway of an all-night supermarket and lights another cigarette, keeping the hand that is holding it outside and upturned, reminding him of how he and his brother used to conceal their smokes like that, in case their parents happened along.

Maybe 'lies' is too strong. The poems are fine. They are good. Everybody said so, bar the one.

A security guard inside the shop is staring at him. He turns to face the street and takes another drag of his cigarette. The poems are as well crafted as any of his earlier work. Better, perhaps, because he is constantly working and perfecting his technique. Yes. They are good. Technically, they are just about perfect.

But he knows, deep down, that this is all whitewash, designed to conceal a truth he is unwilling to face. He glances over his shoulder. The guard is still watching him. He throws the cigarette into the street, where it sends out a trail of sparks like a small firework, then he turns and goes into the shop. He strides towards the guard in a confrontational way but then averts his gaze and walks straight past him and in among the shelves. He picks up a bottle of water, and at the counter he buys a third packet of cigarettes.

{11}

Looking back on it, she can see that her first move towards defining her true self was not exactly revolutionary. He laughed when she told him about No Sandwiches, and at the time it bothered her. It's easy now to see that it was not the great leap into darkness and chaos that she expected it to be, but it was a small step forward and all she was capable of at the time.

The idea grew out of her increasing disenchantment with the sandwich as a lunchtime staple. In the years since she had gone freelance she had eaten lunch out nearly every day, and nearly always in the centre of London. Some clients required fancy restaurants with proper meals, but more often than not her midday meetings took place over a sandwich, and her non-meeting lunches consisted of a sandwich on the run. Despite the changes they had gone through with the introduction of fancy breads, there was still no disguising what they were. And she was well and truly sick of them.

So she came up with the concept of a café that had both eat-in and takeaway sections, and was open from mid-morning to office closing time, and that didn't sell sandwiches. Instead it would offer a huge range of delicious alternatives: pasties, pastry rolls with a variety of fillings, quiches, spanakopita, Spanish omelettes, Indian and Middle Eastern snacks. The only bread would be pita to go with dips, and organic brown rolls to go with the soup.

It took far more research and organisation to get off the ground than she had expected, and there was a time when winding down the old business and winding up the new one overlapped and almost made her ill with exhaustion. There was consternation in the publishing world when word got out that she was giving up, and offers came in that she found all but impossible to refuse. A film star she had worshipped since she was a child was bringing out an autobiography. A writer of comic fiction whom she loved touring with was launching a new series.

Jobs like that might well have elevated her to another level of prestige and income. She wavered, but although he had laughed at No Sandwiches, he was backing her up now. It wasn't only about providing this new option for the office crowd and, hopefully, making a shed-load of money out of it. It was about her and her life; about stepping off the superstar merry-go-round and freeing up some time to get to know herself. So she resisted the irresistible and forged ahead with the new project.

She had never learned to cook and knew nothing about food, so she consulted those who had and did. With painstaking determination, she tracked down the people who could produce what she wanted. No food was to be prepared on the premises, but neither was it to be delivered in tubs or buckets. There was no plastic allowed, because she knew what happened to the taste of any food that came into prolonged contact with it. The only exception was the takeaway cutlery, for which she could find no affordable alternative. The food was stored and displayed in glass and pottery and kept there until it was sold on plates or in cardboard containers. He said she ought to call it No Plastic and compromise on the sandwich ban. He couldn't see what was wrong with sandwiches anyway. He liked them. But he supported her wholeheartedly, and when she was run off her feet he took over some of the donkey work, like supervising the decorators and trudging through the endless volumes of health and safety regulations.

The first few weeks were touch and go. There were teething problems with some of the suppliers and a couple of the young people she employed were all fingers and thumbs and would have been better suited to working on a construction site. Another one couldn't grasp the concept of lunch-sized portions and created havoc with both the balance of quantities and with the future expectations of customers. Of which, initially at least, there weren't very many. No Sandwiches was, as he had pointed out, based on nothing more scientific than her own personal tastes, and for a while it looked as though she might have made a dreadful error of judgement. She was alone in her eccentric preferences. Everyone else was clearly quite happy with sandwiches, and her attempt to rock the boat was a disastrous waste of money and effort.

It was her old industry that came to her rescue. Twenty years' worth of business acquaintances don't go away overnight, and she was still getting dozens of calls and emails every day. She told them all what she was doing now, and some of them came to check it out and found that they liked it. There was no problem getting a table whenever they came in. The food was excellent and the place was quiet, and this was a combination that people in publishing valued. Soon the customers were arriving, and not just any customers, but the right kind of customers. Word began to get around. No Sandwiches was the new 'in' place to eat lunch. She was up and running again, and what's more, it was just the beginning.

{12}

After that warning from the doctor he took to cycling, and over the summer he came up this road nearly every day on his way to Parliament Fields and the Heath. But he has never walked these streets at night before. Not any further than that Japanese restaurant. He has the sense again of going home, and of home being an uncomfortable and challenging place, but one, nevertheless, where he must go. But it isn't easy. All his senses are on red-raw alert, and he knows that in some way he is ignoring the warnings of the gods and striding on to challenge them.

And why not? What else is left for him to do, now that his wife has been transformed into a hag? It feels like their realm, this sudden transmogrification. She left him a beautiful woman and has returned to him a crone. He always knew. She never deceived him about this.

And yet, somehow, he didn't know. For all his powers of imagination, he has never envisaged her as she appeared to him that evening. He has always believed what his eyes told him, not his mind. He has been entrapped by her womanly arts, like a spider in the jaws of its deadly mate. His train of thought offers him a nice bone of resentment to gnaw on, but he stops it there anyway. It is nonsense. They didn't come together on Bondi Beach or at a Hollywood meat market. They met as mature adults. Their relationship is not based upon such superficialities, but on mutual respect. So why should it matter? Why should the colour of her hair make a difference?

It does.

He passes a corner pub. A man and a woman burst out of it, laughing, ducking beneath the rain. The man is wearing a linen jacket, which flies apart as he walks and shows the leanness of his body beneath a soft, white shirt. He has a set of car keys in his hand. The woman is raven-haired, wrapped in a long tweed coat. She takes his arm, tripping along beside him, hurrying from the rain, still laughing. For an instant the man's eyes catch his, and the look in them says, *Aren't you envious, mate.*

As he walks on he understands that he has invented it, this silent exchange, and he sees why he has. It has provided him with the answer to his question. Because he is proud to be seen with her. She draws attention for all kinds of reasons, but her looks are high on the list of them. She has a great body for a woman of her age. She doesn't dress provocatively but she has a unique sense of style; a casual elegance which turns heads. But who will look at her now? He tries to remember other grey-haired women in their circle of friends and acquaintances. He spends some time thinking about this, and lights a cigarette to help him concentrate. Are there any? He can't think of any. Does that mean that there aren't any or that the ones there are have made no impression upon him?

So is that it? Is that the basis of their relationship? The whole fifteen years' worth? The fact that she looks good on his arm?

The rain is coming down harder. He needs to get out of it but he daren't go into a pub. So he ducks into the next takeaway he passes and orders a doner kebab and a black coffee. There are no tables, but there is a ledge running along one wall with stools pushed under it, so he eats there. The kebab is greasy and slimy with mayonnaise and some kind of translucent red goo. He isn't hungry anyway, and neither the smells nor the tastes produce the appetite he knows he ought to have. But eating the food and drinking the soapy coffee is the price of shelter from the rain, so he takes as much time over it as he can.

He is still severely rattled. His heart is going at an alarming rate. He feels its uneven rhythm in his throat, as unwelcome as a neighbour learning the drums and as difficult to ignore. He tries to listen to the conversations going on behind him at the counter, but his internal dialogue is too demanding and soon reclaims his attention.

He can't accept the conclusion he has reached about the nature of the relationship because to do so would be to accept an image of himself that he finds unpalatable. If his interest in her is solely based upon the augmentation of his ego, then he has become the kind of man he despises, concerned only with attracting admiration and envy. He will not accept that judgement upon himself. He declares, silently, that he loves her whatever she looks like, but when the image of her white hair returns to his mind he recoils as strongly as ever.

He asks for water and soaks a wad of paper napkins, cleans his hands and face. He drops the soggy mess into the remains of his food and puts the lot into a bin beside the door. Outside, the rain has slackened. He stands for a moment, looking in both directions. He wants to go back to the house and be comfortable and dry, but he finds he can't. He needs to keep digging until he comes to the bottom of this, and finds the real reason for his reaction to what she has done. And in a strange way, this realisation gives him new heart. It reminds him of his trade and why it has chosen him. He has never gone for the easy option of side-stepping life's challenges and turning on the television. He has always squared up to them and worked to dissect them, and define their nature, and present his findings to anyone with courage enough to read them. That, for him, is the art of poetry.

As he turns his steps towards the north again he takes out his cigarettes, but decides against smoking one and puts them back in his coat pocket. His heart is still frightening him, thudding away; the grim reaper limping behind like a teasing child. So strongly does this image strike him that he turns abruptly in the empty street and yells, 'Fuck off!'

And he sees in himself the archetype of the Irish down-and-out in London, beyond the point of redemption, screaming at ghosts. And he sees, in the same moment, that he really might have ended up like that if it hadn't been for her.

{13}

She pulls up his number on her mobile phone, but she doesn't ring it. He has walked out because he doesn't want to talk to her. He doesn't want to discuss this thing she has done. If she phones he might not answer, and if he does answer, what will she say? There is no point in asking him to come home, because if he wanted to do that he would do it. So would she express her anger at him? Call him a superficial bastard? Tell him he can't handle the truth? Isn't that why she fell in love with him in the first place, precisely because he could handle the truth? Look it in the eye, call it by its real name, reveal it to the world in his poetry?

Could it be that he has changed? Lately he hasn't been working, or at least, he hasn't been working on his own writing, and she knows it bothers him. It occurs to her that perhaps he has lost it; that ability to see beneath the surface of things. And if he has, how does that affect the way she feels about him? Would she still love him if he gave it up? Threw in the towel? Stated that he'd had enough of looking into the underworld and intended to opt for the easy life?

She looks at her phone. The screen has gone dark but she knows his number is still there, waiting to be dialled. The obvious thing to do is apologise for doing this to him. She ought to have asked him first, or at the very least given him some warning. She could tell him it was a joke, or a test; in either case a mistake. She could promise to go to the hairdresser's first thing in the morning and get them to put it back the way it was.

She clears the screen on her phone and stands up, pours the sickly-sweet remains of the coffee into the sink. She rinses the cup and begins opening cupboard doors again, vaguely aware that what she needs is proper food. But the phone still draws her and she wonders whether it's another kind of nourishment she is looking for. She has good friends, several of them, in for the long haul. They have nursed her though bumps and fractures in relationships, and she has done the same for them. She knows she has their support through thick and thin. But she can anticipate their responses too well. They will approve her behaviour and condemn his, and what is happening here is somehow more complex than that. This is a vital step on her journey, and her instinct is to face it squarely, and on her own.

She thinks about the two women who showed her around the New York projects she went over there to see.

One was her age, the other a few years older. Neither of them dyed their hair. And although the subject never arose in conversations, it was their example that gave her the strength to carry out her resolve. It wasn't a sudden decision, after all, but something she had been approaching for a long, long time.

He has cleared up the kitchen but not the living room, which she finds littered with newspapers and coffee cups and the empty packets from trail mix and popcorn. There are DVDs and their brittle cases all around the TV, and there is a snug, cushioned hollow in the centre of the sofa like a nest that some large, heavy beast has made. Is it evidence for her new hypothesis? Are these the signs of a man in a state of defeat, sinking gradually into resignation and torpor?

But in his study she finds comfort. It is a small room, which was her conservatory in a previous life, and it hordes his various smells. The predominant one is of stale cigarette ends, but there are undertones of musk and methane and licorice, merging into a combination that is unique to him. The desk is a chaos of notes and print-outs, but the rest of the room is tidy. The books on their custom-made shelves are lined up in precise order of height, the printer paper and spare cartridges are neatly stacked, and the unruly snarl of computer wires that tangle beneath her own desk are here disciplined into thick, neat bundles with cable ties. It is all in order and it reassures her. He has not disappeared from her life. He will come back here.

She carries her bag up to the bedroom and drops it at the foot of the bed. She needs to keep moving. She is afraid that if she keeps still for too long she will suffocate. It is not a new fear. She has always had it, and it is one of the reasons she chose the career she did. Being on her own never suited her. She has always been lost without someone around to reassure her that she still exists.

It is one of the first things that arose when she entered therapy. Her analyst seldom made suggestions, preferring to allow talk and reflection to bring clients to their own solutions. But this client did not spend time in reflection, and he had to suggest to her that she did; that she build some downtime into her life and spend it on her own.

She saw the wisdom in this but she never did get around to doing it. On the few evenings when she was not out at a party or a dinner she met friends and went to the theatre or the cinema, and on the even rarer occasions when she was alone in the house she invariably used the time to catch up with more distant family and friends on the phone. She thinks of this again now. She could ring someone just for a chat – she needn't even go into her own situation, but just listen and maybe get her mind back into gear for the other things that are happening in her life. But again she resists going beyond herself for help.

She turns on the bedside radio so that she will have voices to listen to, and begins to unpack.

Years of publicity tours have taught her to be a well-organised traveller. She has all her washing in a cotton bag, separated by a section of her case from the clean things. She empties the bag into the laundry basket and drops it in on top, then begins to unpack the rest. She puts her underwear into its drawer, then opens the wardrobe to hang up her dresses and jeans. But something that is lurking in there takes her breath away and she freezes, an empty hanger in her hand.

She had thought that his leaving like that had brought her to the depths of humiliation, but she sees now that there is still further to go. The garment that she sees there pushes her beyond humiliation and into the realms of degradation. It is a short black linen skirt, entirely innocuous. If they were both knocked over by a bus the next day they need have not the slightest fear that their executors would find anything here that revealed any details of their sexual life together. They didn't use sex toys or blue movies. They were a respectable middle-class couple with no dirty secrets. But that skirt, for her, told its own story.

{14}

He was amazed by her interest in him, and at the same time, deeply mistrustful of it. He had a girlfriend of a sort at the time, but both of them knew the relationship was going nowhere and it wasn't hard for him to extricate himself from it. He took great care that this new flame should never see where he lived, in a dingy ex-council flat that he shared with a constant turnover of Irish students and labourers and musicians, all passing through. By day he worked on his poems in one of several favourite libraries throughout the city, and by night he either joined his flatmates on their pub crawls or stayed at home and wrestled with demons. He lived on social security, occasionally supplemented by very small advances, paltry payments from poetry journals or competition winnings. Some months his postage expenditure was higher than his income from poetry. Every year he applied for every award, grant and bursary that was going. Once he got a thousand pounds from the Society of

Authors by forging a doctor's note saying he was suffering from chronic fatigue syndrome and unable to write. The travel grant from the Arts Council that enabled him to go to Australia just about covered his return flight and the barest of hostel accommodation, but it was the largest cheque he had ever received in his life.

So was that why he loved her? Because she had lifted him not only out of obscurity but out of poverty as well? How could there be any possibility of real love developing when the relationship had begun on such an unequal footing? When he had entered it carrying such an enormous debt of gratitude?

He took a long drag from his cigarette, surprised to discover that he had lit one after all, with absolutely no awareness that he was doing it. The gods again. Hades in secret governance of his actions. Was there ever such a thing as free will?

But she loved him. For her own reasons she needed him as much as he needed her. She needed his vision of the world; his willingness to face the blood and guts of existence and grapple with their meaning, and to show her the way to do it, too. She said he was her prince, come to rescue her from the saccharine dream of her media existence. She needed him to help her move forward into a new way of being. Money was worthless when life was meaningless. And so the long talks they had, the walks on the heath, the weekend trips to Ireland and Wales to breathe mountain air or sail inshore waters, these were his repayments to her, and were of equal value to what she did for him.

The playing field was level.

{15}

She was forty-one when they met. She'd had plenty of lovers before, but with him she discovered a passion she had never experienced. She believed it was because of their intrinsic compatibility, and that she had finally met her soulmate. Her analyst agreed, but a straight-talking American author she went on tour with told her it was common among women of her age to feel like that. She said the passion was caused by the body going all out for a last shot at reproduction before the menopause set in.

She chose to believe the first interpretation, but a few years later she was forced to reconsider. He was tolerant of the symptoms of her menopause, although he said they gave him strange dreams; of salamanders; of being boiled alive in a cannibal's cauldron; of sleeping in a tent that had caught fire. He was tolerant, too, of her waning desire, and they talked endlessly about sex and the significance of it in relationships, and for humankind as a whole, and about the different attitudes men and women have towards it. They talked about the sublimation of it as well, and about the potential of unexpended sexual energy as a creative or motivational force. They experimented with tantric practices but discovered, after a few weeks, that they took up more time and stamina than either of them was willing to expend. So they tried a period of celibacy, just to see what would happen.

It bothered him a lot less than it bothered her, or at least, that's the way it seemed to her. She didn't feel much in the way of desire, and she didn't miss the physical act at all, but she couldn't bear it that he didn't appear to miss it either. She had sleepless nights, terrified that he had found, or soon would find, someone else to sleep with. She felt less than human, and that her power in the relationship had evaporated. And so it was that she came up with the idea, and bought the little black skirt to try it out. She put it on one night, along with one of his white shirts and the tie he had bought for a prize-giving dinner. Their celibacy came to a sudden and dramatic end.

{16}

He is thinking about sex as well, but not about the schoolgirl outfit. Every twenty seconds, was it? No. Minutes, surely. Every twenty minutes throughout the day, that was how often men were supposed to think about sex.

But he isn't sure whether this way of thinking about sex really counts. He has an image in his mind of a man who masturbates so frequently that he has no fertile seed left for procreation. The man is himself, but the image does not relate to his sexual proclivities. It refers to his literary ones.

He is thinking again about *The Turf Shed*, and he is thinking about *Salamander*, the volume that followed it four years later. Between them they sold more copies than his other four collections put together, but it didn't necessarily mean they were better. They sold because of what she had done for him, because he was as close to being in the public eye as a poet could hope to be, and because his presence in the media was consistently maintained.

But the things that have brought him success have also sucked the lifeblood from his poetry. He spends a lot of time away from home, teaching courses, attending conferences, giving readings at schools and libraries and colleges. And when he does get a decent stretch of time in London something always comes along and claims it. There are the reviews, which pop up at irregular intervals, and from time to time he gets asked for an article on the contemporary scene or a retrospective overview of some dead poet's work. Or someone will ask him for a contribution to a charitable publication for Amnesty or UNICEF, or to give an opinion on something or other for the BBC, or to judge a competition. And then there are the weekends with influential people in their country retreats, the publishers' parties, and the launches of other people's books; all of it necessary to keep his name and his face in the places where they need to be seen, but all of it drawn from the same pool of energy and time as his writing.

Turf Shed and *Salamander* are fine. They are good. Their sales figures must mean something. The sequence of love poems in *Salamander* is always being talked about because it celebrates the older woman in her passage through menopause. 'Taj Mahal' and one or two other poems from the series pop up regularly in round-ups and on *Poetry Please* on Radio 4, requested by the kind of person who wouldn't have understood a word of his earlier work. His better work. His real work.

He reaches for his cigarettes, stops to light one, walks on through the damp night, mist and smoke mingling now in his exhaled breath. The rain has stopped but it is getting colder. He wishes he had picked up a hat on his way out of the house.

He dislikes the thought of being highbrow but he

equally dislikes the idea that he is being read by suburban housewives behind net curtains who listen to bloody *Poetry Please*. He has not yet stooped to the level of being included on school curriculae, but his poems have been used for the unseen sections of secondary school exams, both in Ireland and the UK. Does he mean 'stooped' or does he mean 'risen'? Suddenly he realises that he is fretting over inconsequential things. Good or bad, read or unread, his published poems are gone. They are making their own way in the world. And his worry about them is neurotic, and covering a far greater problem which he is unwilling to face. He is the masturbating man who has squandered his seed in pursuit of instant gratification, mindless of its real purpose. He is not writing. He has no energy left for it. And a person who does not write poetry has no right to call himself a poet.

It is not the first time he has had this thought. It was, for much of his life, at the heart of his philosophy. He may have even been heard to talk about it in public. Lines on a page are not poetry, no matter what kind of pretty shapes they make, unless there is a true poetic thought contained within them. Poems are not little stories or slices of life. They are not prayers or descriptive passages or songs that have lost their tunes. The job of a poet is to reveal an idea or an observation or an insight that can be described in no other way. It is to forge a bridge with words that can bypass the cumbersome and limited workings of the conscious mind and speak directly from writer to reader; from soul to soul. A poem that works takes the breath away; a poem that works creates a holy shiver which is the closest thing to spiritual rapture that most people will ever experience.

He sees it now, the reason that he is not writing; the weakness in *Turf Shed* and *Salamander* and the poems for Amnesty and UNICEF, and the ones he has written on commission to fill a blank space in an arty journal, and all the snatches and fragments, the once-and-twice drafted pieces piled up in his desk drawers. They are poor imitations. The craft is still there but the substance is not. These poems, even the best of them, are made from pine instead of oak; plastic instead of bronze. They look good at a glance, but there is no weight to them. He sees now that he has departed from his core beliefs and become what his younger self so much despised. He is a sham, a publicist's creation, a poet in name only, a media tart.

At the gates to the park he pauses. Go back or go on? Not back, anyway, not yet. Not back to that. Is she to blame for all this? Has she spiked his bloody bite-sized goat's cheese tartlets? Mickey-Finned his Amé?

But if she did, if she is the perpetrator, then he has been the willing victim. He is ambushed by a sudden wave of love for her, then recalls what she has done to herself. The stark memory diverts the wave but does not stem it. He finds that it is still there, underground, that same feeling that has surprised him again and again throughout the years he has known her. It is a kind of love he stopped believing in when his first teenage relationship bit the dust, and he does not believe in it now. But it is there, undeniably, and if it isn't of his making, then whose? He looks into the heath. It has great swathes of darkness strewn across it. Right under London's nose it is a secret place, alive with heroes and gods. He senses their proximity and sees that his confirmed rationality is as blind as his mother's Catholic faith and just as much of an excuse for lazy thinking. It is an idiot's trick to proclaim, as he often does, that there are more things on heaven and earth, and then to close his mind resolutely against them.

His heart rattles on, an erratic intro to some racy dance tune. He takes out his cigarettes again. He knows they will kill him but he wants just one more, for the level part of the path before it begins to climb. Because he has decided to go in. It is a foolhardy thing to do. The heath is dangerous at night. But it is the closest he can get tonight to home, and there is something waiting for him in there.

{17}

All of a sudden, No Sandwiches was trendy. It got rave write-ups in *Time Out* and two of the broadsheet weekend supplements ran features on it. Soon the place was packed to capacity from the time it opened in the morning until the time it closed. The 'in' crowd moved on to the next wonderful discovery, but their work had been done. In eighteen months the café had paid back its initial capital costs and was in the black. So she promoted her most reliable staff member to the position of branch manager and diverted her energy into opening a second No Sandwiches in Bloomsbury. A year later she opened a third one in Ealing. Her original small suppliers could not meet the increased demand, so she took on additional ones rather than being tempted into the more profitable but ultimately less satisfactory option of approaching bigger commercial kitchens.

Branches four and five opened. People began to approach her looking for franchises. She declined, fearful of falling standards. Instead she upped the ante and began to introduce organic alternatives into the operation. This met with such success that by the time she opened branch six she had decided to make all her cafés completely organic. There was a six-month wobble as the customer base rearranged itself in adjustment to the inevitable price hike, but then it settled down and No Sandwiches forged ahead again.

Despite her change of profession, the parties and book launches and weekend invitations didn't go away. She was still on the invitation lists of all her old contacts, and no one seemed to mind that she was no longer in the trade. Besides, he was on many of those lists as well, and he had not changed his trade. So she still mixed with the old set and kept up with who was in and who was out and who was up-and-coming. And time after time at these gatherings, people who knew of her connection to No Sandwiches asked her why she didn't extend her operations and open a proper restaurant. There was always a need for new places, they said, where publishers and agents could take their authors or have small, intimate dinner parties in peace and quiet. Initially she ignored these enquiries. She had her hands full with the six branches and she had, for the first time in years, succeeded in getting a few evenings a month at home. She was learning to cook and enjoying it, all the more so since she had become so interested in organic and local food. He liked it, too, that she was at home more, and they ate meals together and talked and watched TV like ordinary people.

But as time went by the novelty of that wore off. He was often away, and at those times the long evenings at home were a torment for her. She would almost always find an excuse to go out rather than stay in on her own, still not ready to follow her analyst's advice and take time for reflection or meditation. And what she liked even less was that, when he was around, he began to take her for granted, and headed off to his study to catch up on some work or, even more infuriatingly, went to bed early with a book.

So she began to consider the possibilities and came up with an interesting idea. And she was still at the stage of considering it when an opportunity arose that was tailor-made for the new venture. One of the buildings she was renting came up for sale. It was the Bloomsbury branch, one of the first to open, and by far the most successful. It was a beautiful building, with a cut-stone face and an interior that went back and back from the street, and two upper storeys of offices, all being vacated in advance of the sale. She met with her accountant, who arranged a business mortgage with absurd ease, and put in an initial offer.

It caused the first real row in all the years they had been together. It wasn't that they never disagreed, but that the things they disagreed about were generally trivial and soon forgotten. This was different. He said she was power-hungry and neurotic, and that she would work herself into an early grave if she didn't learn to let go and relax. They had only just carved out a bit of time together and now she was planning to work in the evenings as well as during the day.

'What's the point in me being here,' she said, 'when you go to bed at nine o'clock?'

'Well, why don't you join me?' he said. 'It's one of life's greatest pleasures, lying in bed and reading.'

'I read enough books to last me a lifetime when I was in publicity,' she said. 'One of life's great pleasures for me is not having to read.'

'Well, what about poetry?' he said. 'You told me the first time we met that you loved poetry but you never had time to read it. Now you have time.'

His words hit a nerve and she lashed out, irrationally. 'Well, why don't you bloody well write some, then? What do you do in that study all day anyway, apart from smoking yourself to death?'

He rose to his feet. The TV remote was in his hand and he hurled it to the floor, creating a small explosion of batteries and plastic shards.

'Is that what you want?' he said. 'Your own private scribe beavering away in the back room, producing volumes of adoring verse?'

'Don't be ridiculous. I don't care what you write about.'

'I've told you a thousand times,' he said. 'It doesn't work like that. It isn't something you can turn on and off like a radio. I can't sit down in front of a blank piece of paper and come up with a poem.'

She bent to pick up a battery that had come to rest against her foot. He went on, 'In any case, the whole idea is egregious. A private club, exclusive to the book industry and all its slimy parasites. What are you going to call this one? No Riffraff?'

There was an instant when they might both have laughed and let it drop, but neither of them did, and the opportunity passed.

'And which are you?' she said. 'Industry or parasite?'

When he didn't answer, she did it for him. 'Oh, I'm sorry. You're neither. You're a poet, and therefore superior. In this world but not of it. Is that the way?'

He kicked the eviscerated remote and walked out of the house.

{18}

It is the only other time he has done it. On that occasion he did not prevent his feet from carrying him to his local. He spent the whole evening on a high stool telling the barman, and anyone else who would listen, that he was married to Maggie Thatcher; a woman who only needed three hours' sleep a night and was a jumped-up shopkeeper. He railed against the economic system, the publishing fraternity, the media, the organic sector. He scoffed chicken-flavoured crisps and pork scratchings, both of which he detested, just to prove his street credentials. He bought Woodbines and smoked them, and picked bitter tobacco strands from between his teeth. He drank pints of stout all evening, even though they never kept it cold enough in that pub and had no idea how to pull it anyway. Closing time found him reverting to his roots and expounding the evils of Catholicism and quoting from his first publication, *The Blue Virgin*. Out on the street it took him a while to remember where he was and how to get home, but he found his way and found his key and found, in the end, the hole it was meant to fit into.

She was waiting up for him in the living room but he went straight past and up the stairs and emptied his bladder, which seemed to take an hour, and then collapsed on top of the bed in the spare room. When he woke in the morning she had already gone out to work.

His breakout took him to Ireland, where he spent a few weeks in Dublin, renewing old acquaintances and reminding the organisers of courses and festivals and radio programs of his existence. Then he visited the family home in Tipperary, which his older brother had inherited and had, by then, turned into a health spa. The house had been gutted and extended and dry-lined. In its new incarnation it consisted of a dining hall, a huge yoga room, treatment and massage rooms and a little suite of offices. The courtyard had been rebuilt, tastefully, and held the guest accommodation and the kitchens. His brother had given up the drink and the inmates were all on detox programs, so he went on his own to the pub in the village, where he discovered his fame had travelled ahead of him. He was welcomed as a favourite son and not allowed to put his hand in his pocket all evening.

He slept in a little boxroom in the attic of the house and derived a certain sense of schadenfreude from the discovery that it was heaving with rats. It gave him an idea for a poem and he chewed on it for a while before he went to sleep, but in the morning its soul had vanished, leaving nothing but a thin, desiccated corpse.

He stayed in the house for three days, despite his brother's obvious discomfort. He did not belong in those incensed surroundings. His presence disturbed the hallowed atmosphere. So he made himself scarce during the hours of daylight, and if the house reawakened none of the numinous experiences of youth, then at least the land did. His brother had let it to a neighbouring farmer, with organic conditions attached in keeping with the holy principles of the spa. Clean sheep and shiny cattle grazed the parkland.

The trees in the woods were untouched. They were still as he remembered them. He got up close and down close. He felt the brown soil and the black leaf mould, ran his fingers over rough bark and smooth bark, smelled the bruised leaves underfoot. The first day was blustery and showery. Rain followed sunshine followed rain. He could stand beneath the gloom of heavy cloud and see a nearby hill or copse shining in brilliant light. He could stand in full sun and see the same places dim beneath a blue-green mist. Rainbows blazed into absurd and impossible existence, then faded and died. Across the valley he watched rain fall in silver stripes against the hill.

He remembered games: soldiers and spies and cowboys. The Irish rebel army lying in wait for the Black and Tans. Urgent messages that had to be delivered against impossible odds. He was suddenly back there, scrambling down gullies, darting from cover to cover, leaping over rocks and streams and fallen branches. Until he turned his ankle and remembered himself, and saw himself for what he was: a revenant, plundering the imagination of a child long gone.

He walked across the fields to the village and had lunch – a sandwich – in the pub. Afterwards he returned to the farm and looked for trout to tickle in the stream. There were none, so he spent the afternoon constructing a dam instead which, as the light began to fade, he bombed with massive rocks. He returned to the house and slipped in by a side door, so as not to terrify the clientele with his happy, wet, muddy presence.

Initially, their communications were sparse, brief, cold. But over the six weeks that he stayed away, they defrosted and became longer. She kept him abreast of developments in her new enterprise, and if he never came around to the idea, he did at least learn to accept it. She was who she was and he was not going to change her. In spite of that, or maybe because of it, he loved her and missed her more with every day that passed. And in any event, he knew he couldn't go on the way he was going. He had to pull himself together. His body was rebelling against his abuse of it, and the doctor's warnings bellowed inside his head like the voice of the Old Testament God.

Finally he bit the bullet, swore off the drink again, and returned to his home and to his love.

{19}

He had never suggested that he was leaving her, but his absence had still frightened her. She rejected the advice of both her analyst and her friends, all of whom suggested that she use the time and space to stand back and take stock of herself and her situation. She could not do that. She could not bear a single evening in the empty house. So instead she revved herself up into top gear and drove her new project forward. First she upped the offer on the Bloomsbury premises to a level that she was sure would be accepted. Then she promoted the manager of the first No Sandwiches, who knew the business inside out, to a new position of overall supervisor for the whole chain. Freed from that responsibility, she browbeat estate agents and solicitors to close the Bloomsbury deal and push it through at top speed, engaged a top firm of architects to draw up plans, and bribed a reputable firm of builders with cash incentives to be ready to move in and start work the moment contracts were exchanged. Then she began to head-hunt. She wanted the best chefs and managers and kitchen and waiting staff, and she didn't care where she got them or how much she had to pay them. Inside a fortnight, she had a full complement of staff lined up and waiting for the word to come on board.

In the evenings, no matter how exhausted she was, she put on her face and her party clothes and went out. She went to everything that was worth going to, invited or not. Sometimes she went to two, or even three parties in one night. She used her years of experience to her advantage, knowing which names to drop and precisely when, never initiating a conversation about her project but waiting until she was asked what she was doing. Then she spoke about it casually, and made sure to leave the impression that the new dining club was incredibly exclusive and desirable, and not at all easy to join. And of course, as she had known they would, they signed up in their droves.

{20}

Before the breakout he had been increasingly tempted to believe that he wasn't writing because he wasn't drinking. He had been a fairly heavy drinker since he was in college, and whereas he knew that trying to write poetry tanked up on drink produced disappointing results, a certain blood-alcohol level had constituted his steady state throughout his adult life. It was in its dips that he had generally written his best poems, when financial embarrassment or ill health prevented him from going out to the pub and he was confined to lonely rooms in accommodation that was invariably sub-standard. He remembers those restless, teeth-grinding hours and days. He paced and scribbled, so deep in thought that he reached the thin membrane where conscious and unconscious minds meet, and peered through it, and entered a creative euphoria which is better than anything that alcohol or drugs can manufacture. In those cold, damp rooms he left his body, with all its hungers and discomforts, behind him, and came to a place where his soul was truly at home.

He knows it is an absurd vanity, but he believes that writing poetry is what he was put on this earth to do. Only when he is writing, entering into that deep creative passion, does he feel whole. Nothing else completes him; not the warm and comfortable home he inhabits in Islington, with its expensive hand-printed throws and its beds that masquerade as sofas; not the admiration of others; not the physical satisfactions of good food or good sex. But he can no longer find that perfect state of being within himself. It is the only thing lacking in an otherwise perfect life, but it is essential for him to find it if he is ever going to regain his self-respect.

Which is not the same thing as confidence, not at all. Confidence he has in abundance; in his relationship and in his dealings with the outer world. It is a thing he lacked as a child, throughout his adolescence and well into his adult life. He does not deny that she has been largely responsible for helping him to attain it, and he is grateful to her for that. Confidence is important in life, but it is no substitute for self-respect.

He didn't find his soul's home in the Dublin bars or in the village pub or in the naggin of whiskey he took back with him most nights to tide him through the darkness. He didn't find it either in the old house or in the childhood games or in the smells and sounds of the woodlands or the unlikely rainbows arcing across the Irish sky. Nor did he find it in the agonising climb back to dry land when he returned to Islington. He was assailed by petty irritations and sudden hot rages, most of which he successfully hid from her. Or perhaps he didn't. He remembers that they gave up sex for a while, until she appeared one day in that schoolgirl get-up. He had never gone in for bedroom games and it unnerved him, but he was too vulnerable – they both were – for him to tell her to take it off. And he found that he soon came to like it, not so much because of the clothes, but because of who or what she became when she was wearing them.

{21}

It took another six months for the renovation work to be finished, but when the building was ready she was pleased with it. The kitchen was in the basement and the old chimney that ran up through the centre of the building had been converted into a dumb waiter to carry food to the floors above. On the ground floor was a bar and a series of open dining rooms of varying shapes and sizes. This was a public area and the tables could be booked by club members in the same way as any other restaurant. On the first and second floors, smaller dining rooms opened from large central landings with service and cloakroom areas. These were private rooms, and could be booked for special occasions for any number from two to twenty-five.

It took her most of the six months to come up with a suitable name for the place, but in the end she decided on Elsinore, because she felt it had the right blend of grandeur, bookishness and mystery. But at home he continued to refer to it as No Riffraff, and eventually she conceded and called it that, too. Initially it was not the roaring success she had expected. She had overlooked the caginess of the publishing industry. It wouldn't do for an agent to see a publisher wining and dining an author and all the key media people when one of that agent's equivalent authors had been refused the same treatment on the basis of finance restrictions. Similarly, newspaper arts editors and feature journalists had to be choosy about the invitations they accepted, but they didn't like to be seen to be so. A lot of the people who had sounded off most enthusiastically about what a wonderful idea it was never showed their faces in the place at all.

But luckily, the shortfall from the publishing industry was soon made up by people from other businesses once the word went out on the grapevine. Membership fees were nominal, unlike the more usual kinds of London clubs, and there were plenty of people who valued privacy and quiet and had the money to pay for it. All the same, from day one she had seen that it was a colossal mistake. Far from being another step forward on her way to self-discovery, it was a retrograde move. She had allowed herself to be sucked back into the same old circles, but now she had none of the thrill of the gambler's life. Instead she had taken on the role of perpetual hostess who, after the initial flurry of handshakes and introductions and mutual flattery, was relegated to the background to attend to their needs and excluded from all the most interesting bits.

'Meeting, greeting, seating and retreating,' she told him bitterly, when she finally confessed that he had been right all along.

'Instead of eating and bleating,' he said. 'Are you sure you'd rather be doing that?'

Sometimes she missed it, watching as she was from the sidelines, but no, she didn't want that old life back again. She had arrived, her analyst told her, at a classic midlife crisis. The task of the young adult is to provide for their family, if they have one, and to fulfil the ego's desire for recognition. It is about going out into the world and establishing oneself. It is about careers and achievements. Then comes midlife and everything changes. The outer trappings of life no longer serve the needs of the soul in its journey towards wholeness. New challenges with deeper meanings are needed.

She wasn't so sure about the details, but she had no doubt that the gist of it was true. A quantum leap was what she wanted, and she was ready to take it. The trouble was that she couldn't see either destination or direction. Her animus projection, which over the years and under the guidance of her analyst had been painstakingly withdrawn from the poet, had found no new target and appeared to have reverted to the depths of her unconscious mind. She asked her friends, her analyst and the I Ching what she should do. They all gave her the same answer.

Wait.

{22}

Where the path becomes steeper he tosses his cigarette away and leans into the traces. He always uses this hill as a warm-up. He calls it his pipe-opener.

His father kept a few horses on the farm but no ponies. The children did no riding at all until they were big enough to handle a horse, and then they were all, boys and girls, chucked up on a relatively quiet one and expected to get on with it. There were some terrible falls, usually followed by tantrums and rows, but every one of them learned to ride.

The horses were bred and broken on the farm. Some of them were sold on as yearlings, but most of them were kept back and trained on the farm and given a few runs in point-to-points or over hurdles before their value could be ascertained. They were exercised on the roads and around the farm, and the steepest hill on the place was where they were taken for their pipe-openers.

There were other horses about the place as well, from time to time; horses that were sick or had some bad habit or mental problem. Even his father couldn't fix them all. But he had a handy bag of tricks and people were always calling to the house looking for remedies and advice. It's a thing he regrets now, that all that knowledge died with his father and that no one in the family had enough of an interest to continue with the horse side of things. He would have liked to have done it himself, but it was clear from the beginning that he had no aptitude for it at all. He was such a bad rider that his father stopped asking him to do it, and he hardly ever went to the races with the rest of them. But some of them had been good riders – one of his sisters in particular. He has a memory of her riding a blue roan horse around and around their father, trampling a trough into the sodden ground. The horse moved with stiff, jerky strides, its head high and wild, its tail clamped down tight as though it feared something was going to attack it from behind. His father and his sister both spoke to it, a harmonious mantra intoned inside a muddy mandala of their own making. And the horse, as though hypnotised, slowly relaxed and dropped its head and lengthened its stride and lost its fear of attack.

He doesn't make it all the way up the hill before he needs to stop for breath. His heart is still racing but its rhythm is stronger now, as though it was just fidgety and needed something more strenuous to do. He walks on to where the path levels out and then he stops again. A few weeks ago he walked up here with her – quite late on a long summer's evening. There were some people on the grass with a fancy kite, all strings and streamers, and they had the long, long lines stretched between them and were trying to disentangle them. An hour later, when they walked back the same way, the kite people were still there, still winding strings and fiddling with knots. They looked bad-tempered and miserable, and he had laughed his head off as soon as he was out of earshot.

But now there is no one – just London in its orange veil spread out below him. He hates the lights and wishes someone would switch them off and give him back the stars. It might happen, in some not-too-far-distant energy-strapped future. He hopes so. He has never been afraid of the dark. As a child he often crossed the fields to the village in the dark to take a message to someone, or to collect some bits of shopping from his father when he got delayed in the pub. But this time, when he turns back towards the heath he finds that he is afraid. This is not the benign darkness of Tipperary, where the worst thing he might encounter is a badger out grubbing. This is Hampstead, notorious for its night-time dangers. He glances around him, half blinded by the city lights. What are those dangers, though? Who comes here at night? There were always stories of homosexuals – of politicians and other public figures compromised by being discovered cruising here. But surely not these days, when there are so many easier and safer ways for like-minded people to meet each other. In any event, he is no longer afraid of gay men. Fifteen years of middle-class London has cured him of his indoctrinated homophobia.

So who else is there to be afraid of? Thugs? Hoods? Highwaymen? Do lads still go out looking for 'a bit o' bovver' or its modern equivalent? Possibly. But what is there for them to prey upon if the good citizens of London town keep themselves and their wallets well away from the place at night? Or do they lie in wait for people like him? Idiots who have lost their way in the hustle and dazzle and have come here in search of the old gods?

He has walked this path a thousand times, sometimes with her, more often alone. He knows where it goes – in under the trees and up to the top, then down and around past the pools where the dawn swimmers come, summer and winter. He knows all the path's little tributaries, paved and unpaved, which wind through the more lonely parts of the huge park. He comes here to be alone with the earth and the sky and to sense the long, slow lives of the trees standing around him. It is not a wild place. He has been to wild places and sensed their magic, sometimes sinister, sometimes divine, but this patch of emptiness has long since been sucked dry of its power. It is a flea-bitten mongrel of a landscape, bled to the point of exhaustion by its parasites.

By day it is, anyway. But perhaps it comes alive at night, draws strength from the darkness, reveals forms of magic he has yet to encounter. He wants to go back, but he finds he has painted himself into a corner.

On the face of it he has four options. The first one is to visit the pub, but when he flips open his phone and checks the time he finds it is already too late. He will be lucky if he can find one in time for last orders, and even if he does, one drink will get him nowhere. So option two is to find a hotel, book in, then settle in to the residents' bar. He has a credit card and cash – he could do it, but he has enough self-respect left to dismiss it as a non-runner. It's the easy option, the get-out-of-jail-free card, and he despises himself for even considering it. He is not so far gone, yet.

So he is left with two possibilities. He thinks about her again and finds that the shock is finally being absorbed. This time there are no adrenalin spikes and he can view the remembered scene dispassionately. When he does, he sees it more clearly. The pantomime colours added to the scene by his imagination drop away and he sees her as she really is. Still herself – not a hag or a crone but a woman of fifty-six revealed in her true form. He is aware of his love for her, not as a charge that quickens his pulse but as the steady background current that is essential to his existence. He will not leave her, he is suddenly certain of that. But nor is he ready to go back. There is still something at the basis of his reaction that he has not found and identified.

It doesn't matter to him that he might be less attracted to her sexually. Sometimes he is tempted to blame sex for his creative decline – the literal as well as metaphorical spilling of his seed might be responsible for depleting his vital energy. He found their tantric experiments awkward and frustrating, but not so the celibate phase. He thinks of the schoolgirl outfit with the same mild sense of embarrassment that it produces when she puts it on. He knows that she devised the game to revive her own flagging sexual drive, but he wonders now whether there was more to it. Did she feel obliged to do it for his sake? Out of fear that he might look elsewhere if she didn't provide for his sexual needs? He is not in principle averse to prostitution, though his two experiences with it in his younger days left him feeling ashamed and far from satisfied. Nor is he immune to the attractions of other, usually younger women. But the idea that she should prostitute herself because of a misguided belief about his needs appals him. He ought to have told her that on the first occasion that she dressed up. He should have said he wasn't into that kind of thing. Instead he went along with it, to humour her. But it isn't such a big deal for him – hasn't been for years. He deplores the modern dogma that insists a strong sex drive is essential to life. He has spent large parts of his life sublimating his desires, sometimes out of choice and sometimes out of necessity. Either way, he finds it easier and easier as time goes on. If they never have sex again, he will still stay.

There is the other thing, the thing he finds does matter, about how her changed appearance will reflect upon him when they appear in public together. He recognises the feeling for what it is – an absurd relic of male pride, a throwback to primitive displays of chest-thumping and strutting. The understanding doesn't make the feeling go away, but it does show him a goal towards which he can begin to work.

But it's still not all. There is something else that he has not put his finger on. The shock has passed but there is something which profoundly disturbs him. His fear is that if he goes back to the house now he will pour oil on troubled waters; make his apologies and adjustments; settle back into comfortable patterns without ever discovering what the thing is. Looking into the darkness of the wooded patch ahead, he knows that he is as close to that elusive state of 'home' as he has been for years. Much as he fears what is in there, he can't return until he has investigated it.

{23}

She wanted, she came to understand, to do something for someone else. Throughout her working life she had crossed the street to avoid *Big Issue* vendors or beggars with dogs. She had looked straight through gaunt young people who approached her with hard-luck stories or outstretched hands. She often thought of setting up some charitable standing orders but she never found the time to read the ads in the papers, and chuggers were the only people in the world whom she permitted herself to swear at.

By the time she arrived at this new juncture in her life, gifts of money were no longer the answer. It was too easy and it would not fulfil the deeper need that emerged. She wanted full-scale engagement in something that would make a difference to society, and she set about searching for it with her customary vigour.

She spent hours, mostly after midnight, searching the internet for volunteering opportunities. Locally there were adult literacy programs, hostels for the homeless, charity shops, environmental groups and societies for the disabled and the elderly. Further afield, there were more possibilities. She was amazed to discover that there were schemes for 'midlife gap years', which could be spent counting tigers or saving bats or monitoring the health of coral reefs. You could teach English practically anywhere in the world – to Tibetan refugees in Ladhakh, to street children in Brazil – or you could help to build houses or bridges or schools practically anywhere in the world, all provided that you had the time to spare and the money to pay. It interested her to discover that she could find no opportunities for overseas volunteering that didn't require her to pay for the privilege. This rocked her back on her heels a bit – not because she couldn't afford it, but because it revealed how widespread her particular condition must be. It appeared that the midlife crisis was as inevitable as the knitting of the cranial sutures and the onset of puberty; a fact that was one-up for her analyst and one in the eye for her. She had thought herself unique, and that her sudden desire to give something back to the world was evidence of progress on her path to self-discovery, and of the incredible nobility and generosity of that newly revealed self. But the more she trawled the internet the more convinced she became that this particular phenomenon arose not so much from an innate desire for individuation as from middle-class boredom and guilt.

She soon came to realise that a gap year was not what she

wanted, and nor was a few hours a week of hands-on volunteering in London. She had skills, developed over thirty years, and he agreed that there must be a way in which they could be used that would suit her needs as well as the needs of others. But for a long time, that was as far as they could get. If there was a project that fitted the bill, she wasn't able to find it on the internet.

She had no alternative but to take the advice of her analyst and of her friends, and wait. She remembered how Elsinore had come about – the availability of the building coinciding with her development of the idea – and she put her faith in the same thing happening again when the time was right. In the meantime, she gave some attention to other, more subtle changes that were happening in her life.

Her body was the first concern. As long as she had put the right things into it and onto it, it had always pretty much taken care of itself. Aside from the occasional walk across town, or with him on the heath, she took no exercise at all. Her nervous energy kept her weight down and her GP had always given her a clean bill of health. But now, post-menopause, all that was changing. She had to be more careful about what she ate. She began to skip lunch again, and it worked, or at least she stopped putting on weight. The trouble was, it wasn't just about weight anymore. Her body was changing. What fat she had was redistributing itself in ways she did not like at all. Her skin lost its translucent glow and began to sag. Her hands in particular upset her. Sometimes she caught sight of them, bony and wrinkled, and if she wasn't on guard she was struck by the impression that they belonged to somebody else. She bought into the promises of manufacturers and lathered herself with skin creams. She joined a gym in Bloomsbury, where she could nip out for forty minutes between lunch and high tea at Elsinore. It was good for her fitness and good for her state of mind, but it made no impression at all on her skin or the relentless slippage of her flesh. She couldn't cross-train her way back to youth.

Life was passing her by, and she was condemned to endless, boring days and evenings, manufacturing smiles at Elsinore. She was desperate to throw it all in and jump ship, but until there was some sign of another vessel, she couldn't do it.

{24}

He walks forward. The path enters the trees, but they are not quite as he remembers. They are sparser, for one thing, and they are mangy, half their leaves fallen and the remainder thin and limp. He can see both the sky and the lights of the city between them. It is a slight disappointment.

The path descends again, briefly, then climbs on, passing an empty bench on one side and a circle of them surrounding a tree on the other. There is another copse ahead, and this is the one he remembers; the one he has been expecting. It has more trees, closer together, and there is rough grass and undergrowth between them. There is a little dirt path as well, worn by the feet of walkers, which branches off to the left. He nearly always takes this one. It passes the remains of a painted cast-iron fence, long since fallen and partly submerged in weeds, which always has him wondering what it is doing there. Presumably all this was farmland once, commonage, perhaps. He always means to find out about the history of the heath, but as soon as he leaves it, he always forgets.

When the little path comes into view he hesitates. It leads into a deeper darkness and he can't see far along it. He suspects it is safer to stay on the tarmac, but he can't be sure, because that it presumably what the hoodlums will all be expecting. He laughs; surprises himself with the sound. If it's safety he's concerned about, what is he doing out here in the middle of the night? And where did that word appear from? Hoodlums. Or should it be hoodli? Hoodla?

It is raining again, but not heavily like before. It is a kind of rain that isn't common in London, so light that it's not much more than mist. It permeates clothes gradually but doesn't drench them. It doesn't send rivers down the neck, but gathers quietly in the hair and rolls down the face in warm drops, like tears. At home in Tipperary his neighbours would call it, or the day that brought it, 'soft'. It is Irish weather for an Irishman's journey.

He sets foot upon the path and experiences an immediate sense of rightness, or righteousness, or of something bordering on elation. This is it. This is the way. This path will help him to solve the riddle that so disturbs him. It is the soul's way home, to that lost place within him where integrity and poetry linger in chains like an imprisoned princess.

The path, so ordinary by day, is numinous by night. It is the realm of Hermes and Athene, of Pan and the púca. Above all, it is the tramping ground of Fionn and the Fianna, hunting their magical prey through the forest. This very hill might break open and reveal the golden halls of the sidhe, forever alive within it. A gentle, intermittent wind breathes among the branches. The dying leaves seethe, fall silent, seethe again. The sound is like lazy breakers on a calm shore. The name of the land he is in flits across his mind and is gone before he can catch it. But it is significant. He pauses to concentrate, to summon it back. There is the slightest of sounds behind him; the briefest rubbing-together of two hands, or the quick scratch of a soft brush on the hearth. There is barely time for him to become aware of it. There is no time at all for him to turn and look.

{25}

She gave up on her search for a better life and began to sleep more, going to bed when she came in from work instead of sitting up half the night in front of the computer. On some mornings she was amazed to find him waking her with coffee, instead of the other way round, and he was ridiculously pleased about it, as though she was a stubborn adversary who had finally conceded his point. But it frightened her. She believed that sleeping was a sign of illness or depression, that her body was betraying her and practising for that other, longer sleep. He told her she was being melodramatic, and that she had thirty years of lost sleep to catch up on. Her analyst agreed with him and told her to go with it, and to keep a close eye out for dreams.

She did have some, waking sometimes with a sense of urgency because something was going on that she needed to witness and record, but on those occasions when she could identify some strand of a dream, she was always convinced that it was meaningless, and was embarrassed to write it down. Then, one morning when he was away at a festival in Berlin, she had a dream so vivid and frightening that it woke her. She had killed several people and concealed them in her wardrobe, but it was impossible that they could stay hidden, and the police were at the door. The dream was so vivid that it took her a moment or two to realise that it wasn't actually happening, and the relief, when it came, was enormous. Still she didn't write it down, but she didn't forget it either. When she came home she opened her wardrobe, which was a vast affair, built along an entire wall of her bedroom. There were indeed corpses in there. The clothes were a clear reflection of the state of her life over the years she had worn them. There was nothing wrong with them, except that they were no longer her. She didn't know who it was that she had become, but she knew these clothes no longer represented her.

She ran her fingers along the tightly packed hangers and began, tentatively, to pick out some she no longer wore. Initially it was painful, facing the prospect of parting with them. They were like old selves, with their own particular history and memories. But the further she went, the easier it became, until, suddenly, a landslip occurred in her head. The careful thinning became a virtual clear-fell. The hangers rattled in the vacated space, a sound she hadn't heard since she first moved into the house. The bed disappeared beneath the growing heaps of discards. She moved on to the coats next, and then to the racks and drawers and shelves built in to the right-hand section. New heaps appeared on the floor, of bags and shoes and boots and belts and scarves.

An extraordinary energy flooded through her, mind, body and soul. She pulled her suitcases down from the top shelves, and when they were all stuffed full she pulled his down and filled them as well. There were still mountains of clothes and accessories out on the bed and floor. She sensed her nerve beginning to fail, and she ran downstairs for a roll of dustbin liners and stuffed everything into them, before she could change her mind.

When all the discards were safely out of sight, she looked carefully through the yard or so of remaining garments, huddled nervously in the left-hand corner. Each one got a measured inspection, but the one she lingered over longest was the little black skirt. It ought to go. It made her uneasy and belonged to a phase she wanted to leave behind. But she was afraid that she still needed it, or that he would miss it, and read a meaning into its absence that she didn't intend. Or perhaps, a meaning that she did.

She dreamed that she had been robbed by a mysterious older woman. In the morning, she booked a taxi while she drank her coffee. It came at ten, one of those large ones with a sliding door. The driver helped her to load up and took her to the Sue Ryder shop a few streets away. He helped her unload as well, and she tipped him a tenner. He was delighted, but she got the impression that the volunteers in the shop were not so pleased.

'It's all designer stuff,' she told them. 'It has all been dry-cleaned.'

They looked slightly less beleaguered when they heard this, and one of them said, 'It's very good of you. Thank you.'

She hung around for a couple of beats, expecting something else to happen, some act of closure or finality. There was none. She shrugged and smiled, slightly embarrassed, and left the shop. But as soon as she was on the street she realised she had forgotten about the suitcases, which she didn't intend to give away. She apologised and the same assistant, slightly disdainful, asked her if she'd like to come back for them or wait while they unpacked them, there and then. She knew how hard it would be to find the time to come back, so she said she'd wait, and while the volunteers rummaged around in the back room she wandered idly through the shop.

On the bric-a-brac shelves a small jug caught her eye. It was beautifully shaped with a delicate spout and a lovely round swell of belly. The glaze was a deep, rich, natural green. It didn't fit with anything in her kitchen, which was nouveau-minimalist – all black and white and stainless steel – but she couldn't quite bring herself to put it down, so she kept it in her hand as she moved on round the shop. There were shelves full of videos and a few DVDs, all cheaper than the cost of renting one. She picked out a couple that she thought he might like and tucked them under her arm.

The assistant returned with two of the cases. She looked a lot less disdainful now.

'Won't keep you much longer,' she said, returning to the back room.

There was nothing left to look at now except for the racks and bins of clothes, so she began, almost despite herself, to browse through them. Just out of curiosity, that was all. There was something mildly distasteful about touching things that strangers had worn, and the smell in the place was of an unspecific but distinctly human origin which the air-fresheners failed to disguise. But as she looked she began to forget about it, and became fascinated by the kinds of things that other people bought, presumably wore, and then passed on. Most of the clothes were hideous, but there were some interesting things among the trash. A white granddad shirt in some ultra-soft fabric, maybe cotton mixed with silk. A pair of straight black jeans, hardly worn, which looked well made. She had both these things in her hand when the assistant came out with another empty suitcase.

'Changing room is just there if you want to try anything on,' she said.

'Oh, no,' she said, thrusting the jeans back onto the rail as if they were toxic waste. She had no intention of wearing someone else's cast-offs. But when the volunteer disappeared again she found her attention returning to the jeans. Where was the harm in trying them on? She wasn't going to catch anything from them, and they might give her some clues about the new style she was looking for and how she might replace some of the things she had just brought in. The jeans, it turned out, fitted perfectly, and as she was inspecting herself in front of the mirror the woman came back again.

'They're perfect on you,' she said. 'You can have them if you want. The stuff you brought in is brilliant. It'll make a lot of money for us.'

'No, no,' she said again, but she knew, even then, that she was protesting too much.

'Where did it all come from, anyway?' the assistant asked. 'Has someone died?'

'No,' she said. 'It's all mine. I'm just having a clear-out. Nobody died.'

But it occurred to her that maybe she was wrong. Somebody had died, suffocated by Elsinore. And somebody else, a new and unknown being, was in the process of being born.

{26}

She left the Sue Ryder shop with the black jeans, the granddad shirt and a dusty-blue raw silk jacket with a Nehru collar. She put all the clothes on when she got home and liked what she saw in the mirror, and became aware again of that sense of energy released. At last, for no reason that she could see, her life was unstuck and moving again. Where to she didn't know, but for the moment at least she would keep going with the flow and see where she would wash up.

He was still in Berlin. The next morning she phoned No Riffraff and put the new maître d' in charge. As soon as the shops opened she dropped the Sue Ryder clothes into the drycleaner's and, with a soaring sense of liberation, set out to trawl through every charity shop between Upper Street and Seven Sisters Road. She didn't go nuts – she walked out of most of them empty-handed – but she did collect a few more things, and she exchanged them with the first lot in the drycleaner's on her way home. Back at the house she pottered around, restless and excited. She was used to having energy like this but not at all used to having nowhere to channel it. She checked in with the staff in Elsinore, then phoned an old friend and told her what she had done.

'It's feng shui,' the friend said. 'It's a guaranteed way to change your life and get out of a rut. You just wait and see what happens. You'll be amazed.'

She didn't believe a word of it, but her friend turned out to be right. Tectonic plates were shifting. She had seen nothing yet.

She had an appointment with her hairdresser on her way to work that afternoon. For years he had been trying to persuade her to cut it short and spiky and, still possessed by the changes sweeping through her life, she allowed him to do it. She was thrilled by the way it looked, and left work as soon as high tea was over, so as to be there when he arrived home from Berlin. She put on the granddad shirt and a short Bulgarian waistcoat, and some heavy black trousers in hemp or coarse cotton that she had not had dry-cleaned because it was clear they had never been worn. She was afraid that he would be dismissive and pull the rug out from under her feet, but he didn't. He held her at arms-length and looked her up and down and said, 'Hmm. That old Ralph Lauren trash again, isn't it?'

But she could tell he liked the new look. When he went upstairs to take a shower she told him to look in the wardrobe. He came haring back down and burst in upon her, clutching his head in both hands and saying, 'She's left me! What am I going to do? She's taken everything and left me!'

She laughed and he took her in a great bear hug and lifted her off her feet.

'Why?' she said. 'What are you so pleased about? Why should it matter so much?'

She asked him because she really didn't know, and she wanted to. He put her down and rubbed at her spiky hair and grinned. 'I have absolutely no idea,' he said.

But it was important. It was a thing of huge significance. That night they both discovered a new depth of passion for each other, and the little black skirt hung, unused and unwanted, in all that new, dark emptiness.

{27}

She should have put it out with the rest, she sees that now. She hasn't worn it since. She will never wear it again, either, because it is the image of a woman with grey hair posing as a schoolgirl which has brought her to this state of mortification. Not just how she would look now if she was to wear it, but of the lie it has been on all those other occasions. Because she has been grey since she met him, and it is only that simple chemical artifice that has stopped them both from seeing the absurdity of it all along. It is the stuff of horror films, a man's worst nightmare, a piece of witchcraft that has made fools of them both with its spell.

She drops on to the bed, overwhelmed by a humiliation so deep and so bitter it feels like death. The final layer of her mask has been stripped away and all that is left is thirty years of unacknowledged exhaustion. No, not thirty. Forty. Because this act began way back then, when she was a teenager struggling to be accepted, and it has never once stopped since. She has worked on her mask with relentless energy, painting and powdering and dying, researching her materials, making it ever more sophisticated. And it is not just the make-up and colourants, not just the clothes and the boots and the earrings and the bags. She has masked her whole being for the benefit of how she appears to others. She has smiled and flirted and flattered and pampered and pleasured. She has prostituted herself for this fictional creation, the impossible person she has presented throughout her life. Now she has finally shaken it off, and it has taken her vitality with it and left her empty; the victim of vampires; bled dry.

She has no means left to combat this exhaustion. She claws her way beneath the duvet and falls into oblivion.

{28}

His lights go out, and when they come back on again they aren't working properly. His head is full of bright darkness or black light. There is a weight on his back. He can't breathe. The sky has fallen on him. But it moves. It is someone's knees, and there are hands all over him, in his pockets, front and back.

His face is in gritty mud and his nose is blocked. He gasps through his mouth and says, 'Don't take my cigarettes.'

One of the knees digs in and it feels as though it has found his heart and is squashing it against his breastbone. Fingers in his front trouser pocket are moving beside his balls, and he feels a momentary panic, but they close around his loose change and pull it free. Then the pressure lifts and they are gone, but not as silently as they came. He hears their running footsteps, two sets, hitting the tarmac hard, powering away like sprinters. The sound is full of youth and strength. He tries to lift his head, and is assailed by the sense that he is falling. He cannot be falling because he is flat on the ground, and yet he is, dropping from a height towards a hard, hard landing. He keeps still, terrified by the sensation, and he feels hot fluid running down the sides of his head and pooling around his ears. He knows what it is. It's a trick his father used to use to stop horses from rearing. A bottle filled with hot water, which the rider smashes between its ears as its front feet leave the ground. The blow shocks the horse. The hot liquid cures it of rearing forever because it thinks it's blood.

It is blood. It comes away hot and sticky on his hand. He sits up carefully, feels broken glass on the ground around him. He has been hit with a bottle. What is blocking his nose is blood as well; it has that metallic smell. He feels in his coat pocket for his handkerchief and finds his glasses in there. He puts them on, as though they could help him to see through the darkness, but he makes another discovery and it's the worst one yet. The central field of vision in his right eye has been closed down by the blow to the head. There is a black vacancy, a hole in his vision. He panics. It is a detached retina. It is brain damage. He must get help and quickly.

But he is still falling. He has to move carefully. He puts out both hands, feeling around for the shards of glass, trying to find a clear patch of ground to lean on while he pushes himself up. He feels a familiar shape, a cigarette lighter discarded or dropped by the muggers. His hand is sticky with blood but he gets it to light and is doubly panic-stricken by the discovery that the hole in his vision is blood-red. Something has spiked him in the eye. The eye is lost completely. He reaches up to examine it with his fingers, takes off the glasses and finds that it has miraculously healed. The flame blows out. He sparks it again and, with vision that is only normally deficient, sees the thick red bloody thumbprint on the lens. For an instant he can't imagine how it got there and he still thinks his eyes must be injured, but then he sees the state of his hands and he understands what has happened. As he looks at them and wonders how to clean them, a drop of blood from his nose splashes on to the other lens.

The lighter goes out again and he is totally blinded, deprived of even the limited night vision he had acquired before the attack. He is trembling as well, and still suffering from the vertiginous sensation of falling, which frightens him even more than the blood. He looks for his phone so that he can call an ambulance, but it isn't in the pocket where he normally keeps it and of course, he finally realises, they have taken everything. His wallet, his cash, his cigarettes, his phone. He is surprised they left him his glasses, for all the use the damn things are to him now.

He stands unsteadily and fingers the wound on his head. It is tender but not too painful, and it doesn't feel very big or deep. A bump is growing underneath it. The dramatic blood flow has slowed, leaving gouts and sticky trails across his smooth scalp. He looks around on the ground but there is no white splash which might be a handkerchief. Why would they take a handkerchief, the sadists?

He finds that he can walk, if he takes it carefully. The impression that he is falling is alarming, but it doesn't appear to affect his balance and it is the trembling and the weakness in his knees that keep his steps slow and small. He feels his way with his feet until he comes to the tarmac, and then he is more comfortable. The way is clear now and, provided he meets no unexpected obstacles, he can make it to the gates and find someone to help him.

Halfway down the hill he discovers there is something in his mouth. It feels like a piece of grit or a tiny, rough pebble, and although it doesn't surprise him that it could have got into his mouth while his face was pushed into the mud, he can't understand why he didn't feel it before now. It is during the act of spitting it out that he realises his front tooth is missing, and that the thing that has just vanished into the vast darkness of Hampstead Heath is a crown that cost him nearly seven hundred pounds.

By the time he emerges from the park he is walking almost normally, but he doesn't feel at all well. His head is beginning to ache and the wound is throbbing and he is unaccountably cold. His knees have regained their strength, and he no longer feels in danger of collapsing, but the falling thing is still there, and it worries him more than anything else, because it doesn't make any sense at all. It is not a feeling of dizziness, nor of light-headedness or nausea. It is like falling from a wall and being trapped in that midair point, with the support no longer there and the ground rushing up to meet him. Except that it isn't a wall he has fallen from. It is something else.

But he has made it to light and safety, that is the most important thing. Soon he will be looked after by someone who will be able to explain it to him, this strange sensation, and make it go away. A car approaches. He steps up to the kerb and tries to flag it down, but it goes straight past. He can make out the gist of everything around him without his glasses, but he can't see well enough to know whether the driver saw him or not. Another car comes, but it is speeding along and has a noisy, hot-rod engine, and he lets it go. He tries the third one and he hears the changes in the engine tone as the driver first takes their foot off the accelerator, then firmly presses it back down.

He stares at the car's tail-lights and notices, when they have gone, how quiet the road is. He has never seen it bumper-to-bumper, even in the rush hour. It's a road he has rarely had to wait long to cross. All the same, he is surprised now to see it so empty. He walks over to the other side, to the row of genteel houses that face the park. A car comes from the other direction, but it indicates and turns left before it reaches him. There is another one behind it, but he has by now settled upon a door to knock on, and he lets it go by.

The front garden of the house has been turned into a concrete pad with space for two cars, but there is only one on it now. It's a narrow house, only one room wide, but there are three floors and an attic, and all the windows at the front are lit. So is the shallow glass porch, outside which he pushes on the single doorbell. Almost immediately he hears the thunder of feet on the stairs within, and heavy, confident steps approaching the door. But it doesn't open, and he hears the footsteps recede again, less rapidly. He looks at the door in bewilderment and sees that it has a spy-hole in the middle, a tiny fish eye staring straight at him. Only then does it occur to him how he must look. A tall, bald man with his head, face and hands covered in blood. He doubts he would open the door himself to a man who looked like that. But he has no way to clean himself up, not even a handkerchief. That soft rain is still falling, or drifting, preventing the blood from drying, thinning it and making everything look worse.

{29}

She wakes and lies still for a minute or two, remembering the horrors that preceded her sleep and expecting them to return. But they don't, and she is amazed to discover that her mind and her heart are both clear and unencumbered. She feels as though she has been dragged deep underwater, only to discover that she has gills. She is at home in this new element, and she is quite clear about what she has to do.

She gets up and straightens the bed and sits on the edge to put on her shoes. Then she opens the wardrobe and takes out the black skirt. She would like to burn it and leave no trace of its existence, but the fireplaces in the house are all dummies and the chimneys are blocked off. So she takes it out into the street and up to the litter bin beside the corner shop, and pushes it down as deep as it will go. While she is out she buys a litre of milk and a packet of a kind of stodgy marshmallow biscuit that she hasn't eaten since she was a child.

Back inside, she puts the kettle on and finds herself staring at the lilies. They are way beyond their best, and she wonders whether he has got them cheap somewhere or, even worse, picked them up from some street florist's discard pile. Their petals are splayed wide and there is something profoundly unsettling about that. They are spread-eagled, gaping, exposing their stamens in almost obscene invitation, craving the entry of fertilising insects that are never going to come. She is reminded of what the American author told her, about the body's desire, when it is approaching the end of its fertile years. The memory threatens to plunge her back into despair, and into the thoughts of children she never had, but she catches herself in time, and it is easy. All that is behind her now, along with the black skirt and all it represented.

She goes back upstairs. In the bathroom she washes the remains of yesterday's makeup from her face, then she returns to the bedroom and removes every stitch of clothing. She stands in front of the full-length mirror and looks at her body, really looks at if for the first time in years.

In terror of the effects of gravity upon her softening skin, she has emaciated herself. Her breasts have disappeared and her ribs and her collarbones protrude. She hears his voice inside her head.

'You're all bones. It's like sleeping with Marilyn Monroe.'

'Marilyn Monroe?' she said. 'But she wasn't all bones.'

'She is now, though,' he said.

She pushes the thoughts of him aside. This isn't about him. He has no part in these deliberations. She looks again, and sees that in an effort to hang on to youth she has made herself grotesque. It has to stop. It is time to let herself go.

She looks up at her face. She still doesn't quite recognise herself with her grey hair, and she is interested. This is a face that men will pass in the street without seeing. It's a backstage face, never seen in the spotlights but crucial to the production just the same. She pulls on a pair of white, Indian pyjamas that she once bought for him and that he never wears. She is top to bottom white, now, and she likes it. It makes her smile. She goes downstairs and makes her coffee. In the fridge she finds lasagne that he has cooked, and she cuts a small slice, then doubles it, and puts it in the oven. While she waits for it to cook, she boots up the computer. She has research to do, people and organisations to track down, lists to compile. She has some serious moving and shaking to be getting on with.

{30}

There is no water lying in the street that he can see. There are puddles in the park, around old, makeshift goal mouths, but he is not going back in there under any circumstances. He steps away from the house, so as not to appear threatening if anyone is looking out at him. What would he do in their position? Call the police?

The thought fills him with guilt and dread, but when he turns back to the street and sees the embodiment of his thoughts appear, he realises that the police are exactly what he needs. This is not the nineteen-eighties, when every Irishman was an IRA suspect. He has not stayed too long in the pub and been forcibly removed. He doesn't even have a little silver twist of dope in his pocket tonight. He has been assaulted and robbed. The boot is on the other foot. He is a victim of crime and not a criminal, no matter what he might look like. So he leaves nothing to chance. He doesn't try to flag down the police car. He steps out in front of it instead. It isn't travelling fast, and it comes to a gentle standstill a few feet before it reaches him. Two officers emerge, both of them male.

'I've been attacked,' he calls out. 'Mugged.'

They stop at a significant distance from him, just out of reach of a left hook. 'Where did this happen?'

He waves shamefully towards the park. 'I know it was stupid to be in there.'

'Have a look at you, then.'

One of them turns on a very bright torch and examines first his face, then the back of his head. A car inches past and he sees a woman and a girl inside, rubber-necking, wide-eyed and shameless, as though they believe they are invisible.

'Bottled you, did he?'

'They,' he says. 'I think so. I didn't see them coming.'

'Count yourself lucky. It looks superficial to me. We've already seen worse tonight. Any other injuries?'

'No,' he says, 'but I keep thinking I'm falling.'

'Better get you over to casualty, then, hadn't we?'

He is overwhelmingly grateful to be sitting in that warm, dry car and travelling across London. The driver handles the car beautifully, as if it were full of eggs, wasting no time at all but creating no turbulence either. The other officer sits in the back with him, and hands him moistened baby wipes, one after another, until he has cleaned up his head and his hands and his face and, thank God, his glasses. He tells them his story, but it doesn't give them much to go on. He didn't get even the slightest glimpse of the men who mugged him, not even a foot beside his face. He knows there were two because he heard them run away. They took his cash, his wallet with his bank cards, his phone and two-and-a-half packets of cigarettes.

'Mind my asking what you were doing in the park?'

'I had a row with my partner.' He sighs, and adds, 'My girlfriend,' in case there should be any doubt. 'I was walking it off.'

They have already arrived at the casualty department, and pulled into the ambulance bay. The blue light is flashing. It makes him feel important. The backseat officer accompanies him to reception and takes down his details at the same time as the admissions secretary does. Name. Address. Phone number. Date of birth. He rattles them off mechanically. The secretary tells him to take a seat in the waiting area, and that someone will come and have a look at him soon. In a rare fit of appreciation he blesses England and her blue-breasted bobbies and her national health service, still functioning and still free at the point of need.

'All right now, sir?' the officer says.

'Thank you. You've been very kind.'

'Number would be handy, in case we need to contact you.'

'But you have my number. You took it down, didn't you?'

'Is that a different mobile, then? From the one that was stolen?'

'Oh,' he says. 'No. It isn't.'

Along with the phone has gone his entire contact list, all those important people. They have stolen his whole life, his past, his future. Almost everyone he knows.

'Don't you have a landline?' the policeman asks.

He seldom gives it out these days. It is always his mobile number that he gives people, and it takes him a few moments to remember it. The officer writes it down.

'Like me to give your girlfriend a ring? Tell her where you are?'

He is completely thrown by the suggestion. Since the moment he was hit on the head she has not crossed his mind, not once, not even when he mentioned her to the police. And now, when he thinks about her, it brings him no relief. It should. He should be happy that he has someone who cares for him and can help him through this trauma. Instead it brings a return of the shock and dread that he had thought was all behind him. He is reminded of what he was really doing on Hampstead Heath; the journey he was making; the place he was so sure that he would find. The falling sensation intensifies, and yet again the name of the country he inhabits flits across his memory. Vanishes again. It is not England.

'You all right, sir?'

'Yes,' he says. 'I'll be fine. But please don't phone her. I'll manage.'

'Suit yourself,' says the bobby. 'I'll let you know if there are any developments. And get on to your bank as soon as you can about those cards.'

'Thank you,' he says. 'Thank you for everything.' He pushes through the double doors into the waiting area and meets disillusionment head-on. He isn't sure what he expected. A smiling nurse who would take his hand and lead him into a comfortable room where a doctor was waiting, all white and crisp and freshly ironed. If so, he shouldn't have been. He knows the pressures on the health service. It is headline news about once a week. Exactly this. Dozens of people waiting, some on trolleys, most on uncomfortable plastic chairs, one man lying on a blanket on the floor with a child, looking terrified, sitting beside him. Just inside the door is a young woman with a flushed and listless baby in her arms, and he is glad to see a nurse arrive and lead her rapidly away through another pair of doors. But there are people here who have the helpless look of endlessly waiting. And there are others like him, fresh in from fights or assaults all over North London, bits of rag or hospital gauze pressed against bleeding wounds.

He explores his own cut gingerly. It gapes, but it isn't large. He wonders whether he should go away and stick a plaster on it and not waste his own or anyone else's precious time. If it wasn't for the fact that he is still relentlessly falling, he probably would have.

{31}

Feng shui or no feng shui, the clearing of her wardrobe had the effect of sending a message to the gods. And on the Monday following the trip to the Sue Ryder shop, they sent her an answer. She was in the kitchen, putting together a meal. He was working in his study and she had the radio on in the background while she cooked. It was a Radio 4 documentary about the slow-food markets in New York City, and the idea had immediate appeal for her. There were organic street markets in London – there was one just down the road two days a week – but they were small and expensive and exclusive, for people like her with middle-class sensibilities and deep pockets. The New York markets were quite different.

They were bigger, for one thing, and had a broader base. Instead of bringing them to the wealthy and trendy parts of the city, the organisers had set them up in the most deprived and run-down areas. In each case, regeneration had followed. Small permanent businesses had sprung up around the markets. The foody set were prepared to travel to get their specialities, and money flowed in and spread throughout the community. Ethnic and class diversity took root.

When the documentary was over she let her mind run on. She envisaged a situation where unsold perishables would be donated at the end of the day, to the homeless hostels, perhaps. It needn't all be organic, provided it was fresh and as locally grown as London could manage. All kinds of farmers and market gardeners could be brought in, and bakers, whole-food shops, delicatessens, ethnic-food suppliers of all makes and colours. There might be cookery demonstrations showing what could be done with cheap vegetables or unpopular cuts of meat; that there were viable alternatives to junk food, even for the poorest in society. She saw opportunities for them in the new markets as well; micro-business along the lines of Grameen in Bangladesh. Little stalls offering hot food from all parts of the world, hair braiding, head massage, arts and crafts and services, all with the ethos of slow food and hand-manufacture.

And what would be in it for her? Nothing, so far as she could see, except exactly what she was looking for. The chance to use her skills to engage with a wider community and to give something of herself for the benefit of those in need and society as a whole. It ticked all the boxes. Every one.

But this time she didn't take off half-cocked. She reined in her enthusiasm and prepared to let things take their natural course. She didn't tell him about it, or anyone else, either, but she quietly put the word around that Elsinore might be up for sale. Then, while she waited, she researched the New York markets on the internet and bought books about the slow-food movement, about setting up small businesses and managing micro-credit loans. She sensed the development in herself of a new kind of concentration; a building energy; a plutonium core of potential.

And then the gods provided. Not one, but two interested parties made enquiries about Elsinore. She left the negotiations in the capable hands of her agent, and booked a flight to New York City.

She looks up from the computer. She has a good list already of individuals and small businesses she wants to contact. Market gardeners, organic farmers, growers' associations. Credit unions, homeless organisations, wholefood businesses, existing market organisers. All this is basic groundwork. There will be months of phone calls and meetings and discussions before anything can happen, and the biggest obstacle will be to find the right venues and get the necessary permissions from local authorities. She's aware that it might take years, but she is ready for that. This is not a thing like Elsinore, that can be rushed.

She checks the lasagne and throws together a salad. Her watch says eight o'clock, but that is New York time. The kitchen clock says one. She wonders where he is. It is well after closing time. Has he somewhere else to go in London? Is he staying with friends? Has he got another woman?

She has lived in fear of losing him, but not to someone else. She sees now that it could happen. It is the trend, even the norm in her circles, for men to move on from their established relationships and take up with younger women. Several of her friends and acquaintances have been summarily cast off in favour of some bimbo. She is tempted to plunge into an indignant fury at the injustice of it all, but this new, grey-haired self will not allow her to waste the energy. Fairness is for children's birthday parties. Adults must face reality. So she does.

And part of the reality is that he is no longer the man he was. It is years since he has written a decent poem and, outwardly at least, he seems content to waffle away to students and radio interviewers, and to write about other people's poetry. So what if he leaves her? What if he already has a bimbo, and comes back only to pack up his study and take his things? Can she live without him? Does she even want him if he is no longer the man he used to be?

{32}

He sits and waits. People come and go, but mostly come. He reads the notices on the walls about how to drink safely and how to stop smoking, and when to visit your GP instead of coming into casualty. He reads them again, like those posters in the underground which are impossible to ignore because they are the only things to look at apart from other people, and looking at other people is impermissible. There are newspapers scattered about but he doesn't know if they are provided by the hospital or belong to the people on the seats beside them. And anyway, he doesn't want to read a newspaper. They are irrelevant to what is going on inside him.

He wonders again whether he has some kind of brain injury that is creating this hideous state of midair suspension. He imagines a clot expanding beneath his cranium, slowly choking off the blood supply to his cerebellum. He considers trying to find someone in authority so that he can thump their desk and demand to be taken more seriously. He has no doubt that he is in danger, but unaccountably, he also knows that it is not that kind of danger. His headache is no worse: if anything, it has receded a little. The bump and cut are sore to the touch but he doesn't consider it pain. This fall he is in the midst of will not end on the grubby hospital floor, but on land. On soil. And with that realisation comes the knowledge of what it is he is falling from. Not a wall or a branch or a ladder or a tree. He is falling from a horse.

He hears his father's voice again. 'Just the toe. The toe. If you come off with your foot like that you'll get dragged.'

He never did get dragged, but he came off plenty of times, on grass, on tarmac, on mud. He got dropped in the flagstoned yard, scraped off on gateposts, cannoned into hurdles that horses refused to jump. Is that what this is all about? Is this a flashback, caused by the blow?

A nurse comes over and talks to him. She looks at his head and makes a little face. 'That must be sore.'

But it's the kind of response his mother might have made to a grazed knee or a wasp sting. It isn't serious. She bends her knees and looks directly into his eyes.

'Have you any other problems? Any dizziness or nausea?'

'I feel that I'm falling,' he says.

She straightens up and pats him on the shoulder. 'We'll get one of the doctors to take a look at you. It won't be long.'

There are still people arriving, but not at the same rate as before. Some of the ones who were there when he arrived have been seen and have either gone somewhere else or come back to do some more waiting. A few of them returned from wherever they had been seen and went straight out the front doors, giving him the impression that they had been given an aspirin and sent home. He is slightly irked by the realisation that some people who arrived after he did have been seen before him. He supposes there must be a reason for it. Their problems must be more pressing.

Is he making a fuss about nothing? Is he one of the ones who ought to go home and take an aspirin and see his GP in the morning? He watches, in some apprehension, the arrival of a drunk. The man is covered in blood and staggering, and he lays about him and swears at the hospital staff. Eventually he is mollified and persuaded to sit down, where he dozes and grumbles spasmodically.

The episode sets him thinking about the current debate over rationing in the NHS. He doesn't see why someone so abusive should expect to be treated. But then, if he is denied help, who next? Fat people? Smokers, like himself?

It reminds him of his desire for a cigarette. He is sure he could cadge one at the front door, where there is a constant rotation of smokers, but he's afraid that if he does he'll miss the person who comes looking for him.

He's right, and he congratulates himself. The same nurse returns and bends down with the same sweet manner. She watches him as he walks, and he wishes there was some outward evidence of the symptoms he has described. There isn't. He could walk a white line if he was required to do it. But inside his mind he is still falling. He follows her to a small examination room, where a doctor is washing her hands. But there is another delay, because a different nurse pops her head around the door and takes the doctor away.

He is left alone again. The room is full of steel and plastic and white paper packages. The walls are the kind of green that is only seen in nature when nature is sick. It is the green of deadly algal blooms in polluted lakes. There is a trolley with a folded sheet and a clean white pillow.

There is a chair, but only one. He hasn't been invited to sit down, so he doesn't.

This waiting is infinitely worse than the last. It ought not to be because help is so close, but it is. The falling has accelerated, and the pull of gravity is stronger. A horse is in the act of wheeling away from him. A white horse.

'A grey horse,' his father says. 'You never call them white.'

But it is a white horse, a particular white horse, and it never set foot in his father's yard. He is on the point of recognising it when the doctor returns. She picks up the notes the nurse has left.

'Sit on the chair, please,' she says. 'How are you feeling?'

He sits. 'Not too bad.'

The doctor stands behind him. 'You got hit by a bottle?' Skilled fingers palpate the bump. 'I think you were lucky. It looks quite superficial.'

'I feel as if I'm falling,' he says.

'Falling?' The doctor looks into his eyes. Are you nauseous? Is it like seasickness?'

'No,' he says. 'Just falling.'

'You feel as if you can't keep your balance?'

'No. My balance is fine. I can't really explain it.'

The doctor shines a torch into his eyes. 'Do you know what day of the week it is?'

This was never easy for him, since he doesn't have a regular job. 'Thursday I think,' he says. 'Or Friday morning.'

'Name of the prime minister?'

'Oh, Little Lloyd George Brown Jug.' The doctor looks slightly alarmed. 'And Tony Blair before that. John Who. Maggie Thatcher. My mind is working all right. My memory is fine.'

The doctor picks up the notes again. 'You are probably suffering a little bit from shock,' she tells him. 'These things are more difficult as we get older. We don't bounce back quite so quickly. You are what, sixty-four?'

'Sixty-five,' he says.

The doctor continues to speak but he doesn't hear her. Because he has hit the ground at last, and he is reeling from the impact. The white horse is galloping away and he will never catch it again. He has landed on the solid ground of home.

He hears the sound of his name and he looks up. 'What?'

'I said, we'll play on the safe side. Send you for an X-ray and a scan. We'll just put a couple of stitches in first.'

He hauls his attention to the matter at hand. 'Are stitches necessary? Can't you use those little butterfly things?'

'If you can be sure to keep your head dry. If it opens you could end up with an ugly scar.'

'I don't care about that,' he says. 'Give the pigeons something to aim at.'

The doctor tilts her head sideways in that attractive gesture of assent which is missing from European body language. With deft fingers she cleans the cut and closes it with butterfly clips, then puts a large dressing out of one of the white packets on the top. It's all over before he knows it, and is hardly painful at all.

But the effects of his abrupt landing are still excruciating. He walks along the broad empty corridors to the X-ray department and hands his notes through the small window there. He follows directions, finds himself in another waiting room with four or five other people. This time he doesn't read the posters. He considers where he has been and where he has landed now. He regards his hands, which still have traces of dried blood around the nails. He runs them over the smoothness of his scalp and feels the dressing there. He puts his tongue into the gap left by the broken crown. He has come to the end of his journey and found the answer he was looking for. The shock her grey hair gave him is not caused by her deception. His concerns about how she will appear on his arm are a side issue, or a small aspect of the primary one. The severity of his reaction has, in fact, almost nothing to do with her at all. It isn't her who is growing old. It is him.

Like Oisín, he didn't know that the world he followed her into was Tír na n'Óg. He didn't know that it was so profoundly different from his own world. He didn't see through the glamour to the truth about the land of eternal youth.

He sees it now. The fine living, the parties, the high life. All that flattery and congratulation, the closed and guarded, self-referential circle of the media clique. He has seen its effects on young authors, the chosen few whom the publishers have connived with the media to promote. He has watched them lose touch with reality as they buy into the hype; come to believe that the things said about them are true: that they are demigods, with the gift of bringing insight to humankind. He has seen writers ruined by it, their skills destroyed because they have lost contact with the real, flesh-and-blood world. He never dreamed that it could happen to him, but it has. And while he moved in this fictional world of fame and ease and wealth and beauty, his own world has continued to grow older, and his body along with it.

A name is called and he looks up. A teenaged boy in a wheelchair goes out, pushed by an older man. There are still three people ahead of him. The air is stale, as though it has been breathed too many times already. He doesn't want to be there. He doesn't need to be there. He has no symptoms now that give cause for concern. The falling is over. But he supposes that the good doctor is probably right, and that he should have those tests, to be on the safe side.

He contemplates the truth he has been hiding from. He remembers turning fifty just after he met her. They went out to dinner to celebrate. He remembers fifty-five and refusing to go out or do anything. From then on he developed a number of techniques to avoid noticing his birthdays. On his sixtieth he was away at a conference and no one knew. She did, of course – she never forgot – but he was so determined not to mark his birthdays that she learned to disregard them. And so did he. It's not that he doesn't know how old he is, but that he has chosen not to think about it.

Now he has to. He chose to go looking for home. The decision was his, every step of the way. He knew it was dangerous to go into the park, but he went. He chose to ride the white horse in search of his own land and, like Oisín, he has paid the price.

He stands up and leaves the waiting room. He walks past the reception window and back along the broad corridors, following the signs to the exit. No one tries to stop him.

The night air is sweet and cool in his lungs. He sees a taxi parked in a drop-off bay with its light on, and he is on the point of opening the door when he remembers that he hasn't any money. He stops to think. She is at home. He can get money from her when he gets there. It won't be a problem, but still he hesitates. There is something about the air. There is something about the sounds of London, the distant sirens, the low, animal snore of cars and taxis and night buses. The city feels wide awake and so does he. He has fallen from the horse, but unlike Oisín he has not turned to dust. He is still alive.

He begins to walk. How long does he have? His father's heart gave out when he was sixty-seven, but these are different times. People live longer now. He has plenty of life left in him.

As he walks he finds that his senses have come alive. When did they desert him? He didn't even notice it happening. But suddenly the air is full of smells and tastes and textures. There are changing zones of temperature and tone between one street and the next. There are stories and struggles, upheavals and resolutions happening all around him, in and beyond the silent houses. The city is undulating with human energy. And beneath his feet there is another world. The ground feels solid but it is not. Under London is a network of tunnels and conduits and cables and drains and sewers, the arteries and bowels and neural pathways of a prodigious city. He is a small thing, a drone in a heaving hive, but he is where he belongs.

His poetry is with him again, and he knows there will be no more *Turf Sheds* and *Salamanders*. This is the real thing. Images arise that defy description, but which he will describe. Words and lines bubble up, arrange and rearrange themselves. A raw excitement courses through his marrow. He is so intent upon these marvellous new beginnings that he barely sees the streets through which he is walking. But he is not lost. For the first time in years, he knows exactly where he is.

{33}

She has found a place of unprecedented calm within herself. She knows that there are busy times ahead, but she knows there will be silences as well. It's time she took her analyst's advice and stopped running from herself. She is ready for it, now that she is white-haired, now that she has gills. As for him, absent or present he will cause disturbances, the way squalls and storms stir up the sea. But they will only affect the surface waters of her life. In the deeps, where it really matters, she is secure.

Her watch is still showing the time in New York. She sets it to London time and turns off the computer. She is halfway up the stairs when she hears his footsteps outside the front door and then a pause, and then a knock. Why would he knock?

Because he is drunk again, that's why. But when she looks at him through the spy-hole she's not so sure. He calls through the door. She opens it.

'A ghost!' he says, when he sees her. 'And wearing my pyjamas!'

He turns to put the bolt across and she sees the white dressing on his head.

'What happened?' she says. 'What have you done?'

'It's nothing. I was wrestling with my demons and they won. Kind of.'

His face is pale, but there is a familiar light in his eyes, the return of an energy that she hasn't seen in him for years.

And for the first time in as many years, she finds she is intrigued by him, and she leans against the wall as he hangs up his coat.

'No, really,' she says. 'What happened? Where have you been?'

He puts his arms around her and breathes into her soft, white hair. She gets a faint whiff of alcohol from him, but it's only the surgical kind, she is sure. The last of her resistance fades. She returns his embrace.

'I'm sorry,' he says. 'I got lost, but it doesn't matter now. I've found my way home, at last.'

She is asleep within minutes but he lies awake for what is left of the night, his mind reaching and stretching, his soul crossing mountainous terrain, up and down, passing through hope, despair, enthusiasm, fear. But it is where it belongs, and he is already wringing words and lines and stanzas out of it all, and it is only an unwillingness to disturb her that keeps him from getting up and searching for a notebook.

When the first light leaks between the curtains it reveals form, but no detail and no colour. Her hair might as easily be blonde as white. She might be forty still, or sixty, or twenty-five. It makes no difference. What matters is that she is herself, entirely and uniquely. And so, thanks to the gods and the heroes which somehow still move between the heavens and the earth, is he.

AFTERWORD

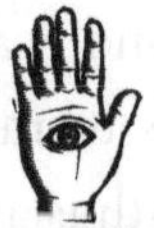

{BASED ON THE STORY OF OISÍN AND TÍR NA N'ÓG}

I don't remember ever feeling pressurised for time when I was a child. When my children were born time seemed to accelerate, and the hours, days and years began to speed past. It took me by surprise, and I became intrigued by the phenomenon. But it wasn't until I began going to schools as a visiting author that I realised how pervasive the lack of time was becoming. When I asked classes of eleven- and twelve-year-olds whether they felt they had enough time, large numbers of them informed me that they didn't, that they were already having trouble fitting their busy schedules into the available time.

I thought about this for a couple of years, and gradually an idea for a book began to form. This book was *The New Policeman*, which is set in the west of Ireland where I live, and concerns a scarcity of time in the human world and an unwanted excess of it in the parallel fairy world of Tír na n'Óg [*Teer-nah-nohg*].

I had read various tellings of the Irish fairy mythology, just for my own pleasure, but now I revisited them for research purposes. I was amazed and delighted to discover how well my invented hypothesis – that Tír na n'Óg is a land without time – worked with the stories. The story of Oisín [*U-sheen*], in particular, appears to confirm it.

For those who aren't familiar with it, the story is about Oisín, one of the Fianna [*Fee-anna*], who falls in love with a fairy woman and goes to live with her in her land. It is wonderful there and he is very content, but he misses his friends and family and expresses his intention to return home for a visit. The fairy people try to dissuade him, but when they can't they give him a white horse and tell him that on no account should he get off the horse when he is back in his own land.

When he gets there, he discovers that three hundred years have passed. All his friends and family are dead. He passes through the changed land, appalled by what he sees. As long as he is on the horse he remains immune to the passage of time, even though his own lifespan in this world has long since been used up. His undoing comes about when he encounters a group of men trying to move an enormous rock in a field. They ask him for his help, and as he leans from the horse to push the rock, he loses his balance, falls, and turns to dust.

I love the story, and have used it as the basis for the third part of the New Policeman trilogy, entitled *The White Horse Trick*. I have also examined there, as here, the concept of *glamour*, which comes into a lot of fairy stories, from Ireland and elsewhere.

The fairy folk have the ability to alter the form of things, to make that which is plain, ugly or dangerous look beautiful, in order to entice and deceive. I see this idea as having great relevance to our consumption-driven societies, and most of us are victims of it to a greater or lesser extent. It isn't the fairies who are responsible for it now, of course, but business, media and fashion interests. The result is largely the same, though. We have become dazzled by celebrity and possessions. We pursue these modern versions of glamour, often losing our unique identities in the process. And most of those who achieve the dreams of celebrity status or great wealth soon discover that they have been fooled, and that the expected satisfaction and fulfilment promised by glamour do not exist.

My story is about two people going in opposite directions – one moving away from the glitzy celebrity world and the other who has, largely unwittingly, entered into it. When one of them finally makes a gesture which casts it off, the other is thrown into crisis and forced to recognise the difference between what glamour has made of him, and what he really is.

Some terms may be unfamiliar: **bladdered** – drunk; **Amé** – high-class carbonated fruit-drink; **dry-lined** – old walls covered with studs and plasterboard; **naggin** – small bottle of spirits; **chuggers** – charity workers collecting on the street; **púca** [*poo-ka*] – Irish goat-god; **Fionn** – Fionn Mac Cumhaill [*Finn Mac Coo-well*], mythical Celtic hunter-warrior, father of Oisín; **sidhe** [*shee*] – the fairy folk.

Lastly, a brief note about the length. I'm aware that this story is a lot longer than the others in the collection, and I'd like to explain. Isobelle's original idea was to have a series of novellas, published in separate volumes. When she mentioned this to me, it immediately resonated with an idea I had been mulling over, so I set to work straight away and came up with something in or around 25 000 words. When the concept of the collection changed, I submitted the story anyway, with the promise that I would shorten it later if it was accepted. However, despite my best efforts, and those of editor Nan, it has proved impossible to get it any shorter than this. My apologies – I did not set out to take up more than my fair share of space!

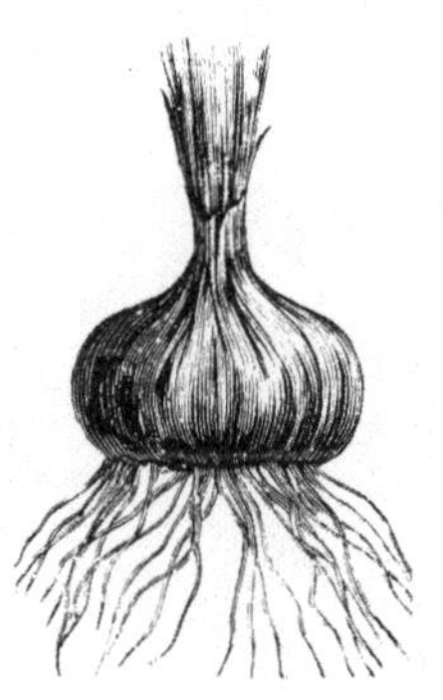

ABOUT *the* AUTHORS

Cate Kennedy grew up in a magical kingdom of books which ran adjacent to the real life of suburbia and school. Even now, she can't open a wardrobe without pushing her hand through the coats to see if she could possibly step through. She is wary of apples that look too perfect, fast-talking strangers and not keeping promises, but has come to be persuaded that the writing life is not much different from sitting in a room late at night, trying to spin straw into gold. She has published poetry, short stories and a novel, as well as a number of essays and articles, and she lives in north-east Victoria next to a forest full of bats, lizards and owls. She has a garden full of pumpkins, just to be on the safe side. It's porridge every morning at her house.

Nan McNab was born on a farm and spent her school holidays within sniffing distance of a bacon factory. One unforgettable day, she and her cousins watched in appalled fascination as pigs were slaughtered. Now she lives by the sea in a house built of straw, sticks and bricks, with her son and two fine dogs. Nan works as a freelance editor and writer, and has published over two dozen books in Australia and overseas (non-fiction, fiction plus a few stories). No pigs were harmed in the writing of this story.

Catherine Bateson grew up in a family of writers and editors who were gently appalled when she became a poet. She ran away from Brisbane with a broken heart and spent some time living in a tower in Melbourne filled with beautiful art. She wrote bad love poems and waited for a prince to rescue her. The prince never came, but the poems improved. Since then she's written young adult and children's novels as well as poetry. She lives in the hills outside Melbourne where she teaches professional writing and editing online so she can pay her overdue library fines.

Maureen McCarthy has published ten books and is currently working on the eleventh, a historically based novel about the Abbotsford Convent in Melbourne. She is very chuffed to be included in a story collection dealing with fairytales not only because her story was great fun to write, but because she has always thought of herself as a very naturalistic writer. Maybe that will change. Maureen lives near the Yarra River in Melbourne. Now that her three sons have left home to fight dragons, rescue princesses and search for treasure, she is thinking about getting a dog.

Victor Kelleher was brought up in the East End of London by semi-literate grandparents and attended a string of appalling back-street schools. Not surprisingly, he didn't read, didn't love books, and didn't long to become a writer. At age fifteen, he had just enough sense to escape to Central Africa, where he felt that he'd been reborn into a fairytale world of sunlight and plenty. As all fairytales should, it changed him completely, opening magical portals/casement windows/wardrobe doors, etc., onto vistas he'd never dreamed of. Now, many years later, with an academic career behind him, and more books than he dares to count, he still blesses the 'good' fairy who waved her wand over his boyhood self. Though ever wary (he knows about fairytales!), he also keeps a lookout for the 'bad' fairy. She hasn't turned up yet, but she's sure to be lurking somewhere.

Up in the hills one day, **Kate Thompson** smelled tobacco smoke when there was nobody there to be smoking it. She has been searching for the fairy folk ever since. She has published twenty books and won many awards, including the *Guardian* and the Whitbread (Costa) children's book prizes.

ALSO AVAILABLE:

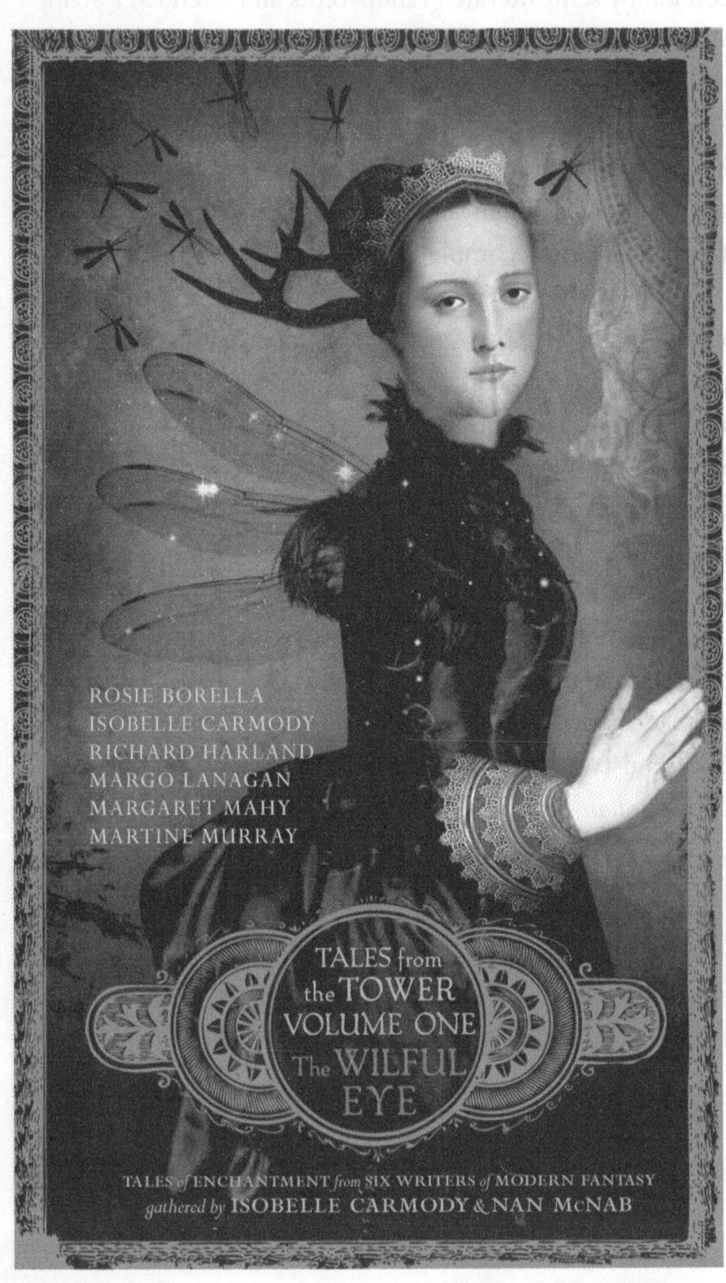